# Mass Deception

A Novel by

Hallema

*Mahogany Publishing*

Published and distributed by Mahogany Publishing
P.O. Box 170952, Hialeah, Florida 33017-0952
www.hallema.net

10 09 08 07 06 05 04' 2 3 4 5 6 7 8 9 10
Library of Congress Cataloging-in-Publication Data

Printed and bound in the United States of America.

Edited by James B. Sims of inkeditor@aol.com

PUBLISHER'S NOTE
This book is a work of fiction. Names, characters, places, and incidents are either the product of the author's imagination or are used fictitiously, and any resemblance to actual persons, living or dead, business establishments, events, or locales is entirely coincidental.

ISBN 0-9746909-0-2

ATTENTION ORGANIZTIONS AND BOOK CLUBS
Quantity discounts are available on bulk purchases of this book. For more information contact Mahogany Publishing at P.O. Box 179052 Hialeah, Florida 33017-0952, or visit us on the Web at www.hallema.net.

# Dedication

*For my parents, Jimmy and Lorraine, for your unconditional love and support. Thank you for giving me roots to keep me grounded and wings so that I could fly. I am soaring like an eagle. I hope I've made you proud.*

*And*

*For my last surviving Grandparent, Mattie "Big Mama" Hunter. You are still all of that and a bag of chips.*

*And*

*For Benjamin L. Crump, I thank God for you everyday of my life. You are truly a blessing. Thanks for believing in me and supporting this work of art.*

*In Memory of my fallen heroes and sheroes*

*Lillian "Boot" Mc Clain 1992*
*Calvin "Twinkle" Simmons, Jr. 1992*
*Nathaniel "Nat" Hunter 1992*
*Turner "Granddaddy" Simmons, Sr. 1994*
*Richard "Ricky" Moman, Jr. 1996*
*Eddie Lee Mayo 2002*
*Maggie "Granny" Simmons 2003*

# Acknowledgments

For those of you who know me, you know that "*life for me ain't been no crystal stair.*" Thank you, God for pointing me in the right direction and surrounding me with the people who could help me get there. Thanks for my prayer partners **Linnette Fuller, Angelene "Sunshine" Terry, James Perryman, Garfield Jackman, Vicki Gallon, and Judy Jackson** who prayed unceasingly with and for me. *I finally found my purpose ya'll!* Thank you for **The Universal Truth Center**, my church family who keep me spiritually fed and uplifted every Sunday. Most of all, I thank you for my immediate and extended family and friends. I couldn't have done this without them. I am so BLESSED!

## Special shouts out to the following people:

**Preston Allen**, my creative writing teacher, mentor, and friend. Toni Goodwin was born out of an exercise in your class. Thanks for pushing me beyond my comfort zone. **Jacqueline D. Brown**, my sister, my friend. You have been there for me and Toni since I gave birth to the idea of her. Thank you for listening to me read to you page by page for the last three years. I love you. **The Dream Team: Benjamin Crump**, thanks for being my Earth angel. You will let me sway, but you never let me fall! Thanks for having my back 24/7/365 for the last 16 years. That's a long time to love a friend. Thank you for doing it unconditionally; you know I love you to infinity and beyond! *Arf-oop!* **Treva Johnson Marshall**, girl, you have been pushing me since law school. Thank you! Thank you for being the first to accept my invitation to join The Dream Team and the last to complete your assignments. Thanks for being that true sistah friend on whom I know I can depend. You have always believed in, encouraged, and inspired me. I appreciate you. Remember the DD Club. **Judith-Ann Johnson**, my home girl, my road dawg, my walking buddy, my confidant, my sistah, my friend. *You are still not the boss of me.* Thank you for constantly harassing me to finish this book. Three years is a long time to sweat somebody about something, but I knew you had my back. **Natalie Preston**, girl, your diligence has always served as inspiration for me. Thanks for being my biggest critic, your advice made me grow. Thanks for keeping me in the job market when I didn't want to be and for always coming to my annual birthday party. Let's keep it going. **Marcye Slutsky**, you are my total opposite, but one of my closes friends. I truly believe we were born to be friends. Thanks for all of your support and feedback. Thanks for introducing me to you know who. Most of all thanks for all of the good times we have on girlfriend day. I can't wait for our trip to *Italy!* **Eddie Holman,** my shared play husband. Thanks for trying to hook a sistah up with an employed, intelligent BLACK MAN. I expect you to keep searching until we find him. **Ada P. Oli Onyia,** Eleven years and counting… we go way back sistah girl. Thanks for being my sister at heart. You are my true friend and confidant. I can't wait to meet our new baby Ejike. **Annette Breedlove**, my publicist. Thank you so much for stepping up to the plate and offering your love and support. Girl, we are on our way.

### Family

**Big Mama "Mattie Hunter"** you are my shero! I am so glad that God blessed me with you. I love you Big Mama. You have thought me a lot about life and men. Thank you. **Mama "Lorraine,"** thank you so much for keeping me fed and my hair looking good. You made me look like I had money even when I was broke. You know that's priceless. I love you with all my heart. **Daddy "Jimmy,"** thank you for constantly supporting me. Because of you, I know what a real man looks like. This year really tested our relationship. I am glad we both passed with flying colors. I love you. **Cassandra**, girl, you know you mean well. You are the best oldest sister in the world!!! Your heart is really made of gold. I love you so much. **Valerie**, girl, you know you have an attitude. But you are such a teddy bear. Thank you so much for keeping me fed, finding my lost chapters, and just being you. I love you, sis. **Jacqueline**, I already gave you a shout out, but here is another one for being the first of my siblings to sign my guest book. You better represent, sis! I love you. **Elijah,** thank you for demonstrating your support by being the first family member and the third person to buy my book. I love and appreciate you. **Rashada**, my sister, my soror, my legacy, thank you for helping a sistah out. You gave me unconditional support when I needed it. Thanks, twin. I love you. **Jimmy Jr.,** my baby brother, my friend, my twin, my laughing buddy, my co-star. Thank you for listening to me read. You are a big man with a giant heart. I think you're special. I love you. To my nephews **Christopher and Craig Michael Allen**, and **Elijah, Jr.**, I love you. To my precious niece, **Lorraine "Lo-lo,"** girl you know you make Auntie Lema proud. That's why you're my favorite niece. To my in-laws: **Troy "T-roy" Brown,** you know we go way back to your halo days playa! **Craig Allen**, I couldn't have gotten Pasé without you. **Eboni Horner**, girl you have been a member of our family for a long time. Thank you for loving my brother unconditionally. I love you girl! **Tanisha**, girl, my banana pudding is off the hook thanks to you. I love you guys. If I had this life to live all over again and I was given an opportunity to pick my family I would choose each of you again. I am so honored to be a member of such a dynamic group of people. It is my privilege to love all of you.

The people who kept me laughing:
**Natalie Everette Jones**, you keep me rolling. **Robert Hughley**, you are just too funny! Thanks for making me laugh when I needed a break. **Loriann Opara** and **Larcenia Turner,** "the ladies who lunch" crew. I am so glad the three of us are back together again. Lunch was never the same without y'all. **Lori,** Dallas will never be the same without us! Grapevine Mills or bust!

The people who lent me their voices:
**Esme Russell** I hope I made you proud. Thanks for letting me peak inside of your world. **Kelli,** thanks for trusting me enough to tell me your story and share your pain.

For the people who lent me their male voices:
**Raynard "Ray-Ray" Harrington,** thank you for giving me the inspiration for the Morehouse scene. That's one of my favorites. **Alexander Proctor**, your speaking voice is phenomenal. Thank you for setting the tone for my early male characters. I can still hear them talking. **Brian Culmer**, thanks for providing me with the male vernacular.

For the people who kept me nourished and entertained:
**Gregory Raines**, boy, you know you took good care of mama at the Essence Festival. That is, until Frankie Beverly and Maze came on. Thanks for providing me with food and entertainment when I wasn't working. You understood that I had to write. **Karen Green,** you are a good friend. Thanks for feeding me while I was editing, and for the sneak previews when I needed a break. Karen you know *free* always works for me.

For the angels who flew in to save me when things went wrong:
**Kevin Douglas,** you are my shoulder to lean on. Thanks for being a strong, positive force in my life. God knew I needed you. Now here is a little bit of tough love: *get rid of the black leather!* **Mario Cadenas**, BRAVO, Mario! My cover is off the hook! The six hours we spent designing it was well worth the investment. I can't wait to see the next one. **David McPherson**, meeting you was one of the best things God ever did for me. You have consistently proven that you

are a GREAT friend. I am so glad we met. Thanks for pulling me through. **Moses Bell,** thank you for doing such a good job with my photo shoot. You did what others couldn't do. I love your dependability. **Sheila Slutsky**, you really saved me. Thank you so much for dropping everything to help a friend. I love you. **Leroy Clare**, you called just when I needed a friend. Thank you for volunteering to help out. You did a great job! I owe you one. **Clark Solomon**, you hooked a sistah up! You did a FANTASTIC job on my web site. Thanks for putting up with me and giving me what I wanted. **Darlene Christie**, thank you for staying up with me until the wee hours of the morning to help me finish my final edit. **Toya "TJ" Johnson**, thanks for knowing what I needed without me having to ask you for it. I'll never forget it.

To my fellow authors who have shown me much love throughout this process: **K. Elliott, Preston Allen, Candice Harris, Shonda Cheekes, and D.L. Christie,** I have nothing but love for you. We are truly climbing the ladder of success together. I'll see all of you at the top!

To my fans:
I know that without you I would not have a writing career. I would like to say a special thank you to **Charlie Jackson,** for being the first person to purchase my book. Charlie you jump started my career, I'll never forget that. Thanks for believing in me. To my cousin and biggest promoter, **Reginald "Reggie Black" Thomas**, thank you for supporting my project. You treated it like it was your own. You have always had my back. I love you cuz! **Sistah Girl Reading and Investment Club,** you all have shown me nothing but love since I met you. I appreciate all of your support and dedication. A very special shout out to **Sisters Book Club** in Clearwater, Florida: **Kim Gaines, Velma Butler, Maritza Reyes, Carlini Rivers, Christine Burrows, and Loretta Calvin,** I appreciate you all being the first club to select *Mass Deception* as your book of the month. You go, girls! I can't wait to meet all of you at the signing.

Finally, to all of my family in Georgia, Florida, California, Washington DC, and South Carolina, I love you. To all of my friends everywhere, especially **Valerie Ivory Ferguson, Chavell Jones Thames, Keenya Johnson Roberts, Yvette Sands and Marion "Jones" Graham III**, I couldn't mention you all by name but I do appreciate each and every one of you. To my **Sorors of Delta Sigma Theta Sorority, Inc.,** thank you for the love and support that you've shown me. Especially my line sister **Sharon Wilson,** my pen pal, **Dr. Cecile "Cece" Miller,** my internet pen pals **Jane Fox Long** and **Ellen Brown,** my homegirl **Davida Matchett,** and my little sister **Erica Phillips,** *OO-OOP!* **Sorors,** I look forward to seeing lots of red and white at my book signings.

**Thank you all for supporting me!**

# Chapter 1
## Tony or Toni?

I sprang out of bed earlier than usual, excited about starting my [...] at Carlton International. This is the beginning of a whole new life for m[...] brushed my teeth, my thoughts drifted. I imagined myself walking into my [...]w office, and sitting in the high-back Italian leather, chair behind the beautiful cherry wood desk. I saw myself listening to the soothing ocean tunes of the fountain I'd had custom-made for my office. My navy blue suit fit smoothly over my perfectly rounded breasts and ample behind. No one would miss my long flawless legs peeking from underneath my expertly tailored, trademarked, three-inches-above-the knee skirt. Although I'm professional, I want to be thought of as sexy too.

*I'll be the talk of the office.*

The telephone rang and jolted me back to reality. I finished brushing my teeth and sprinted out of the bathroom to grab it before the answering machine picked up.

"Hello, Toni Goodwin speaking," I answered, practicing for my new job.

"Good morning, sweetheart," my mom said. "Are you ready for your first day as the new Vice-President of Carlton International?"

"But of course. You know Toni T. Goodwin is always ready, willing, and able to take on new challenges." We giggled like schoolgirls at my confident reply. "Mom, on the outside I am going to exude strength and look like perfection personified. On the inside, however, my stomach will be doing back flips."

Mom burst into a chorus of laughter, and I chimed in with an alto pitch laugh of my own.

Me and my mother are best friends and have been for as long as I can remember. She has always wanted the best for me, so she does everything she can to elevate and uplift me. Even when I admitted to her that although I was a *he*, I really felt like a *she*. And I wanted to have an operation to free the feminine voice inside me. Linda did what any unsuspecting mother would do....she passed out.

After discussing with me all of the possible ramifications of the procedure, and after researching sex change operations thoroughly, Mom cautiously agreed to support my decision. So for my twenty-first birthday, she gave me the gift of freedom.

After all of my surgeries were completed, the two of us packed our bags and moved to Atlanta. We haven't looked back since.

"Mom, thank you so much for calling me this morning. You always know how to put me at ease. I've gotta finish getting dressed now, but I will call you later."

"Okay sweetheart. Have a wonderful day, and knock 'em dead."

, ..om....I love you."

I love you, too, baby. Bye-bye."

I finished dressing, checked my makeup in the mirror, grabbed my keys, and strolled out of the door.

\*\*\*

*Just like clockwork*, I thought. It was 7:45a.m. I was fifteen minutes early. I opened the door to my two-seater BMW, grabbed my briefcase, took a deep breath, and headed into the office.

An attractive man greeted me.

"Good morning, Mrs. Goodwin. I am Sean, your executive assistant."

"Good morning Sean, it's a pleasure to meet you. And that would be *Ms.* Goodwin," I replied, as I extended my hand and smiled. He shook my hand and donned a genuine smile in return.

"Are you ready for me to see you to your office and help you get settled?" Sean said.

"Yes, that would be nice."

We walked through an elegant mahogany corridor that had an Asian motif. All of the vases were larger than life. The bamboo plants were beautiful and well cared for; the Feng Shui was on point. While we waited for the elevator to arrive, Sean filled me in on what was going on in the company. I was taking a complete inventory of him while he was talking.

*Hmmm*, let's see: He's about 6'3, *check;* broad shoulders, *check;* flat stomach, *check;* Possible six- pack, *check, check;* nice butt, *check, check, check, check, check;* beautiful smile, pretty teeth, manicured nails, and well groomed hair. *He's earned an "A" in the looks category,* I thought to myself, as I smiled politely at whatever Sean was talking about. *Humph!* He has style, too. Versace shirt and tie with matching cufflinks, perfectly tailored black pants, Gucci shoes with a matching Gucci belt. Yes, he truly has it going on! I will have to keep my *good eye* on this one.

"Here we are, the eighteenth floor," Sean indicated. "Your office is to the left. Everyone here is excited about you becoming a member of the Carlton family."

"Thank you, Sean. I am excited to become a part of the Carlton family. And I'm especially looking forward to working with you."

"Thank you, Ms. Goodwin" Sean smiled.

"Please, call me Toni."

"Okay, Toni I'll get you some coffee while you are getting set up."

"Thank you, Sean."

2

I watched him as he exited the room. I thought to myself, *humph*, if I were half the *man* I used to be, I would make a move on him. I shook my head, smiled, sat back in my new Italian leather, high-back chair, closed my eyes and listened to the sounds of the soothing ocean tunes being played by my fountain.

Sean returned with my coffee, and knocked on my office door. I jumped, looked at him somewhat embarrassed, apologized for my jumpiness, and thanked him for the coffee. I decided to unpack.

"What would you like me to help you with?" he asked.

"How about unpacking those two boxes in the corner and placing the contents on the bookshelf?"

"You have a lot of books," Sean commented.

"Yes, I love to read. I especially love fiction. How about you, are you an avid reader?"

"Yes, I try to read at least a book a month."

"Really? Who is your favorite author?"

"My favorite female authors are Hallema and Terry McMillan, and my favorite male authors are K. Elliott and E. Lynn Harris."

"Impressive. I love all four of the authors you named. As a matter of fact, I'm considering starting a book club and inviting different authors to attend our meetings. I know a few of them live in the Atlanta area."

"I think that's a wonderful idea, Toni. I have a friend who knows E. Lynn, maybe he could get him to attend one of your meetings."

"That would be wonderful, Sean."

\*\*\*

By the time we finished unpacking, the rest of the staff had arrived and were already working. My door was open. I overheard a female voice say, "I bet she is going to be a major bitch." My ears instantly tuned in. I didn't want Sean to know that I was eavesdropping, so I pretended to read the piece of paper I had in my hand. Then I heard a more mature woman's voice interject.

"Janae, why would you say something like that about her and you haven't met her yet? That's what's wrong with young black women today; you all are too quick to judge one another. Instead of you introducing yourself to Mrs. Goodwin, and offering your assistance, you are out here talking about someone you know absolutely nothing about. I am really disappointed in your behavior. Now, I suggest the two of you stop gossiping and get to work." I smiled to myself. "*You tell 'em, girl,*" I mumbled.

"Toni, why don't you let me introduce you to some of the office staff."

I looked up from the paper I was pretending to read and smiled, "Oh, Sean, I

3

would love that." *Now I can match a face with a voice and see which one of them called me a bitch.*

As we entered the hallway outside of my office, I noticed two women talking. Another young lady was walking away as we approached them. *It's inventory time again.* The younger one was about 5'6" tall, with shoulder-length weave that resembled R&B singer Ashanti's hair, acrylic nails, a mocha-colored Ralph Lauren outfit that accentuated her small waist and ghetto booty. Matching Nine West pumps, and a Coach purse. I estimated her age to be between eighteen and twenty years old. *I'm guessing she is the one that called me a bitch.* The other lady was an older more distinguished-looking woman. She, too, was around 5'6" tall. She had her hair pulled back in a bun. Her angelic face was framed by touches of gray around her edges. She had a very pleasant demeanor and her clothes were definitely stylish. Her stunning black suit looked like an Ann Taylor design. Her figure was that of a black woman in her early fifties and her eyes told a story. I was extremely anxious to meet her. I knew in my heart that she was the sistah that had my back a few minutes earlier.

"Good morning, ladies, I would like to introduce you to our newest family member. This is Toni T. Goodwin. She is the new vice president of marketing. Toni, this is Mrs. Elaine Stevens and Janae Johnson. Mrs. Stevens is the Director of Communications and Public Relations, and Janae is her administrative assistant."

"Good morning, ladies. It is a pleasure to meet you both. I look forward to working with you."

"Good morning, Mrs. Goodwin. The pleasure is all ours."

"Thank you, Mrs. Stevens, and that would be *Ms.* Goodwin. But I would prefer it if you just called me Toni."

"Okay. Toni it is."

I decided that the best way to break the ice with Janae and to get a better feel for Mrs. Stevens would be to have lunch with them. Women tend to bond better whenever food is involved." Ladies, Sean and I are on somewhat of a tight schedule this morning. I have to meet the rest of the office staff, but I insist on the two of you join me for lunch, my treat. I would love to sit and talk with both of you and get your thoughts on the company and our upcoming campaigns."

"I would like that," Mrs. Stevens said as she gave Janae a look.

"Me, too," Janae added, with a strained smile.

*Great.* I handled that little predicament with sincerity and a smile.

\*\*\*

I chose to take Janae and Mrs. Stevens to lunch at Café de Italy. It's one of my

4

favorite Italian restaurants. While we were there, we bonded over pasta and garlic bread. I'm not certain whether or not I won them over. I realized, however, that between Mrs. Stevens's knowledge of the company and Janae's fresh ideas for ad campaigns, that they would probably be my best allies at Carlton. Having lunch with them was definitely a good idea.

"Ladies, thank you both for joining me for lunch, but I'd better get back to work before Mr. Carlton wonders why he hired me." I said, as I walked away laughing. Mrs. Stevens and Janae were laughing, too, as they returned to their offices.

Throughout the day I met directors, managers, and personnel from different parts of the company. By 5:00 P.M., I was ready for the day to end. My adrenaline was pumping and my dogs were barking. Girlfriend was ready to kick off her two-inch pumps and slip into a warm bath, cotton robe, and cashmere slippers. As I drove home, I thought about candlelight, jazz, jasmine bath salts, and peppermint tea.

The first thing I did when I walked inside the house was turn off all of the ringers, because I knew my mother would be calling to see how my first day was. Then I dimmed all the lights, turned on the teapot, grabbed extra candles, and headed upstairs. I started the water running for my bubble bath. As I sat among the thousands of bubbles caressing my smooth, chocolate skin, I thought to myself, *look at how far I've come. This is truly heaven on earth.*

My mind retreated from today's activities and drifted back to when I'd first arrived in Atlanta. I had hooked up with a group of ladies whom I'd met in Luxurious Locks, a beauty salon in Buckhead. Everybody who is anybody or who wants to be somebody gets their hair done there. I had met Michelle, Cynthia, and Ebony while sitting in the waiting room. We bonded over the latest edition of Ebony Hunks magazine featuring Shemar Moore and Morris Chestnut.

"Girl, Shemar is my baby's daddy," Ebony had shouted as she looked at his swimsuit picture. "Y'all know he has a new workout video, it's called 'Six Weeks to a Six Pack'. Mine should be arriving in the mail tomorrow."

Michelle and Cynthia laughed.

"See, y'all laughing, but when I take this forty ounce stomach I am sporting right now and turn it into a six pack, don't start sweating me then. And don't ask me for the telephone number to call and order the tape, either. If I catch either one of you heifers calling my baby's daddy, I will not hesitate to scratch your eyes out. Then how are you going to get a six pack if you can't even *see* your stomach?"

The three of them died laughing and I chimed in. They have been my girls ever since.

The four of us started hanging out, clubbing, shopping, and exhaling together.

One night on our way to Atlanta Live we heard the song, "*Whoot, Whoot...pull over that ass is too phat*"

"Hey, girl, turn that up, that's my jam," said Ebony.

"Awe shucks now, it's girls night out in Hotlanta and me and my girls are about to turn it out tonight. Cynthia, this convertible Benz is phat! Girl, you must be doing something right."

"Ebony, honey, it's called dating men with money. You should try it. It will be a new and different experience for you," Cynthia said, laughing, while me and Michelle gave each other high-fives.

"*Screw all y'all heifers. Just wait until me and Shemar get together. I'll show you who's who.*" Ebony defended, while rolling her eyes at us, and still getting her jam on. As we pulled up to the valet stand, we noticed the brothers waiting to get inside the club. Their eyes were going *from the rides to the hides.*

"Look at all the *mens*," Michelle said.

"All right, ladies, it's time to work it. *Divatude!*" said Cynthia as we exited the Benzo.

Four sophisticated-looking ladies stepped out of a brand new convertible platinum package, limited-edition Mercedes.

"Are y'all somebody important?" some dude shouted.

"That's what my mama always told me," I replied, as I winked at the men and walked inside the club through the VIP entrance. The four of us looked absolutely flawless. We'd spent the better part of the day at Luxurious Locks getting the works: hair, manicures, pedicures, facials, and waxing. I had on a black form-fitting dress that stopped at my trademark, three inches above my knee. I wore my new sandals that tie all the way up my long, coffee-colored legs and stop at my calf. I knew those shoes drove men crazy. Especially whenever I had a fresh pedicure. They were my sexy secret weapons. Michelle had on a baby blue fitted pantsuit that accentuated all of her curves and gave her cleavage ample attention. She was sporting her new Halle Berry haircut, and some killer Versace sandals. Cynthia wore a strapless, elastic cocktail mini-dress with a see-through chiffon mid section. Her outfit screamed Dolce & Gabbana and her expression shouted *platinum preferred—all others need not apply!*

"Ebony, girl, you are going to set the place on fire with your bad-ass red mini skirt; and what's up with the plunging neckline? Your legs look longer than Lil Kim's weave," Michelle said, laughing.

Ebony accessorized her outfit with Sade-style hoop earrings and a matching choker. All four of us looked tasteful, elegant and expensive.

"Toni, isn't that Andre over their talking to the light skinned sister with the long hair?" Michelle said.

"Yeah girl, that's his tired ass. He's a trip. Andre is truly an opportunist. He takes every opportunity he has to hit on every woman who he thinks has money. I remember when I dated him. Girl, that brother was reading me poetry and singing to me over the phone. I just knew he was the man. Until I found out he was living with his grandmother, and driving a Yugo with no air conditioning and no radio. I had to drop that phony, fronting brotha like a bad habit. I bet you he is over there reciting a poem to her right now."

"Okay, girlfriend, you're on. In fact, let's make this bet interesting. I bet you your next manicure and pedicure from the salon if you can guess which poem he is reciting."

"I'll take that bet, girl, because I know him like a book. He's reciting 'Fine as Wine.' That is always his introductory poem. Let's walk past them without him seeing me, and make sure you are listening to what he's saying. Michelle, I intend to get my free manicure and pedicure."

The two of us strolled through the club, casually smiling and flirting with men as we made our way over to where Andre stood. As we passed by the couple we heard Andre saying *"Red or white, either is fine with me, when my eyes focused on you I couldn't believe what I could see. An angelic face, heavenly body, I prayed that God would give me time… to get to meet a woman like you, who is as fine as wine."* Michelle and I could barely hold our laughter long enough to get outside of earshot of Andre. The last thing I wanted was for him to recognize me. We laughed so hard we had tears streaming down our faces. We had to go to the ladies room immediately to freshen up our make-up. On the way to the ladies room, we passed a brotha who had obviously had a little too much to drink. We overheard him saying, to a sistah with a short dress on, *"Damn, baby, that dress is shorter than a midget on his knees."* That sister looked at him with an attitude that said *fuck you.* Me and Michelle burst out laughing all over again.

"Well girlfriend, I have to admit you were right and your next manicure and pedicure are on me."

"Thank you very much, Michelle. Your generosity is always appreciated" I smiled.

"Girl, we have truly gotten our laugh on tonight. Where is Ebony and Cynthia?" Michelle asked.

"The last time I saw Ebony she was on the dance floor getting her jam on. Cynthia was at the bar talking to a guy who looked like he thought he was somebody."

"Cynthia knows how to pull men with money. Now that's a gift," Michelle said, laughing.

"I know, girl. I wish it would rub off on me."

"Toni, girl, I don't know about you but I have had my fill of excitement for the evening. I am ready to collect the rest of our posse and retire for the night."

"I hear you girl. Let's go find Cynthia and Ebony and head home."

We walked out of the bathroom, and passed the drunk brotha again. This time he jumped in front of Michelle, looked at her chest, and said, "*Damn, mama, it looks like you're smuggling two midgets under your jacket.*"

Michelle backed up looked at his crotch and retorted, "*damn, daddy, it looks like one of the midgets escaped and is hiding in your pants!*" Then she gracefully walked away. We grabbed Ebony off of the dance floor, summoned Cynthia from the bar and left Atlanta Live. We'd had a great time that night.

By the time I finished daydreaming, I had been in the tub over an hour. The teapot was whistling, and my skin was wrinkled, but I felt relaxed and rejuvenated. I got out of the tub and massaged mango-scented body butter all over my newly cleansed body. I slipped into my cotton bathrobe, slid my feet into my cashmere slippers and went downstairs. Once I turned off the teapot and poured myself a cup of peppermint tea, I called Mom to tell her all about my first day at work.

# Chapter 2
## Sean's story

I'm Sean Carlton, the executive assistant to VP of Marketing at Carlton International. I attended Morehouse College here in Atlanta, Georgia, where I received my Bachelors degree in Marketing. I went on to further my education at Yale where I received my M.B.A. I'm twenty-nine years old, single; with no children. Women approach me all the time, but I am very careful about who I date. You see, my father is constantly watching over the heir to his empire, because I am an only child. In fact, the last name is no coincidence. My full name is Jeffery Sean Carlton IV. I tell everyone my name is Sean because I don't want anyone to know that I am the boss's son.

There are only two people who know the truth about my identity at work and I plan to keep it that way. When I came to work at the company four years ago, my father wanted to make a formal announcement that I was his son. But I was really uncomfortable with the idea. I told him I wanted to work my way from the bottom up. So I asked him not to make a big fuss. The only people who know the truth are Mrs. Stevens, the Director of Communications and Public Relations, and Henry, our building maintenance man. My father has employed the two of them since he started this business 30 years ago.

My mother says my father got tired of being trapped by the "glass ceiling" that exists in Corporate America. So he saved his money, made good stock investments, applied for a small business loan, and quit his job. The day he quit he vowed that his son would never have to experience the heartache, rejection, and prejudice that he'd faced in Corporate America. He now lives is his dream as the CEO of a multimillion-dollar advertising firm.

My new boss just started a month ago. Her name is Toni T. Goodwin. I really feel an attraction to her. It's not a physical attraction but a spiritual one. There is something about her spirit that I am drawn to. It's almost as if I have seen her some place before. She is very bright and extremely personable. I am sure we will work well together.

"Good morning, Sean" Toni interrupted.

"Good morning, Toni" I replied.

"I stopped by Krispy Kreme and picked up some coffee and donuts for our staff meeting this morning."

"Sean, you are heaven-sent. I didn't have breakfast this morning, and I am starving. Thank you."

"You are quite welcome. Toni, what time would you like me to schedule the driver to take you to the airport?"

"*Oh!* I almost forgot about my trip to Tallahassee. Please ask him to be here by five o'clock, and thanks for the reminder."

"No problem. Why are you going to Tallahassee?"

"My high school reunion. I can't believe it has been ten years since I graduated."

"I know what you mean. I went to mine last year. It was fun yet stressful."

"What do you mean, Sean?"

"Well, although I was looking forward to seeing all of my homeboys, I wasn't looking forward to answering all of their questions."

"What kind of questions?"

"Like why aren't you married, where is your girlfriend, are you running your daddy's company yet?" *Oh Damn!* I hope Toni didn't pick up on what I said.

"I understand what you mean, Sean, but what's this about running your father's company? What kind of company does your father own? I hate to be like everybody else, but why aren't you running it?"

*Shit!* I was afraid she would ask me that! I had to think quickly on my feet. As much as I like Toni, I can't let her in on the family secret.

"He is in the janitorial services business. He has 10 teams of cleaning people that clean downtown office buildings, and he also has 25 invisible butlers."

"Really? That's a pretty large staff."

"Yes, he has 130 employees including his office staff."

"Wow! Now let me get this straight. I'm assuming this at the risk of making an ass out of myself. The invisible butlers are a maid service?"

"That's exactly right."

"Sean, this is good to know. I have been looking for someone to clean my place every two weeks. I would be happy to throw some business your father's way."

*Damn!* This hole is getting deeper and deeper. I feel like Joe Frazier fighting Muhammad Ali. She really has my back up against the ropes. I have to come out fighting or else I am in big trouble.

"Toni, that's very sweet of you; I'll let my father know."

"Sean, that's the least I can do. I believe in supporting black businesses."

"Me too."

"By the way, you never told me why you aren't working for your father."

*Shit!* She sucker-punched me again. Just when I thought I was about to get away...

"Oh, yeah, well, I decided while I was in college that it would be beneficial for me to work for someone else for a while. That way, I would learn to appreciate what my father has done for me. I do intend to work for him one day though."

"That's pretty admirable, Sean. Most kids would take the easy way out and go work for daddy. If I was in your shoes, I would probably be working for my daddy."

"Well, thanks for the pat on the back, Toni, but I'd better try to get in touch with the driver before he makes other plans."

"Sure, go ahead, I'll see you at the staff meeting."

*Whew!* That was a close call. I barely got out of that one. I have got to be more careful around Toni. She is too sharp for me to make mistakes like that in front of her. Now I have to figure out how I am going to get my ass out of this one. I better call Mike to help me get out of this.

Mike was my roommate at Morehouse my freshman year. I can still remember the first day we met. I arrived on campus a week early for freshman orientation. My parents and I attended all the meetings and activities held on campus for incoming freshmen. I felt like such a nerd walking around campus with my mother and father. Not many of the young men entering Morehouse had their parents hanging out with them. I was so embarrassed. My father put everything into perspective for me, however, saying that I was fortunate enough to have parents who are still married and able to send their child to a Historically Black College.

"Morehouse has produced many great men such as Martin Luther King, Jr., Spike Lee, Samuel L. Jackson, and Edwin Moses," my dad had once said. "These men and others like them who have graduated from this institution have transformed the way Black people are treated in society. They have not only revolutionized Black people, but they have transformed the sports, film and entertainment industry. You should feel blessed and proud to become a part of such a rich tradition and you should never feel anything other than pride when walking across this campus, especially while being accompanied by two loving and supportive parents."

Dad really had a way of bringing everything full circle. After that sermon, I never felt embarrassed about walking with my parents on campus again. In fact, I made sure they attended Parents' Weekend every year.

That evening, after my parents had left, we had the freshman welcoming ceremony. This ceremony was traditionally held in Sale Hall, which is named after one of the former professors at Morehouse. It was the most remarkable thing I'd ever experienced. We entered the hall to the sound of bass, baritone, and tenor voices reciting African chants and singing folk songs. Our feet marched to the soft ancestral beat of an African drum. Once inside, two-hundred strong African-American men dressed in all black surrounded us, welcoming us with open arms into their 100-year-old tradition of producing strong Black leaders, teacher, doctors, lawyers, scientists, and entrepreneurs. The ceremony continued with a mellow baritone voice reciting a speech from Martin Luther King Jr. He was interrupted by the sound of a bass voice performing a monologue from Marcus Garvey, and then the voice of a tenor narrating a speech from Malcolm X took center stage and captivated us all.

As the voices speaking to us from our ancestors quieted to a whisper, the lights dimmed to darkness. The room was lit only by candlelight. The president of

Morehouse seemed to rise out of the darkness to command our attention center stage. He explained to us the significance of the three-m's, Martin, Marcus, and Malcolm. "Martin stands for non-violence," he exclaimed. "Marcus, for those of you who are unfamiliar with him and all his greatness, stands for wisdom," he proclaimed. "And Malcolm, affectionately referred to by "*The house*" as the X-factor, stands for strength," he intoned.

He preached to us about the three "necessaries" every true Morehouse man should have in his possession. Someone shouted "You mean necessities, don't you sir?" The room quieted to a hush. The President answered, "No, young man, I meant exactly what I said. You see, son, it is absolutely *necessary* for you to have a watch, because if you arrive anywhere on time, you are late. So, make sure you always arrive fifteen minutes early," he insisted. The second is a pen, "You need to always be prepared to network," he emphasized. Lastly, you should always have a quarter for a phone call. "Never be afraid to call for help. Your Morehouse brothers are all you have to depend on," he declared. By the time he was finished, the only sound you heard was the whimpering of over two-hundred male voices. The entire room was overcome with emotion. This was black male bonding in its finest hour.

We all left the ceremony in silence, too wrought with emotion to speak. That evening, while walking on campus, if you encountered another brother no words were exchanged, only a solemn and heartfelt embrace, as you continued on your way.

By the time I got back to my dorm room, I was drained from the emotional ride I had been on all evening. When I entered the room, there was a 6'4", dark chocolate, football-player-chiseled brother standing in the middle of the room with a towel wrapped around his waist, brushing his teeth. For a moment, I thought I was in the wrong room. I backed back out of the room and looked at the number on the door.

That's when Mike said, "You must be Jeffery" and extended his hand.

"Yes, I am, and you are?"

"Michael Charles Alexander, and I am your new roommate." He smiled.

"It's a pleasure to meet you, Michael."

"You can call me Mike."

"Okay, Mike, am I interrupting something?" I asked as my eyes darted down to his towel.

"*Oh, Dang, man, excuse me!* I forgot I was standing here half naked. I am so used to holding conversations in a towel it slipped my mind."

I raised one eyebrow, and gave him a strange look. Then he said, "What I mean is I am used to doing this in the locker room. I play football."

"Okay, I gotcha. Well, why aren't you staying in the football dorms?"

"Because I got accepted to Florida State on an athletic Scholarship, but I really wanted to go to Morehouse. So I'm going to try out for the team as a walk-on."

"Good for you, man. I hope you make it."

"Thanks, Jeffery."

"You can call me Sean, that's my middle name. All of my friends call me Sean."

"Okay, Sean it is."

Mike did make the team that year. He ended up having a great season. He rushed for 1200 yards, and managed to sack every quarterback he played against. He was voted an All-American. He started being heavily recruited by the NFL. But he was not willing to entertain the thought of pro-ball until he obtained his degree. He always focused his attention on the Morehouse truths: the three-M's and the three necessaries. Whenever either of us became unfocused, it was the others responsibility to make his brother recite the Morehouse truths, regardless of who was present. One night, when we were on the campus of Spelman College, Mike was rapping to this nice-looking young lady. Meanwhile we only had ten minutes to make curfew, or he wouldn't have been eligible to play in our homecoming game. I nudged him and told him we had to leave, but he kept on macking. I sat there anxiously watching the clock tick. Little beads of sweat started to form on my forehead. Mike kept on talking. Finally when it got down to five minutes, I stood up and shouted, "*Morehouse truths!*" Mike stopped mid-sentence, and looked at me with pleading eyes as if to say, "*Naw man, don't do me like this in front of this fine babe.*" I ignored his look and said it again, "*Morehouse truths!*" Mike stood up, pulled out his pen, and wrote his phone number down on a piece of paper. Then he gave the young lady his quarter to insure that she would call him. He kissed her on the cheek, said goodnight, and fell in line like a good solider. As we raced back to the dorms, he recited the Morehouse truths. When we got back to the dorm, we had three seconds left to spare. We both fell on to our beds, breathing hard and laughing.

"Man! That was a close call, Sean. Thanks."

"Hey, what are brothers for Mike?"

He's had my back ever since.

\*\*\*

"Hey, what's up, man? This is Sean."

"Chillin,' man. What's up with you?"

"Not a whole lot I'm just dealing with a couple of things right now."

"Talk to your brother, man, what's happening?"

"Well, you know the new supervisor that I told you about?"

"Yeah, the fine one."

13

"This morning, she caught me slipping, and I had to tell her my father owns a janitorial and maid service."

"You what!"

"Yeah, man, and it gets worse. She told me she wanted to throw some business my father's, way so she wants to hire his company to come clean her house! *Man*, Mike, how am I going to rectify this shit?"

"You really messed up this time," Mike said, laughing. "Okay, check this out: tell her you called your father and he said he is not taking on any new clients because he is thinking of phasing out the residential portion of the business. Then give her a referral to another maid service."

"You think that'll work?"

"What other choice do you have?"

"None."

"Well, then, bro, I suggest you try it."

"You're right, I better roll with that. Are we still on for basketball tomorrow?"

"Yeah I'll swing by your crib around two o'clock tomorrow."

"Okay, Mike. Thanks man."

"No problem. I hope it works."

"Me, too, man. Me, too."

"Let me know how it turns out."

"For sure."

"I'll catch you tomorrow, bro"

"Okay. Peace out."

I sure hope Toni buys this story. Otherwise I am in big trouble. I'll just tell her after the staff meeting that I called my dad, and he told me he wasn't taking on any new clients. I better call the service I use and tell them I'm sending them a referral and that they are not to discuss me or my father's company with her under any circumstances. I feel really bad about lying to Toni, but what choice do I have? I hope this is the only lie I have to tell her. Hell, I've spent enough time trippin' on this today. I better call and order the driver to come pick her up to take her to the airport before I forget and screw that up, too. Damn, it's only nine-thirty and I feel like I have put in a full day's work already! Thank God it's Friday. I'm looking forward to the weekend. Tonight, I have plans for dinner and jazz with my friend Jackie. She'll certainly brighten up my day. Jackie is going to *die* when I tell her about what happened today. Especially when I tell her about Toni wanting to hire my dad's company to clean her place. I can just hear her scream, "WHAT!" and then fall out laughing in my face. I'm sure I'll be laughing with her.

"Sean," Toni buzzed. "Would you please round everyone up for our ten o'clock meeting?"

14

"Sure, Toni, no problem. Do you need anything else?"

"No, thanks."

"You're welcome."

# Chapter 3
## Going Back To Tally

When I looked at the clock it was already 4:30p.m. The limo driver would be here promptly at 5:00p.m. to pick me up. I had to make one last phone call before I dashed out the door.

"Hey, girlfriend, it's me. I just wanted to call and confirm my flight times with you."

"Now, Teaser, you know I have that information memorized. When has Ms. Divine ever let you down?"

"Never"

"Exactly. So you just stop being nervous and get on that plane. Mama will be there to meet you and help you get through this weekend."

"Thank you, Ms. D. What would I ever do without you?"

"I don't know, honey, but let's hope we never have to find out."

"Amen to that."

"Okay, love, I will see you in two hours. Have a safe flight."

"I'll try, sweetie. Love you."

"Love you, too, boo, bye-bye."

I hung up the phone, called Sean to see if the driver was downstairs, and bolted out of the door. *Oh my God! I forgot to call mama.* She will have an absolute fit if I don't call her before I leave town. Okay, Toni, stay cool. You can do this. I'll just call her from my cell on the way to the airport. Whenever I get nervous about something, I always have to talk myself through the situation. I am sure I will be doing that a lot on this trip, because I am more nervous right now than I have ever been in my life. Well, maybe with the exception of my operations.

I'm on my way to my high school reunion to see people whom I haven't seen in ten years. These are people who knew me when my name was spelled with a Y, not an I. They knew me when my penis was just that, and not a simulated clitoris. When my chest wasn't breast, and when my voice had bass in it. No one, with the exception of Ms. Divine, will know who I am! This is going to be one hell of a reunion. Thank God Ms. Divine will be there with me.

Ms. Divine is my best friend, Devon. We met our freshmen year at Leon High School in Tallahassee. We bonded instantly. We were both only children being raised by our single mothers. We were both considered outcasts. There was just something about us that was a little different from most boys. After about a month of hanging out together, Devon told me he had a confession to make. So he invited me over to his house after school. When we got there, he went into his bedroom closet and pulled out his collection of Barbie dolls. He told me he always had an affinity for girlish things, and that pink was his favorite color.

16

"Why are you showing me this?" I had asked.

"Because I have a feeling you are just like me, Tony."

"No! No, I'm not."

"Tony I have seen the way you look at cute boys. I have caught you looking at boys in the locker room, and you have yet to try and hit on a girl. So just admit it."

"You don't know what you're talking about!"

"Are you sure about that?" he pressed. "Or are you too afraid to face the truth? You can trust me, Tony. Believe me when I tell you your secrets are safe with me. We are in the same boat, and we need somebody who understands what we're going through. I promise you from this day forward anything you share with me is between you, me, and God."

*Devon's right. I do need to have someone to talk to about my feelings. I'm going to take a chance on him.* "Do you cross your heart and hope to die?"

He drew an imaginary X over his heart. "Yes, cross my heart and hope to die!"

"Okay...Yes. I do think I'm gay. I am not attracted to girls the way I am to boys. I am attracted to girl clothes and the attention they get from boys, but I am not physically attracted to them. I've never acknowledged this before. You are the first person I am confiding in. Usually I write in my diary about it or just talk to God."

"Do you think your mom knows?"

"I'm not sure. However, I do think she became suspicious when I asked her for a fuchsia diary. What about you, does your mom know?"

"Who do you think supplies me with all the dolls?"

We both started laughing, hugged, and vowed to take each other's secrets to the grave. Devon was the only person I told when I had my first sexual encounter. He was also the first person I confided in when I decided I wanted to have a sex change. I'll never forget the look on his face or what he said.

He looked at me and said, "Sweetie, dick is far too good to cut off! Are you out of your ever-loving mind? I don't care if you're hetero or homo, a good dick is hard to find. You have the nerve to want to cut yours off!" Then he grabbed my hands, looked me in the eyes, and said, " Can I have your leftovers?"

After we finished laughing, he gave me his blessing and promised to be by my side through my transformation and beyond. To this very day, he has never broken a promise to me. To tell you the truth, I don't know how I would have ever made it through high school or my operations without him.

*I'd better call mama; we're almost at the airport.*

"Hey, Ma, it's me. I'm just calling to let you know that I'm on my way to the airport."

"Hi sweetheart. How are you feeling? Are you nervous?"

"Yes, Ma, I am."

17

"Well, don't be. You have every right to go to your reunion and be proud of who you have become."

"I know, Ma, but it's scary."

"Then, darling, what you have to do is feel the fear and do it anyway. Is Devon going to pick you up from the airport?"

"Yes, he is. I can't tell you how glad I am to have him there. Next to you, he is the most important person in the world to me."

"I know, sweetheart, that's what good friends are all about. Now, go have fun and don't forget to call me as soon as you land to let me know you made it. Give my love to Devon and his mom."

"Okay, Ma, I will."

"Have a safe flight, sweetheart, and try to enjoy your reunion."

"Thanks, Ma. I will. I love you."

"I love you, too, baby. Bye."

By the time I hung up with my mother, we were pulling up to the Delta Airlines curbside check-in counter. I got out of the limo, checked my bags, and tipped the driver fifty dollars. Then I started that long journey to my gateway. Hartsfield Airport is so large and so busy that you really need to arrive two hours before your flight is scheduled to leave. I had more than enough time so I decided to stop in Starbucks for some hot tea to calm me down. There were quite a few gentlemen in there drinking coffee and cocktails and checking out the ladies. They were all businessmen, and most were wearing wedding rings.

I said to the woman standing next to me, "Isn't it a shame that you never know what your man is doing when you're not around?"

She looked at me and said, "That's exactly why I cheat on my husband. You have to always assume they are going to cheat on you. Honey, I learned that lesson from my first husband."

I looked at her and said, " I hear you, girlfriend. Enough said."

I sat there talking with her for fifteen minutes while I drank my tea to calm my nerves. Then I shook her hand, thanked her for her company, and continued on my journey to my boarding gate. As I arrived at the gate, the ticket agents were announcing that the flight was full and asking for volunteers to give up their seats.

*I could give up my seat, not face my fears of seeing all of my old classmates as a woman now, and just run like the wind.* Two things stopped me from doing it: One, I was flying in first class, and you never give that up. Two, Ms. Divine would have a fit and go off on me if I didn't show up. And that alone will make you stick to the plan.

Landing at the Tallahassee airport brought on a surge of emotions. I felt the butterflies forming in my stomach as the flight attendant announced that we would be deplaning momentarily. The moisture pooled in the palm of my hands. I had to take a few deep breaths and experience a moment of silent meditation. I unbuckled my seat belt, grabbed my carry-on bag from the overhead compartment, and exited the plane. As I walked up the ramp to the gateway entrance, my mood instantly changed from fear to excitement. There stood my best friend in the whole world with a bouquet of exotic flowers and a banner that read, *"Welcome home, Teaser."*

I dropped my bag, ran, and gave Ms. Divine a big hug. "What a wonderful welcome, Ms. D," I whispered.

"Teaser, you look absolutely marvelous!"

I stepped back and gave D the once-over and said, "Ms. D, you look simply divine, as only you could."

We hugged again. "Girl, I missed you so much."

"I missed you too."

"We are going to have a ball this weekend."

"What do you have planned? I know you have something up your sleeve, D."

"You know you would be disappointed if I didn't."

"You got that right, so let's hear it."

"For starters, we are going to the Martini Bar tonight. I have already made arrangements for some gentlemen friends to meet us there. But before we do that, we have got to go shopping. Tallahassee has really grown since the last time you were here. Tallahassee Mall is just as nice now as the Governor Square Mall. So I figured we would hit both of them."

"Ms. D, I know you are not trying to do all of that in one night."

"Yes, I am, unless you have something short and tight in this beautiful Louis Vuitton luggage of yours."

"As a matter of fact, yes, ma'am, I do. And I look fabulous in it, too."

"If that's the case, then we can just head back to my place and chill for an hour before going out."

"That sounds good to me."

"Then my place it is. By the way, did I mention I hired a driver for the weekend?"

"Ms. D, no, you didn't!"

"Oh yes, I did!"

"Girl you are too much."

"Now you know how we Divas do it! First class baby, just like I'm sure your seat on the plane was."

"Touché. I will happily shut my mouth now and ride in our limo with pride."

"Thank you. That's what a true Diva would do."

"Girl, I can't tell you how happy I am to see you. Thank you for this."

"No thanks necessary. What are friends for?"

Ms. D recently had a home built in the suburbs of Tallahassee known as Plantation. Although she hates the name of the suburb for obvious reasons, she has to live where the "people in the know" live. Ms. D prides herself on *being* "The Joneses." According to her, everybody is trying to keep up with her.

The driver approached a beautiful stately home accentuated by a cobblestone driveway. The house was situated at least a half a mile from the roadway and was surrounded by an acre of land.

The land was well groomed and her garden was absolutely breathtaking. The inside of the house left me speechless. Ms. D had taken care of every detail all the way down to the waterfall that you could see and hear from the dining room. Her living space would put Martha Stewart to shame. From her imported African leather rugs to the cobalt blue accent lights lining her staircase. She even had a built-in jazz system that started to play as soon as the key entered the lock on the front door.

The entire second floor was the master bedroom and bathroom. And it was, bar none, the best room in the entire house. Ms. D continued the African motif in her bedroom, using softer colors. A California king-size platform bed sat in the center of the room. Her comforter set alone had to cost upwards of $5000. A leather chaise lounge was placed neatly against the wall adjacent to a huge walk -in closet that looked like the one Angela Bassett's husband had in the movie, *Waiting to Exhale.* Beautiful French doors opened out onto the balcony, with a view that is astonishing. The cool breeze was equally as pleasing. D had a cus-tom-made swing built for two out here, along with hibachi style grills that were actually lit to give off the illusion of candlelight. All of the potted plants were healthy and exotic, just like her parrot, which swung effortlessly in his cage.

The bathroom was definitely the serenity room. All of the lighting in it was dim. The garden-style tub spoke volumes about the room. Candles surrounded the tub, and a waterfall actually trickled down into it. The inside of the tub was equipped with powerful looking jets. Her bathroom put mine to shame. However, D put the final nail in my coffin when I saw the bidet. Enough said.

"D, this home is unbelievable! You not only have an eye for fashion, Diva; you have an eye for all things beautiful. You go, girl! I am overwhelmed and proud. You have certainly done well for yourself. Hell, let me just go ahead and bow to the queen." I kneeled down.

"You know I'm a queen in more ways than one." She said, laughing. "Girl, get your crazy self up off the floor and let me show you to your room."

"After you, queen." I curtsied.

The guest quarters were just as lovely as the rest of the house. Just walking in here gave my energy level a major boost. It felt light and airy. Her choice of colors made a bold statement: fuchsia, tangerine, and a hint of gold. The view from the window seat showed the large oval-shaped swimming pool and hot tub. The bathroom had a Roman tub encircled by scented candles and mocha-colored marble floors. Ms. D didn't miss a beat in decorating this room, either. I guess good taste runs deep.

"D, I feel at home already. This room is just as wonderful as every other square inch of this gorgeous home."

"Thank you girl. Do you need me to get you anything?"

"No, thank you. I am just going to lie down and rest a little bit before we go out. Would you wake me up in an hour?"

"Of course, get your rest, girl, I'll see you in a little while."

*** 

The limo arrived to pick us up at eight o'clock. We arrived at the Martini Bar at 8:30. I was wearing a brown leather bustier with a low slung a long straight skirt that hugged my hips and showed off my belly button, and brown leather boots that matched my top. I had my hair pinned up so that my diamond teardrop earrings would get the attention they deserved. Ms. D had on a winter-white pants suit. The pants were palazzo pants and her shirt was the exact same color with wide sleeves. We both looked like a million bucks, if I do say so myself.

Now is probably a good time to tell you a thing or two about Ms. D. Devon is still a man for all intents and purposes. He has not had any operations, nor does he intend to. He likes his penis--a lot! He is what we call "Puss". That's gay lingo for a sissy. He dates men and he does answer to his name. I call him Ms. Divine, or Ms. D, for short. That was his stage name, back in the day, when we were performers. I thought it fit him so well that I continued to call him that. The only time I call him Devon is when we are in front of company or if I have something serious to tell him. On occasion, he will dress up like a woman, but for the most part, he wears semi-feminine clothes.

"Teaser, I just spotted our dates sitting at the bar."

"Quick, girl, give me the scoop on them before they walk over here."

"John, the taller one, is an investment banker. He owns a home here in Plantation and a condo in Miami. He drives a Mercedes Benz, and he has a Yacht. He's divorced and doesn't have any children. He is 35, and from what I hear he has dick for days. He is yours."

"Bless you, D."

"Roger, the slightly shorter one, is an attorney, he is married but he likes boys. I have been seeing him off and on for the last six months. We try to keep it on the DL because if this got out it would ruin him. I can't have that happen, girl,

21

he is my 401k plan, if you know what I mean."

"I hear you, I guess a boy has to do what a boy has to do."

"You got that right, sistah."

John and Roger walked over to us.

"Good evening, gentlemen. This is my friend, Toni T. Goodwin. Toni, this is John Collins, and Roger Bryant."

" It's a pleasure to meet you." I grinned as I extended my hand.

"The pleasure is all ours," they replied in unison, and they each kissed my hand.

"Okay, cut that shit out. Y'all are making me jealous. You all know I need attention too," D protested.

We all looked at him and laughed. Then they both escorted us to our reserved table. The Martini Bar was warm and elegant. The lights were dimly lit and candles adorned each table. I heard my favorite artist, Tami Davis, playing. While John and I sat talking and sipping our drinks, track number seven off of Tami's "Only You" CD interrupted us.

"Excuse me, John, but that is my song. Would you mind escorting me to the dance floor?"

"It would be an honor to dance with such a lovely young lady."

"You are too kind, John," I blushed.

"Did I tell you how breathtaking I think you are?"

"No, you didn't, but I thank you for the compliment. It's always nice to hear a man acknowledge how much trouble we women go through to look this good. So, on behalf of all the women in America, I thank you."

All John could do was look at me and chuckle. He didn't know whether to take me seriously or not. So I left it like that. One thing I know for sure is that you have to keep men guessing. I decided since this one seems to be worthwhile, I am going to keep him guessing about a lot of things.

John's body was pressed against mine so closely that I could feel his heartbeat. It seemed to beat to the rhythm of the song. His cologne made me want to just lick him. His hair was cut low and wavy like he has Indian in his family. His pants were black and hung just right over his perfectly round butt. As we swayed to the music, my soul felt like it was being penetrated by those amber. Colored gems he called eyes. His mustache was perfectly groomed, and his skin was flawless. The more Tami sang, and the more I smelled him, the more I wanted him. Apparently he was a little hot and bothered, too, because I could feel his penis swelling. And let's just say that it feels like the kind of dick that will make you drop down to your knees and thank the Lord! But y'all don't hear me, though. Can a sistah get an amen?

"Toni, you are a pretty smooth dancer."

"Well you are not doing to bad either, Mr. Smooth Operator."

Five tracks later, we realized that the music was no longer Tami Davis. Will Downing was now crooning, as only he can, and John and I were still swaying. His bulge had swollen to hernia size now. I wanted to grab it and tell him to cough. I had to resist temptation and remain a lady. However, a lady does know her limits.

"John, would you mind if we sit this next song out. I think I saw the waiter arrive at the table with our food."

"I do mind, because I don't want to let you go. But if you promise that this will not be the last time we dance, I'll honor your request."

"You know you're twisting my arm on this one, but okay, I promise." I whispered flirtatiously to him letting my lips *accidentally* brush against his ear.

We left the dance floor and I returned to the table alone. John excused himself to go to the bathroom. I know he must have had to adjust that rock-hard dick of his. He should've just asked me; I would have done it for him.

"Are you having a good time, Toni?" Roger asked.

"Yes, I am. John is a nice man."

"Good. I am glad you like my partner. I have been trying to hook him up with a nice lady. I have to confess, you came highly recommended."

"Oh really? Devon, I wouldn't suppose he is referring to you."

"Girl, you know mama does what she can."

"I know you do. Thank you for this one." I winked at Devon. "So, Roger, are you originally from the Tallahassee area?"

"No. I moved here five years ago. I have aspirations of running for office. So I figured, what better place to live than the capital city?"

"Good for you. What office do you plan to run for?"

"I'm still torn. I'm interested in the Governor's office as well as the Senate. I figured I would give myself about two more years before I make a decision."

"That's very admirable. Good luck with it."

"Thank you, Toni. That's very kind of you."

John came back to the table just as the waiter arrived with the ground pepper for my salad. He looked at Roger and said, "You haven't been telling Toni all of my secrets, have you?"

Roger looked at him with a straight face and said, "of course I have. She knows all about your bed-wetting problem."

Me and Ms. D almost choked on our drinks. The look on John's face was absolutely priceless. He was stunned for a moment, then the four of us burst out laughing. We continued to eat, drink and talk. Both of them were great conversationalists and very easy on the eyes. I have to give Ms. D her props; she definitely has a knack for selecting all things beautiful. Roger is a very handsome man. No one would ever suspect him of being family. He has skin the color of Taye Diggs, and it looks just as smooth too. His body is built like Alonzo Mourning's, and he has a smile that would brighten up your darkest hour. I can see why Ms. D is doing him, although it is out of character for her to date married men. She usually has a "just say no" attitude when it comes to them. More importantly, Ms. D does not play second fiddle to anyone. So I know we are going to have a serious talk about this one; she is breaking two of her cardinal rules. All I know is his money has got to be long, and his dick must be even longer. That's the only way I can see my girl going for this.

"How are you enjoying the food Toni?" John asked.

"It's delicious. This was a great choice."

"What about you, Devon? Are you enjoying your food, too?"

"Yes, very much so. I hate that we are going to have to cut this evening short."

"Why are you cutting it short?" John inquired.

"Didn't Roger tell you? Toni is visiting because our ten year class reunion is this weekend, so we have to get our beauty rest because we have a big day ahead of us tomorrow."

"No, Roger didn't tell me that. It sounds like fun, though."

"I am sure it will be."

John touched my hand. "So, Toni, is this the last time I am going to see you?"

"Gosh, I hope not. Besides, I owe you another dance, and I expect you to hold me to it."

He flashed that colgate smile. "Oh, believe me...I will."

"Good, I want you to," I flirted as he walked me to the car. "I will be at Devon's the rest of the weekend.  Feel free to call me there, although with the schedule we are on, I'm not sure how much I will be there. But if you leave a message I'm sure I will get it."

"Then that's exactly what I'll do. Toni, it's been a pleasure," John said as he kissed me on the cheek.

"Devon, it was good to see you again."

"You, too." D replied.

"Good night, you two," they said as they tipped the driver and closed the door to the limo.

* * *

"Rise and shine, Ms. Thing, it's time to get up. Breakfast is ready."

"Good morning D. What time is it?"

She snatched the covers off me. "Time for you to get up and get moving. We

24

have a very busy day ahead of us."

"What do you have planned for us?" I asked, somewhat irritated as I pulled at the covers.

"The spa, of course. The driver will be here by 10 a.m. to pick us up. I have coffee and orange juice sitting on the table waiting for you. So get in there and eat before everything gets cold."

"Okay, D," I snapped. "Can I at least brush my teeth first?"

"Yes, you may, heifer. Did someone wake up on the wrong side of the bed this morning or what?"

"No, I didn't. I think I'm just jet lagged. I feel really tired."

"You'll perk up as soon as you see the surprise awaiting you in the kitchen."

Brushing my teeth and washing my face felt like a chore in and of itself. Upon completion, I dragged myself into the kitchen. To my surprise there were my favorite breakfast foods. A cute little bistro table sat delicately in front of the bay window in the kitchen. It was accented by a vase filled with sunflowers and a bowl of fresh fruit, pancakes, turkey sausage, coffee, orange juice, and a note that read:

A grand breakfast for a grand Diva. Welcome home, Toni with an I not a Y. Love, D.

Tears flowed as I thought about how I was mistreating D this morning. She always knows the right things to say or do to cheer me up. I feel really bad about being such a bitch this morning. Most of it is because I am scared to death about going to my reunion tonight. I got up from the table without tasting one delicious morsel. "Thank you sweetie. That was very thoughtful of you, and I apologize for my grumpiness this morning. Along with being jet lagged, I am nervous about tonight ,too. I hope you know I didn't mean to act ugly."

"You don't have to apologize, honey, I understand. I hope you enjoy the breakfast, and don't worry, we are going to get through this reunion together."

"I know we will. Thank you so much for everything, D I really appreciate you."

"Well if you really appreciate me you will let go of me and go eat that breakfast I spent an hour slaving over a hot stove to prepare."

"Okay, girl, I'm going."

D can really throw down in the kitchen. Breakfast was *sooo* good I almost licked the plate. Getting up from the table was a challenge because I was so full. This was a classic overeating situation. It was worth every ounce I probably gained. By the time I left the kitchen, D was already dressed for the spa and ready to go. I took a quick shower, popped a vitamin, threw on a tennis skirt and a pair of sneakers, then put my hair in a ponytail. I headed for the limo. D was already in the car on the phone, confirming our plans for the day.

"John and Roger called," she said, as I entered the limo.

"Oh yeah, girl, what did they say?"

"They called to thank us for a lovely evening. John also wanted to thank me for the hook up. He said he can't wait to see you again."

"Really? Girl, I can't wait to see that man and feel his concrete dick again myself."

"*Ooh, Ms. Thang*, you didn't tell me about the dick! Girl, what's the tee? Dish the dirt."

"Honey, while I was dancing with that fine specimen of a man, I could feel his dick swell to the size of Mount Everest. Girl, when I tell you I wanted to mount that man like a jockey and ride off into the sunset. *Believe it*. That's why I came back to the table alone. John had to go to the bathroom and tame that Trojan."

"Well hush my mouth, Diva. *You Go, Girl!* So I take it you really like him."

"I more than like him. I want him to be my baby's daddy!"

"If that happens I'm selling your story to the National Enquirer, and I'm booking you as a guest on Oprah." D chuckled.

"You are so silly," I said, laughing.

"So does this mean you're going to tell him?"

*Is the sky purple?* "Tell him what?"

"Don't play Toni, you know what I'm talking about."

*Damn. Why do I have to have this conversation with D? We never agree on how to handle this subject.* "You mean tell him about my operation. Hell no!"

"Why not?"

*Ding! Round 1, here we go.* "Because I don't know him well enough yet."

"But you do intend to sleep with him right?"

"Yes."

"Then don't you think you owe it to the man to tell him?"

"No. I think I owe it to myself to get laid. Hell, I need dick in my life, too." *It's been a long time since a mechanic tuned me up.*

"Well, suit yourself. I just don't want to see you get hurt."

"Do you think he would hurt me? Is he a violent man?"

"No. To my knowledge, John is a kind, generous man with a big heart. But when you start playing around with a man's sexuality that can be dangerous. You need to really be careful."

*Who died and made you the moral majority? Aren't you the same person who is sleeping with a married man?* "Are you saying you don't approve?"

"No. I'm saying you need to exercise the golden rule: 'Do unto others as you would have them do unto you.' Toni, you and I both know how painful this lifestyle can be. All I am saying is be fair with him. Allow him the opportunity to choose."

"I feel you, D. Thanks for the reality check. I will tread lightly with this one. I am not saying I'm going to tell him. But I will consider it. I have to feel him out a little more before I decide."

"Good."

*It's time to turn the tables.* "So what's up with you and Roger? I noticed you are breaking two of your cardinal rules."

"It's simple arithmetic, sweetheart. Let's just say it took 12 inches and $500,000 in stock options to convince me he was worth it. Who do you think helped me pay for this house? Girl, if he walked out of my life tomorrow, I'm set for life. I had John diversify my portfolio, and some of the stocks he invested in split and made me a millionaire."

"What! Diva, you have got to be kidding me. You have always been extravagant, so I knew to expect something flamboyant like the limo. But I never suspected this!"

" I kid you not, darling. Ms. Divine is truly divine. I told you, I'm the Joneses. I will never have to work another day in my life."

"Why didn't you tell me?"

"I wanted to wait until you got here so I could see your reaction. Believe me, it was worth the wait," D said, giggling.

"So does that mean this Spa day is your treat?"

"Absolutely!"

"Then thank you very much, and I forgive you for breaking the rules. I knew it had to be a damn good explanation for it. This calls for a toast." I poured some champagne for both of us. "To the flyest millionaire Diva I know."

"I am the only millionaire Diva you know."

"Yeah, that's true, but you know you're fly as hell."

"True, true," D said, laughing as we clinked our glasses and drank our champagne.

"Girl, I'm still trippin'. I can't believe it. I can't wait to tell mama. She's going to holla."

"I know. I was trippin' when it first happened, but now I'm settling into my role. You should have seen the look on my mama's face when I told her. She literally passed out. But now she's constantly finding ways to spend my money. I opened a trust fund for her at the bank. So now she can buy what she wants when she wants. Girl, every time I turn around mama is at the spa or the mall. I wouldn't be surprised if she's at the spa when we get there. She thinks she is Ms. High Society now. But I have to admit it's nice to see her enjoying her golden years. I'm glad I'm able to give her at least that much after all she has given me."

"*Hmmm,* maybe I should get John to make some investments for me."

"If you know like I know you will."

"Hey, I'll drink to that." I exclaimed, as I poured both of us another glass of champagne. " John sounds like a real gold mine. I think I will try to play my cards right with him."

"Now, that's the best idea you've had all day." D chuckled.

The driver let down the glass partition and interrupted our conversation.

"Excuse me, *Ms. Jones*, we will be arriving at the country club within the next five minutes. Would you like me to wait for the two of you until you are finished with your appointments, or would you prefer me to leave and come back at a particular time?"

"I would prefer you come back and pick us up at 3 o'clock. We'll be finished by then."

"Okay, *Ma'am*, I will do that. Is there anything else you would like me to do while I am out?"

"No, Joseph, that will be all. Thank you."

"You are quite welcome, *Ma'am*. Ladies, enjoy your day at the spa."

"Thank you, Joseph," I said as I stepped out of the limo. "D, did you notice that he referred to you as *Ms.* and *Ma'am*?"

"Yes. I told him when I hired him that I may look like a man but I'm a lady! He got with the program immediately. He has been calling me '*Ms. Jones*' and '*Ma'am*' ever since."

"You go, girl!" I laughed as we entered the club. "D, does he have any idea that your last name is really Davis?"

"Nope, not a clue!"

***

Caressing hands massaged my burning spine and elevated my spirit. Oil dripped down the small of my back as I lay there virtually paralyzed, not wanting to move an inch. I slowly drifted off to a place and time that was all too familiar-when life was different and the hands that touched me were not as gentle. It was springtime, May 13, 1990, a day that shaped the rest of my life. That was the day that Paul changed the course of my existence as a man. Tall, dark, and handsome was an understatement. Paul was an elongated version of Adonis. Standing six feet, six inches tall, walnut-colored skin, eyes that sparkled like rhinestones, and a cock that cut glass like diamonds. So I named it Diamond. Paul played basketball for Jefferson High, which was our rival school. We met through our girlfriends at the time. You see, when you're a gay male, and you haven't come out yet, you always have what we call a "cover", translation, "girlfriend". Paul's cover was Lashonda, and mine was Kiesha.

It was Lashonda's birthday, and her parents threw her a party at the rec center. Kiesha brought me along as her date. While the girls were off talking and doing their thing, Paul and I conversed. There was something about the way his eyes sparkled when he spoke to me that made me feel like he was *family*, if you know what I mean. From what I remember of that conversation, we made mostly

28

idle chitchat. The only thing I know for sure is that his eyes undeniably mesmerized me.

During the course of our conversation, we exchanged telephone numbers and made plans to get together and shoot some hoops. The drive home was filled with thoughts of him. To this very day, I have no knowledge of what Kiesha was talking about. The only reason I know she was present was because she drove. I wrote in my diary that night:

"Dear God,

Forgive me for what I am about to say, but the man of my dreams walked into my reality tonight. I'm not sure if he is gay but I hope so. Please make him gay, Lord. I know he is the one. But I need a sign from you to confirm it. So if you would please let him do something while I'm playing basketball with him that will give me the green light. I would appreciate it. Let him lick is lips, or pat me on the butt or something. Thanks for listening God. Goodnight."

That night I got in my bed and dreamed only of my Adonis. The next day, I called D to tell him all about it.

"Hey, Devon, what are you doing?"

"Waiting for you to call me and give me the scoop on the party."

"Then your wait is over, that's why I'm calling."

"Okay, boyfriend, don't keep me in suspense. Give me the dirt. Before you start, tell me, was he there?"

"Yes, he was."

"Are you serious? Ronnie was there?"

"Ronnie who? What are you talking about?"

"I'm talking about Ronnie from the football team. He is only the finest boy at the school, Ms Thing."

"Oh, I don't remember seeing him. I'm talking about my Prince Charming." I sucked my teeth. "Can we focus on me for once?"

"Then go ahead, no need to get snippy. Tell me who is he. What's his name? Does he go to Leon?"

"His name is Paul, and he plays basketball for Jefferson. He is gorgeous!"

"Is he family?"

"I'm not sure, but I think he might be. If he is he has a cover, too. He is Lashonda's boyfriend, the girl that threw the party."

"*Noooooooo!*" Devon screamed. "I guess you won't be getting invited to anymore of her parties." He laughed.

"No, I guess not. Anyway, I'm supposed to meet him to play basketball."

"Basketball?"

"Yeah."

"Uh, *hello*, you don't play basketball, Ms. Thing. Or did you forget?"

"No, I didn't forget. I told him I wasn't any good at it, and he offered to coach me."

"Oh really? Did he offer to let you play with his balls, too?"

"Shut up, D! Can you be serious for a moment? I need your help."

"Okay. What do you need from me?"

"Your gaydar. I want you to go with me to the courts to meet him. I need your expertise."

"So what am I, your gay sidekick?"

"No. But you know your gaydar is always on the money. I need you to check him out and see if he's family."

"Okay, I'll do it since you're my birl."

"Birl, what's that?"

"It's boy and girl combined."

"You are *sooo* stupid." I giggled.

"Okay, what color should I wear?"

"It doesn't matter, but whatever you do, don't wear pink, please!"

"Does that mean I can't get my nails done?"

"Absolutely not!"

"Okay, if you insist."

"I do, and please do me a favor and try to look like a real boy."

"When are we going to meet him?"

"Today at two o'clock."

"Dawg, you didn't waste any time did you? Come pick me up at 1:30. I'll be ready."

"I'll be there. Thanks, Devon."

* * *

At 1:25p.m. I pulled into Devon's driveway and blew the horn. He came sashaying out of the house and down the walkway. We both laughed at how silly he was acting. As I put the car in reverse and backed out of the driveway, Devon's mom yelled, "wait!" I stopped the car while she ran down the driveway with Devon's inhaler. "Devon, you forgot your medicine," she said, handing it to him. "Thanks, Mom," Devon said as we drove off.

We arrived at the park at 1:55p.m. I parked the car and we devised our plan.

"How are we going to do this, D?"

"This is what you're going to do: Introduce me as your cousin."

"Why?"

"Because we don't want him to think we're partners, you know, like homeboys. If he's family and we appear too masculine, that will make him reluctant to show his tendencies."

"If my gaydar goes off, I'll have a sneezing attack and excuse myself. I'll go to the bathroom and stay there for a while so you'll be free to make your move."

"What if it doesn't go off?"

"Then I will sit and watch the game the whole time and I won't move. If you feel uncomfortable and need to get out of there, wink at me and I'll remind you of my curfew."

"Sounds like a plan. Let's go play ball"

"You mean play with balls, don't you?" Devon remarked.

"Please behave yourself, D. Try to act like a real boy."

"Okay, if you insist."

"I definitely do, thank you!"

"Don't thank me, thank GOD for that fine thang over there."

"Where?"

"To the right."

"Oh, I already thanked God for him. That's Paul," I whispered.

"He is beautiful!" Devon shouted.

"*Shhhhhhh!* He might hear you."

Devon dropped to his knees and prayed.

"Dear God, please let that boy be gay. And Lord, if he's not interested in Tony, then please let him be interested in me. Amen."

"Devon, get up before he sees you. You promised to behave," I whispered through clenched teeth.

Devon stood up and brushed the dirt off his knees. "Okay, okay. I was just playing." He laughed. "Go ahead call him over here."

"Hey, Paul, over here." I waved.

Paul walked over to us dribbling a basketball. "Hey, Tony, what's up?" We dapped each other up.

"Nothing much. This is my cousin, Devon."

"What's up, Devon?" Paul said, giving Devon dap.

"'Sup, Paul?" Devon replied with bass in his voice.

It was all I could do to keep a straight face. I knew it was killing Devon to act like a real boy.

"You play ball, Devon?"

"No, I like to play with them. I mean watch them. I mean I like to watch basketball players play the game."

"I hear you, man. It's nothing wrong with that. Tony, I'm ready to play if you are." Paul said.

"Then let's play ball."

"Yes, let's," Devon mumbled.

We played a game of one-on-one in 90-degree heat. Paul dribbled circles around me. When the first game ended with a score of 15-0, Paul realized I wasn't lying when I said I couldn't play. So, he started over with the basics. While playing the second game, I couldn't concentrate. Out of the corner of my eye, I saw Devon winking at some guy sitting on top of a car. Meanwhile, Paul was rubbing up against me as he demonstrated different guarding techniques. Every time his body touched mine, shock waves ran down my spine. I didn't know how much more I could take. And Devon hadn't given me any signs yet.

"Um, um," I coughed to get Devon's attention.

"Are you okay?" Paul asked.

"Yes, I just need some water, give me a minute to get a drink."

I ran over to the bleachers, where Devon was sitting, to go off on him for not paying attention. I was standing right in front of Devon and he had no idea because he was too busy getting his flirt on.

"Excuse me loverboy, but you are supposed to be paying attention to me and not sitting your ass up here flirting with every Tom, Dick, and Larry that passes by."

"No, excuse me! What is with your stank attitude, Ms. Thing?"

"Correct me if I'm wrong, but I thought you were supposed to be out here helping me. But it looks like you are too busy helping yourself!" I had massive attitude.

"Tony, don't go getting your panties in a bunch. I *am* here to help you. I just got distracted, I'm sorry," he said, giving me that sad puppy dogface. "You have my full, undivided attention now."

"So are you telling me you haven't picked up on anything yet?"

"Unfortunately, love, I wasn't paying attention long enough. So you're just going to have to get back out there and do your best Michael Jordan impression until I give you the signal."

"Please don't let me down again, Devon. I don't know how much more I can take. He keeps rubbing up against me."

"You say that like it's a bad thing."

"Well it will be if he's not family and I get a fuckin' hard on out there playing basketball."

"Ah yeah... I can see how that would present a problem. I have your back now. Go ahead and play; I got my good eye on you."

"All right, wish me luck."

D gave me a pat on the back. "Good luck," he said.

I ran back onto the court. "Sorry for the holdup Paul."

"No problem, I needed a break. Are you ready to continue now?" He inquired as he got up from the ground.

"Yes, I think I am getting my second wind."

"Good. Then let's play ball."

We started game three. I was getting better at basketball. Paul wasn't running circles around me this time. He was, however, continuing to rub up against me. I was really trying hard to concentrate. But how could I with his dick constantly hitting me. Just as I was beginning to feel the rock of Gibraltar forming in my pants, Devon started sneezing. That was it! That was the sign I was praying for. God bless that Devon, he always comes through in a crunch.

I stopped playing ball and turned my attention to the bleachers. "Devon, are you okay?" I asked.

"Yes. I think my allergies are acting up," he yelled back. "I'm going to the bathroom. I'll be right back."

"Okay."

"Is everything okay with Devon?" Paul asked.

"Yeah. He'll be fine, man. He just has allergies."

"Tony, now that we're finally alone for the first time, I need to ask you something."

"Yes, Paul, what is it?" I felt my body grow tense. *Lord please let him ask me to be his boyfriend.*

"I wanted to know...how serious your relationship is with Kiesha?"

"Kiesha is cool. Why do you ask?"

"Well, I noticed that you and I spent more time together at the party than either of us spent with our girlfriends."

"Yeah, I noticed that, too."

"So, I was wondering," he said nervously, "if you were feeling a connection with me like I'm feeling with you?"

I exhaled. "Yes, I am, but what do we do about it? What about Lashonda?"

He looked puzzled. "Who?"

"Lashonda," I repeated. "Your girlfriend."

"Oh, she's just my cover."

"Your cover."

"Yeah, I thought you would know what I meant by that."

"I do know what you mean. I'm just so happy to hear you say it. That's what Kiesha is to me," I confessed with a smile.

"*Whew!* You had me worried for a minute, Tony. I thought I had blown my cover."

"No. Your secret is safe with me. But let me ask you something. What made you feel comfortable enough to approach me about this topic."

"Your cousin."

"Devon?"

"Yep."

"Why Devon?"

"Are you kidding?" Paul laughed. "He screams sissy. I saw him flirting with the brotha sitting on the car."

"Oh, you saw that?" I said, laughing.

"Yeah, man, I saw it. Tell Devon he needs to work on being slicker. But he is all right with me."

"I'll be sure and let him know."

"So, where do we go from here?"

"I was hoping you would tell me that. You have been doing a pretty good job of guiding this conversation so far."

"Tony, I know that I want to go out with you, but we have to keep it on the DL. If the news got out that I was gay, that would hurt my chances of getting an athletic scholarship to play basketball. I can't let that happen."

"I completely understand. I'm not out of the closet myself, so I have no problem keeping this between the three of us."

"The three of us?"

"Yes. Me, you, and Devon."

"Can Devon keep a secret?"

"Yes. He is my best friend and confidant. I trust him with my life."

"Okay, but I thought you said he was your cousin."

"We lied. We weren't sure if you were family, and we wanted to appear to be straight just in case."

"I feel you. Speaking of Devon," he said, looking around." Do you think he is all right? He has been gone a long time."

"He's probably somewhere flirting, but I guess we should go check on him."


Paul and I walked into the bathroom and found Devon laid out on the floor. He was wheezing and turning blue.

I ran to him. "Oh my God! Devon! What happened?"

Devon couldn't speak. He just kept wheezing and looking pitiful.

I put his head in my lap. "What's wrong with him, Paul?" I asked.

"I don't know. Does he have asthma? He looks just like one of the players did when he had an asthma attack on the court."

"Yes, he does. I have never seen him have an attack before but that has got to be what's happening. His inhaler is in the car. Here are the keys, please run and get it. Hurry, Paul!"

"*Oh, D*...I'm so sorry. Please don't die on me! Please just try to breathe, D. Please breathe, please breathe!"

Paul came back within minutes with the inhaler. Devon was starting to lose consciousness. I shook the inhaler feverishly, put it in Devon's mouth and pressed. His breathing changed slightly. I repeated it until he was able to do it himself. After what seemed like hours, Devon's color came back, and he was starting to breathe normally again.

"Devon, can you talk?"

He shook his head affirmatively.

"Then say something, dammit!"

"What took you so long?" he said.

The three of us bellowed out a hearty laugh.

"Oh, D, you scared me! Don't you ever do that again!"

"Hell, I scared myself. I'll try not to let it happen again, but you know I'm a drama queen so I can't make any promises." He laughed.

"Yep, Paul, he's fine. That's the Devon I know." I assured him as Devon got up from the floor. "Fellas, I think we better call it a night. I need to get Devon home."

"Okay, I'll walk you guys to the car."

"Thanks, Paul," Devon said.

"That's the least I can do after the scare you gave us."

"Sorry about that, but now you two know better than to leave me alone for too long," Devon joked.

"Believe me, I've learned my lesson. That won't happen again."

"Paul, thanks again for the game. Call me so we can hook up again."

"I will. Devon, you take it easy and feel better."

"Thanks, Paul, I will. Goodnight."

"Goodnight fellas."

I dropped Devon off and told his mother what had happened. She told me to always make sure Devon has his inhaler with him. Otherwise his asthma attacks could be fatal. From that day forward, I became the official inhaler carrier. It was just like American Express: We didn't leave home without it. That evening, I went home, took a shower, and wrote in my diary:

*Dear God,*

*Today's events took me on an emotional roller coaster ride. Just as I was mad at Devon for not paying attention to me he gave me the signal I asked you for. Then when I became happy about me and Paul, I discovered my best friend on the bathroom floor in trouble. The only thing I could think of was that he could have died right there in my arms. Thank you so much for not taking my earth angel away to fly with you in the heavens. I need him here, Lord. I think you know I do, and I appreciate you for letting him stay. Just between you and me, that was the scariest moment of my life. But thanks to you it all turned out fine. I appreciate you for all that you do for me, Lord.*

*Goodnight.*

*PS: By the way, thanks for the hook up with the Paul situation.*

# Chapter 4
## The Reunion

"Ms. D, thanks for a wonderful spa day. That was just what the doctor ordered. I am so relaxed right now. I can go to our reunion with my head held high and be proud that I'm now Toni with an 'I' and not a 'Y'."

"No, that's the Toni I know!" Ms. D shouted, giving me a high-five.

"What time does the reunion start?"

"There's a pre-cocktail reception at seven-thirty, and dinner is served at eight."

I folded my arms a looked at D. "And what time do you have us scheduled to arrive, Diva?" I asked with a smirk.

"You do know me well, don't you?" D grinned. "I told the chauffeur we need to arrive at exactly 7:45. We need to make an entrance that will make jaws drop and toes curl, *if* you know what I mean." He winked.

"Oh, I see you're up to your old tricks, girl friend. But I ain't mad atcha."

"Don't be. Just let me do what I do best." We giggled.

"Then work it, girl. I'm following your lead."

For the next three hours, we looked through old yearbooks and pictures reminiscing about the good times we had growing up. We memorized faces and flaws of everyone in our graduating class. Then we made a list of people we loved and the ones we loved to hate. We wanted to make sure that anyone who picked on us or called us sissies growing up would receive a lady-like snub this evening. Truth be told, we would prefer to give them a good ghetto-style beat-down. But we have to maintain our Diva status, so there won't be any beat-downs tonight.

"D, if there was anyone you could run into tonight, who would it be and why?"

"That's easy, girl. I would love to see Tyrone Phelps!"

*Hmm,* I thought for a moment. "I'm not sure I remember him, D."

"Honey, how could you forget him? He was on the football team, number 69. He had abs of steel and a cock that looked like it belonged to Mr. Ed."

"*Now that sounds like a piece of chocolate the Hershey factory could be proud of.*" I squealed, fanning myself like I was having hot flashes.

"*Baby...* I can't tell you how bad I wanted that man. The funny thing is I think he wanted me, too. But you know how those athletes are. They're always concealing the fact that they are family."

"Yeah, girl, they can pat a man's ass in front of millions of people on TV, but they can't buy you drink at a club. What is that about? They really need to stop fronting."

"Okay, Toni, it's your turn," D said, pouring himself a drink. "Who would you like to run into?"

"I have two people I would like to run into. One would be Paul."

"Paul. Who is Paul?"

"Surely you haven't forgotten my first love."

"Oh, Paul…No, I haven't forgotten him. I was just thrown off because he didn't go to Leon. Now that's a blast from the past. I haven't heard you mention his name in years."

"I know but I would love to see him again. As a matter of fact, while I was getting my massage today, I was reliving the moment I first met him. Do you remember when I went to play basketball with him so that you could check him out for me?"

D plopped down on the sofa next to me. "Child, yeah. That was the day I almost died while you were out there getting your mack on, Miss Thang."

"Oh, D, don't even bring that up. That was the scariest moment of my life. My heart starts beating fast just thinking about it. I had no idea anything was wrong with you. I thought you were just giving me ample time to make my move."

"What move?"

"Remember when you excused yourself from the court? That was the signal right?"

"No, child, I was really sneezing… and I had to pee."

"You mean to tell me after all of this time, that your gaydar hadn't gone off yet! Are you saying that was a false alarm?"

"Yep."

I jumped up off the sofa. "*Girl, no!* I paced back and forth. "I had no idea! I could have really embarrassed myself, or worse, gotten beat up on the court!"

"Child, sit down." D patted the seat next to him. "Don't go getting yourself all worked up for nothing. Everything worked out for the best."

"It sure did. Paul and I had some wonderful times together." I smiled.

"Okay, enough about him. Who is the second person?"

"The other person would be Tommy Jones. Do you remember him?"

"Yeah, I remember him. How could I forget him? He was only the biggest jackass at Leon!" D had an attitude. "What do you want to see him for?" D snapped.

I raised one eyebrow, looked at D, and replied, "Revenge, my dear."

"Okay, see, now you're talking. Continue," D said as he slid to the edge of the couch. He was all ears.

"See, D, my fear is that I am going to die without teaching a few deserving students a much-needed lesson."

"Child, this is getting good. Do tell."

"Tommy is one of those men who thinks he can tell everything about a woman by looking at her. He was always making jokes about gays and calling people *faggot*. Tommy never realized I was one of those people. Honey, if I get my perfectly manicured hands on him, I am going to leave him feeling cheaper than a two-dollar whore."

"Well hell, if that's the case, I'm praying he shows up tonight! I want to see Ms. Toni T. Goodwin work it," D shouted, snapping his fingers two times up in a circle.

"Believe me, if he shows up I intend to. In fact, I won't be coming home tonight if he does show up, so feel free to leave me at the party whenever you're ready to go."

"Only if you promise to give me the play by play in the morning, girl."

"That's a deal." I winked.

"We'd better get dressed; the driver will be here any minute." D got up from the couch and headed for the stairs.

$$***$$

D is so full of surprises. Instead of going to the reunion in a standard limousine, D had a chauffeur-driven Bentley serve as our chariot for the evening. I was speechless. I felt just like Cinderella. We arrived at 7:45 exactly. The driver opened the passenger door in the rear of the car and escorted D and me out. For us, this one moment in time was priceless. Everyone around us seemed frozen. It was as if the earth had stopped revolving on its axis and had started revolving around the two of us. Men who were escorted by their wives stole glances at me and the single ladies were giving D the once over. Little did they know, my boy don't swing that way. D and I looked at each other, winked, and said in unison, "Let's do this."

I entered the reception area first looking like a royal descendant of Queen Nefertiti. By female standards, I'm already considered tall, but wearing my hair up elevated me to supermodel status. My dress looked like it was tailor-made for me by Lillie Rubin herself. Although it was a simple long black strapless dress, the cleavage in the front and the split up the back would make any man's mind play tricks on him. For me, tonight was all about tricks and treats. I wore my dress with the confidence of a runway model and the elegance of a queen. All eyes were on me...and for good reason. Toni T. Goodwin was looking good!

"Ms. Thing, you are working that dress," D whispered.

"Am I, darling?" I teased.

"Girl, do you hear the people whispering under their breath?"

"No. I see their lips moving but I can't make out what they are saying?"

"Honey, I heard one heifer say, '*Who does she think she is, and her friend replied, 'I don't know, but I need her workout program and her tailor's phone number!*"

"*Are you serious, D?*" I laughed.

"Yes, girl. I wanted to *holla.*"

"Do you see anybody you recognize off of our list yet?"

"Not yet, girl, but I do have my good eye out for Tommy Jones. I'm praying he shows up."

"Do you think we should go in the ballroom and get a good table before the program starts?"

"Yes. I don't want to miss a thing, and I definitely don't want to sit with people I don't like. So let's get in there and claim a table so we can choose, use and refuse whoever we want to." D walked toward the door.

I grabbed his arm. "D, *wait.* Do you think anyone has recognized me yet?" I said nervously. Suddenly, I was feeling really insecure. D stopped me dead in my tracks with his reassuring response.

"No, Toni. How could they? You look totally different...remember?"

"Yeah, you're right. I think I'm just a little nervous." I said trying to calm myself.

"Well honey, don't be. You got it going on. Now, can a sistah get some *Divatude* out of you, or I'm going to be forced to leave you out here acting common."

That did it! I snapped back into my confident self real quick. D had a way of shedding light on a situation that would make you get your act together quickly.

D and I entered the ballroom and selected an vacant table towards the front. We strategically placed ourselves so that we could view everything that was going on in the room. Our main focus was seeing who was entering with whom, and who was wearing what. As we sat there observing the crowd and complimenting those who were fashion savvy, we also gave tickets for fashion faux pas. The band was playing many of the cuts off of Boney James' *Body Language* CD. As *Boneyizm* played, D and I sipped champagne and chilled.

The master of ceremonies took his place center stage. D and I turned to face him. That's when it happened. My eyes landed directly on Tommy Jones. *Hot damn!* I said through my phony smile and clenched teeth. I held my gaze on him and elbowed D with my right arm.

"What? Why are you elbowing me, Toni?"

"Just look in the direction I am, and you will see that your prayers have been answered."

"*Oh shit!* Is that who I think it is?" D said with nervous excitement in her voice.

"Yes, sistah girl, it's Tommy," I confirmed.

"Is he with anyone?"

"I did see a lady sitting at that table with them. I'm not sure who she's with. I'm guessing she went to the ladies room, so we'll find out in a minute."

Before the words could finish rolling off of my tongue, the lady returned. When she noticed me looking at her she leaned over and kissed the guy sitting next to Tommy, *I guess that do-not-touch gesture* was aimed at me. Little did that heifer know it's not her man I'm interested in. Now D, on the other hand, might be. You know how he is.

"Well, girlfriend, it looks like the coast is clear."

"Yes, it does. So you know that means you'll be going home alone."

"Not necessarily, Ms. Thang. It just means I won't be going home with you!"

"Oooh, D, no, you didn't."

"You're right, I didn't. Not yet anyway! But watch mama work it honey. I just haven't found my victim yet, but the night is still young."

"Well *all righty* then; you better work it mama!" I laughed.

"Ladies and gentlemen of the Class of 1993, welcome to our ten-year class reunion. I'm Gordon Sparks, your senior class president. It is with great pride that I stand here before all of my Leon High School classmates. Many of us have gone on to do great things with our lives and careers. If the information we have gathered on you all over the years is correct, we have a very successful class. Many of you are lawyers, doctors, policemen, teachers, pro-athletes, congressmen, and corporate executives. Nearly all of you have moved out of our hometown and relocated to new cities and states. Most of you are married or starting a family. Even though you all were given name tags when you came in, I would like to move from table to table and have each person tell us their name and what has changed about them in the last ten years."

"*Oh my god, D!* I panicked. What am I going to do?"

"Just stay calm, Diva. Don't draw any attention to yourself," he said calmly.

"How can I stay calm at a time like this. I feel like a fraud that's about to be exposed."

"Toni, *stop it!*" D commanded. He was trying his damnedest to be discreet. "Girlfriend, I love you and I'm not about to let you embarrass either one of us, so sit tight and stop with all of this damn drama! When I say go, gently get up and slide out of here and into the ladies room stay there until either I come in and get you or until you hear Gordon talking again. That will signal to you that the introductions have been completed and that we are moving on in the program. Then simply glide back in here and take a seat."

I nodded with agreement. "Okay, girl. That's a good idea. You know I'm usually cooler than this right?" I said, trying to make D smile. It worked. He squeezed my hand and said, "go now." I got up and gracefully walked out one of the side doors. *Whew!* That was close, I thought to myself as I searched for the bathroom. I hurried into the ladies room and patted the perspiration from my face. The last thing I needed was for my makeup to run. I was already a nervous wreck on the inside; I didn't need to look like one on the outside, too. I stayed in the ladies room watching the little hand on my watch tick slowly, one second at a time.

I tried to keep myself busy by freshening up my makeup. Okay, that took all of five minutes. Do you know how short five minutes is when you're waiting for an eternity? I paced the floor back and forth, reminding myself that I was Toni T. Goodwin, a.k.a. Ms. Cool, Calm, and Collected. Yeah, right! Who am I fooling? I am standing here shakin' in these tight-ass Gucci pumps. I have got to calm down. I am really trippin'.

Just when I was getting ready to begin round two of officially stalking myself in the ladies room, I heard Gordon's voice floating through the air waves. I glanced down at my watch. I have been in here exactly 1200 seconds, Translation…twenty minutes. That was my cue to leave the ladies room before someone mistook me for a bathroom attendant, and asked me for a paper towel and a mint.

I tried to slide back in through the same door I had came out of but it was locked. I tried another side door and that one was locked, too. Gordon kept talking and I kept struggling. I was struggling to retain my inner calm, which had all but packed up and moved out of my body to an undisclosed location. I was struggling to get back into that room and into my seat without being noticed. Most of all, I was struggling to suppress my true identity. I could feel the knots in my shoulders which the masseuse so brilliantly worked out of my body earlier today, returning to their favorite resting place. My palms moistened. I was on the verge of a panic attack. *I have to get back in there. Where is D? Why hasn't D come to get me?* I wondered.

In the midst of my panic attack I noticed a cleaning lady walking towards me. "Excuse me, Ma'am, do you know how I can get back into the ballroom?" I tried to sound calm.

"Yes, Ma'am, you can enter through the center doors," she said, pointing towards the main entrance of the ballroom.

"Is there another more discreet entrance," I glanced down at her nametag, "Charlotte?"

"No, Ma'am. For security reasons, we keep the side doors locked from the outside."

"Oh, I see. Thanks for your help, Charlotte." *Hell, that's what I was afraid of.* The moment she left my panic returned. This Cinderella story is turning into a nightmare right before my eyes. I know that the majority of this is in my head. I also know that I have to calm down and pull myself together. *I should have escaped the worst of it by now anyway.* All I have to do is make it through the rest of the evening drama-free.

I opened the center doors and entered. As I maneuvered to my seat, Gordon announced that dinner would be served momentarily.

That's when Mr. Jackass himself stood up. He announced to Gordon that there was someone who'd missed the introductions. He pointed towards me and smiled. If I wasn't two seconds from having a heart-attack right there on the spot, I might have thought he was cute. This had to be bar none the worse moment of my life. This was worse than standing in front of an audience with your zipper down. This was worse than talking to a good-looking man and having lipstick or food in your teeth. This was worse than failing college algebra four times. This was my greatest fear personified.

Everyone began to clap as Gordon asked that they give me a round of applause to make me feel welcome. I searched the table where D and I were for the comfort of D's face, and his strength and courage, only to find that...*Elvis had left the building!* D was gone!

A wave of panic washed over me, soon replaced by a soft, flowing calm. This calm breathed new life into my spirit. It was the calm that you have when you know what you know, and no matter what, you are not going to change your mind. It was time. Time for Toni T. Goodwin to walk the walk.

I smiled and nodded my head at the crowd and thanked them for being so warm and welcoming. Then I spoke.

"My name is Toni T. Goodwin. I am a proud member of the graduating class of 1993. Since graduating from high school, I moved to Atlanta and received my bachelor's degree and MBA from Georgia State University. I am currently the vice-president of advertising for Carlton International. I am honored to be here."

The room erupted into applause as I strutted back to my table wearing my dress and proverbial crown well. After all, it's been bought and paid for...if you know what I mean.

Shortly after I took my seat, still feeling like the cat's meow, door number one opened and my favorite jackass walked through it. I watched as Tommy slithered his tired ass over to my table. I sat there wondering what was going to happen next. It had become more than obvious to me that this evening was totally out of my control. The most I could do was stay present in the moment and go with the flow. Tommy arrived at my table displaying all thirty-two. He was working his single breasted navy blue suit. If I didn't despise him so much, I might actually find him stimulating.

Upon reaching my table he extended his hand. "Hello, allow me to introduce myself. My name is Tommy Jones."

"Tommy, is it?" I glared at him. "I think we've already met." I didn't return his handshake, but I did turn up my attitude.

"Have we?" He smiled, and then he lowered his right hand and pulled out a chair.

*Who told this Negro he could have a seat?* "Yes, about five minutes ago when you embarrassed the *shit* out of me. Please excuse my French," I mumbled under my breath.

"Oh," he said laughing. "I apologize for my abruptness, but I was dying to know who you were."

"So, you just couldn't come over and approach me like a normal gentleman?" I said with attitude.

"To be honest, I was scared to death. The last thing any man wants to do is get rejected in front of a room full of people. You have no idea what taking the walk of shame feels like."

"So instead, you decided to make me your sacrificial lamb. *Wow.* That really won you points." I said, rolling my eyes.

"Again, Toni, please accept my humble apology. At least let me buy you a drink as a token of my sincerity."

"That won't be necessary. Aren't the drinks free?"

He looked defeated. "I just can't seem to make this right. What can I do to earn your forgiveness?"

I knew I couldn't completely dis him because that would ruin my plans. So I had to think of something quick. "*Hmmmm*....Let's see...the night is still young, and I do believe everyone deserves a chance at redemption. So I'll tell you what I'm going to do. I will give you until midnight to correct this situation. Then, I'm leaving. If you can't come up with a solution by then, please don't ever speak to me again."

"Okay, I think that's fair enough. I'll come back to you this evening when I can come at you correct, like the real man that I am." He said patting his chest.

I looked him up and down and said, "That's debatable." Then I snickered, just to be nasty for the hell of it.

"*Ouch*, that hurt."

"Oh did it? Then welcome to my world."

"I see I better come up with something good, quick. You have the sting of a scorpion. I really don't want to be on your bad side."

"Now that's the smartest thing you've said all evening," I laughed.

He lifted my hand. "Toni, for what it's worth I'm really sorry for putting you on the spot and embarrassing you like that. But if it's any consolation to you, you handled the situation like a pro. You looked like a natural."

I softened. "Thank you."

He bent down lifted my hand and kissed it. "Until later, my queen," he said as he turned and walked away.

D rushed over to the table the moment Tommy was out of sight. "*Girlllll*, what was that all about?" D asked as he took a seat.

"Never mind that. Where were you?" I demanded.

"Looking for you. When you didn't come back in, I went out through the side door to find you. Then I knocked on the ladies room and there was no answer. So I figured maybe you had gone back inside, and I tried coming back in through the side door but it was locked. By the time I got to the center door, I heard you standing there introducing yourself. I slid in and stood to the back of the room. I am *sooooo* proud of you! You really handled your business, Ms. Thang."

"You just don't know how petrified I was, D."

"What happened? How did you end up doing it?"

"You won't believe this, but as I was coming into the dining area, maneuvering to my seat, Tommy stood up and pointed out to Gordon that I hadn't introduced myself yet."

"*Girl, shut-up!* No he didn't!"

"Yes, he did."

"Then what?"

"After talking myself out of a heart attack, I realized that it was time for me to stand on my own two feet and face the music. So I began speaking and it just flowed."

"Wow! You really proved something to yourself tonight, didn't you?"

"Yes, I realized that all I really need is already inside of me. It's something I have always known, I guess, but I just never had to test it out because I always had you and mama to rely on."

"So, I guess this reunion is not as bad as you thought it would be, huh?"

"No. I think the worst is over now. I had to face my fear head-on and I did it. Ms. D, I really did it."

"Yes, you did. I think this calls for a toast. Raise 'em up. To the strongest, sexiest, wearing the-hell-out-of-that-dress shemale I know."

"*Oooh child, stop it!* You know you are wrong for that." I said, laughing my ass off. D laughed, too.

"I'll drink to that." I said, as we clinked our glasses in a toast and drank.

*** 

"Dinner is served, Madame," the waiter said as he sat a plate of lobster in front of me.

"Thank you," we both said to the waiter. "D," I whispered, "I think he is talking to me."

"Oh, child, I forgot where I was for a moment. He doesn't know I'm a lady huh?" I couldn't help but laugh at D. He is *soooo* silly.

Our table remained the center of attention for most of the evening. Many of our classmates approached the table to talk to Devon. They remembered him because he was voted most school spirit our senior year. A few of them asked me if I was Tony's twin sister. My response, of course was no. A few of them looked puzzled but I just smiled and shrugged it off. Devon and I continued to talk and mingle until the band began playing the *Electric Slide.*

"Awe shucks, girl, you know that's the jam. We have to get out on the dance floor and get the slide started."

"Lead the way, D, I am right behind you. You know I am going to show you up, don't you?"

"I'd like to see that, girlfriend." D said, dancing his way to the dance floor.

D and I got out on the dance floor and set the standard for working the slide. We were jammin'. The floor filled up quickly. Everyone was laughing, singing, and having a ball. It looked like the last scene in the movie, *The Best Man.* D became the official slide director. "Take it back now, y'all, freeze. Everybody clap your hands....work it, class of 1993, work it!" D shouted. He was the life of the party. We stayed on the dance floor all evening. We did the electric slide, the hustle, and the cha-cha slide. Before everything was said and done, D had everybody backin' that ass up, and droppin' it like it's hot.

Can you say party starter? D won the award for most outgoing personality. Tommy Jones won the award for most improved. If I do say so myself, he has definitely improved, but he is still going to have to pay.

The time now is 11:30, and Tommy has yet to file his papers with the Supreme Court of Toni T. Goodwin for his stay of execution. I hope he comes up with something halfway decent. I really need an opportunity to warm up to him. I have to leave here with him tonight. As I was starting to get lost in thought, the lights dimmed and the band began playing slow songs. The first one featured the lead singer of the band doing his best James Ingram imitation. He sang a heart-felt version of *Give Me Forever (I Do).* As I turned my head to look around the room, I was slightly startled by the image of Tommy kneeling next to me with a single white rose in his hand.

"May I have this dance?" he asked with his head bowed to the Queen.

"Yes," I said, as he took my hand and escorted me to the dance floor. As the singer sung and the band played, my mood begin to soften. "He's a wonderful singer," I whispered in Tommy's ear.

"Yes, he is, and you are a wonderful dancer."

"Thank you. Is this part of your attempt at redemption?" I asked jokingly.

"Yes. How am I doing so far?"

"Well, you haven't gotten slapped, cursed, or a drink thrown in your face. So I would say you're doing pretty good."

Tommy laughed and I joined in.

Then he spun me around. "You're really a tough lady, Miss Goodwin."

"That's what they tell me," I replied, batting my eyes at Tommy. He smiled and pulled me in closer. He smelled heavenly, and he felt even better. I decided to close my eyes and enjoy the moment. When my eyes opened again, the music had stopped, the band was packing up, and Tommy and I were the only two left on the floor.

"I guess we got caught up in our own music."

"Yeah, I guess we did. Toni, I know this evening started out a little rough, but I would say it has gotten better. I really don't want it to end. Would you think I was being too forward if I invited you back to my place for drinks?"

*Hot damn! I hit the bullseye!*

"No, I wouldn't think you were being too forward. I would think you were reading my mind." I am getting just what I wanted but I kind of like Tommy now. *What's a girl to do?*

Tommy and I went outside in search of D. When we finally found him, he was sitting in the front seat of a brand new Hummer. "Excuse me, Devon, I need to speak to you for a minute."

"Toni, hey, girl, have you met Lester McMillan?"

"No, I don't think we've met."

"Lester, this is my best friend, Toni Goodwin. Toni, this is Lester McMillan, an old friend of mine."

"Nice to meet you Lester. Would you please excuse Devon and me for a moment?"

"Of course."

We walked a few feet away. "Devon, what are you doing with Lester?"

"Hopefully fucking him if I get lucky. Girl, he is hung like a horse!"

"Well, miss hot ass, I just came to let you know I won't be coming home tonight. Tommy has invited me over to his place for drinks."

"I see I'm not the only hot ass standing here, am I? Are you going to continue with the plan?"

"I am not sure yet. I kind of like him."

"Well, go with the flow and do whatever your heart desires."

"Okay, honey. You be careful with Lester, you know how those pro-football players can be."

"Yes, I do, and they know how good I can be," Devon said boyishly.

I walked back over to Lester's Hummer, touched Tommy in the small of his back and whispered, "Let's go." He turned around and gave me a sexy smile. He took my hand and escorted me to his car. I was shocked to see that Tommy was driving a Jaguar. *I guess he is doing well for himself.* I can't wait to see what his place looks like. I'm finding myself more and more intrigued by Tommy.

I prayed as we drove down Tennessee Street, *"Lord, help me to do the right thing."*

# Chapter 5
## The Morning After

By the time I'd awakened, Tommy had prepared breakfast and had smooth jazz playing on his Bose sound system. Breakfast consisted of the most beautifully golden brown pancakes I have ever seen. He even prepared veggie sausage links after finding out that I'm trying to give up meat. He also prepared sliced fruit, and vegetable omelets. He topped it off with fresh squeezed orange juice.

"Good morning, sleeping beauty," he said as he kissed me on the lips.

"Good morning. Did you cook all of this for me?"

"I sure did, and I hope I will get the opportunity to cook a lot more meals for you in the future."

"This is really sweet, Tommy, but what are you saying?"

"I'm saying that I want us to spend more time together."

"I don't even live here."

"I don't care."

"But, Tommy..."

"Listen, Toni, when I first laid eyes on you last night, I had a feeling in the pit of my stomach that was unexplainable. Although I knew I'd never met you before, there was something so warm and familiar about you. I knew in that moment that I had to meet you. I have been searching all of these years to find the right woman. Someone who will make me laugh, and comfort me if I cry. Someone who's spontaneous yet ambitious. Now, Toni, I know we just met, I am not trying to pressure you or propose to you. However, I am trying to proposition you. I want you to at least entertain the thought of you and I exploring the possibility of a relationship together. I know that when you first meet someone things aren't always what they seem."

*You are right about that,* I thought as I let him continue.

"We all put our best foot forward at the beginning of dating. What I'm saying to you, sweetheart, is that I want to see how far we can go when the mask comes off."

*My guess is your ass will be long gone when this masks comes off.*

"Toni, before you say no, at least consider it? I know we don't live in the same city but I'm willing and able to travel as much as I need to. I think you are so worth the effort."

"Wow, Tommy, that was totally unexpected. I must admit that I am flattered. I enjoyed our evening as well. Even though it started out extremely shaky, you did a great job of redeeming yourself. I am, however, very skeptical about starting a long-distance relationship. They tend to be very stressful and in the end they don't last. I'm not sure I 'm willing to invite that kind of stress into my life. Especially since I just became the Vice-President of my company. I still have a learning curve with my job that will probably cause me a fair amount of stress. To  add a long-distance relationship on top of that would just be asking for trouble. Besides, you don't even know who I am."

"That's just it. I want to get to know who you are. You don't know who I am, either. But don't we owe it to ourselves to at least try?"

"Maybe."

"Maybe? Well I guess that's better than a flat out no.  I'll tell you what, Ms. Goodwin, you take a seat and enjoy the breakfast I prepared for you, and we can continue this discussion later. Agreed?"

"Agreed. *Ummmmm*, Tommy, this food is delicious! You really out did your-self."

"Thanks, sweetheart. Would you like something else while I'm up?"

"No thanks, I couldn't eat another bite. So what do you have planned to do today?"

"That depends."

"On what?"

"On what you had in mind."

"Oh really? I said, grinning."

"Yes, really, so let's hear it."

"Well, to be honest I'm not sure. I need to call Devon and see what he has planned for us today.  Since I'm his house guest and best friend I have to give him the first right of refusal."

"I hope he refuses you," Tommy whispered under his breath.

"What was that, Mr. Jones?"

"Nothing," he said, laughing.

"For your information, I heard you and I hope he refuses me too." We both laughed.

"What if he doesn't?"

"Then we will just have to get creative with the remainder of my time here. But right now I need to take a shower and call Devon."

"Let me get you a towel. The phone is in the kitchen on the wall."

"Thanks, Tommy. I'll just be a minute."

"Take your time. I'll be in the weight room. I want to make sure I get my workout in before we get our day started."

\*\*\*

"Hey, D, Good morning," I said.

"Good morning, princess, how are you?"

"I am wonderful. How are you, Queen?"

"Spectabulous!"

"Well, I guess you win," I said, laughing at D. "I guess your evening went according to plan."

"Yes, you could say that. I still have company," he whispered. "Lester is in the other room. He is getting dressed to leave."

"Oh, okay. I won't hold you, I just wanted to let you know I was fine and that I will be at your house in about an hour."

"Okay, I'll be here but don't you have something else to tell me?"

"Yeah, but I'll tell you when I see you. By the way D, do you have anything planned for us today?"

"Perhaps. Why?"

"Because Tommy was hoping to steal some of my time today."

"Damn diva, you must have put it on his *ass* last night."

"Anyway, D, do you or don't you?"

"Anyway, Toni, did you or didn't you?"

"A lady never tells."

"Oh no, you didn't! Hoe, I will beat your ass! You know you have got to tell me. We are in this thing together. So stop playing and just tell me."

" I told you we would discuss this when I get back to your place. So you're just going to have to suffer for an hour."

"Now you know that ain't right. I wouldn't do you like this, diva. This is unnecessary pain and suffering."

"Oh, D, quit with your drama and just tell me if you have something planned for us or not."

" As a matter of fact we do have plans. We're meeting Roger and John for lunch. Did you forget you told John you would try to see him before you leave. If I recall correctly you told him, and I quote, 'I owe you another dance and I expect you to hold me to it.' Well, sweetie, John is holding you to it. He and Roger called me this morning while Lester was in the shower and invited us to lunch. I accepted for us."

"Dang, D, I forgot all about John. He's a nice man but I'm kind of feeling Tommy right now, too."

"Well, playa, I say don't put all your eggs in one basket. Go out with both of them. Hell, you're single, independent, and available; it's your prerogative to date whomever, and how many men you choose to. Besides, you don't live here anyway. You might as well enjoy it. You know when it rains it pours. So enjoy your mini hurricane while you have it. Because you know you'll be in a drought again before you know it."

"D, you know what? You're right. Before I got here my love life was nonexistent, but I'm really feeling sexy and alive again. Thanks to this little trip. So I'm going to take your advice. I'll go out to lunch with you, John, and Roger. Then I'll spend part of the evening with Tommy and finish out my night with some good old-fashioned girlfriend time."

"Sounds good to me. I'll see you in an hour. I have to run, I hear Lester coming."

"Okay, sweetie, go tend to your man. I'll see you in a few."

Just as I was hanging up the phone, Tommy came back in to check on me. "Is everything ok?"

"Yes, everything is fine. Devon does have plans for us for the first part of the day, but you and I will be able to hook up later this evening if that's still cool with you."

"Yes, that's fine with me."

"Good. Well I'm going to go take a shower now. I'll be ready to leave to go to Devon's in about thirty minutes."

"Okay, sweetheart, take your time."

***

I arrived at Devon's looking a lot like yesterday. Devon opened the door grinning from ear to ear. He even had a little glow. "I guess Lester really whipped it on you, missy," I said as I kissed D on the cheek and waved goodbye to Tommy as he pulled out of the driveway.

"Churl, forget about me; tell me what happened with you and Tommy Jones. The two of you look awfully cheery. I take it you didn't tell him yet. Well, then again maybe you did and his ass is just freaky like that. Hell, I don't know! Just tell me before I lose my mind, Toni."

"I would tell you if you could stop talking to yourself long enough for me to get a word in."

'Okay, okay, I'm quiet. Go ahead."

"Tommy and I arrived at his place, which is gorgeous by the way. He walked in and put on some Kim Waters and poured me a glass of wine. Then he slid my shoes off and massaged my feet while we sat there talking and laughing. He was really entertaining and interesting. He is not the same Tommy Jones from high school, D. There is a soft tenderness about him. I can't quite put my finger on it ,but something about him has really changed."

"Yeah, it sounds like he lost his asshole quotient."

"I thought you said you were going to be quiet."

"Okay, okay. Get to the good part."

"Who is telling this story, me or you? Anyway, we continued to laugh and talk and listen to jazz for about two hours. Then I'm not sure if it was the wine or

51

whether I was just plain tired, but I became extremely sleepy. I asked Tommy for some pajamas to sleep in, and he obliged me. He was the perfect gentleman. He didn't try anything. He asked me if I would be comfortable sleeping with him or in the guestroom. I told him I would be fine sleeping next to him. His kissed me goodnight we laid in the spoon position and went to sleep."

"I know this story is going to pick up, right? What in the hell...Never mind, just finish the story."

"It gets better; don't worry. This morning when I woke up Tommy had already prepared a full breakfast for me. Everything was perfectly prepared. If I didn't know better, I would have thought he had it catered."

"Well, how do you know he didn't? You did say he did all of this while you were sleeping, right?"

"Right, but I just know in my heart that he didn't do that."

"Oh spare me."

"I thought you weren't going to interrupt anymore."

"Alright already, get to the juicy part."

"During breakfast Tommy asked me about he and I forming a relationship."

"*Whaaat!* So I guess you did whip it on him."

"That's just it, D, I didn't whip anything on anyone. All we did was kiss. I didn't have the heart to deceive him. He was so nice and such a gentleman that I lost my desire for revenge. Somewhere during the evening I let go of the high school hurt and started living in the moment. D, I exhaled! I guess I just learned to let it go. Last night turned out to be such a defining moment in my life. First, I was able to go to our high school reunion and introduce myself as Toni with an I, and not a Y. I was able to heal those old hurts and forgive the people that caused them. I think I really seized the moment and took the opportunity to grow. I'm really proud of myself. Now, you can talk."

"That's it? That's the whole story? Toni T. Goodwin, did you just tell me the truth, the whole truth, and nothing but the truth, so help you God?"

"Yes, D, I did."

"Well, what happened to the part where he whipped his dick out and you rode it like a jockey? What happened to the part where you went down on him and gave a new meaning to the phrase 'deep throat?' What happened to the SEX?"

"There wasn't any."

"Well why the hell not?"

"I told you I had an epiphany."

"Well couldn't you have an epiphany and an orgasm in the same night? I mean really, what are we doing here?"

"Gosh, D, I didn't know you had so much invested in my pussy."

"I don't. I just want you to let your guard down for once and have yourself a freaky good time."

"And I will when the time is right."

"Seeing as how you don't have a period, it seems to me the time is right quite often."

"Point well taken. I'm just not as comfortable as I should be with my sexuality as a woman yet. Remember, D, I'm dealing with heterosexual men. Not bisexual or gay men. You of all people know we have to deal with them a little differently."

"Yeah, I guess you're right, but I still want you to go ahead and get laid. I mean you are starting to make me feel like a whore. I'm out here having the time of my life. One-night stands and all, and all you're doing is getting a forehead kiss."

"Very funny, D, but for your information, I'm getting French kisses."

"Well excuse the hell out of me then." D laughed.

"You're excused," I said, joining her in that silly little laugh of hers.

# Chapter 6
## All Good things must come to an end

Roger and John arrived to pick us up before I had an opportunity to tell Toni about my night with Lester. They were both wearing chic-looking linen pantsuits. Roger's outfit was winter white which looked heavenly against his dark skin. I licked my lips when I saw him. John had on a mocha-colored outfit and he looked equally delicious. Toni wore a halter dress, and I had on a summery pants ensemble.

"Where are you taking us, fellas?" I asked.

"We're taking you to St George's Island. We're going to go out on John's yacht for the afternoon. Make sure you pack your swimsuit and plenty of sunscreen," Roger said.

"Then give us a minute to throw a few things in a bag."

"Sure," Roger said as he took a seat.

A few minutes later, Toni emerged wearing her wide brim hat and sunglasses. I had on sunglasses, too, and carried a tiny little bag in my hand.

"What's that?" Roger asked, referring to my bag. "Oh, this is my swimsuit. It's a thong." I grinned.

"On that note, shall we go?" Toni asked, nudging me.

I looked at her and winked.

We put the top down on John's car and drove up the coast. Roger did the driving, I sat in the passenger seat feeling like Whitney Houston in the opening scene of *Waiting to Exhale*. The only thing I was missing was the scarf. The scenery was lush and peaceful. I reclined my seat and let myself be transported by the music and the ambiance. My mind drifted back to the previous night and the wild time I'd had with Lester.

I must admit that I was a little nervous at first about Lester. Although I'd heard rumors about him in the past, I wasn't convinced that he was "family". Most of the rumors I'd heard came from women. They were usually about how well hung and freaky Lester was. Some of the rumors were about bisexual activity but nothing was confirmed. So when Lester had approached me at the reunion, I knew I had to proceed with caution. This lifestyle can be very dangerous if you bark up the wrong tree. I was more than relieved when I realized that Lester was down with the program.

Given the fact that I've had more than my share of athletes in my day, I knew what to expect. Most athletes are bisexual instead of straight-out gay. So in order to protect their delicate egos, their partners have to assume a very feminine role behind closed doors. However, when you're in the public with them you have to be the epitome of masculinity. So I played the role while we were at the reunion. Basically I was mimicking all of the other men in the room. I have

54

been gay so long that being macho escapes me. I did slip up once during the evening when I told Jeff that his shoes were cute. I recovered quickly by deepening my voice and saying, *"yeah, man, those are some bad-ass shoes you're sporting."* Jeff raised an eyebrow at first, then he just shrugged it off. He shook my hand and walked away. I knew it was time for me to go sit in the car. That's where I was when Toni came to tell me she was leaving.

Once Lester and I had arrived at my house, he laid down the house rules. Rule number one: "I am not gay."

*Yeah, whatever you say, big daddy,* I thought to myself.

Rule number two: "I do you, you don't do me."

*No shit, Sherlock, I don't want to stick my dick up your muscular ass anyway.* Rule number, three: "When we see each other in the public you have to act extremely macho."

"Anything else, Lester, or can we get this party started?"

"One more thing, Devon: Don't ever call my house."

I rolled my eyes. *As if I would want to. He is really starting to get on my nerves. Let me do what I do best and shut this muthafucka up,* I thought.

I knelt down, unzipped Lester's pants, and unleashed the dragon. His cock was thick and juicy. I was deep-throating it like I was starring in a porno. Hell, Jane Kennedy didn't have anything on me. Lester was moaning like a little girl. All of that macho shit he was talking a few minutes earlier was thrown out the window. When he couldn't take it anymore, he pulled me up, flipped my ass over like I was a gymnast and stuck it in. At first my ass was burning like Lester's dragon was really spitting fire, but once I adjusted, it was on! Lester and I went at it for hours. By the time we were finished, I felt like an Auntie Anne pretzel. We did so many positions that I lost count after an hour.

For someone who claims he's not gay, Lester is pretty well versed in man on man positions. He's certainly not new to this game. I don't know who he thinks he's fooling. But you have to get up a little earlier than that to fool Ms. D. I have to give it to him, he was a good lover, but I'm not sure if I would consider hooking up with him again. He had a few too many rules for me. Men like him, who are in denial that deeply, usually spells trouble. Trouble is the last thing I need in my almost perfect life, especially from a jock with issues. Thanks, but no thanks. I know I'm better off kicking it with Roger. We have an understanding that works for us and for the time being, that's good enough for me.

"Devon, why are you so quiet?" Toni interrupted my thoughts.

I lifted my sunglasses and turned around to look at her. "No reason, I'm just enjoying the scenery. Besides, I'm still trying to recover from last night."

"Then you're getting old my friend. You've always been able to party all night and the next day, too. Now you sound like you need a couple of hours of recuperation time."

*That's easy for her to say; she wasn't up all night with a linebacker's dick up her ass*, I thought.

"No, honey, I'm not getting old at all. I just think I partied harder than you did."

"That's true; you did have the whole room on the dance floor," She said.

I smiled to myself. *That was a very smooth save by Toni. I knew she'd caught my drift, but she played it off like a pro. I see my girl has got skills.*

"Toni, how rude of me, I forgot to ask you if you enjoyed the reunion." John interrupted. "I remember you telling me you were kind of nervous about seeing your old classmates."

"Actually, John, I had a great time. I think most of my fears were in my head. I guess when you're young, and not necessarily part of the *"in crowd,"* you feel like the whole world is staring at you, just waiting for you to make a fool out of yourself. But last night I realized no one is paying me any attention."

He touched her hand. "Oh, I find that hard to believe. You're a good-looking lady; I am sure you turned quite a few heads."

She blushed. "John, you flatter me. But that's not what I meant."

"I know exactly what you mean. I was just trying to win points. So how did I do?"

"I have only one word to describe how you did: *Score!*" she yelled.

Toni and John fell out laughing in the backseat.

"The two of you are making me really ill," I said as I turned around. They were so caught up in their own thing that they weren't paying me any attention. But that's just as well because I was straight up playa hatin'. That's right, I'm *woman* enough to admit when I'm hatin'.

I turned my attention back to my Boo. "So Roger, what have you been doing all weekend?"

"Sonya and I attended a few political receptions. They were mostly fundraisers for the Democratic Party."

"Aren't those fundraisers usually overpriced and full of fluff."

"Pretty much. Most of the time it's a room full of people with deep pockets. They pay anywhere from $5,000 a plate and up to attend. You shake hands, smile politely, and try to pretend you don't see an elected official there with his secretary-girlfriend instead of his wife."

I pulled my sunglasses back on and reclined again. "It all sounds so pretentious to me."

"It is."

"Then how can you stand it?"

"I know it's a necessary evil to get me where I want to go," he explained.

"Better you than me. I would never make it in a room full of people who think they have it going on more than I do."

"Ain't that the truth?" Toni offered from the back seat.

I snatched my sunglasses off, turned around and gave her the diva version of the evil eye, which is basically a one-minute stare down followed by a smile.

"Ms. Toni," I said, "I don't think you were included in this "A" and "B" conversation, and I trust you can "C" your way out." I put my glasses back on and turned around.

"Well, D, I never!" She said in a southern drawl.

"I know, and Lord *knows* I wish you would."

The whole car erupted in laughter. Toni hit me on the shoulder and said, "D, I'm going to get you for that."

I turned and looked at her over my shoulder and said, "watch the merchandise, diva, you know I bruise easily."

By the time we stopped laughing we'd arrived at the pier.

"Here we are," Roger said." I hope everybody is ready for a fun day in the sun."

"Sounds good to me."

"Me too," Toni said.

"My yacht is the fourth one over." John pointed.

"Do you mean the one named Lady Love?" Toni asked, looking toward the dock.

"Yes, that's her. That's my lady love," John said with a wide grin.

"Well, let's go see what all the fuss is about. I want to know what this boat has that I don't," Toni said.

"What makes you think my yacht has something you don't, Toni?"

"Because your eyes lit up brighter than the New York skyline the moment you saw her. I want to know what her secret is so I can bottle it and sell it."

"Naw, Toni, it's not like that. You know how men are; we love our toys. What can I say?"

Toni wrapped her arms around John's waist. "You don't have to defend yourself, John; I'm not trying to playa hate If anything, I want to imitate. I'm just trying to figure out how can I be down," she joked.

"You already are. I am sure my eyes light up just as bright when I see you." John assured her.

Toni threw her arms up in the air, as if John had just scored a touchdown, and yelled "*Score!*" Then she grabbed my hand and waltzed down the pier leaving John standing there with his hands in his pockets, smiling.

John's yacht was spectacular. A blind man could see why he loved it so much. John had had everything down to the minor details taken care of. As Toni and I boarded the yacht, we received a warm greeting from some of the crew members.

"*Dayum*, Toni, I knew John had it going on, but I didn't know his shit was this tight."

"Me neither girl. Thanks for the hook up!"

"Hell, if I would have known this I might have tried to persuade John to cross over to the other side and kept him for myself." I laughed.

"Then I'm certainly glad you didn't know." Toni giggled.

"Madame, may I take your bag and show you to your quarters?" The butler asked Toni.

"Well what in the hell am, I chopped liver." I mumbled under my breath with a serious attitude.

"Monsieur, may I show you to your guest quarters?" The maid asked.

"Yes, you may, and that's *Madame*," I corrected her.

"My apologies, Madame."

*Now that's what I'm talking about. It's about time a lady got some respect around here.*

The cabin was really cozy. The lights were dimly lit and the curtains were closed. There was a bottle of champagne and a note on the dresser addressed to me. The note read:

Dear Devon,

Thank you for being my guest today. I trust that you and Roger will enjoy your stay. If you need anything, remember, my crew is here to cater to your every need. I pay them handsomely to make sure you feel special. So just relax and enjoy.

PS: Thanks again for introducing me to such an exquisite woman. I owe you one.

John

What a thoughtful man John turned out to be. Toni should take her time with him. He is the catch of the century. I only hope when she tells him, he is able to deal with her situation without acting a damn fool. It would be a shame to lose him on a minor technicality.

There was a knock at the door.

"Who is it?"

"Madame, we are ready to set sail. The gentlemen would like for the two of you to join them on deck."

"Has Madame Toni joined them yet?" I asked.

"She is on her way up right now."

"Okay, I will be right there."

"Oui, Madame, I will inform the gentlemen."

"Merci."

The little bit of French I remembered from high school is coming in handy today. I hope the maid doesn't get the wrong impression and actually try to hold a conversation with me in French. She's heard the extent of my French already. The only thing I have left in my repertoire is croissant, French fries, French toast, crepe, and *Voulez-vous coucher avec moi,* but she is not my type, so that won't work."

I tucked the note inside my pouch and joined the trio on the deck. I met with them just as we were setting sail. It was a beautiful day. The ocean air was refreshing, and the waves completely relaxed me. I took a seat on one of the loungers and closed my eyes. I was so lost in my own serenity that I didn't even notice that the others had left.

Roger snuck up behind me. "Are you having a good time?" he asked.

"You startled me," I said, clutching my chest. "Yes, Boo, I'm having a good time. What about you?"

He sat down next to me. "Absolutely, and wait until you see what's on the menu for lunch."

"I can hardly wait. I see the two of you have really paid attention to details."

"Yes, we're trying to make sure you and Toni's reunion weekend turn out to be one you won't forget."

I leaned over and kissed him. "That's very thoughtful of you. I appreciate that."

"You know I aim to please." He grinned.

"Yes, I do, and might I add, your aim is good, big boy," I flirted.

"John and Toni went to the entertainment room to play black jack. Would you like to join them?"

"No," I answered. Let the two lovebirds have their fun. You and I can lie here and just chill. It's a refreshing change to be able to sit here and hold each other and not have to worry about other people seeing us. I want to lay here in your arms and enjoy the moment."

"That sounds good to me," Roger said as he lay down beside me.

***

"I win, I win!" I heard Toni shouting.

"I think my dealer must be partial to pretty ladies, Toni. I've never been beaten this badly in Black Jack in my life!"

"If you need a break to lick your wounds I'll let you take a time out." She grinned.

"Oh, it's like that, huh?"

"Yep. Don't try to hang with the big girls if you don't have what it takes to sustain your position, Mr. Collins."

John turned to her and said, "If I didn't know better, Toni, I would think that was a challenge."

"It is. So, whatcha got for me?" she replied with a smug look on her face.

"It's on now! I had been trying to take it easy on you since you're my guest. But all bets are off now. I challenge you to three games of pool. The person who wins two out of three will walk away with bragging rights and the right to call the challenger on a moments notice for a rematch anywhere in the world. The loser must not only oblige the request, but he or she will have to foot the bill for the entire trip."

"Okay, let me get this straight: *When* I beat you in pool, I get to call you whenever I want, and you have to stop what you're doing and fly wherever I want to go and play me again. *And* you're going to pay for my plane ticket, too. That's a sweet deal, John. I almost feel sorry for you."

"Why?"

"Because I'm about to beat you like you stole something. Don't you know I'm Toni T. Goodwin, the reigning pool queen of Atlanta?" She said proudly.

"That maybe so, sweetie, but you're on my turf now, and I'm not having it," John told her.

They were making so much noise I couldn't sleep. I decided to sit quietly on the stairs and watch them.

"Well, then let's get ready to rumble! Africa, here I come!" Toni shouted.

"*Ha, ha, ha,*" he said, laughing. Oh, is that where you want your rematch *if* you win?

"Not *if,* my brotha, *when* I win. And yes, that's where you'll be taking me."

The two of them were talking so much trash that I couldn't wait to see who was going to win the game.

"Time to put your cue stick where your mouth, is. "John warned." Would you do the honors and break, Toni?"

Toni calmly positioned her cue stick on the table and replied," My pleasure."

Before she took her first shot Roger had joined me on the stairs. The two of them had no idea that we were watching.

Toni's first shot didn't go too well. None of the balls went into the pockets. John took his shot and three of the striped balls went into the side pocket. On Toni's next shot she knocked one of John's balls in.

"Thanks, Toni, I appreciate the help," He said sarcastically.

"You're welcome. My mama always told me to help the less fortunate," she retorted.

"*Ouch!* That was cold, but that's okay; I'll take my revenge out on you on the table."

John sank another two balls before it was Toni's turn. She made her next shot. John got down to his final shot, which was the eight ball in the corner pocket. Poor Toni was still standing there with all but one ball on the table. John took his shot and made it.

"How you like me now?" he said, dancing.

"I'd like you better if you stopped doing the cabbage patch," she answered.

"Don't hate the playa, sweetheart, hate the game."

"Right about now, I'm hating the playa and the game."

"You are cold-blooded when you're losing," he said, still dancing.

"John you need to quit dancing and rack'em. Let's not prolong this whoopin' I'm about to give you." There was venom in her voice.

"I see the lady has heart," he said, smiling. "So you still think you're going to win huh. That's real cute." He laughed.

"We'll see how cute you think it is when I spank that booty," she said, tapping him on the butt with her cue stick.

"Go ahead. Ladies first."

"I broke them the last time. You can break them this time."

" Are you sure you want to do that? You may not get a chance to play this game if I break," John bragged. "I want you to make sure you pay attention, you might spend the next five minutes learning something."

"Okay, Mr. Big shot, go ahead. Show me what you workin' with."

"Remember you asked for this," he reminded her.

John held true to his prediction. Toni did not get a shot. John broke and never missed a shot. Toni looked a little stunned as if couldn't believe he was really that good.

"John, one thing I am not, is a sore loser. You kicked my butt and I have to give you your props on that." She extended her hand. "I guess I owe you a trip huh?"

"Yep." He grinned.

"Go ahead and gloat. It's written all over your face." She smiled.

"*Whew!* Thank God you're okay with it, because I am dying to do this. *Go, John, it's your birthday, it's birthday, it's your birthday!*"

"Boy, I can't take you anywhere," Toni said, laughing. "I was cool with you until you broke out with the running man."

"You didn't know daddy had it in him, huh?"

"I still don't know it, daddy."

"That's cold." He laughed.

"John, you are hilarious. I don't know the last time I had this much fun. I never would've guessed you could be this silly and carefree."

"How did you think I would be?"

"I just thought you were a serious romantic."

"I am serious, and romantic, but I love being silly, too. I guess looks are deceiving, huh?"

"Yeah, you can't judge a book by its cover?"

"That's why I keep my library card updated. I like to check my books out, then open them and read the pages."

"That was pretty smooth, Mr. Collins." She smiled.

"Well, you know I'm still trying to win points."

"Very funny, Joe Cool."

"I aim to please." He said conceitedly.

"*Score!*" she yelled.

\*\*\*

Roger and I tip-toed back up the stairs. We didn't want Toni and John to know that we'd been watching them. I looked at Roger with a frown on my face.

"What's wrong, baby?"

"I'm hungry. What time are we having lunch?"

"We're scheduled to eat at one o'clock. What time is it?"

"It's about ten minutes 'til."

"Do you think Toni and John are going to come up any time soon?"

"After what we just witnessed, who knows?"

"Let's go get them for lunch," Roger suggested.

"Lead the way, Roger, my blood-sugar level is dropping by the minute. If I don't eat soon I'm going to flatline."

When we walked into the entertainment room we saw John doing a sad rendition of the runnin' man.

"Toni, what in the hell happened here?"

Toni could barely speak. She was laughing so hard that tears were streaming down her face. Finally she said, "John just beat me in pool and won our bet."

"Too bad you didn't challenge him to a dance contest; you would have won hands down."

"Devon, stop it. You're about to make me wet my pants!" Toni screamed holding her stomach.

"John I'm sure you've worked up an appetite. And I'm starving, so if you're finished, Mr. Danny Terrio, I would love to eat lunch."

John stopped dancing and regained his composure. "Of course, Devon. Follow me." John turned around and looked at me. "Oh, and, Devon, I'm going to let you slide with that little remark about my dancing, but don't think I didn't pick up on it."

"*Chile*, whatever. Just feed me before I pass out."

Lunch was delectable. The chefs really outdid themselves. They served a four-course meal. By the time dessert came I could barely sit up straight. I was so stuffed I needed a siesta. So once we finished eating  Roger and I excused ourselves to our cabin. Toni went and put her swimsuit on and said she was going to catch some rays. John joined her of course.

* * *

When Roger and I emerged from our nap, Toni and John were still on deck. They looked like they were engaging in a deep discussion. Roger and I couldn't resist eavesdropping so we sat on the loungers near them and pretended not to listen.

"John, thank you. All joking aside, you have really made this a weekend to remember. I'm eternally grateful."

"You are very welcome, I am glad you are having a good time."

"Correction. I'm having a great time!" she said, hugging him.

"Toni, you know it doesn't have to end just because you are leaving tomorrow."

"*Oooh*...this is getting good," I whispered to Roger.

"I know, Devon,  now be quiet so we can hear."

*No he didn't just try me like that. I'm going to let him slide this time because I really want to hear what Toni and John are saying.*

Toni looked puzzled. "What do you mean?" she asked.

"I would like to continue seeing you, that is, *if* you are interested."

"I'm interested John, However, I'm not sure that starting a long-distance relationship is in my best interest right now."

"Why? Are you seeing someone else?"

"No, not really. It's just that long-distance relationships can be stressful and I'm not sure that I want to invite that kind of stress into my life right now." "You're right, they can be stressful if the people involved aren't focused on the relationship. They are a lot of work, but I feel we have a connection. I think we should explore it."

John was making her an offer she shouldn't refuse. At least that's what Roger and I thought.

He continued, "Toni, I certainly have enough money to fly to see you every weekend or at least as often as you will allow me to see you."

"John, I'm flattered. Really I am.  But I'm not sure I want to put myself out

63

there like that and risk getting hurt."

"Toni, I would never do anything to hurt you."

"John I'm sure your intentions are good, but you really can't promise me that. Neither of us knows what the future may bring."

"Exactly. So let's seize the moment and go for it. Please trust me. This is not about trying to get you in bed or anything like that. There is plenty of time for that. This is about a cosmic connection between two kindred souls. I know you feel it too," he insisted as he looked at her with sincerity in his eyes.

Dang, that was powerful. I couldn't control myself. I blurted out, "You tell her, John!" *Hell I'm feeling it and I'm not even a part of their conversation.*

"Devon, be quiet before they realize we're listening."

"Sorry, Boo, but you know how moved I get when I see Black on Black love."

Toni continued, "I do feel it, John. But I'm still skeptical."

"Okay, then what can you commit to?"

"I'm open to telephone conversations and a date on my turf in two weeks."

"Why two weeks?"

"Because that will give me a chance to see if I miss you."

"And if you do?"

"Then I'll let my heart be my guide."

"Sounds fair to me."

"Then do we have a deal?" she asked.

"Yes, we certainly do." He smiled.

***

The four of us spent the rest of the day with our respective partners lounging around. At four o'clock we docked. On the drive back home we sang rap songs from the eighties. Toni and I did a sad version of Salt and Pepa's hit song, *Push it.* John and Roger did an even sadder version of LL Cool J's '*Round the way girl.* Once we got home we thanked them individually and collectively. Toni gave John her number and a very passionate kiss before telling him goodbye. Roger and I made plans for Wednesday night. We stood outside and waved goodbye until John's car disappeared over the hill.

"So, Ms. Goodwin, did you have a good time today?" I asked as we walked arm in arm up the driveway.

"That would be putting it mildly. I had a great time!"

"I see." I looked at her with a raised eyebrow. I knew she was holding out on me about something. "You know I'm waiting for you to tell me what's up with you and John. Baby Doll, I was checking out that kiss between the two of you, and it didn't look like a forehead kiss to me."

Toni pinched me. "Oh, I see you got jokes." She laughed.

"Yeah, plenty of them. Now stop stalling and give me the scoop."

"To make a long story short, D, I laughed more today with John than I have with a man in a long time. For once I was able to let go and be silly. It felt wonderful!" Toni shouted as she twirled around with her arms extended, and head slung back. "Ms. D, I felt youthful and alive. John is amazing! He is so well-rounded and fun. I could get used to him."

"*Girl, hush your mouth.* I know this is not Toni T. Goodwin getting serious about a man."

"Wait a minute," Toni said with her hands on her hips. " Wasn't it you who told me I needed to have fun and play the field?"

"Yes, and..."

"And I am following your directions. John is at the top of my list. But don't forget I have a date with Tommy Jones tonight."

"*Lord,* I've created a monster. Somebody stop her before she has too much fun and refuses to leave tomorrow."

"*Awww, D.* That's right, I am leaving tomorrow. I wish I could stay longer."

"Well, honey, as long as Delta keeps flying, you can come back as often as you'd like. So don't go getting sad on me now."

"You're right, I can come back anytime. Even if it's only to see you."

"Alright, you better watch it, diva. A few more comments like that and my self-esteem will be so low, I'll be on Dr. Phil telling my story." I joked.

"Oh yeah, I can see it now." Toni giggled. "Dr. Phil I'm a gay male millionaire who sometimes likes to dress like a woman. I had extremely high self-esteem until my transgendered best friend came into town and stole all of the straight men."

Before Toni could finish, we were laid out in my driveway crying-laughing. If the neighbors could have seen us they might have thought we were crazy.

"Toni, girl, you are a *fool!* I don't know when I have had this much fun, either. I'm so glad you came. Even if you did steal all of the straight men."

"I'm glad I came, too, D. Thanks for twisting my arm."

"Okay, missy, let's get up from here before somebody calls the police on us. You know the neighbors haven't gotten use to me living here yet. We better get inside and get you dressed and off to your next date, Cinderella."

"I need to call Tommy and ask him where we're going. After that big lunch we had, I'm not interested in food. Maybe we could go have a drink in a nice piano bar."

"Just make sure you're home in time for our ending ritual. I've already purchased the goods."

"D, I can't believe you remembered. You left no stone unturned this weekend. You really thought of everything."

"Now, Teaser, how could I forget that of all things? When I come to visit you in *Hotlanta*, I'll be expecting you to be just as thorough I as I am."

"You got it."

***

Tommy arrived for Toni at seven-thirty. He and I made small talk in my living room until Toni walked in.

"Tommy, what do you have planned for the two of you this evening?" I asked. "I picked out a cute little piano bar to take her to. It's nestled away in the hills of downtown Tallahassee," he said.Toni walked into the room. Tommy's eyes bulged.

"Hello sweetheart. How was your outing today?" he asked.

"It was fun." Toni smiled.

"That's good. Where did you go?"

"We went to St. George's Island."

"Do you know someone that lives there?"

"No. Devon has some friends who have a boat; they invited us to go out out on the water for a few hours."

"Sounds relaxing."

"It was. It was a good way to wind down after a fast and furious weekend."

"Have you given any more thought to my question?"

"Yes, I have."

"And?"

"And I don't think we should be discussing this in front of Devon. Can we talk about it over drinks?"

"Of course we can." Tommy extended an escorting arm out. "Shall we go?" he asked.

"Yes, we shall," Toni replied as the two of them headed for the door.

Toni kissed me on the cheek. "I'll see you in a couple of hours, D."

"Okay, sweetie, have fun. Tommy, it was good to see you again."

"You, too, Devon. Take care."

***

When Toni returned she told me all about her date with Tommy. And how she decided that they could try long-distance dating but without a commitment. She told Tommy that she was open to it as long as there was no pressure. She said that Tommy was relieved. He told her that was the kind of news he'd spent all afternoon hoping for. He also promised her that there would be no pressure.

66

"D, you have got to go to that Piano bar. The atmosphere is so soothing, and the sunsets are gorgeous! If I didn't have to get back here in time for our ritual, I would still be there admiring the view."

"Admiring the view or Tommy? You seem a little smitten by Mr. Jones, Toni."

She blushed. "I do kinda like him, D. The drive home with him was fabulous, and we didn't even talk. We rode down Monroe Street in complete silence. Bob James' sax took the place of our voices. The crisp night air filled our lungs and smiles brightened up our faces. I gave him all of my contact information before we said our goodbyes. He pulled me close to him and kissed me passionately. Before I knew it he was gone. Girl, I was standing in the driveway dazed and confused!"

"Snap out of it and get changed, It's ritual time now. I'll put the movie in. Your pint of Chunky Monkey is sitting in the den with a spoon and a napkin waiting for you. I'm headed back into the kitchen to get my New York Super Fudge Chunk right now."

"D, my mouth has been watering all night just thinking about that ice cream!" Toni yelled from the bedroom.

"Mine, too," I responded. "It was all I could do to keep from counting the minutes until you came back."

Toni came rushing into the den in her bathrobe. "Okay, D, I'm ready. Let's exhale!"

We grabbed each other's hand and took in a deep breath. Then we let it out right in time for the opening scene of *Waiting to Exhale*.

\*\*\*

"This is the perfect ending to a perfect weekend." Toni said as the movie credits rolled.

"Amen, Teaser." I yawned. What time do you have to be at the airport in the morning?"

"My flight leaves at eight-thirty. What time did you tell the driver to pick us up? I know you ordered a car."

"Damn, you know me so well. I told him to be here at seven."

"That should be fine. You know Tallahassee is so small that it will only take us ten minutes to get there. Okay, sweetie, I'm going to turn in. Thank you for the movie and the ice cream. I'll see you bright and early."

"Goodnight, Toni."

"Goodnight, D."

\*\*\*

"Here we are, Madame," the driver said.

"Thank you, François. Would you give us a minute alone, please?" I asked.

"Of course, Madame."

"I see that you told him to call you Madame, too."

"You know how I do it, girl."

"Oh, D, I can't ever repay you for this weekend. You helped breathe new life into my dying spirit. The sad part is I didn't even know it was dying. I thought I was doing fine. But being with you made me realize I haven't been fully present in the moment in a long time. Thank you, sweetie."

"Now, Teaser, don't you start getting teary-eyed on me. You know I even cry over commercials. And I really don't want to ruin my eye-liner."

"Oh, D, I love you so much," Toni said with tears streaming down her face.

"I love you, too, Teaser. Please stop making me cry."

"Okay, I'll try to pull it together. But I'm going to miss you D. When are you coming to visit?"

"I'll plan a trip for next month."

"Great! I will call you when I get back and tell you what my calendar looks like."

"Perfect. And Toni... Thank you for coming. It was wonderful to have my old friend back."

Toni put her hands on her hips, rolled her neck and said, "who you calling old?" All I could do was laugh. "Thanks T, I needed that. Now go catch that plane girl." I gave her a big hug and a kiss.

"I'm gone D. Love you!" She said as she walked away.

"Love you too Teaser," I waved.

***

As soon as Toni's plane landed she called to tell me what happened.

"She said, she was sitting at the boarding gate reading the latest issue of Essence when she felt someone standing over her. As she laid eyes on the figure in front of her tears streamed down her face. It was John holding a huge tropical floral arrangement."

He walked up to her and said. "I couldn't let you leave without saying good-bye, at least for now. I brought you these to remind you of the beautiful rainbow we saw yesterday while we were laying on deck."

Toni said she couldn't say anything. She sat there silently, in awe, listening to him.

"Well, can I at least have a hug?" John asked. Toni nodded affirmatively and stood up to hug John. As she kissed him she said she heard cheering in the background. She let go of John and looked around. That's when they realized that the whole terminal was cheering. They looked at each other, laughed, and continued kissing.

Just between you and me, I think Teaser is falling in love.

## Chapter 7
## Another day another dollar

"Good morning, Toni. How was the reunion?"

"Good morning, Sean. It was fun."

"Did you and your friends spend a lot of time catching up?"

"Not really. I spent more time meeting new people."

"Why is that?"

"I'm not sure why it worked out like that. But I'm not mad about it."

"You look well rested for a woman who should be exhausted."

" It was a whirlwind weekend, but I did manage to slip in a spa day and some R&R on the ocean."

"Sounds like you had it going on, Ms. Goodwin."

"I did."

"Well *excuse me*, boss lady. And on that note would you like your morning cup of coffee?"

"Yes, Sean, thanks."

"No problem."

*All right boss lady you better get to work. You know you have a lot to catch up on. Let me see what Sean has placed on my to-do list. That will help keep me on task. But before I do that, I need to check all of my messages from yesterday and put out any fires that might have started.*

*Ring, Ring.*

*The phone would start ringing as soon as I sit down to get busy.*

"Toni Goodwin," I answered.

"Hey, girl, welcome back!" the voice on the other end shouted.

"Thanks. Is this Ebony?"

"In the flesh. How was your trip?"

"Hey, Ebony. It was great."

"Do you mean class-reunion great or I-met-a-man great. You know those are two totally different greats."

"Okay. Then what is I-met-two-men great?"

"That's just straight up scandalous! Ms. Goodwin, are you serious?"

"Yes, Very."

"*Oh, child,* I can't wait to tell the girls on you. We let you out of our sight for a weekend, and you turn into a straight up hoochie mama."

"I don't know about all that," Toni said, laughing.

"What are you doing tonight? The crew wanted to get together for a little welcome back dinner. Then you can fill us in on all the details from your trip."

"I didn't have anything planned. That sounds good. Where are we going?"

"How about the Cheesecake Factory?"

"What time?"

"Since I started my Shemar workout program, I can't eat too late. So how about six o'clock?"

"That works for me. I'll see you there."

"Okay, hoochie mama. Have a good day."

"You too. Bye, girl."

Knock, Knock.

"Come in, Sean. Thanks for my coffee. Is there anything I missed yesterday that I should know about?"

"Everything went pretty smoothly. I did book a few appointments for you. They're in your calendar. Other than that, we had a quiet day in the office."

"Oh, Sean, before I forget again-I need to get the number from you for your dad's cleaning service."

*Oh hell! Not that again.* "Didn't you get the message I left for you on your voice mail before you left town?"

"No, I never got a message from you."

"Really? I'm sorry about that. I'd asked my father about adding you to his client roster. He told me to give you his apologies. He's no longer accepting new clients, because he is phasing out that portion of his business. He's referring all of his new clients to another very reputable service. I've used them before; I'll get you their information."

"Thanks. Tell your dad I appreciate the referral. By the way, Sean, are they black-owned?"

"I don't think so."

"Oh well, I tried."

"You can't win them all."

"Ain't that the truth?" Toni muttered.

"I'll let you get back to work. I know you have some catching up to do. I'll get you the number before the day is over."

"Thanks."

Let's get back to work, Toni. You have a ton of things to do, and you have to leave on time tonight to meet the girls.

***

Damn, I can't believe she didn't get my message. Here I am thinking that this whole nightmare is over and I have another close call. I was really hoping Toni had forgotten about my dad's cleaning service altogether. But I see she has a memory like an elephant.

When I told Jackie about what I did, she did exactly what I knew she would do. She laughed all in my face. But we had a good time Friday night in spite of her childish behavior. I mean, what kind of friend would laugh at another friend's lie that fell apart? Okay, I'm trippin'. I do have to admit it was pretty damn funny. I'm just glad it's over with. Now I can call my boy, Mike, back and tell him he can quit with all the jokes.

We went to play ball on Saturday. Mike, Trent,and I play against Ilandus, Stan, and Danny every weekend. The six of us use basketball as a means of keeping in shape. We go to *Hooters* afterwards for some male bonding, unless it's football season; then the male bonding takes place at one of our houses. We usually order wings and pizza, drink a few beers, and talk about the ladies. Instead of focusing on women, the conversation this week focused on me and my boss.

"Sean, man, tell us about the new hottie in the offic,." Trent said.

"Who?"

"Brotha, don't even try it. You know exactly who I'm talking about. The fine babe with the Tina Turner legs, J-Lo ass, and Serena Williams breasts."

"Oh, you mean my new VP, Toni. She's cool, I like her."

"That's it? She's cool and I like her? C'mon man what are you a member of the Village People now? Why are you holding out on us? Since when did you stop checking for the honeys?  Give up the goods bro."

"What exactly would you like to know, Trent?"

"Are you trying to hit that or what?"

"No, I'm not trying to hit it."

"Mike, what's up with your boy? Why is he acting so tight lipped about his boss?"

"Probably because he almost got caught in a lie."

"Man, what happened?" the fellas said, laughing.

"Our boy, Sean, fucked up and told his boss that his Pops owned a company. She asked him why he wasn't working for his daddy. You see, it's a secret that Sean's old man owns Carlton International. So when he let it slip that his daddy owned a business, he had to come up with a quick lie. Next thing I know I'm getting a call from Sean asking me to help him out of a situation. We came up with a decent lie to tell her."

"What's the lie?"

"Tell them, Sean."

"I told her my father ran a cleaning service."

"You mean like dry cleaning?" Danny asked.

"No, like come and clean your house," Mike said, laughing.

"What's so funny about that?" Trent asked.

"It's funny because she told him she wanted to throw some business his way. She wanted his daddy to come clean her place!"

When Mike said that, Ilandus and Trent accidentally spat beer. Danny jumped up from the table and ran to the men's room. I sat there trying not to draw any more attention to our table or myself. The waitress came over to see if we needed anything else. I think she was trying to be nosy. You know how women are. When they see a table full of fellas having a good time, they want to join in. I quickly sent her away. I didn't need anybody else laughing at me. The five of them were enough. I 'm starting to wonder if I will ever live this down.

Once they pulled themselves together, I told them how I got out of it by using the story Mike gave me.

"And she bought it?" Trent asked

"For sho'. Hook, line, and sinker. But that was a close call."

"Yeah, it was, you better not get caught slippin' like that again, partner."

"Don't sweat it, I won't."

***

"Sean," Toni buzzed. "Would you come to my office for a moment?"

"Sure."

"Sean, I'm just about ready to leave for the day. I wanted to update you on a few things that came up today. Would you bring the number for the cleaning service with you, too, if you don't mind?"

I walked into her office with my calendar, notepad, and pen. Without looking up, Toni continued.

"I have been a very busy woman today. We have quite a few new developments. I'm going to start with October 1st. I will be out of the office all day I'll be visiting the La Cola plant. We're looking at bringing them on board as one of our new ad campaign clients."

"That's great Toni! When will we know something?"

"Well, we're looking at an October 31st deadline. Once I visit the job site, we will put together some ideas for a new campaign for them. They really want to target the African-American market. I'm expecting this department to pull together and knock them off their feet. Landing this account will put us in a whole new arena, Sean."

"It sure would. I'm sure the higher ups will be impressed with your work, Toni."

"I hope so. I know I still have to prove myself. It's one thing to be given an opportunity; it's another thing to take the opportunity and run with it."

"I hear you."

"On October 15th, Mr. Santos and Mrs. Slutsky from La Cola will be here. They would like to take a tour of our company and speak to a few of the employees. We must make every effort to ensure that their visit goes smoothly. I want you to schedule a staff meeting for Thursday at three o'clock. That will give everyone a day to clear their schedule. Please let the staff know that this is a mandatory meeting."

"Is there anything else?"

"Yes. November 1st, schedule me an appointment for a nervous break down," Toni said laughing.

"I'm sure you'll be fine."

"Thanks, Sean. Have a goodnight."

"Oh, here is the number for the cleaning service; I almost forgot to give it to you."

" Thank you. I'm going to have them come out this weekend."

"Let me know how you like them."

"I will."

"See you tomorrow."

"Okay."

They better do a good job; my reputation is on the line. I hope Mrs. Waters will remember what I told her about not discussing me with Toni. If Toni ever found out that I-- lied that's my ass.

# Chapter 8
## It's all in the details

Six o'clock on the dot, I walked into the Cheesecake Factory. I spotted my girls right away. They were already talking and having a good time.

"Mind if I join you?" I asked.

"Well, look what the wind blew in."

"What might that be, Ebony?" I inquired.

"The Tallahassee hoochie mama," She answered, laughing.

"Excuse me, ladies, I'm not feeling the love in this room. Can a sistah at least get a hug before she becomes the live entertainment for the evening?"

"Of course you can," they said in unison.

"Then come on and give me my group hug. Now that's the way you greet a friend, Ebony, with your slick mouth."

"I was just kidding, boo, you know mama loves you. Now quit stalling and give us the low down on the two men you met."

"Let's not get ahead of ourselves, Ebony, I want to hear about the whole trip from beginning to end. Don't you leave out a single detail, Toni," Michelle interjected.

"Listen up, ladies, and listen good. Toni T. Goodwin is back in full effect. I am telling you, that was the most exhilarating time I've had in a long time. My spirit came alive."

"Hell, I didn't know it was dead."

"Me neither, Ebony. Not until I got there and had the time of my life. D picked me up from the airport in a limo. Took me to his new estate. Child, Devon is now a millionaire. He invested in some stocks that soared and made him a ton of money."

"Girl, you need to introduce me to him."

"You all will get a chance to meet him in a couple of weeks; he is coming to visit. But, Cynthia, darling, you can forget about trying to hit on him for his money. Because although Devon is good-looking he is no more interested in woman than I am. You're not his flavor, sistah. Sorry."

"His loss," Cynthia replied.

"I'm sure he won't suffer too long. Now, can I get back to the story?"

"I guess she *told* you," Ebony added.

"As I was saying, Devon's house is phat! The décor is exquisite. We chilled at D's for a few hours then went to the Martini Bar. Devon arranged for us to meet our dates there."

"Dates? You mean to tell me you were only in the city for a few hours and you had a date? Dang, playa, I wanna be like you when I grow up," Cynthia interrupted.

"Girl, it wasn't me it was Devon. He really worked it this weekend. My date was John. He's an investment banker; he owns a home in Plantation and a condo in Miami. He drives a convertible Mercedes, and he has a Yacht that he leaves docked on St. Georges' Island. We went out on it Sunday. I had a ball with him. He's divorced and doesn't have any children. He's 35, and from what D has told me, he has dick for days."

"Wait a minute, Toni. How does Devon know about the dick? He hasn't tried it out has he?" Ebony quizzed.

"Are you out of your mind? Hell no, he hasn't tried it out! We don't play like that. We maybe be best friends and share everything, but not the dick! You tried me then, Ebony. For your information, Devon found that tidbit of information out from a female friend of his. Now if you are through with your insulting questions, I'll continue."

"Go 'head, girl. I didn't mean to piss you off."

"I'm not pissed, I'm just really sensitive when it comes to Devon."

"My bad."

"It's cool. So, anyway, John and I hit it off and you all may get a chance to meet him in the near future."

"How near?"

"Very near. He asked me if we could start a relationship and I told him we could take it slow."

"*Girl*, you must have put something on that man. I need you to teach me that trick."

"Michelle, believe it or not, all we did was kiss a few times. John was a perfect gentleman. He didn't try to get me into bed at all. We had good, wholesome fun."

"What does he look like? And does he have a rich available friend?"

"Actually, Cynthia, he is gorgeous. He's over six feet tall, and he's buff. He has low cut wavy hair, amber colored eyes, a mustache, and perfect white teeth. His ass is so round and tight you could bounce a quarter off of it. As for the friend, Cynthia, the only friend I met of his is married and seeing Devon on the side. Sorry, girlfriend."

"Back up, sistah. Did you say married and seeing Devon on the side?"

"You heard me right, Michelle."

"*Ooooh*, y'all are straight up scandalous!" Michelle said with her hand over her mouth."

"Hey, it is what it is. I was just a willing and innocent participant. Now for part two of my weekend. My class reunion was lots of fun. Devon had us a chauffeur and in a Bentley. When we arrived everyone was staring at us and whispering, and might I add, we earned those stares. We were looking fabulous. We'd spent the day at the spa getting massages, facials, and the works. By the time we got to the reunion our skin was tight and glowing. I had a hairdo that was so fierce I looked like a runway model. And let me just say that mama was working her black dress."

"*Go ahead, mama!*" the girls chimed in. "We're proud of you, girl."

"I haven't told you the best part of the evening yet. How about I went to the ladies room during the introductions because I was too nervous to participate? I was hoping to miss it by the time I came back. When I entered the room the introductions were over. I breathed a sigh of relief and headed to my table. That's when it happened."

"What happened?" Ebony asked excitedly.

"That's when Tommy Jones stood up and told the host that they had missed somebody in the introductions. The room grew so quiet you could hear a pin drop. I was petrified at first. But once the applause, started a calm washed over me, and I handled my business like a pro."

"Now that's my girl!" Michelle shouted giving me a high-five.

"Then what happened?" Ebony asked.

"Then I sashayed back to my seat and sat down. The next thing I knew, Tommy brought his ass over there trying to holla at me."

"*Oh no, he didn't!* Not after the stunt he pulled."

"*Okay!* Cynthia, that's what I was saying."

"That brotha had a lot of nerve. What did you do?"

"I made him grovel the whole night. He did apologize for embarrassing me. He said he was dying to know who I was so he did that to find out."

"So he couldn't just come up and introduce himself like a normal person."

"That's the same thing I told him. But to make a long story short, I told him he had until the end on the evening to make it up to me. He did a good job smoothing things over. He came to my table on bended knee, with a single white rose, and asked me to dance. We spent the rest of the night in each other's arms."

"You said *night,* did you mean *evening?*"

"No, Ebony, I know what I said. I went home with him."

"*You what!*" the trio shouted.

"Ladies, do you mind? We're in the public, and I don't need the whole restaurant knowing my business."

"We're sorry, Toni, but all of this is so out of character for you."

"I know. I shocked myself. But I'm glad I got down there and lived a little."

"I told y'all she turned into a hoochie mama."

"Yeah, I think you're right, Ebony," Cynthia said.

"Toni, I can't believe you had a one night stand."

"I never said that, Michelle."

"You said you went home with the man."

"I did, but I didn't fuck him."

"Well what in the hell were y'all doing? Playing chess."

"Ebony, I think he was playing with her chest," Cynthia said, slapping Ebony five.

"Okay, simmer down, heifers...I went back to his house to have a drink and talk. He gave me a foot massage and then we went to bed."

"Now we're getting somewhere."

"Wrong again, Ebony. We went to bed and went to sleep."

"So are you trying to tell us that nothing happened?"

"That's exactly what I'm telling you. Why would I have to lie? Y'all know we don't keep secrets from each other. If I would have slept with him I would tell y'all."

"Then how did the two of you leave it?"

"Actually, I wasn't finished with the story. The next morning I woke up to a freshly prepared breakfast. He cooked pancakes, veggie sausage an omelet, fresh fruit, and he topped it off with fresh squeezed orange juice."

"*Damn.* All of that and you didn't give him any?"

"I am definitely doing something wrong. I can't get those cheap men I date to take me to IHOP after I've fucked them all night long. And Toni's got men cooking for her and she ain't giving up nothing."

"Ebony, girl I am telling you, you better take notes. The Toni T. Goodwin School of Dating is now in session."

"I'm taking notes, trust me."

"Hell, so am I," Michelle added.

"Me, too, for that matter." Cynthia concluded.

"Continue with the story, girl, you have our full undivided attention."

"Sunday afternoon was spent with John and Sunday evening was spent with Tommy at a Piano bar. At the end of our date, Tommy asked me for the answer to the question he'd asked me over breakfast."

"What question was that? You didn't say anything about him asking you a question at breakfast."

"He asked me if we could explore the possibly of a relationship."

"Hold up! Stop the damn presses! This chick had two men ask her in one damn weekend for a relationship. I can't get one man to ask me out for drinks twice in a month."

"Michelle, don't hate. Congratulate."

"You're right, Cynt, I'm hating. My bad, Toni, go ahead."

"I told Tommy the same thing I told John. That we can start talking over the telephone and visiting each other. Then we'll see what develops. I told him I did not want any pressure. So, you all should be meeting him in a few weeks, too."

"Well, go on, sistah girl! I guess you did handle your business this weekend."

"I appreciate the praise, but I think you're premature. I haven't finished yet."

"You mean to tell us there's more?" Michelle asked." What are you trying to do, drive me to drink?"

"Speaking of drinks, what happened to that skinny heifer with my margarita? Hell, I'm going to need it after this hoochie finishes."

"Ladies, do you all realize we've been here for over an hour and we haven't ordered dinner yet?"

"We'll order as soon as you finish your story, Toni."

"I only have one more part to tell you. Devon had the limo drop me to the airport. Well, once Devon and I finished our good-byes, I went to my boarding gate. While I was sitting there, I felt someone standing over me. I looked up and it was John with a beautiful floral arrangement. The flowers were the same color as the rainbow we saw while out on his yacht. He said he bought them like that to remind me of the rainbow."

"Okay, Toni, now you have me crying. This is not right. You don't have to do a sistah like this while she is PMSing and feeling vulnerable."

"Ebony, honey, I'm not trying to make you cry. Hell, all I did was cry when I saw John standing there. I couldn't even speak. He asked me for a hug and I stood up with tears streaming down my face. I gave him the biggest hug and kiss that I could muster up.  The next thing I heard was the terminal erupting in applause. That was one of the most romantic gestures a man has ever made towards me."

"Toni, I hope you're finished now because I can't take anymore."

"Fortunately, for you, I'm finished."

"Good. Let's eat. I'm starving," Cynthia suggested.

## Chapter 9
## Home sweet home

It feels so good to be home. I called Mama to let her know I got back safely. We talked about my trip for nearly an hour. She questioned me about all of the old gang from the neighborhood. I told her about how Devon had struck it rich and how much his mama is enjoying his money. Mama was really happy for them; and a little envious, too, I suspect. But who could blame her. Truth be told, I wish I had some of Devon's money, too. It's all good, though. Having Devon strike it rich is just as good as me striking it rich. I know if I need anything Devon has my back.

My mind has been replaying my trip over and over in my head. Seeing John's eyes piercing mine. Feeling Tommy's hands massaging my feet. Tasting all of the food that was prepared especially for me makes me want to pack my bags and move back to Tallahassee. But I know better than that. Tallahassee is not the place to be for a career minded woman like myself; I would never find a job or company equivalent to mine.

The telephone rang.

"Hello?"

"Hello, Sweetheart, how are you?"

"Much better now."

"How are you, John?"

"Sad."

"Why? What happened?"

"You left."

"Oh, John, you're so sweet."

"I'm not trying to be sweet. I'm just telling the truth."

"I guess that means you miss me, huh?"

"More than you know."

"Then when are you coming to see me?"

"I thought you would never ask. Have you checked your calendar?"

"Yes. I have a really busy month at work. I have an opportunity to land La Cola as one of our accounts."

"That sounds wonderful, Toni. I'm proud of you."

"Don't be proud of me just yet. I still have to sell Cola on our ideas."

"If you put a spell on them, like the one you put on me, they may not only give you the account, they may put you on their board of directors."

"Oh John, stop it. You're embarrassing me." I giggled.

"I'm serious, Toni. I can't stop thinking about you. If I didn't know any better, I'd swear that you put a spell on me."

Well, Mr. Spellbound, pull out your calendar; let's schedule a weekend for your visit so I can put you out of your misery."

"I have my calendar right here. Go ahead."

"Okay, then how about in three weeks."

"That's not good for me."

"Why? Are you away on business?"

"No. I just don't think I can wait that long to see you."

"Then what about in two weeks?"

"How about this weekend?"

"John, don't you think that's too soon. I was just there."

"No. I think it's not soon enough. Toni, I was serious when I told you I wanted to really get to know you. I feel the chemistry between us and I know you do too. I think I'm just a little more at ease with expressing my true desire than you are. But that's cool with me, because I know when you're ready you will."

"Okay, John, you win. You can come this weekend, but I already have plans to have my place cleaned. We're going to have to either spend a lot of time away from my house or we'll have to rent a hotel."

"Either one is fine with me as long as I'm with you."

"If you keep this up, John, you're going to spoil me."

"I hope so."

"Be careful what you wish for; you just might get it."

"Wouldn't that be nice?"

"I suppose it would be."

"Toni I know you have to get up early, and today was your first day back, so I won't hold you. I'm going to make my reservations. I'll call you tomorrow with the details."

"Okay, John. Have a wonderful evening."

"I will, now that I know I have something to look forward to. Goodnight, sweetheart."

"Goodnight, John."

I can't believe I let John talk me into letting him come to town this weekend. I have so much to do to get ready for him. I have to go grocery shopping. I need to make a hair appointment to get my roots done. I need to get a manicure and pedicure, and I can't let him see me wearing the same old polish from this past weekend. Oh my God, I don't have a thing to wear! I'm going to have to run by the mall, too. Why did I let him put me under all of this pressure? I only have two days to prepare. I'm really going to be stalking myself the rest of the week about John's visit.

Gosh, wait until I tell the crew that John is coming to town. They're going to flip out, especially Ebony. I can't wait to see the look on their faces when I drop this bomb on them. I can just hear Ebony now, asking me how did I manage to get John to come here if I'm not giving him any. The truth is I'm not sure what I did to him to make him infatuated with me. I know D didn't give my secret away, so I don't know what's up with John but I do know that I like it a lot. At some point I'm going to have to tell him the truth. But how do you determine when the time is right to tell a man something like this. The last man I told nearly killed me.

Chill bumps appear out of nowhere when I think about that particular period of my life. The memory still haunts me to this day. I'd just arrived in Atlanta after living in Paris for two years. It was cold outside and I was standing in front of Peachtree Plaza, in downtown Atlanta, jet lagged and exhausted. I remember looking around and thinking about how much the city had changed during my absence. Even though I'd only been there once when I was in high school. The buildings seemed taller than I recalled, and there was a lot more traffic than I remembered. As I was walking up to the counter to check into the hotel, I spotted a 6'9" 280 pound brother headed my way. His mustache and beard combination gave him a mysterious look. To say I was intrigued would be an understatement. He strolled over to me moving with the grace of a leopard. When he spoke to me, Barry White's voice came out of his mouth.

"Hello, pretty lady. My name is Robert. I don't normally walk up to women in hotels and introduce myself. But the moment I stepped off the elevator I spotted you standing here. You are absolutely stunning. I hope you will forgive me for being so forward, but I couldn't help myself."

"No forgiveness needed, Robert. My name is Toni, and I like your introduction."

"Again, I hope I'm not being too forward, but would you have dinner with me tomorrow night? That is, if your husband wouldn't mind."

"I see somebody has been reading their players handbook. What page is that move on, 196?"

"I am not trying to run a game on you. I only want to take you to dinner. What's so bad about that?"

"Nothing. It was the comment about my husband that killed your rap."

"I wasn't trying to rap to you, either. I'm just trying to make sure there isn't going to be an angry husband coming after me for flirting with his wife."

"Then you should have simply asked me if I was married."

"My bad. Toni, are you married?"

"No."

"Then would you do me the honor of joining me for dinner tomorrow night?"

"I would love to. Are you staying in the hotel as well?"

"Yes. I'm in room 316."

"I am not sure of my room number yet. Let me finish checking in and when I know I will call you with my room number."

"That sounds fair enough. I'll get out of your way now and let you handle your business. I'll see you tomorrow."

"What time is dinner?"

"Seven o'clock."

"Perfect. I'll see you then."

* * *

The next day I woke up and called Robert to give him my room number. We reaffirmed our dinner plans. I would be dressed and ready to go by seven o'clock. Our reservations were at Surin of Thailand. I spent the whole day unwinding and relaxing. I was still a little jet lagged from the flight. My interview with the ad agency wasn't until Thursday, so I had two days to rest. The day seemed to fly by. In fact, once my massage was over, I had just enough time to jump in the shower and be ready to go by seven.

At seven o' clock sharp I heard a knock on the door. It was Robert. He was impeccably dressed. That big, fine man had on a long, thirteen-button taupe-colored suit. His tie was crème with taupe accents. His hands were perfectly manicured and his brown shoes were shining. That brotha looked good! I felt like my outfit was from Wal-mart. The minute he said "Good evening, Toni," my panties got moist. To say I was overly attracted to him is a gross understatement.

"You look lovely, pretty lady."

"Thank you. You don't look too bad yourself."

"Thanks. Are you ready to go?"

"Yes, I'm starving."

"If you like Thai food then you're going to love this restaurant."

"I love Thai food. I've heard good things about Surin of Thailand, and I'm looking forward to trying it."

In the car, we began the getting to know you process.

"So, Toni, what do you do?"

"I just got back from doing a stint in Paris. I'm interviewing with an ad agency here on Thursday."

"What were you doing in Paris?"

"I worked with high-fashion models and top designers. Basically, I was learning the industry."

"How long were you over there?"

"Two years."

"That's a long time. Weren't you homesick?"

"At times, but once I got use to it I was fine."

"What company are you interviewing with in Atlanta?"

"Mademoiselle."

"Are you nervous?"

"A little."

"Then, tonight, I'm going to do everything I can to make you relax and have a good time."

"Wonderful."

***

While we were at dinner, Robert told me all about his business. He is the CEO of his own company, Baskin Technology Inc. I'd heard of it. They had been recently traded on the NYSE. From what I'd read they were doing very well.

Robert talked to me about everything from ballet to world peace. He was well spoken and had a diverse background. Dinner seemed to fly by. The conversation was so good that I can barely recall the taste of my food. By the time our dessert was served, I knew more about Robert than I'd known about most of my friends. He was twenty-eight and a divorced father of two. His children's names are Malik, who is 13, and Zoë who is 5. They different mothers. Malik was the result of Robert's first sexual encounter. which made him a dad at the age of 15. Zoë was a product of his marriage. Robert had been married to his college sweetheart for six years. According to him, they divorced because they stopped being each other's friend. Now they are just parents. Robert had sole custody of Malik because Malik's mother died of sickle cell when he was two years old. He shared joint custody of Zoë with her mother. Being a good father was one of his passions. From what I could tell, he was doing a good job at it.

"Robert, dinner was delicious!"

"Good. I'm glad you liked it. Are you ready to go back to the hotel, or do you feel up to hanging out for a while?"

"I think I could hang. What do you have in mind?"

"I heard there is this new poetry set in Buckhead. It's supposed to be like the club in that *Love Jones movie*. I was thinking that we could swing by and check it out."

"I love poetry. Let's go."

Upon entering the club, we heard the host introducing the next poet.

"Give it up for Ms. Ebony Jackson."

"Thank you, everybody. Tonight I am going to do an original piece I wrote entitled *Their Lying Asses*, and it goes a little something like this:

Speaking the King's English and opening doors

Tell me somethin': Why you always frontin' in front of your boys?

Taking three days to call; trying to have sex on the first date
Thank God I didn't make that mistake!

Coming to my dinner table to get fed
Questioning me about why I don't give head
Telling me lies about how you plan to marry
Well I ain't Meg Ryan and this ain't *When Harry met Sally*

Constantly plotting to get the kitty cat
Chances are if I gave you the opportunity you couldn't hit it with a bat

Trifling is an understatement---
Playa keep trying
I think I speak for all my sistahs when I say brothas, *please* stop lying

Trying to impress me with things you don't posses
Brotha, why don't you just confess?

Leading an invisible life, always on the phone
As soon as I turn my *back* you calling Tyrone

Buying fake diamonds passing them off as gems
Sitting on the third pew singing all those hymns

The bible says, 'he who findeth a wife findeth a good thing'
Brotha, you didn't even buy me a real diamond ring

You knew right then you were being underhanded
Now you claiming it's all a misunderstanding

Get a grip; stop trippin'
No sistah worth her salt would pay you any attention

We're smarter than you think, so you might as well stop fakin'
If you think you're fooling somebody then you're sadly mistakin'

In case you haven't figured it out yet
This poem wasn't written for the masses

It's strictly for those phony, frontin' brothas--- with *Their Lying Asses!*

The crowd erupted in applause and snaps from the ladies. Ms. Ebony took a bow and left the stage. Me and Robert looked at each other, then we left the building.

"Robert, I think I better call it a night."

"Yes, I think you're right."

On the drive back to the hotel we listened to Luther Vandross sing *A House is Not a Home.* Again my panties got moist as I sat their just inhaling Robert's cologne and wondering what his hands would feel like against my skin.

Before we got to my room door Robert swung me around in the middle of the hallway and kissed me deeply. I was speechless. He caressed my back until his hands landed on my hips. Then he pulled away.

"Toni, I apologize I don't know what came over me."

"I guess it was the same thing that came over me."

"I'm embarrassed."

"Don't be. I'm just as attracted to you as you are to me."

"What do we do about that?"

"I don't know, Robert. What do you suggest?"

"I suggest you give me a half an hour and meet me in my room."

"I'm not sure that's a good idea."

"Why not?"

"Because a lady should not be in a gentleman's room at this time of night."

"Then I'll come to your room in a half an hour, but it will ruin the surprise."

"Now that's not fair. I'm a sucker for a good surprise. You're playing hardball with a sistah."

"So what's it going to be? My room or yours?"

"You got me. I'll come to your room."

"Thirty minutes."

"Yes, thirty minutes."

Robert kissed me and disappeared down the hallway.

I went into my room to freshen up and grab a few condoms--- just in case. I knocked on Robert's door at midnight, which was exactly thirty minutes from the time he'd left. As the door opened I saw the golden glimmer of candlelight. The fragrance coming from his room was clean and tropical. The music was low and mellow. What looked like one hundred helium balloons filled the air, and multi-colored rose petals covered the bed.

Robert stood there shirtless, watching the expression on my face.

I was in awe of his body and him. I had no idea how he'd set such a scene in thirty minutes. Robert's chest was smooth and glistening; he had obviously freshened up, too. All I could see in the candlelight was dark, silky-looking skin. He didn't have any chest hair. Actually, the only hair I saw on his body was the little happy trail that was slightly peaking from underneath his silk drawstring pants. I felt like I was having an out-of-body experience.

"*Surprise!*" he said with that Barry White voice of his.

"Yes, I am surprised."

"How do you like it?"

"I love it. How did you do this?"

"I can't tell you. Let's just say I know people."

"Apparently. Thank you for going through all of this trouble for me."

"It was no trouble at all. Toni, may I kiss you?"

"I thought you would never ask."Robert grabbed me that and unzipped the back of my dress in one quick motion. It was obvious to me he had done this before. He swept me up into his arms and gently placed my naked body on top of the rose garden that used to be his bed. The petals felt cool and soft against my warm flesh. I felt little tremors in my spine as I anticipated his next move.

Robert stood there for a moment, scanning my body like a metal detector. The only difference was the fact that he was using his eyes.

I sat up and gently tugged at the string on his pants and watched them as they fell to the floor.

He stood there looking deep into my eyes. I surveyed his body to see what his package looked like. When saw his penis I knew he could be a dildo model. I had a mini orgasm just looking at it.

Robert knelt down to kiss me with his soft wet lips, and I laid back down. He slid gently on top of me and started sucking and nibbling on every inch of my body. He stroked my inner thighs like the strings on a guitar.

I could feel his warm breath working its way down toward my newly formed clit. I was nervous. *Would he be able to tell the difference? Am I going to be exposed right here, right now?* Those thoughts threatened to ruin my evening. I had to fight to keep them out of my head. I wanted this man in the worst kind of way, and I refused to lie there and sabotage myself with feelings of fear and insecurity. The tension was mounting and I decided to let it. He made his way to my clit and sucked that baby like a pacifier. Then he licked it layer by layer, back and forth. His tongue darted in and out, and my body shook. I experienced the greatest sensation of my life as I came uncontrollably. *Oh my God! The operation was a success*, I thought.

Before my surgery the doctors told me that there was a 50/50 chance that I would no longer have sensation down there. In fact, while I was in Paris, one of the other girls who had her operation done before me committed suicide. She'd had her penis removed and tried having vaginal sex with a man and she couldn't feel anything. Her suicide note read: "Life is no longer worth living if I can't fully enjoy all of the benefits of being a woman." That incident scared all of us. A few of the girls changed their minds and decided to keep their penises, but I went through with my transformation. I stepped out on faith.

Tonight I can officially proclaim mission accomplished.

*\*\**

Robert and I had made love until the wee hours of the morning. We'd done it from the front, the back, the side, and all those spots in between. Thank God I used to have a big dick. Because if I didn't there would have been no way for him to fit inside of me. Unfortunately, one of the drawbacks to having a sex change is that the hole in your new vagina is only as big as your dick was as a man. Therefore, if I'd had a five-inch dick as a man, my hole as a woman would not accommodate anything over five inches. Only natural women have vaginal walls that can expand and contract. Therefore, if you get a man that is bigger than you were, sorry, Charlie, you're out of luck. It's a major disadvantage because you're constantly playing a guessing game. Fortunately for me, I guessed right this time. Everything checked out a-okay.

*\*\**

That night with Robert was the night I discovered I was one hundred percent woman. He made me feel like I was the most desirable person on earth. I went to my job interview glowing. They made me an offer right on the spot. I accepted and asked for a start date a month later. I needed time to get use to being back in the States. I had to pack mama up and move us to Atlanta.

Robert and I continued to see each other for the rest of my stay in Atlanta. We both finished up our business around the same time. On our last night together, I decided to tell him whom I used to be. He had already assured me that I was the only woman for him and that our relationship would continue even after we both left Atlanta. I waited until we finished making love to make my confession.

I laid my head on his chest and stroked his abs. "Robert, I need to share something with you."

"Go ahead, baby, you know you can tell me anything."

That's what he said, but that is certainly not what he meant.

I proceeded to tell Robert about how I always had this feeling deep down inside of me that I was born to be somebody else; that my mother named me Tony for a reason.

"I'm sorry, baby, but I'm not following you," he said.

*I knew I must have been rambling on and on.* My nervousness was getting the better of me. Finally I just blurted it out. "Robert, I used to be a man!"

His eyes darkened for a moment then he laughed.

"*Oh*, you almost had me, Toni." He chuckled. "Now quit playing and tell me what's on your mind."

"I'm not playing, Robert, I wish I were."

The smile faded from his face. The rage in his eyes reappeared and I started to tremble. He got up from the bed and moved away from me. He searched the floor for his boxers and put them on. Then he turned around and looked at me like a raging bull. His brow was furrowed, his eyes were red, and his fists were clinched. Without a word he swung at me and knocked me to the floor.

"What kind of sick-ass game are you trying to play with me, Toni?" he asked in a scolding tone of voice.

"I'm not trying to play games with you," I cried. "I wasn't the one who approached you. You came up to me in the lobby, remember?"

He hit me again. This time blood came pouring out of my mouth.

"I ought to kill your punk-ass!" he shouted, spit flying everywhere.

In that very moment I was terrified but I was also angry. I don't know where it came from but the testosterone in me must have kicked back in. My knees were shaking but I gathered myself up off the floor and looked him in the eye and said, "Look, muthafucker, I'm not your Goddamn punching bag! Now just because your ass is feeling like a straight up sissy right now, that does not give you the right to hit me." That's when he hit me for the final time and knocked my ass unconscious. I woke up in Grady hospital. My mother was standing by my bedside when my eyes opened. She said I had been in ICU for three days. I had a concussion, a couple of broken ribs, and stitches in my lip.

"What happened to the guy who did this," I asked?

"The mugger got away, sweetheart."

"What mugger, mama?"

"The mugger that robbed you in the alley."

"What alley? What are you talking about?"

"Toni, I got a call from the City of Atlanta Police Department telling me that you had been mugged and that you were unconscious."

"Mugged?"

"Yes. I caught the first flight I could and came straight to the hospital."

"What day is it mama?"

"It's Tuesday, sweetheart. Why?"

"Then that means he is long gone by now."

"Who, Toni?"

"The guy who did this to me."

"What guy? The mugger?"

"No, mama. I wasn't mugged."

"What do you mean you weren't mugged?"

"I was beaten up in my hotel room."

"Then how come the police found you in the alley?"

"He must have put me there."

"Who?"

"Robert."

"Who is Robert? Toni are you sure you're feeling okay?"

"Yes, I'm sure. Robert is a guy I met at the hotel."

"You mean the one who took you out to dinner?"

"Yes, that's the one."

"Are you saying he did this to you?"

"That's exactly what I'm saying."

"But why baby? Why would he do a thing like this? I thought you two were hitting it off."

"We were until I told him."

"Told him what?" Mama paused. Then you could almost see the light bulb come on in Mama's head. *Oh*, Toni, you told him?"

"Yes. I felt so comfortable with him that I thought I could be honest and tell him. I didn't think it would matter to him since he had gotten to know me. He said he was falling in love with me, mama; I thought I could trust him."

"Oh, baby, I'm sorry." Mama took me in her arms and held me close while I cried.

"Mama, we can't let him get away with this."

"No, we can't, sweetheart. Do you have any information on him?"

"I have all of his information. We exchanged telephone numbers and addresses before this all happened. His business card is in my purse."

Mama grabbed my purse pulled out Robert's business card and read it. "Baskin Technology Inc. Robert Baskin, CEO. You mean to tell me this fool is the CEO."

"Yep, can you believe it? He has two kids, too mama."

"He has two kids, is a CEO, and he goes around beating up women. Oh, yeah, we're definitely going to make him pay."

"Mama, did the doctor say when I would be released?"

"He said he couldn't tell me until you woke up. He needed to run another CAT scan."

"We need to get him in here."

Mama pressed the button for the nurse and told them to alert the doctor of my newly conscious status. The doctor came rushing in to examine me.

"Ms. Goodwin, you are a lucky woman. Thank God someone found you in that alley and called 911. You could have died. Do you remember what happened?" Mama looked at me and shook her head. I looked at the doctor and said, "no. What does the police report say doctor?"

"It says that a gentleman by the name of Baskin found you passed out in the alley. He told the police he thought you had been mugged."

"Was he there when the police came?"

"No. He called in the report and told the police he had a flight to catch."

"Did he leave his information? I would like to send him a thank you note."

"I'm not sure, but I do have the officer's card who wrote the report. You can give him a call and find out."

"I will. Doctor, when are you going to release me?"

"I have you scheduled for a CAT scan at one o'clock. If everything looks good you should be able to go home tomorrow."

"Will I be okay to fly?"

"No, I don't recommend flying. You need to stay put for at least a week."

"Okay. Thank you doctor." I might not be able travel, but mama and I have enough connections to make Robert's life a living hell. *They say payback is a bitch, and right about now so am I!*


As soon as the doctor left the room mama and I started working on our plan---a scheme that required Mama to come out of retirement. Most people don't know it, but Mama worked for the FBI as an executive assistant for many years. She knows computers and how to use high-tech equipment like nobody's business. Quiet as it's kept, Mama dated her boss for years, and let's just say she learned a lot from pillow talk.

We called the police station to find out if they had any information on Robert. They had the same info we already had.

At one o'clock I went in for my CAT scan, and everything was fine. The hospital released me the next day. We checked into a new hotel and started making calls. By six o'clock that evening the plan was set. Since I couldn't fly, mama booked a round-trip ticket to Dallas for herself. She called our cousin Junior and told him we needed his help. She filled him in on everything that had happened, and the two of them formulated their course of action from there. Mama left on the five a.m. flight to Dallas. Junior was scheduled to meet her at seven.

When mama saw Junior, he was far bigger then either of us recalled. He hugged mama and said, "Let's go do this." At eight o'clock, mama and Junior were sitting outside of Baskin Technology waiting for Robert to arrive. I was talking to them by cell phone. I described Robert perfectly. I didn't want them to mistake anyone else for him. Robert arrived around eight-thirty. Junior sat there and studied him. He watched his every move. He scoped out the car he drove. He had a friend of his run the license plates on it. My friend, Ralph, ran a credit report for me. We found out everything there was to know about Robert Baskin. We even knew where his children went to school.

Mama and Junior rented a suite across the street from Robert's office. Mama applied for a job as a cleaning lady in his building. She was hired. We needed a way to gain entry into his offices. They followed Robert around for three days. They wanted to study his habits and learn his pattern. He drops his daughter off for school at eight o'clock in the morning. He goes through the drive thru at Dunkin Donuts to get coffee and a bagel. He arrives at his office at eight-thirty. His day is spent working and running his business. He usually has his lunch delivered. He leaves work at five o'clock to pick his daughter up and take her home. He even prepares dinner for the kids while they do their homework. From the outside looking in, he is a perfect gentleman and father. I almost felt guilty about what we were going to do to him.

On day four it was time to put our plan into action. Mama finally had access to Robert's office. All of our background investigations were complete. We now had access to all of Robert's bank accounts, credit cards, and even his cell phone access code. You name it we had it. Junior managed to call the school and impersonate Robert. He told them that a good friend of his named Linda would pick Zoe up at four-thirty. The school told him they would have her ready to go but that they had to call him back at the number they had on file to verify it was him. Junior had already anticipated that move and was able to intercept Robert's calls. The school called back, and Junior answered.

Mama called Robert's office and said she was the nurse at Martin Junior High School. She informed Robert that Malik was sick and needed to be picked up immediately. When Robert left the building, Junior set off the fire alarm. As everyone vacated the building Mama ran into Robert's office and downloaded all of his files then deleted them from his system. For extra insurance, she put a virus on all of his machines. She broke into his safe and stole all of his backup files and recovery disk. Then she left him a note. The note read: "*How does it feel?*"

Mama left the building while everyone was coming back in. She changed clothes, jumped in the rental car, and headed over to the school to pick up Zoë. She recognized her from the outfit she'd seen her wearing that morning. She walked up to Zoë and her teacher like she knew them.

"Hello, I'm Linda. I came to pick up Zoë."

"Hi, Linda, I'm Mrs. Gibson. We've been expecting you."

"Oh good, Robert did get a chance to call you."

"Yes, he sure did. Is everything alright?"

"Yes, everything is fine. He had to pick Malik up today and was afraid he wouldn't make it here on time, so he asked me to help him out."

"Oh, I see. Okay, Zoë, I'll see you tomorrow. It was a pleasure to meet you Linda."

"Likewise." Mama took Zoë by the hand and walked her to the car.

"Zoë," mama said as she stooped down to look her in the eye. "My name is Linda, I'm a friend of your daddy's. I'm going to take you to get some ice cream and then I'll take you home. Is that okay?"

"Yes ma'am, Zoë said. "Linda," Zoë said as she surveyed her surroundings.

"Yes, Zoë."

"Why do you have all of that stuff in your backseat?"

"Because I make movies."

"For real?"

"Yes, Zoë, for real."

"Can I be in one of your movies, Linda?"

"Sure. As a matter of fact, I'm getting ready to make a movie with a little girl who is just about your age. Do you want to read her part while I film you?"

"Yes!" Zoë screamed jumping up and down and clapping her hands.

Linda pulled over and stopped the car in a secluded area. She got out and set up the scene.

"Here, Zoë, put this on." She handed Zoë a torn and stained dress similar to the one she was wearing.

"What's this?" Zoë asked, referring to the ketchup stain that looked like blood?

"Oh, that's nothing. You have to look like a little girl who has been kidnapped and abused. So you have to look really sad. Do you think you can do that?"

"Yep. I can do it."

"Okay. When I say *action* you have to start crying and saying 'daddy I'm scared please come get me. Please come get me.' You got it?"

"Got it."

"Action."

Zoë went into action. She played her role better than mama could have imagined. She was a natural. Mama even messed her hair up and took one of her shoes off to make it look real.

Twenty minutes later, Zoë was overjoyed with her work. Mama took Zoë to get some ice cream.

\*\*\*

Meanwhile Robert made it out to the school to pick up Malik only to find out that Malik was at football practice and feeling fine. Robert scratched his head. Something wasn't right.

He raced over to Zoë's school to pick her up but luck was not on his side. There was an accident on the 213 Expressway, and he was stuck in gridlock. By the time he got to Zoë's school it was six o'clock and everyone was gone for the day. Robert began to panic. He had no idea where his daughter was. He picked up the cell phone to call her mother but hung up when he heard her voicemail message reminding callers that she was on a seven-day cruise to the Caribbean.

Just as he was about to head home to see if Zoë had caught a ride with the teacher his phone rang.

"*How does it feel?*" the voice on the other end asked.

"Who is this?"

"*How does it feel?*" the voice asked again.

"How does what feel?"

"*How does it feel to lose control of your life?*"

"I haven't lost control of anything. Who is this?"

"Oh, so you think you haven't lost control? Then you haven't been to your office."

Robert did a 180-degree turn in the middle of the road and raced back downtown toward his office. He had completely forgotten about Zoë for a moment. The voice on the other end had him caught up. Robert jumped out of his car and ran up thirteen flights of stairs to his office. He found that his screensaver had been changed. In bold red letters, the words YOU HAVE BEEN INFECTED scrolled across the black screen. Robert searched his system only to find nothing there but a virus. All of his company files were gone--- including his client roster. He went to his safe to retrieve his backup disk. The only thing in his safe was a note that read: "*How does it feel?*"

He screamed in frustration and knocked everything off his desk. His stapler flew across the room and broke the antique mirror hanging on his wall. One of his client files flew up in the air. Each sheet floated to the floor covering it. He ran back down stairs and jumped in his car. His cell phone rang again.

"Are you *still* in control?" the voice asked.

"*Fuck you!*" he yelled. "Who is this? Why are you doing this?"

"Because I want to know *how does it feel?*" The voice said.

His anger penetrated the phone. "Okay. I'll play your little game, *you* fucking asshole! It feels fucked up. Is that what you want to hear?"

94

"*Robert, where is Zoë?*" the voice asked calmly.

"Home."

"Are you *sure* about that?"

"Look, man, I don't know who you are or what you want, but if you hurt a single hair on my little girl's head, I will hunt you down like a dog and kill you my damn self!"

"Now, Robert, do you really think you're in a position to make threats? Remember, you are not in control. Don't you think you should stop and get some gas? Your fuel light is on."

Robert looked at his gas gauge. He was nervous now. The fuel light was on. He pulled into the Shell station and got out of the car looking over his shoulder.

"I *wouldn't* use my credit card if I were you." The voice said.

"*Fuck you!*" Robert yelled and threw the phone down on the floor of the car.

He put his platinum American Express Card in the machine and it instructed him to go inside and see the cashier. Once inside the cashier swiped his card and it came up stolen.

"Sorry, sir, but this card was reported stolen. I'm going to have to keep it."

"What are you talking about? I'm the owner of the card. Here is my ID," Robert said.

"I'm sorry, sir, I'm just doing what I'm told. You might want to call your credit card company to straighten this out. However, if you have cash or another card I'll be happy to take them. Robert had fifty dollars on him.

"Give me twenty dollars on pump seven," he said as he slapped the twenty down on the counter and stormed out of the store. Robert pumped his gas and got back in the car to head home.

His phone rang.

"Listen, muthafucker, I'm not in the mood to play games with you!"

"Okay, dad, I guess we can shoot hoops another time."

"Malik, I'm sorry. I didn't know it was you."

"Is something wrong dad?"

"No, nothing for you to worry about. Where are you?"

"I'm just leaving practice. I'm headed home."

"Do me a favor, don't go home. Can you go to Jamal's house and hang out until I come pick you up?"

"Sure, but is something wrong, dad?"

"Malik! Just do it!"

"Okay, okay, my bad."

"I don't mean to yell, son, but today has been very stressful for me."

"It's cool, dad. Later."

Robert ended the call and punched the steering wheel with his fist, causing his knuckles to crack. Then he got on the 213 southbound and headed to his house. As he drove home he replayed the events of the last few hours over in his mind. Someone was definitely fucking with him. *But why?*

Robert sped into the driveway unaware of his skid marks as he ran into the house. No one was home, but it was obvious that someone had been there. Robert walked into his daughter's room and found a videotape and a note lying on her bed. The note read: "*If* you want to see your daughter again, *play me.*" Robert put the videotape in and sat on his daughter's bed. Zoë appeared on the screen looking bruised and frightened. Zoë cried, "Daddy, I'm scared. Please come get me, please come get me." Then the tape faded to black. Robert put his head in his heads and wept.

The telephone rang. Robert jumped to answer the phone.

"*How does it feel?*" the voice asked.

"It feels fucked up! How do you expect it to feel? Who are you? Why are you doing this? Where is my little girl?"

"One question at a time, pretty boy."

"What do you want from me? Just tell me and give me my little girl back damn it!"

"I want you to suffer." the voice hissed.

"Why?"

"Because you made me suffer, asshole!"

"When?"

"That's not important. This is what you need to do if you want to see your daughter alive again. You need to go down to the old YMCA building on 3rd and Blanding. Be there by seven P.M. I'll call you for further instructions when you get there."

"But that's fifteen minutes from now."

"Then I suggest you drive like your life depends on it."

Robert hung up the phone, grabbed his cell phone and his keys, and raced over to the Y.

As soon as he pulled up his phone rang.

"I see you made it," the voice said.

"Now what? Is my little girl inside?"

"Get out of the car, go inside, and take off all of your clothes."

"For what?"

"Do it or Zoë dies!" The voice shouted and hung up the phone.

Robert heard Zoë's voice again saying, "Daddy, please I'm scared." This time her voice was coming out of the building.

"Okay, I'm doing it. Just don't hurt her," he pleaded.

Robert went inside the abandoned building and took off all of his clothes.

There was a note and a blindfold lying on the floor. The note read: "*Put me on.*" Robert put the blindfold on and stood there. That's when Junior and his boys came out of nowhere and beat Robert down. They kicked and punched him. One of them stomped him in the ribs and said, "*This is for my cousin.*" Those were the last words Robert remembered hearing before he passed out. While he was lying there naked, Junior had his friend tattoo I love boys on one of Robert's butt cheeks and I hit women on the other one. They turned him over and put a wig and lipstick on him and took lots of pictures of Robert in compromising positions. Then they put him into the car and drove off.

Linda and Zoë spent their day eating ice cream and playing in the park. Linda dropped Zoë off and waited to tuck her in bed. While Zoë bathed and got ready for bed, Linda went into action. She hid a Nanny Cam in Zoë's room and two microscopic cameras and microphones in other parts of the house. One of them was in Robert's room, of course. She sat outside in the car until she saw Malik walk inside the house. Then she left, right on schedule.

Around eleven o'clock, Junior and his crew dropped Robert and his car off at home. Robert came to about midnight. The sight of his naked body startled him.

He mumbled something as he snatched the wig off. Then he moved. "Ouch! *Somebody beat my ass!* Oh my God, Zoë! he shouted as he jumped out of the car, rushing toward the house.

When he got in the house, both Malik and Zoë were sound asleep in their beds. Robert breathed a sigh of relief and went to take a shower. A note and a video-cassette were taped to his bathroom mirror. By now he knew the routine.

He put the tape in the VCR and pressed play. His mouth dropped open at the sight of his naked body with his face in a man's lap. He instantly vomited. Robert jumped up and ran to the bathroom and started scrubbing his body and brushing his teeth. He felt sick. Once his stomach settled down he began to dry off in the mirror. That's when he noticed his butt. As he backed up closer toward the mirror he could read the tattoo. He vomited again. Then he fell on his bed and passed out.

*** 

"Daddy, wake up." We heard Zoë say as she stood in the doorway to Robert's room.

Robert jumped up at the sound of Zoë's voice. "Hi, baby. Come and give daddy a hug," he said.

Zoë entered the room giggling. "You don't have on any clothes, daddy," she said, pointing and laughing.

Robert looked down and threw the comforter across his body.

"Oh, Zoë, you're so silly," he said, tickling her.

"How was your day yesterday, daddy?"

"Very busy," he lied.

"That's what Linda said."

"Who is Linda?"

"Your friend that you sent to pick me up, silly."

"Oh yeah, *Linda.* So what did the two of you do?"

"We made a videotape and she took me to get ice cream and then we went to the park and played on the swings."

"*Really?* It sounds like you had fun."

"I did. Linda said I'm a good actress too."

"Well how would she know that?"

"Because when we made the video she had me act like I was crying and begging you to come get me."

*Aw, hell, she is a good actress*, he thought. "So how did you get home?"

"Linda dropped me off."

"Where is Malik?"

"In the shower."

"I guess I better get in the shower, too, or we're going to be late Zoë.

Go and fix yourself some cereal; I'll be in there in a few minutes."

"Okay, dadd,." Zoë said as she skipped out of the room and down the hallway.

Robert took a shower and started replaying the events of the previous day in his head. He was starting to piece things together, but he was still unclear as to who was doing this to him. He was certainly glad that his family was all right.

"Malik."

"Yeah, dad?"

"Would you come here for a minute, son?"

"Hey, dad, good morning."

"Good morning, Malik. How did you get home last night?"

"Dad, don't you remember? You called Jamal's mom and asked her if she could drop me off."

"I did? Oh yeah that's right, I did call her." Robert snapped his finger, pretending to remember.

"Dad, are you sure you're all right? You've been acting strange since yesterday."

"Yeah, son, I'm fine. I've just been under a lot of pressure at work, that's all. Go ahead and finish getting ready for school. I'll be out in a minute."

"Okay. Dad, try to take it easy."

"I will; I owe you a game of hoops this weekend."

"Cool."

Damn, somebody has been doing a good job of impersonating me. I know damn well I didn't call the school and release Zoë to no lady named Linda. And I know I didn't call Jamal's mama and ask her to drop Malik off last night because I was too busy getting my ass kicked. Speaking of ass, what the hell is up with these tattoos? I've got to get this shit removed.

\*\*\*

Robert got dressed for work and did his morning routine. He dropped Zoë off, went by Dunkin Donuts, and arrived at his office by eight-thirty.

"Good morning, Cindy."

"Good morning, Mr. Baskin. A package came for you."

Robert stopped dead in his tracks. "Where is it?"

"I placed it on your desk."

"Thank you, Cindy."

"You're welcome."

Robert entered his office cautiously. He looked at the package and then locked his door. "*God, please don't let this be a bomb*," he prayed.

Robert opened the package and pictures fell out. They were of his butt cheeks. The note read: "*There are plenty more where these came from.*"

"Why, God? Why is someone doing this to me," he asked?

Then he sat there and studied the pictures. *I like boys. Woman beater. This is for my cousin,* he repeated, over and over in his head. Just as the phone rang he shouted, "Toni!"

"Yes, Robert, it's Toni, and I want to know one thing."

"What's that?"

"*How does it feel?*"

"You fucking bitch! Why are you doing this to me?"

"Oh, did you think you could break a few of my ribs, give me a concussion and make me miss out on three days of my life, and get away with it? You must be out of your damn mind! You don't know who you're messing with."

"Toni, I'll kill you!"

"Oh yeah? Look out the window. You see the fella sitting on the bus bench reading the newspaper? He has a gun aimed at you. Look on top of the hotel across the street. You see the sniper on the roof? And let's not forget Linda is sitting outside of Zoë's school."

"What do you want from me, Toni?"

"I want an apology, then I want you to deposit $350,000 in an account I have set up at your bank. It's for all of the pain and suffering you caused me. All you have to do is call the bank and transfer the money. I linked an additional account to your current bank account so it will look like you are just moving your own money around."

"How did you manage to do that?"

"Let's just say I know people."

"Then what?"

"Then I want you to go to the post office on King Boulevard. There will be a package waiting for you. Follow the instructions inside," Toni said then hung up.

"Shit, Shit, Shit!" Robert screamed.

"Mr. Baskin, are you all right?" Cindy buzzed

"Yes, I'm fine, Cindy. I'm just letting off a little steam."

"Do you want me to get you something?"

"No, that won't be necessary. Just cancel all of my appointments for today, and hold all of my calls."

"Consider it done, sir."

"Thanks, Cindy."

Robert sat there for a while, gathering his thoughts. Then he grabbed his car keys and headed for the post office.

*** 

"Next!" the clerk yelled. "May I help you, sir?"

"Yes, there is supposed to be a package here for Mr. Robert Baskin."

"Do you have the yellow claim form?"

"No, I wasn't told I needed one."

"Wait just a minute, sir; I'll go in the back and check."

"Today must be your lucky day; I have your package right here, and you don't need a claim check. Here you are, sir, have a nice day."

"Thank you," Robert said and left the building.

Robert raced home feeling nervous. After what he'd experienced in the last 24 hours, he didn't know what to expect. He pulled his car into the garage and carried the package very carefully. Then he closed all of the blinds just in case somebody was watching him.

"I wonder what's in here. Well, Robert, it's only one way to find out," he said to himself, "so stop being a punk and open it."

Robert carefully opened the package. Once again there was a note and a videotape. Robert inserted the video and pressed play. At first he didn't understand why or how someone was videotaping his daily activities. Then he saw his children going about their day-to-day lives. Next, his daughter was on the video saying, "Daddy, please save me. I'm scared!" Finally, he saw himself getting beat down and tattooed. Then the tape faded to black, and he heard the same voice that had been calling him say, *"How does it feel to know that your life can be changed in an instant?"* Another voice added, *"How does it feel to know that someone has touched your little girl?"* A third voice asked, *"How does it feel to get your ass kicked by someone stronger than you?"* The last voice was the original caller, and she asked, *"How does it feel to get knocked unconscious and then robbed of your dignity?"*

Robert was stunned. He sat there with a vacant look on his face.

*** 

Some men have a need to be in control all the time. For Robert, his need to be in control was based on all of the many responsibilities he had. The mere thought of doing something that wasn't *manly* threatened to crush the very foundation that his life was built upon. Most straight men are homophobic--- so much so that they aren't comfortable in the presence of gay men. I guess for Robert, the thought of being "tricked" into sleeping with a transsexual was more than his male ego could take. I'm sure that's why he brutally beat me. However, his calling 911 let me know he still had a shred of human decency in him. That's why I decided to teach him a mild lesson rather then having him straight up hurt. I even wrote him a letter explaining why I did what I did to him.

*My Dearest Robert,*

*How unfortunate for us that we had to end it this way. We had such a great time together. I trusted you. I know you felt betrayed, but I hope you believe me when I say that was never my intent; I am not a malicious person. Nor am I out to hurt anyone. I know you must hate me on some level, but I'm sure you still love me on a much deeper level. I just want to be Toni with an I, not a Y. I hope you can understand that. If not, maybe in time you will. Please know that Zoe was in the best of care during her time with Linda. She has no idea what she was a part of, and neither does Malik. So if you continue to act like nothing ever happened, then in their minds nothing did happen.*

*We have reactivated your credit cards so you can feel free to use them without suffering any embarrassment. The moment you deposit the money into the dummy account we have set up, you will receive a package. Inside will be the instruc-*

tions on how to get rid of the virus we put on your computers. Also, you will find all of your computer files and your client roster. Basically you can return to your normal life.

I have kept a copy of everything including the pictures and the videotape just in case you're stupid enough to try to have me arrested or create some kind of revenge plot of your own. Don't be a fool, Robert. This was a very mild lesson. Let's just call it even and go on with our lives. You have two very beautiful children to raise, and I have a new career ahead of me. I think we should both move on. Take care of yourself and know that I will never forget you.

Toni

\*\*\*

Robert followed my instructions down to the last detail. Mama got back on the plane and flew to Atlanta. We divided the money amongst all of us. Me, mama and Junior each got $100,000. We divided the other $50,000 amongst the fellas that helped us pull this off. Everybody returned back to their normal lives as if nothing ever happened. Mama and me flew back to Tallahassee to pack up and move to Atlanta just in time for me to start my new job.

# Chapter 10
## John's visit

"Ouch!" I screamed as Sharon ripped the hair from under my arm. "Waxing should not be this painful."

"I know. It's a shame we have to endure so much pain in the name of beauty."

"Preach!"

"So what time does Mr. Wonderful's flight land?"

"His message said five-fifteen."

"Are you excited?"

"Thrilled!"

"What are the two of you going to do this weekend?"

"I'm not sure yet. We discussed renting a hotel for the weekend because my place is getting cleaned. I know I want to take him to the Love & Jazz concert in Piedmont Park."

"*Ooh* that sounds nice. I might check that out myself. Have you gotten all of your outfits together yet?"

"Girl, no, I'm under the gun to get everything I need done by five."

"I know how that is. That's why I can't wait to meet my husband so I can let myself go. All of this working out, staying fit, waxing body hair, perming natural hair, and getting manicures and pedicures will have to cease. Honey, my husband is going to roll over one morning, and I'm going to be lying there looking like big foot. Just hairy and happy with ingrown toenails."

"*Stop!*" I hollered. "Girl, you know you are wrong for that!"

"Hey, a sistah has to do what a sistah has to do."

"I heard that. Are we almost finished?"

"That depends?"

"On what?"

"Whether or not you want the bikini wax, too."

"The thought of it brings tears to my eyes, Sharon."

"You being too hairy down there may bring tears to his eyes."

"Who said he was going to be down there?"

"Girl, who do you think you're fooling? I know you're going to give the brotha some," Sharon said while applying wax to my eyebrows.

"You're right, I'm going to give him some--- of my attention."

"Are you kidding me? After what you told me about him. How wonderful he is. How he couldn't wait to see you. You mean to tell me sex is not on your list of things to do?" She freed my body of more unwanted hair.

"Nope. Ouch!" I screamed again.

"Why? Are you scared?"

103

"A little. I don't want him to get the wrong impression and think I'm easy."

"Girl, please. The way women are dropping their panties these days. Any woman who keeps a man waiting five days is considered a challenge."

"Are you serious?" *If that's the case then I must be a major obstacle course.*

"Toni, where in the hell have you been?"

"I guess out of the loop. Damn, I didn't know it was like that."

"You better ask somebody."

"I guess he must be thinking I'm old fashioned, huh?"

"Probably."

"That's a good thing, isn't it?"

"It depends."

"On what?"

"On the type of man he is."

"How old did you say he was?"

"Thirty-five."

"Then he's probably old school. You making him wait a little bit won't be that big of a deal."

"Are you sure about that?"

"No, but you better believe if he was one of these men in their twenties, he would be trying to get you, and every other honey he met, in the sack."

"That's a damn shame. What about AIDS?"

"What about it?"

"Don't men know it's running rampant in our community?"

"Girl, those fools don't give a damn. They think it's never going to happen to them."

"Well I hope it never happens to anyone I know, including me."

"For real. So what's it going to be?"

"Give me the wax."

"Oh so you *are* going to give him some."

"No, I haven't decided yet, but I want to be prepared just in case."

"Better safe than sorry."

"Absolutely."

I spent another thirty minutes with Sharon, getting the hair ripped away from my body. All I know is John better appreciate the look and feel of my hairless body. Two hours is all I have left to complete my errands before I need to head to the airport. That gives me just enough time to pick my clothes up from the cleaners, purchase a really cute outfit from the mall, and get a new pair of sandals. Then I need to run by and drop my house key off to Mrs. Waters so her staff can get into my house tomorrow to clean it. John booked a suite for us at the *W*, which just happens to be one of my favorite hotels. I also arranged for us to have drinks tonight with the girls, so that he could get a chance to meet my friends. My intent is to give my friends a chance to scope him out and tell me what they think. I know they are really going to like John. He's a sweetheart.

\*\*\*

"John, over here," I yelled, waving to him through the crowd. The moment he spotted me his face lit up like a fireworks display on the fourth of July.

"Toni, baby, you look marvelous," he said as has greeted me with a big hug and a kiss. "Wow!"

"Now that's the kind of welcome a girl can appreciate," I joked. "How was your flight?"

"It wasn't bad at all."

"Are you ready for some fun, Hotlanta style?"

"Lead the way, beautiful."

John and I walked to the car and placed his bags in the trunk. I put the top down on my Beemer and we sped away.

"Toni, I like your car. It's very sporty."

"Thanks."

"Where are we going?"

"I thought I would take you by my house first for a quick tour. Then we're meeting three of my friends for happy hour."

"Let me guess: Cynthia, Michelle, and Ebony."

"Very good, John. How did you remember their names?"

"Believe it or not, I actually listen when you talk."

"Well that's a first."

"What is?"

"A man listening when a woman is talking."

"That's a low blow."

"You know it's true."

"What is?"

"What I just said."

"Oh, I'm sorry, I wasn't listening."

"*Ha, ha, ha,* very funny, John."

He stroked my hair. "I'm kidding. I heard you, and yeah it's true to some extent."

\*\*\*

We pulled into my subdivision after our thirty-minute gabfest, coming from the airport.

"Nice neighborhood, Toni. How long have you lived here?"

105

"Four years in this area but eight months in my house."

"How do you like it?"

"It's peaceful, well kept, and out of the way. I love it."

"Have you ever considered living anywhere else?"

"No."

"Didn't you say mom lives in Atlanta, too?"

"Yes."

"Will I get the opportunity to meet her, too?"

"Yes, we will see her in Church on Sunday. You did bring a suit for Church, didn't you?"

"Of course I did."

*That's what I'm talking about. There's nothing like a brotha who loves the Lord.* "Good. I think you will enjoy Reverend Thompson. He is very dynamic."

"What makes him so dynamic?"

"The way he delivers the Word. He's dramatic but easy to understand. He interprets the Bible better than anyone I've ever encountered"

"Sounds like an interesting brotha."

"He is. We're here."

"Your landscaping is beautiful," John commented as he got out of the car and handed me his suit bag. "I'm not sure if you've figured me out yet, but I have a thing for flowers," he said, admiring my garden as we walked toward the front door.

"Really? When did you develop your love for flowers?"

"I have loved them since I was a little boy. I used to help my mother plant her flowers and cultivate her vegetable garden."

"I would have never figured you for a man who likes to get his hands dirty."

"Why not?"

"Because you're a business man. You don't see too many businessmen in the backyard getting down and dirty."

"That's true, but some of us are just good old fashioned country boys."

"There's nothing wrong with that. Actually I find it charming."

"Oh, do you now?" John whispered as he grabbed me from behind, wrapped his arms around my waist, and kissed me softly on the neck.

"*Umm,* you keep that up and we may not make it to happy hour."

"If that's an offer, then let's go inside, and I'll make you happy in less than an hour."

"That's very tempting, lover boy, but my friends would never forgive me if I stood them up. They have been dying to meet you."

"Well can a brotha get a rain check?"

"I'll think about it."

106

"You'll think about it? Now is that any way to treat a guest? What happened to good old-fashioned southern hospitality?"

"You' re absolutely right. What was I thinking?"

"Now that's what I'm talking about."

"Baby, come on inside and let me fix you a nice tall glass of lemonade. Then we can go to happy hour. How is that for southern hospitality?"

"That's a start but, Toni, sweetheart, if that's the full extent of your southern charm, we are going to have to strip you of your southern bell title."

"Well, John, I never!" I said, doing my best Scarlett O'Hara imitation.

"At this rate, sweetheart, you never will," he replied, doing a very convincing Rhett Butler imitation.

We went inside and I poured John a nice cold glass of lemonade. I gave him a tour of my house and a moment to freshen up. Then we headed for the club called *Libations*, the new hot spot in Atlanta. It's a Neo-soul, R&B, and Jazzy-type of atmosphere. It's the place to be for the upper middle-class, twenty-and thirty-something professional crowd. The music is always tight. From the moment you walk in the door you're grooving to singers like Glenn Lewis, Kem, Jill Scott, and our own Atlanta native, India.Arie. When John and I entered, the DJ was playing *Close* by Next. We went straight to the dance floor because that is my jam. Besides, I wanted to see what kind of dancer John was. John's moves, when we slow danced in Tallahassee, were on point. I had fet all of him, and let's just say I wasn't mad at him. I knew he was a real man by the way our sway made his soldier stand up and salute me. The thought of that night made me chuckle.

"What's so funny, Ms. Goodwin? I know you're not laughing at my dance moves."

"No, not at all. I was just thinking about something."

"Do you care to share?"

"No, I think I better keep this one to myself."

"Oh, so it's like that, huh?"

"Trust me, you don't want to know."

"If you say so."

"I see you can hold your own on the dance floor, Mr. Collins."

"Yeah, I do aw'ight."

"Now look whos's being modest. You know you want to breakout with the runnin' man again."

"Now that was a private show that day."

"Thank God."

"Oh how are you going to play me?"

"You played yourself, my brotha. You know you were wrong for that."

"I see you can't appreciate dances from the eighties."

"Yes, I could--- back in the eighties when they were popular."

"Now you have gone and hurt my feelings. No more dances for you," John said as he played like he was leaving the floor.

"Oh don't be like that. I was just kidding."

"Then let me hear it."

"Hear what?"

"That I am the best dancer you ever met, and no one does the runnin' man like John Collins."

"You've got to be kidding me."

"Yeah, I am. Are you ready to take break?"

"Yes, I think I saw my friends come in. Are you ready for the interrogation?"

"Bring it on. I'm not scared of a few girlfriends. Now your mama…that's another story."

"Well you still have a little over twenty-four hours to get ready for her." *I know mama is ready to meet him.*

"I know, and I'm going to need every hour I have to get my mind together. It's something about meeting parents that always makes me nervous. I don't why, because they always love me. But that initial meeting makes me a little uneasy."

"You will be fine. I'm sure Linda is going to love you. However, the three ladies you are about to meet will give you a run for your money."

"Then let's go find them and get this over with."

I grabbed John's hand and led him through the crowd. Libations had gotten pretty crowded while we were on the dance floor. I didn't want to run the risk of losing my man in the crowd, especially in a room full of good-looking, desperate, single women.

"Toni, over here!" Ebony shouted over the sound of the crowd and the beat of the music.

When I spotted her, I waved back to acknowledge her. John and I snaked our way through the crowd to the other side of the room. Cynthia, Michelle, and Ebony were looking great. All three of them were wearing black. Cynthia had on the signature little black dress that all women should own. Ebony wore a body-hugging, Lycra tank top that showed off her mid-section with some tight black slacks.

"I see somebody is trying to show off the results of their new workout program," I said as we walked up to them.

"You got that right, girl," Ebony replied, hugging me.

"Ebony, I have to give it to you. You're working that top."

"Un-umm," Cynthia said, clearing her throat. Excuse me,but what are we, chop liver?"

108

"No, what you are is a hater," Ebony remarked. Now let the girl give credit where credit is due."

"Go ahead, Toni. You were saying?"

"You look marvelous, Ebony!"

"Thank you. I try."

"Ladies you all look marvelous. Michelle, I love that skirt. I have been looking for a long black skirt, now I know where I can get one."

"I'm going to have to ask that you stay out of my closet and get your own, missy."

"Fine, be that way. Remember, payback is a bitch."

"Enough with the clothes. Aren't you going to introduce us to your friend, Toni?"

"I was just about to do that, Cynthia. John Collins, I would love for you to meet three of my closest friends. This is Cynthia, Michelle, and Ebony."

"It's a pleasure to meet you ladies." John took each of their extended hands and kissed them.

"Ummm, I like him already, Toni."

"Yeah, Ebony, so do I," I said, smiling and wrapping my arm around John's.

"So John, what do you do for a living?" Cynthia asked.

"I'm an investment banker."

"Really? That's interesting."

"I think so. I enjoy my work."

"That's a good thing."

"Ladies, would you like something to drink?"

"How thoughtful of you. I'll have a Miami Vice," Michelle said.

"Rum and Coke for me."

"White wine for me," Cynthia added.

"Toni, I didn't get an order from you."

" I'll have an ocean cocktail."

"What's that?"

"A tall, cold glass of water. I'm designated driver, remember?"

"I gotcha."

John moved down to the end of the bar to order our drinks. It gave me a few minutes to check in with my girls to see what they thought.

"So, ladies, what do you think?"

"He seems like a keeper. Have you seen his dance moves yet? You know that's an important criteria to meet."

"Yes, Michelle, I've seen them, and he has it going on."

"Then I vote yes."

"What about you, Ebony?"

"Hell, anybody who kisses my hand and offers to buy me a drink seems like good people to me. I say keep his ass and fuck him, too."

"Thanks for the added instruction." I laughed.

Ebony winked at me and said, "You know I'm just keeping it real."

"Yeah, *real* ghetto."

"Go to hell, Cynt."

"I would but your ghetto ass might be there."

I jumped in to break them up. "Okay, ladies, enough. So, Cynt, what do you think?"

"He seems well groomed which is usually a definite sign of money. I say keep him until his bank account runs low."

"Girl, money is not everything."

"The hell you say."

"I guess I forgot who I was talking to."

"You must have."

"You know I'm all about the Benjamins."

"Ladies, we need to change the subject; he's coming."

"Good looking out, Michelle. I don't think he would appreciate hearing us discussing his bank account."

"Here you are, ladies. Enjoy," John said handing out our drinks.

"Thanks, John," the four of us said in unison.

We stood there drinking and having a good time. The girls continued to question John. They were thankfully enjoying his company. I didn't get any negative vibes from them at all. Not until Ebony and Michelle started pointing out the gay men in the club. John seemed really surprised.

"Are you sure he's gay?" he asked.

"John, we have the best gaydar this side of Atlanta."

"Gaydar?" John asked.

"Yes, gay radar," Ebony answered.

"Oh. "How can you tell that brotha's gay? He looks straight to me."

"So does Roger" I whispered in his ear.

"Touché."

"Gaydar is a gift that God has blessed us with. Trust me, living in Atlanta, a sistah needs it," Ebony confirmed.

She went on to tell John about how she got tricked by this one guy she was dating her senior year at Clark.

"John, the brotha was tall and good looking. I thought he was just a little in touch with his feminine side because he had mad decorating skills. He could also dress his ass off. But a little voice inside me kept telling me something wasn't right. I guess I should have picked up on it because he had a lot of girlfriends. But he also had guy friends that didn't act suspect.

But one day while I was over his house, this guy called and sounded like a straight up punk. I got suspicious. I told him to call back and leave a message on the answering machine because I didn't think I would be there when Paul came home. That sissy must have called back thinking it was voice mail instead of an answering machine. I heard the whole message. He told Paul that him and the girls were going to their special hangout spot, and to meet them there at nine o'clock that evening.

So me being the no-nonsense sister that I am, I called one of my girls and we planned a stakeout. We got there early because we wanted to make sure we could hide out in a spot where we could see everything but no one could see us. Man, I was so nervous, because I did not know what I was in for. The fellas started showing up one by one around nine o'clock. Some of them I recognized from Morehouse. A few of them fools had on their fraternity shirts.

Then I saw Paul pull up with a guy I never saw before. I heard one of the guys say 'are y'all ready to get this party started?' The fellas all went wild saying 'yeah, bring them on.' Then I heard the guy say 'get your dollars out.' The music started to play and a boatload of sissy's came parading out of the back. They had on thongs, lingerie, you name it. Them fools went crazy. They were giving them lap dances and going down on them. It looked like a gay-ass bachelor party. My girl and I were stunned. We sat there watching in horror. You could have knocked us over with a feather.

We left and went to the corner drug store and bought a disposable camera. I still have copies of the pictures we took of those fools. The next day we got them developed and mailed a copy of them anonymously to the fellas we knew, including Paul. We set up a fake P.O. Box and had them send checks to it every Friday. The money we made off of them was better then the money we made on our work-study jobs. Tanya and I were able to finance all of our extracurricular activities through our blackmail scheme. The funny thing is none of them ever found out it was us. Not even Paul."

"What happened with Paul? I know you didn't stay with that brotha."

"Hell no. I told him that I was getting ready to go online for a sorority, and I wouldn't have time to dedicate to the relationship so I thought it would be best if we broke up."

"Did he buy it?" John asked.

"Yeah, he sure did."

"He even bought me presents when I went over."

"Dang! That is jacked up."

"Tell me about it."

"So why didn't you bust him."

"I figured being gay in a straight man's world has to be it's own silent hell. I

111

can't imagine what it's like to walk around pretending to be something I'm not all of the time. I mean, if I couldn't be me and keep it real, I would go crazy. I could only imagine what he must have been going through. It wasn't worth it for me to add to his anguish. I decided to leave him with his dignity. I figured it was the least I could do. Especially since I had him paying me back financially for the hurt and embarrassment he caused me. To this day he still has no idea that I know. I still run into him from time to time, and he's still in the closet. Last I heard he was thinking of getting married to one of the Atlanta Falcon's cheerleaders. I hope the sistah knows what she is getting."

"Me too."

"So anyway, that's how I first developed my gaydar. It hasn't failed me yet."

John looked amazed. "Wow! That's some story, Ebony."

"Tell me about it."

"Enough with the stories. Ladies, I think it's time we take John on the dance floor and make him show us what he's working with."

"I'm ready when you are. Toni, lead the way."

"Are you sure you're up to this? John, we have been known to hurt a man on the dance floor."

"Well, I'm willing to take one for the team."

"Just remember you asked for it," Michelle reminded him.

John handled his business on the dance floor. Dancing with four good looking sistahs and having a great time had to make John the envy of every brotha in the club. I caught a few brothas shooting John an evil look. He was so busy trying to keep up with us that I don't think he even noticed. At one point a crowd formed around us and we started a soul train line. Everybody got in to it and we ended up turning Libations out.

"Ladies, I think it's time for us to call it a night," I said as we left the dance floor and headed for the door. "John has been such a good sport, I think it's time for me to take him home and pamper him a little."

"Now that's what I'm talking about." John blushed.

"I agree. I think Mr. Collins has earned a little pampering," Michelle insisted.

Cynthia extended her hand and said, "It was a pleasure to meet you, John. If you have any friends that are just like you, please bring them with you on your next visit. I'll be happy to show them some southern hospitality."

"I'll keep that in mind."

"Please do."

"John, you are alright with me. This is the most fun I've had with a brotha in a long time. I am glad to see you know how to have fun. Thanks for the drinks."

"You are very welcome, Ebony. I enjoyed meeting you, too. We'll have to do this again sometime."

"You got it." She smiled.

"Goodnight, girls. I'll catch up with y'all next week."

"Goodnight, Toni. Don't do anything we wouldn't do."

"Then that gives me a lot of room to work with."

"Very funny, heifer. We'll see you later," Michelle said as she hugged me and ran to catch up with Cynthia and Ebony.

"Shall we, Mr. Collins?"

"After you, love."

\*\*\*

We got back to my house around eleven o'clock. I fixed John a nightcap and collapsed on the sofa next to him. I was exhausted.

We stayed there for about an hour talking about the evening and my friends. At some point we must have fallen asleep. It wasn't until the doorbell rang that I woke up.

"Who is it?"

"Waters' cleaning service."

"Oh my God. What time is it?" I mumbled to myself as I ran to wake John.

"John, baby, wake up."

"Huh?"

"Wake up, baby, the cleaning service is here."

"Oh, what time is it?"

"Eight o'clock. We must have fallen asleep here last night."

John's eyes popped open as he sprang to his feet. "We better get moving then. Toni, where is your overnight bag?"

"Sitting by the door in my bedroom."

"Do you have everything you need in it?"

"Yes, I think so."

"Give me a minute to wash my face and brush my teeth and then we can get out of here."

"I headed for the front door." "Hi, Come on in. I'm sorry we're still here, but we accidentally fell asleep on the sofa last night."

"It's okay, ma'am we understand."

"Did Mrs. Waters give you the key?"

"Yes Ma'am."

"Great, then we're going to get out of here and let you get to work. I left my cell phone number on the counter in case you need me."

"All right."

"John! Sweetie, are you ready to go?"

113

"Ready."

"I'll need a few minutes to get myself together and we're out of here."

"You too Ma'am."

\*\*\*

"Can you believe we fell asleep on the couch?"

"No. The last thing I remember was talking about Ebony. Can you believe the story she told us about Paul?"

"I know. What a trip?"

"I have to give it to her, though, I don't think I would have handled the situation as graciously as she did."

"What do you mean, John?"

"If I was dating a woman and found out she was gay, I would want to watch of course," he said jokingly. "But putting all jokes aside, I would feel betrayed."

"That's understandable." *Hump! I understand that I might have to keep my little secret to myself a little while longer.*

"My belief has always been honesty is the best policy. So I think people should just be honest from the beginning about who they are and what they want."

"That's true, but you know sometimes that's not as easy as it sounds. With all the pressure that society places on you to conform. Anyone who is a little different is usually subject to major scrutiny."

"You sound very passionate about this, Toni."

"I am. I was picked on a lot as a child."

"Why?"

While we waited for the light to change I continued to explain to John about my childhood. "Because I was different."

"Different how?"

"I didn't come from a two parent home like most of the kids in my neighborhood, and I was an only child."

"That's not a big deal."

"It was back then. The other kids used to tease me and tell me I didn't have a daddy. Whenever they saw me walking down the street, they would sing *Papa was a rolling stone.* It was a lonely, horrible feeling. That's how Devon and I became so close. We were living similar hells. The difference was that Devon used humor to cope with his pain."

"What did you use?"

"Books. I worked really hard in school and became an overachiever."

John looked solemn. "That's a sad story, Toni."

"What can I say? I was a sad child."

114

***

We pulled up to the *W* around nine-fifteen. The valet unloaded our bags and parked the car.

"John, why don't we explain to them what happened last night? Maybe that'll keep you from having to pay for two nights."

"That's a good idea. It's worth a shot."

"Welcome to the *W*; may I help you, sir?"

"I certainly hope so, young lady. My name is John Collins. I have a reservation."

"One moment sir. Yes, I see you have a reservation for two nights."

"That's correct. However, I was unable to take advantage of my reservation last night due to unforeseen circumstances. Do you have the authority to credit me for that night or should I speak with your manager directly?"

"*You go, boy!*" I whispered silently to myself. He was taking care of business.

"No, sir. That won't be necessary. I have the authority to credit you for that night."

"I would appreciate that."

"No problem."

"Also would you please make sure we're on the highest floor and away from the elevator?"

"Mr. Collins, I took the liberty of upgrading you to our presidential suite. Will you need one room key or two?"

"Two is fine."

"Here you are. I hope you enjoy your stay. Someone will bring your bags up momentarily."

"Thank you."

"You're welcome."

"You go boy!" I said to John on the way to our room. "You handled that beautifully."

"Thank you." He smiled. "You know I learned a long time ago that when you truly believe that you are important and act accordingly, people will respond to you in kind. I always handle my affairs in a very dignified manner."

"Duly noted."

" What do you say we get showered and changed and go have some breakfast."

"I say yes, I'm starving."

"This is our room right here."

"John, hurry up and open the door. I have to go to the ladies room."

Our suite had the cozy feeling of home. Every inch of the room was picture

115

perfect. The interior decorator made great use of color, too. From the black and white framed photographs on the wall to the warm neutral tones of the Berber carpet to the most enchanting part of the room--- the king-size feather bed and goose down duvet cover. Not a single detail was missed. A flat screen TV hung on the velvet-covered wall. A CD and DVD player completed the entertainment center. Flavored teas and imported coffee and a gigantic fruit basket filled the snack bar. What a wonderful home away from home.

"Toni, look at this suite!" John said excitedly. "You have great taste in hotels."

"So I've been told."

"Oh yeah, by who?"

*Oops! I didn't mean to let that slip out.* "Nobody, sweetie, I was just kidding." I kissed him on the cheek and ran to the bathroom.

"John!" I yelled from the ladies room.

"Yes, sweetheart?"

"I'm going to jump in the shower while I'm in here. I'll be out in a few minutes."

"Okay. I'll go in right after you, then we can go have breakfast."

***

"Breakfast was delicious," he said kissing my hand as he helped me into the car. "What do you have planned for us today, sweetheart?"

"I figured we could go for a nice drive. That way you'll get the grand tour of Atlanta. Then we're going to Piedmont Park for the Love and Jazz festival."

"That sounds romantic."

"It usually is. Tonight's line-up is spectacular. Kenny G, Kirk Whalum, David Sanborn, and George Benson are the featured artists."

"What a great line-up!"

"I thought so, too. I'm sure you'll enjoy it."

"What kind of seating arrangements do we have?"

"For this type of concert everyone brings their lawn chairs or blankets."

"Oh, so it's like lying on the beach under the stars."

"Yep. The only exception is we are not on or near a beach."

"Then we'll just have to pretend, won't we?"

"What do you have in mind?"

We pulled into a hotel parking lot and parked next to a huge fountain. I told John to close his eyes while I painted a picture for him of what our evening would be like. "I'm envisioning us lying on a very beautiful blanket under the stars. Our picnic basket is filled with fresh strawberries, whip cream, chicken kababs, a tossed salad, and a bambino watermelon."

"*Ummm*, that sounds mouthwatering." he said. "What are we drinking?"

"Watermelon Martini's."

His eyes popped opened. "Count me in!"

"John you have got to be one of the most romantic men I have ever met."

"I don't take compliments like that lightly. Thank you."

"Believe me, you have earned it. You are welcome."

"What's the dress code for this evening's main event?"

"There isn't one. I'm sure we will see a little of everything out there."

"Then I have a great idea."

"What's that?"

"Since I"m the architect for this evenings atmosphere, my fantasy consists of you and I both wearing white. I see you in a white sheer sundress and bare feet, lying in my arms while Kirk Whalum serenades us. I, on the other hand, am wearing an all-linen outfit with some *Cole Hann* sandals. A tranquil breeze blows and extinguishes some of our scented candles. But the sweet smell of coconut lingers long after the flame is gone. We sway to the rhythm of the sax. So caught up in the moment that we don't notice our candles are dying out one by one like fallen soldiers. Nothing matters in that moment but you and I."

"You have a very vivid imagination. I was so wrapped up in the moment that I felt like I was really there."

" You'll be there in about three hours."

\*\*\*

John and I had a magnificent time at the concert. The evening was surreal. Everything looked just as John had described it in his fantasy. We returned to the hotel, opened the French doors to our balcony, laid a blanket on the ground, turned on the smooth jazz station, and extended our evening under the stars.

"Rise and shine John" I said in a barely audible voice. We were sleeping quite comfortably on our feather bed. I could feel John's erection against my back, thanks to the extremely comfortable spoon position we had assumed sometime during the night. He didn't respond to my command verbally.

He pulled me in closer to his body and kept on sleeping.

Although I was reveling in the moment, I knew if we didn't get up and start getting dressed for Church, we would be late. This time I nudged him and said, "John, Mama is waiting to meet you." That did the trick.

John's eyes opened wide. He sat up in the bed and massaged his temples.

"What's wrong? Do you have a headache?"

"No, I'm trying to get my mind right. What time is Church?"

"Eight-thirty."

117

"How much time do we have to get ready?"

"One hour."

"Then would it be okay if I lie here for another fifteen minutes, please?"

"Of course you can. I'll go jump in the shower; that should give you enough time to get your mind together."

"Thanks, baby."

"You're welcome. John, try to relax. I think mama is really going to like you."

We got to Church in time for the praise and worship service. Mama entered the service about ten minutes late, wearing a fabulous, wide brim hat and lavender suit. She arrived just in time to fellowship. Since John was on her right, he was the first person she met during the meet and greet.

"Good morning, God bless you." Mama greeted John.

"Good morning ma'am, and may God bless you, too."

"Mama, this is John."

"Well aren't you a handsome young man," Mama said. "How are you enjoying your visit to Atlanta?"

"I 'm having a wonderful time, ma'am."

"Please, call me Linda."

"Mama, I think you and John will have to continue your conversation after service. Fellowship time is over. Everyone is returning to their seats."

"Okay, Toni. John, we'll get to talk more over brunch."

"I'd like that."


The Reverend preached his sermon on forgiveness. His message was powerful and easy to understand as usual. It's funny how no matter what the topic of the day is in Church, it always seems to apply to you and your present circumstance. The whole time I sat in church listening to him speak, I couldn't help but think about how I'm going to need forgiving some time in the near future. Although I told Ms. D. that I would consider telling John the truth before things get too serious with him, I'm not sure I can do that now. I'm already having very strong feelings for him, and I know sex is inevitable. I want him so bad till I can't stand it. Since I'm sitting here in the church having this conversation with myself I guess now is a good time to say. *Thank you Lord for making John a patient gentle man. Lord, I hope you have made him as forgiving as he is patient. While we're talking Lord, please forgive me for not being honest with John. I'm not ready to reveal my true self to him,--- not yet anyway. I know I'm being selfish but if you would indulge me just this once, Lord, I would appreciate it, and I promise I will tell him eventually. Thanks for listening, Lord.* Just as I finished my talk with God, I heard the Reverend say "...and let all the saints say Amen."

"Amen, amen." Mama declared. "The Reverend surely knows how to deliver the Word. Did you enjoy the sermon, John?"

"Yes, I sure did. He's as dynamic as Toni said he was."

"Isn't that the truth? So, John, are you hungry?"

"Starved."

"Toni and I wanted to take you to brunch. Have you ever been to Gladys' Chicken and Waffles?"

"No. Is that the restaurant owned by Gladys Knight?"

"It sure is."

"I've never eaten chicken with waffles, but I've heard great things about the food there."

"You are in for a treat. The food there is finger-licking good."

"Then I guess the Colonel better watch out."

Mama laughed at John's quick-witted response.

"I like him already Toni." She exclaimed through her laughter. "John, I like a man with a sense of humor. You have made a very good first impression."

"Thank you Linda. I like you too." John smiled.

After nearly two hours and what looked like five pounds of food John paid the bill and we left the restaurant.

"John thank you for brunch. It's always a pleasure to be in the company of a true gentleman. Make sure you come to see me on your next visit."

"I will."

"I am going to get out of here and let you and Toni enjoy your last couple of hours together. I really enjoyed meeting you."

Kissing mama on the cheek, John insisted, "the pleasure was all mine."

"Okay sweetheart go enjoy that man. I'll call you tomorrow."

"Alright mama drive safely and enjoy the rest of your Sunday afternoon."

John and I stood there waving until Mama turned the corner.

"See John I told you she would like you."

"You sure did. I think I was nervous for nothing."

***

Entering the hotel made me feel sad. I knew it meant that my weekend with John was coming to an end. We went back to our suite and changed clothes. Then we lounged around for the rest of the afternoon. At three o'clock we checked out and headed for the airport. I dropped him off feeling like I was losing my best friend. As I watched him disappear in the crowd a single tear rolled down my

119

cheek. I drove home in complete silence. When I walked in my bedroom, content to wallow in my misery, I noticed an envelope on my nightstand. At first I thought the cleaning crew left it but I could smell John's cologne on the envelope. I ripped it open and read those three little words 'What a weekend.' I turned the note over and there was three more words 'Thank you Toni.' Once again a tear rolled down my cheek. But this time it was filled with a little bit of guilt. *I don't mean to lead John on, but I can't seem to let him go.* I fell back on the bed and stared at the ceiling until I fell asleep.

# Chapter 11
## The site visit

On my drive to the La Cola plant in rush hour traffic, I listened to the Tom Joyner morning show. J. Anthony Brown was doing his Reverend Richard Adenoid skit. Even though I was stuck in traffic and a little anxious about my site visit, I laughed hysterically at how crazy J is. The morning show is always a great way to start off your workday. By the time "*It's your world*" came on, I was so caught up that I forgot about being nervous. Before I knew it, I was pulling into the underground parking lot at La Cola. Mr. Santos was standing in the lobby waiting to greet me.

"Good Morning, Toni, How are you?"
"I 'm doing terrific. How are you?"
"I'm Great. Are you ready for your tour?"
"I sure am."
"Wonderful. I will start the tour by taking you throughout our corporate offices. Then Mrs. Slutsky will join us for lunch, after which you will have an opportunity to change clothes for your plant tour."
"Sounds good."
"We have coffee and bagels in the main conference room for you."
"Thank you."
" Please make yourself comfortable. I'm going to give you a few minutes to relax and have something to eat. I'll come back in about fifteen minutes to start your tour."
"Okay. I'll be ready to go by then."
Mr. Santos left the room, which gave me a much-needed opportunity to put some food in my stomach. I hadn't eaten since brunch yesterday, and my stomach felt like it was turning against me. I sat in one of the chairs surrounding the huge mahogany conference table and enjoyed two Einstein bagels and a cup of Blue Mountain Coffee. Mr. Santos came back to get me just as I was finishing my coffee.
"Toni, we're ready for you."
"Then lead the way," I said, getting up from the table to join him in the hallway.
"How was your weekend?"
"It was relaxing. I went to a jazz concert in Piedmont Park."
"I heard something about that on the radio. How was it?"
"Extraordinary! I think it was one of the best concerts I have ever been to."
"I hate I missed it."
"Are you into jazz?"

"Yes, it is one of my favorite forms of music. I'm a closet musician, you know?"

"Really? what instrument do you play?"

"I play a little sax."

"That's my favorite instrument. How often do you play?"

"Not often. While I was in college I played in a band. But I don't get the chance to play that much anymore."

"That's too bad. I would love to hear you perform."

"Well, you know how it is when you get a family. Your personal dreams take a backseat to the dreams you have for your family."

"I guess so. Maybe one day you will have the opportunity to pursue it again."

"Maybe. Stranger things have happened I guess."

We exited the elevator on the penthouse floor.

"Toni, we like to start our tours off at the top and work our way down. I'm going to escort you to our CEO's office and then I will take to you the fiscal department for a quick briefing. Carmen, is Mr. Blackwell ready for us?"

"Yes, go right in."

"Bill Blackwell, this is Toni Goodwin of Carlton International."

"Toni, this is our CEO Bill Blackwell."

Mr. Blackwell extended his hand.

"It's a pleasure to meet you sir." I said as I shook it.

"Consider the pleasure all mine, Ms. Goodwin."

"Please, call me Toni."

"Only if you'll call me Bill."

"That's a deal." I smiled.

"Toni, please have a seat. I'm not a man who likes to beat around the bush so I'll get straight to the point. We have been watching your company for quite some time. Quite frankly I like the way you do business. The only concern we've had is that you all are one of the smaller firms based on industry standards. The type of campaigns we're planning to introduce into the marketplace will call for lots of manpower. And I don't know if your ftrm will have the manpower and the resources to pull it off.

However, La Cola is committed to developing or expanding our minority base. Our three-point thrust for this year is to reach out to our African-American, Latino, and Jewish communities. We already have a presence in all three of these communities, thanks to branding. However, we're not satisfied with our percentage of the market share. Our immediate goal for the African-American market is to sponsor the Essence Music Festival in New Orleans.

We're currently in negotiations with the team at Essence. If we land that account, in my opinion, your firm would be the perfect firm to handle that campaign."

"Why, because we're black?"

"Mostly. Forgive me for being direct, but who better to target the African-American audience than an African-American firm?"

"Bill, I have to interject. I hope you don't mind."

"No, please go right ahead."

"I've listened to everything you've said, and quite frankly I'm elated to have this opportunity. I realize that Cola is one of the industry giants, and partnering with you will really send our firm into a new arena. However, I am not sure I like what I'm hearing."

"What do you mean?"

"I hear you saying that you have researched and watched our firm."

"That's correct."

"Then if that's the case you should know that we have handled big accounts before. Now granted, none of them were as large as you are. However, if you review our track record, you'll find that when Carlton International is faced with a challenge, we rise to the occasion. I understand your concerns because you are targeting three large markets and you want to be the product of choice for those consumers. I submit to you that at Carlton International that is exactly what we want to be. We want to be the firm of choice for all of your advertising needs. Not just for your African-American market. Are you prepared to offer us the opportunity to work on campaigns other than the ones that target your African-American consumers?"

"Toni, I like your spunk. Not many people stand up to me and tell me what they are really thinking. I appreciate your doing so. However, I have a board of directors that I'm accountable to. I cannot make that kind of a decision on my own. I do suggest that you continue your site visit, and at the end of the day come back and see me before you leave. I have a few calls to make."

Mr. Santos and I shook Bill's hand and headed for the elevator.

"What was I thinking? I hope I didn't blow our opportunity."

"Do you want my opinion?"

"Yes."

"Between me you and the walls of this elevator, I think you were terrific."

"Are you serious? That was your CEO."

"I know. That's what's so terrific about it. Listen, Toni, not many people speak their mind to men in positions of power. Most of the people who come here are so busy kissing his butt, that I don't think they even have minds. But you stood up for your company. You didn't let them play the race card and try to pigeonhole you into the African-American community. As a fellow minority, I understand how you feel." He leaned in close to me. Just between us," he whispered, "we are in negotiations for the Latin Grammys, held in Miami, too. If I were you I would try to get that account as well."

"Mr. Santos, I appreciate your candor. But right now I'm not even sure I still have a shot at getting the Essence account, much less the Latin Grammys."

"Don't worry about it, Toni; I think you do. I've seen him when he's angry, and trust me he wasn't. He seemed impressed if you want to know the truth."

"Impressed? Are you kidding me?" I said, shaking my head and folding my arms as I leaned against the wall of the elevator.

"No, I'm not kidding you."

"Then I hope you're right."

We walked out of the elevator and entered what looked like a room full of accountants. Five white men, all of whom were wearing dark blue suits and glasses, and one white woman wearing the same thing the men were. except hers was a skirt. An Asian man, who could have easily been related to Jackie Chan, invited us in to have a seat. The tension in the room was so thick, you couldn't cut it with a chain saw.

"Shall we get started?" The woman asked.

"Certainly," I responded.

They went around the room introducing themselves and stating their titles. Not one of them smiled or offered an endearing gesture. I sat there hoping this meeting wouldn't last long. The accountants handed me a prospectus that had to be about two hundred pages thick. I wanted to laugh at them and ask them if they really expected me to read all of that. Instead, I made a mental note to drop it off to our Fiscal Department as soon as I got back to work.

The meeting continued with them spewing out facts and figures. They explained the results of a feasibility study that they had conducted, and they tried to impress upon me the accuracy of their research. Although I'm sure they put a lot of time and effort into their presentation, my mind could not focus on what they were saying. I was still caught up in what had just taken place in Bill's office. By the time I snapped out of my own little world, I heard one of them saying, "We hope you will find our numbers favorable. We look forward to partnering with your firm."

I nodded politely and went around the table shaking hands before Mr. Santos and I headed out for lunch.

"So, Toni, what did you think?"

"I thought they were pretty impressive," I lied.

"Then you're the first person to think so. Most people think they look like clones and are bored to death," he said, laughing.

Even though I thought he was cool, I knew better than to join him in any neg-ative bantering about the company or the people who worked for it. I couldn't forget for one moment that I was still a black woman living in a white man's world. I knew what lines not to cross.

***

Lunch was catered. Mr. Santos, Mrs. Slutsky, and myself dined privately in one of the exclusive lounges on site. I have to admit that La Cola set it out for me. They know how to treat a girl. We had three carving stations and white glove service. I was impressed. Lunch lasted nearly two hours. We spent it mostly talking about our backgrounds and where we went to school. Mrs. Slutsky made it known to me that she had been briefed on what had transpired earlier in Bill 's office.

"Have your feelings changed toward La Cola?" she asked.

"Not really," I lied. "I'm still as excited about working with Cola as I was when I woke up this morning." That was another lie.

"That's good to hear. I'm sure Mr. Blackwell is just as excited, too."

*Now who was doing the lying?* I thought.

Mr. Santos interrupted, thankfully. "Toni," he said standing up from the table. "Today has been a pleasure. I look forward to seeing you on your turf on the 15th. I sincerely hope you get the account," he added, shaking my hand.

"Me, too, and thank you very much for all of your assistance and insight. I had a good time."

"With that said, I will leave you two ladies to finish the rest of your lunch. I hope you will enjoy the rest of your visit."

"I'm sure I will. Thank you."

"Toni, would you like anything else to eat or drink?"

"No. I couldn't touch another bite."

"Then are you ready to change clothes and go to the plant."

" I sure am."

"I'll show you to the ladies locker room. You can change clothes in there."

"My bag is in my car."

"No problem. I'll walk with you to get it."

We went to my car, retrieved my bag and then to the locker room. I had on my jeans and sneakers in a matter of minutes. I guess I'm still able to change my clothes fast from my days in the business. They say old habits die hard.

***

Mrs. Slutsky and I spent two hours yelling at each other. The noise in the plant was so loud that that was the only way we could hear what each other was

125

saying. Watching what goes on was an eye opening experience. When you pick up a bottle of La Cola, you have absolutely no idea what all went into getting that bottle to the shelf. It's not something that anyone would ordinarily think about. Be that as it may, I know I will never look at Cola the same. It takes about thirty people to produce one bottle of Cola. First, you have the team that mixes the secret formula. Then you have the taste testers that make sure it passes inspection. Then there are the bottle makers and the labelers. Another crew operates the bottle top fasteners. Lastly, you have the forklift crew and the delivery drivers.

"Gee, Mrs. Slutsky, that was incredible," I said, pulling off my goggles.

"I'm glad you liked it. Most people are surprised at how much work goes into making a bottle of Cola."

"I can see why. I had no idea it was that involved. No wonder the product is so good."

"That's very flattering, Toni. Are you ready to see Mr. Blackwell now?"

"I would like to change back into my suit first."

"You don't have to, he knows you were visiting the plant."

"I'm sure he does. Nevertheless, I would feel more comfortable in my suit."

"Then by all means, please feel free to change."

"I'll only be a minute."

"Take your time."

Once again I freshened up and was ready to go in a matter of minutes. Mrs. Slutsky escorted me back to the penthouse floor. As soon as we stepped out of the elevator, Carmen told us to go right in.

"Mr. Blackwell, Toni and I have completed our plant visit."

"Toni, please tell me you didn't visit the plant dressed like that. I wouldn't have wanted you to mess up that lovely suit."

"No, Bill, I didn't wear this. I changed clothes."

"Oh, so why did you put your suit back on. You could have left your other clothes on."

"No, sir, I couldn't have. One of the Toni T. Goodwin rules of doing business is to always look the part. I never let my business colleagues outmatch me in wit, skill or dress."

"That's an interesting perspective you have. I like it. Toni, like I told you before, I like a person who is not afraid to speak his or her mind. You have proven to me twice today that you are such a person. For that reason alone, I called a few of my board members and conducted a poll on the possibility of offering to your company, accounts other than just the Essence account.

I know you're not aware of this, but La Cola is currently in negotiations to sponsor the Latin Grammy Awards in Miami, Florida. Based on the feeling I got from my board of directors, we would be willing to consider Carlton International for that campaign as well. Of course, right now all of this is just speculation. The board will meet following Mr. Santos and Mrs. Slutsky's visit to your firm. After we've evaluated their findings and read their recommendations, we will have a meeting to determine who will win the contract."

"That's great news," I said, brandishing a nervous smile. "How many firms are in the running?"

"Four."

"How many of them are the size of Carlton?"

"None. You are the smallest. So you have a tough battle ahead of you."

"Your point is well taken. I'm going to make sure we wow you."

"I look forward to seeing what you come up with."

"Bill, thank you for this opportunity," I said, shaking his hand.

"You earned it. Have a nice day, Toni. Mrs. Slutsky will show you out."

Mrs. Slutsky walked me to the front of the building, smiling. "I hope you enjoyed your visit."

"I did."

"Good Luck to you, Toni. I will see you on the 15th."

"I look forward to it."

I shook her hand, got in my Beemer, put the top down, and drove off into the sunset.

# Chapter 12
## Across the tracks

I walked into the office with my game face on. After what had occurred yesterday during my site visit, I knew if we wanted to wow Cola, we had to operate a tight ship for the next month. I had Sean call an emergency staff meeting.

"Good Morning, team. I apologize for calling this staff meeting on such short notice. However, I'm sure you will find it necessary. All of you were made aware of the fact that La Cola could become our biggest account. Yesterday, I spent the entire day at Cola. The visit had its high points and low points. The good news is that we are still contenders for this account. However, we are the smallest firm and the only minority firm. Initially, I thought being the only minority firm would work to our advantage. Until I realized that that was the main reason they wanted us. The original intent was for them to consider hiring us to work only on campaigns that targeted African-Americans.

I went out on a limb and told CEO Bill Blackwell that Carlton has an impeccable reputation and that our company has the manpower and resource's to handle a large account such as Cola. I also told him we would need for them to offer us accounts other than just the ones that targeted African-Americans. Thankfully, he took what I said in the spirit in which it was meant. By the end of the day, he let me know that he appreciated my spunk. He had polled his board of directors to find out if they would be in favor of giving to us campaigns other than just African-American ones. They were."

I stood up and walked around the room like a coach talking to his players. "This is where you all come in!" I said with excitement. I knew I needed to show them how excited I was in order to get them pumped up.

"I'm sure everyone in this room knows what it means to be considered from the other side of the tracks. Well that's what we're faced with. Our challenge is to live up to our name. We are Carlton International, thus we have to give the appearance of an international firm. Granted, we're all black. Nevertheless, we do not want them to think of us as the black firm. We need to appear to be global. Just because all of the faces in this room happen to be of a darker hue, we're not all from the same culture. I'm going to rely on all of you to resurrect your uniqueness from your different cultures and backgrounds.

We are going up against the big boys for Colas' business. The first account would be for the Essence Music Festival." Everyone started cheering. "I know it's exciting. That's why we'll have to pull together as a team to get this done. Hence, all request for vacation time between now and the end of the month will be denied. I hope this is not too much of an inconvenience. However, I think it's necessary. If you are sick or have an emergency please see me. I will grant or deny on a case-by-case basis.

"In thirteen days we will be conducting a site visit for Mr. Santos and Mrs. Slutsky. They are the diversity team from Cola. Among other things, they will be here interviewing some of you on a random basis. If you are picked, speak honestly but remember the goal. If they try to engage you in any form of negativity, do not oblige them. Also, I would like for everyone to look the part. So make sure you have on either a suit or some sort of business attire. I will be working very closely with the ad team to make sure we produce a product that will knock them off their feet. Are there any questions?"

Ronald raised his hand. "Toni, when will we know if we got the account?"

"That's a good question. We will find out by the end of the month."

"Will the hourly employees get overtime pay for this?"

"I will have to work that out with Mr. Carlton, but I'm sure that won't be a problem."

"If we get the account, do we get free tickets to the Essence Music Festival?"

"I'm not sure but I doubt it. Those kind of perks are usually reserved for management. Are there any other questions?"

"When do we start?"

"Immediately. I will have individual team meetings with all of you today to determine who is doing what."

"Toni, I don't have a question, but I do have a comment."

"Please share it, Sean."

Sean had a serious look on his face. "Toni, I think I speak for all of us when I say that we are glad you're here. In the short period of time that you've been with us, you've repeatedly shown us that you have our backs. I would personally like to thank you for speaking up for us yesterday. You really took a risk, and I want you to know that I recognize and appreciate it."

"Me too, Toni," a voice shouted from the back of the room.

"Me too," another one shouted.

Finally someone stood up and said, "We all do."

Everyone stood up and applauded. My heart sank as I stood there smiling at all of the support I had. I knew, in that very moment, that I was officially a member of the Carlton family.

# Chapter 13
## Not a moment's peace

"Hello?" I answered, knowing I sounded a little irritated.

"Hi, beautiful. How are you?" John's wonderful voice crooned.

"Much better now that you called."

"What's wrong?"

"Fatigue and nervousness."

"Are you nervous about the site visit tomorrow?"

"Yes. I've so much riding on this, John."

"You do, but haven't you put a lot into it?"

"Yes, I have given it my all."

"Then what are you worried about?"

"This could make or break my career."

"Now you're not being realistic. Toni, your company hired you because they believed in your ability to get the job done. I don't think they will fire you if you don't get this account. Besides, aren't you the one who's always saying 'if you've done your best, then that's all you can do?'"

"Yep."

"Have you done your best?"

"I think so."

"Then you know the rest."

"You're right."

"What time are you going to bed? You sound so defeated." I felt really defeated too.

"As soon as we finish our conversation, I need to get all the sleep that I can."

"I heard that. I won't keep you too long. Have you spoken to Devon?"

"Not in a few days. Why? Is something wrong?"

"No, I was just asking. How is mom doing?"

"She's fine. She asked about you earlier. You know you won major cool points with her when I told her about the note you left on my nightstand Saturday morning."

"What did she say?"

"She still can't get over how positive and forward-thinking you are. She keeps asking how could you be so sure you were going to have a good time. You know I had to straighten her out and tell her you knew that because you were going to be with me."

"You go, Ms. Goodwin. Now that's the confident Toni I know. Well, Sweetie, I'm going to get off this phone and let you go to bed."

"I am glad you called. I feel better now."

"I'm glad I could help."

"I'll call you tomorrow and let you know how it goes."

"I'll be waiting," I said, trying to sound sultry. "Goodnight, John."

I hung up with John and jumped in the shower.

As soon as I stepped out the phone started ringing. I hurried to get it, dripping water all over my carpet. "Hello?"

"Hi, sweetheart," a man's voice said.

"Who is this?" *I know it's not John because I just hung up with him.*

"Tommy."

"Sorry, Tommy, I didn't catch your voice. How are you?"

"I'm fine. The more important question is how are you?"

"A little fatigued but I'm making it," I said, trying to wrap a towel around me.

"Are you ready for your big day tomorrow?"

"I guess as ready as I'll ever be."

"Were you getting ready to go to bed?"

"In a few minutes. I was just stepping out of the shower."

"Oh, so I caught you while you're dripping wet."

"You could say that."

"I'm having a major visual."

"Stop being voyeuristic and focus."

"Okay, okay. So when am I going to see you again?"

"Probably sometime in September."

"That sounds so far away."

"I know, but I have to get through this site visit and land the La Cola account first."

"I know. Have you spoken to your friend, Devon, lately?"

*Hmmm, he's asking about Devon too.* "That's funny."

"What is?"

"You are the second person to ask me that tonight."

"Am I? I guess everyone knows how tight you two are."

"Maybe that's it. But I think I'll call him tomorrow just to check on him."

"That sounds like a good idea."

"Tommy, I hate to cut this conversation short, but I really need to finish drying off and then go to bed."

"I understand. Good luck tomorrow. I'm sure you're going to be spectacular."

"Thanks, and thanks for calling to check on me."

"You're welcome. Just remember, if you need a little stress-buster, I can be there tomorrow night."

I laughed. "I'll keep that in mind."

"You do that. Goodnight, Love."

"Goodnight, Tommy."

I hung up the phone with Tommy and finished drying off. I brushed my teeth, wrapped my hair, set the alarm and got in the bed. As soon as my head hit the pillow the phone rang. I contemplated, then I looked at the Caller ID and saw it was mama.

"Hello?"

"Hi, baby, are you okay?"

"Yeah, I'm just tired."

"Are you ready for tomorrow?"

"As ready as I'm going to get."

"Have you heard from John?"

"Yes, he called about an hour ago."

"Is everything alright?"

"As great as ever. Tommy called too."

"How is he?"

"He's fine. He called to wish me luck."

"That was thoughtful of him."

"Yes, it was."

"Have you heard from Devon?"

"Okay, now this is getting scary."

"What is?"

"You are the third person to ask me that tonight. It's starting to freak me out."

"Don't go getting yourself all upset. It's probably just a coincidence."

"Were John and Tommy the other two people that asked about Devon?"

"Yes."

"Then what are you worried about? They both know him. That's a common question when you know somebody."

"I guess you're right."

"Although, Toni, Devon's mom did call and leave a message for me today."

"Did you call her back?"

"No. I thought it was too late. I'll call her tomorrow."

"That's it. I am definitely calling Devon in the morning. I'm surprised he didn't call me tonight. It's really unlike him not to call the day before a big event. I was so tired, I hadn't really thought about it, but now I'm really worried."

"Honey, try not to upset yourself. I'll give his mom a call in the morning. Then I'll call you and let you know if I hear something."

"Okay, Mom, but if I'm not in my office leave a message and I'll call you back after the site visit."

"I sure will. Try to get some rest, Toni. I'm sure this is all a coincidence."

"I hope so. Goodnight, Mom."

132

"Goodnight, Baby."

# Chapter 14
## In a league of their own

Today is the big day. I put on my red Donna Karan power suit with the gold buttons and headed into the office. I had breakfast and lunch catered in for the entire staff. I wanted everyone to know how much I appreciated all the hard work and long hours they were putting in. Our senior marketing team really put their heads down and got to work. When I saw the final product for our presentation, I was speechless. The ad consisted of the young and old...the fat and skinny...the rich and the not so rich...the straight haired and the nappy kinks...dreadlocks and bald heads...the King's English to Ebonics...the lightest of light skin to the darkest of dark skin... it was a virtual rainbow of brown skin and black people. The message the ad conveyed spoke volumes about our culture. The subliminal message was that Cola is for everyone. It ends with male and female voices saying: One world...one drink...COLA!

I was awestruck. I stood up and gave them an ovation. I immediately called Mr. Carlton down to the screening room for a private viewing. He was so elated that he called a quick, company pep rally in the viewing room. Then he announced to everyone that they were all going to be given a bonus for their hard work, and two extra vacation days this year. "Whether we get the account or not," he said, "I want all of you to know that each and everyone of you represent a spoke on the wheels of this company, and without each of you we would be unable to continue rolling forward. From the bottom of my heart, and on behalf of my senior staff, I thank you."

Everyone applauded.

"Now let's put our game faces on and show the representatives from La Cola that we are in a league of our own!"

I announced, "Excuse me, everyone. Before we return back to our departments, I would like to brief you on today's schedule. So if I could have your attention for five more minutes I would appreciate it." I continued, "Mr. Santos and Mrs. Slutsky will be here at nine o'clock. You all should have received a memo informing you that the company is having breakfast and lunch catered. So by nine-fifteen everyone should be seated in the main dining room. I'll escort our guests into the dining hall and make a formal introduction of the two of them. Please stand and give them a hearty welcome, after which they will be served and then the rest of us. By ten-fifteen everyone should conclude their dining and return to their departments, ready to work. Remember, they will select ten of you at random to interview. Just be yourself, and answer the questions honestly. Thanks, everyone."

I concluded the meeting and returned to my office for a moment of silent meditation. I wanted to get calm and centered before my guests arrived.

"Toni, our guests from La Cola have arrived and are downstairs in the lobby. Do you want me to escort them up?"

"No, Sean, that won't be necessary. I'll take care of it."

I gave myself a quick once-over and strolled toward the elevator. I was confident. I was poised. I was ready.

"Good morning, Mr. Santos and Mrs. Slutsky."

"Good morning, Toni," they spoke in unison.

"How are you?" I asked.

"Truthfully, we are excited," Mr. Santos said.

"About what we have to offer I hope."

"You hit the nail on the head. Ever since you visited our facility, Carlton International has been the buzz among the big wigs. We are really anxious to see what you came up with."

"Then let's not prolong your agony any further. Are you ready to meet the team?"

"Ready."

I lead the two of them up to the executive dining room. Everyone was already in there and seated. The moment we walked in, a round of applause started. The look on Mr. Santos and Mrs. Slutsky's faces was priceless. They were in complete shock. I could see that this surprise was going over well.

"Toni, we don't know what to say. We weren't expecting this," Mr. Santos said with a look of enthusiasm.

"I know. We just wanted to show you how we do business." I smiled then continued, "Everyone, please take your seats." I gave them a moment to get seated.

The entire dining room took a seat immediately.

"It is my pleasure to introduce two of the visionaries from La Cola. I have invited them here today to dine with us and to see what it's like to be a member of the Carlton family. Would you please give another hearty welcome to Mr. Miguel Santos and Mrs. Marcie Slutsky?"

Everyone gave them another standing ovation.

"Please, take your seats," Mr. Santos instructed. "You are too kind. From the moment I had the pleasure of meeting Toni, I knew there was something special about her. And any company who had the foresight to see her gift and snatch her up has to have something very special about them as well. This welcoming celebration alone has proven to me that I was right about Toni, and I was as equally correct on my assessment of this company. Thank you very much for having us here today and for welcoming us into the Carlton family."

"Mr. Santos, Mrs. Slutsky--- I hope you brought your appetites because we

135

have quite a spread. After you."

"Toni, you weren't kidding. Look at all of this food. There goes my diet. I guess I can start Weight Watchers tomorrow."

"Oh no, Mrs. Slutsky. I anticipated that there might be some diet restrictions, so we have lots of fresh fruit, low fat yogurt, and rice cakes."

"Are you kidding me? I wouldn't miss out on tasting this spread for the world," she said, laughing.

"Then by all means, help yourself."

We made it through the buffet line effortlessly. Mrs. Slutsky wasn't kidding when she said she didn't want to miss out on the spread. I think she had a little of everything. Mr. Santos threw down too. Once we were seated, Mr. Carlton came over, introduced himself, and joined us. The trio really hit it off. I could see everything was going according to plan.

Breakfast ended right on schedule. Everyone was out of the dining room and back working by ten-fifteen. We finished our coffee and started the tour at ten-thirty.

"Toni, I'm already impressed by the discipline of your staff. They are already working. Most employees tend to talk and linger for another thirty minutes after a group function. But everyone here seems to be back in their offices actually working."

"One thing we impress upon our employees is that each of them is an integral part of the team. So if one of them isn't doing his or her job then it affects the overall performance of the whole team. I assure you, no one wants that burden."

"That's a very interesting way to place value on the job that everyone does. I like it."

"Me too," Mrs. Slutsky added.

"After I finish giving you a tour of our offices, you have a choice of either selecting the employees you would like to interview or you can have your meeting with the Fiscal Department. Which would you like?"

"I think I would like to meet with the employees first. I can't wait to hear what they have to say. What about you, Mr. Santos?"

"I'm with you. I'm anxious to hear what they have to say as well."

"Then that settles it. You select the employees you would like to interview while we're touring, and I will have them sent up one by one for your interviews."

"Great."

We finished the tour around eleven. I arranged for five of the employees, who were chosen for interviews, to come up before lunch. The interviews were held in our conference room. While they were being conducted, I went back to my office to call Devon. In all of the excitement this morning, I forgot to call him earlier.

*This is Devon. I'm probably somewhere doing something fabulous. Leave me a message if you are so inclined, and I'll return your call if I'm so inclined Ciao. Beep.*

"Hey, D, it's me. I was calling to check on you. I didn't hear from you yesterday or this morning, so I wanted to make sure you're all right. Give me a call at work. Love you."

*Hmmmm. Let me call mama and see if she has spoken to Devon's mother yet.*

"Hey, Mama, it's Toni. I was calling to see if you heard from Devon's mom yet. Give me a call at work and let me know. By the way, Ma, everything is going really well so far. I'll tell you all about it when I speak to you. Love you."

"Toni," Sean buzzed.

"Yes, Sean?"

"A package just came for you. Do you want me to bring it in?"

"Would you, please?" I waited until Sean entered my office. "Look at the size of this box. I bet this is from Devon. That's probably why he hasn't called; he didn't want to spoil the surprise."

"I don't think it's from Devon, Toni. The name on the return address says John Collins."

"That was my second guess. He's so thoughtful."

"Hurry up and open it. I'm dying to know what's in it."

"You seem more excited than I am. Do you have the scissors with you, too?"

"Right here."

"I should have known." I cut the tape off of the box and opened it up. Inside was another smaller box. I opened that one up and inside of it was the prettiest serenity garden I'd ever seen.

"Oh, Toni, that's nice."

"Isn't it?"

"Now that's a brotha who pays attention. You better keep him, sistah."

"Was there a note with this, Sean?"

"Yes, it's right here."

*To the Lady who lights up my life, I offer you serenity. Good luck on your presentation. I'm in your corner. Love, John.*

"Sean, this has got to be the most romantic man I have ever met in my life. He always knows the right thing to say."

"I see. Well, you better hold on to him; there aren't many of us left."

"Us? Are you implying that you're a romantic too?"

"I sure am. Is that hard to believe?"

"No. I just never thought about your personal life."

"I guess that's fair enough. I'll give you a minute to call John or do whatever you need to do then you need to get back to work, Ms. Goodwin. La Cola is waiting."

"Roger, boss." I said as I saluted Sean. How much time do I have?"

"About five minutes if you want to stay on schedule. The staff is starting to make their way to the dining room right now."

"Okay. I'll just be a minute." I watched Sean leave, then I dialed John's number. "Hello, John, it's Toni. I received your lovely gift. I'm flabbergasted. Thank you for always thinking of me. I'll call you tonight and tell you all about the site visit. I hope your day is going as well as mine. Smooches." After leaving John a message, I went down the hall to get Mr. Santos and Mrs. Slutsky. They were just finishing their last interview.

"How are the interviews going?"

"Wonderful. Your staff is delightful, Toni."

"I'm glad you think so."

"Are you two hungry?"

"I am."

"Me too."

"Then let's eat."

We walked into the executive dining room and it looked like a repeat of this morning. Everyone was seated and waiting for us to arrive. This time, it was a little more formal. The head table had personalized menus with our names printed on them. All we had to do was put a check mark next to the items we wanted for lunch.

The waiters would then collect the menus and bring us our meals. Again Mr. Santos and Mrs. Slutsky were impressed.

"Toni, this is really a first-class firm. If you keep this up you are going to spoil us."

"I concur," Mrs. Slutsky chimed in.

"I'm glad you're enjoying yourself. Please feel free to try as many of the dishes as you like."

"We will," they said in unison.

Lunch went off without a hitch. We talked, ate, and laughed for an hour and a half. Then I set up the next five interviews. While the interviews were being conducted, I went back to my office to check my messages.

*Hey, girl. Good luck today. Give me a call and let me know how it goes. This is Ebony. Beep.*

*Hey, Toni, you are my shero. I know you are knocking them dead, and I bet you are dressed to kill too! Call me when you get a chance. This is Michelle. Love you Beep.*

*Who is the worlds best advertising executive? You are! This is Tommy I hope everything is going well. I will call you back tonight. Beep.*

I had three messages and still nothing from Devon or mama. What's up with that? I better try Devon's cell phone.

*This is D and, as you can see, I'm busy. Leave me a message if you wish. Beep.*

"Hey, Ms. D, it's Toni. Where are you? Now is this anyway to treat your best friend? You better not be somewhere having the time of your life while I'm here working and looking for you. Call me when you get the message, Diva. Love you."

"Toni, the Fiscal Department called. They would like to know what time they are meeting with the Cola execs."

"Buzz them back and tell them two-thirty. By the way, Sean, did my mother or Devon call?"

"No, I didn't take any calls from them. Did you check your messages?"

"Yes. They weren't on there."

"I'm sure they will call before the day is over. Meanwhile, you stay focused on the task at hand. You're rounding third base and too close to sliding into to home to lose focus now."

"You're right. Thanks for the reality check. Do me a favor and call down to the conference room and see where we are with the interviews."

"No problem."

I sat at my desk, tapping my pen. *Where are you, D?*

*Buzz.*

"Yes, Sean."

They're on the last one. They should be finished in another fifteen minutes."

"Thanks." I sat in my high-back, Italian leather chair for ten minutes, taking a mental break. I needed to return back to my center. Sean was right. I was too close to home plate to lose focus now.  I don't have much left to do today. The last two presentations will sell themselves. I can just sit back and enjoy them.

*Buzz.*

"Yes, Sean."

"It's time."

"Thanks."

As I escorted Mr. Santos and Mrs. Slutsky to the Fiscal Department for the budget meeting, they rambled on and on about how wonderful my staff was. I took that as a definite sign that we're receiving high marks with them. As long as the numbers look good, I know we are definitely still in the running.

"Toni, I feel comfortable telling you so far, so good. I think Mrs. Slutsky agrees with me."

"I sure do."

"So far we're excited about everything we've seen and everyone we've talked to. We can't wait to see the actual ad."

"Immediately following this meeting you will get to see the main attraction."
*You have no idea what's in store for you.*

"I can't wait!" Mrs. Slutsky beamed with her hands clasped together and a big
Kool-Aid smile.

"Lisa, are they ready for us?" I asked the receptionist.

"Yes. Go right in."

What a big difference in the look and feel of our accountants versus the
accountants over at La Cola. When we walked into the room, each of them stood
up wearing expensive designer suits in several different colors. They all smiled
and made small talk as they shook hands and introduce themselves to the team
from Cola. Nothing about our accounting team was identical or clone-like. Not
even their accennts or skin complexion. I felt really good about that. I could see
from the intrigue on their faces that the Cola team had picked up on the diversity
of the group as well.

"Shall we get started?" the senior accountant suggested.

Numbers are not my thing. So while they gave a very compelling presentation,
I zoned in and out depending on the words that caught my attention. The meeting
lasted forty-five minutes. The entire room seemed pleased with the outcome.

"Now, are you ready for the main event?"

"Wild horses couldn't keep us from it."

"Just a second. Let me buzz my assistant to make sure they're ready for us."

"Sure."

While I was talking to Sean, I noticed the Cola team talking to each other and
giving each other the thumbs up. My energy level shot through the roof from
witnessing that. I knew it was time to slide into home plate.

"They're ready for us. Please follow me, right this way."

We entered the main screening room. Mr. Carlton had had this room built with
stadium seating. He wanted perspective clients to really feel like they were in for
some big-time entertainment. He'd even had a small concession stand built in for
the clients. The first time I saw it, I thought it was the most ingenious idea I had
ever seen. From the expression on the Cola team's face, they thought so too.

"Please sit anywhere you like."

"Toni, this is spectacular!"

"Thank you, Mr. Santos."

"It really is Toni."

"Thank you. Mrs. Slutsky."

"We feel no premiere would be complete without snacks, so we have popcorn,
candy, and La Cola floats for you."

"You have got to be kidding!" they said with their mouths wide open.

"I kid you not. Sean, will you do the honors?"

Sean presented each of them with a menu. They were allowed to choose what they wanted on their popcorn --- butter or no butter, flavored salt or no salt. Then they got a chance to select the type of candy they wanted and what size drink they wanted. The two of them were enjoying themselves so much that they looked like two big kids in a candy store.

Mr. Carlton came in and joined us. "How is my staff treating you?" he asked.

"Better than our own staff," Mr. Santos replied.

"You wouldn't happen to have two vacancies available for former Cola execs, would you?" Mrs. Slutsky joked.

"I'm afraid not, but I'll keep you two in mind if something becomes available." He laughed.

"Ladies and gentlemen, introducing the main event: La Cola's best ad yet. May I have a drum role please?" I asked.

Everyone started taping the sides of their seats, making it sound like a real drum role. Even Mr. Santos and Mrs. Slutsky participated. I was so caught up, I was feeling like a movie director. I think I really crossed the line when I said, "And action!" The curtain went up and our forty-second spot played. When it ended Mr. Santos and Mrs. Slutsky stood up and gave us a standing ovation. "Bravo, Carlton International, bravo!" They clapped.

"Mr. Carlton, Toni, and the Carlton Family on behalf of myself, Mrs. Slutsky, and The La-Cola Company, we say job well done! That spot was magnificent! Thank you so much for your warm hospitality and your hard work."

***

Before we left the screening room, the company was buzzing with speculation. The news about the standing ovation and praise traveled fast. I think the whole company was on cloud nine. I walked Mr. Santos and Mrs. Slutsky downstairs. They were still smiling.

"Toni, you all outdid yourselves and most of your competition. We still have one more site visit to conduct before the final decision will be made. But I want you to know that Mrs. Slutsky and I are in your corner. We have never been treated with so much warmth and enthusiasm before. Today didn't feel like work at all, it felt like Disney Land."

"It sure did, and Toni thanks for giving me an excuse to put off starting Weight Watchers. The food was delicious."

"You're welcome," I said, laughing. "Thanks for being in our corner. I'll be anxiously awaiting the news. Have a good evening," I said, shaking their hands.

The ride in the elevator was quiet and peaceful. The only noise was the chatter in my head. Most of my thoughts were about mama and Devon. I was also trying to make sure I remembered to give Sean all of the names for the thank you baskets I ordered for the staff. I had too much on my mind. The doors to the elevator opened.

"So what did they say?" Sean asked.

"They said they had a wonderful time and that they were in our corner."

"That's great news! By the way, Toni, Mr. Carlton wanted you to call him."

"Okay. Sean, could you give me a little privacy? I need to unwind for a minute and check my messages."

"Of course."

*Beep.*

*Hey, Toni, it's me, Cynt. I know you thought I forgot about your big day, but I didn't. Call me and let me know how it went. You know I also want to know if the Cola representative is single, with some change in his pockets. Call me.*

"She is such a gold digger," I said, shaking my head.

*Beep.*

*Hi, Sweetheart, it's John. I'm glad you liked your gift. Hopefully you can use it tonight along with a nice bubble bath. Call and let me know how everything turned out.*

*Beep.*

*Hi, Baby, it's mama. I'm sorry I didn't get to talk to you earlier. But I spoke to Devon's mom, and Devon's in the hospital. Call me.*

*Beep.*

# Chapter 15
## 911

"Toni, are you okay?" Sean asked as he shook me.

"Huh? What happened? Where am I?"

"You passed out."

"I passed out?"

"Yes, right here in your office."

"Why?"

"I have no idea. You asked me for some privacy so you could unwind and check your messages. A few minutes later I heard the intercom buzzing. I came in here and you were slumped over the desk."

"Oh, Sean, I have to go! I remember what happened now. I got a message from my mother telling me that Devon was in the hospital. I must have fainted from the shock and the fatigue. I have to get out of here and find out what happened to Devon. Do me a favor and tell Mr. Carlton I wasn't feeling well, and that I will call him from my cell phone."

"Okay, but are you sure you feel well enough to drive? I could take you home."

"Thanks, Sean, but I think I can manage."

"Call me if you need me. I hope everything is okay with Devon."

"Me too. I'll call you and let you know whether I will be in tomorrow."

"Call me at home if you need to. Drive safely, Toni."

"I will."

I jumped in my car and sped out of the parking lot. All kinds of horrible thoughts ran through my mind about what could have happened to Devon. I saw that my message light was on just as I was about to call mama. I checked the messages first, just incase it was mama giving me an update on Devon.

"Hey, sweetheart, it's John. I was calling to see if anyone has told you about Devon. Roger just called me. Give me a call as soon as you can. I have my cell on." *Beep.*

I hung up immediately and dialed John's cell number. The whole time I was dialing I was saying a little prayer. " God, please let this be something minor. Please, God, Please, God."

"Hello?"

"John, it's Toni. What happened to Devon?"

"Sweetheart, try to calm down. He..."

"He what? John? Hello?" The phone went dead. These goddamn cell phones always cut off at the wrong time! If I didn't need this piece of shit right now I would throw the muthafucker out the window!

I tried to calm down and call John back. While I was dialing the number, my phone rang.

"John?"

"No, girl, it's Ebony. Damn that man got you Jonesin' like that? You answer the phone saying his name. Are you sure you haven't slept with him?"

"Not now, Ebony. I have to call John back."

"Is everything all right?"

"No. Something happened to Devon. I don't mean to be short with you, but I gotta go." I said and terminated the call. I called John back and he answered on the first ring.

"One of our phones must have cut off."

"What were you saying about Devon? What happened to him?"

"He's in the hospital. I don't have all the details, but it has something to do with his asthma and a car accident."

"Oh my God! How is he?"

"He's still unconscious."

"Unconscious! John, is he going to be all right? How bad is it?"

"I don't know. That's all the information I have."

"I need to call the airlines. I'm flying up there tonight."

"Are you sure you don't want to wait until we find out more about his condition?"

"Am I sure? I have never been more sure of anything in my life! If something happens and I'm not there, I'll never forgive myself. Poor Devon." I began to cry uncontrollably.

"Oh, Baby, I'm so sorry. I wish there was something I could do. Please pull your car over. Don't try to drive until you stop crying."

John had a good point. I didn't need to drive in the condition I was in, so I pulled over. Crying gave me the release I needed. My life has been so full of activity, that I hadn't taken time to nurture Toni. So on top of my already fatigued body and mind, fell sadness. That was the emotion that opened the floodgates. What makes this even worse is that I've just had the best day of my career and I have no desire to share it with anyone. My best friend is in a hospital bed hundreds of miles away, and I can't hold it together long enough to drive myself home. I feel completely helpless. I wish someone would wake me up and tell me this is all a bad dream.

"Toni, are you still there?"

"Yes, I'm here, John. I'm sorry; my mind was wandering."

"I understand. Are you okay to drive now?"

"I think so."

"Do you want me to stay on the phone to keep you company while you drive home?"

"No, you don't have to."

"I don't mind, if you want the company."

*He's such a good man.* "Thanks, John, but I think I better try to call mama again. She may want to come with me to Tallahassee. She and Devon's mom are good friends."

"Will you need a place to stay?"

"I'm not sure yet."

"You are welcome to stay with me if you want to."

"Thanks, John. I appreciate what you are trying to do. I'll call you after I make my reservations."

"I'll talk to you then."

***

After John and I hung up, I immediately called mama. This time she answered.

"Ma, it's Toni."

"Did you get my message?"

"Yes. Since then I've talked to John. He told me what little he knew. He said Devon had an asthma attack and a car accident, and that he was unconscious. Do you know the details, Ma?"

"That's basically all I know too."

"Ma, I am going home to pack a bag and book a flight out tonight. Are you coming?"

"Definitely. My bags are already packed. After I spoke to his mom and saw how hysterical she was, I told her I would fly down there to keep her company."

"I'm glad you're going too. I will swing by and pick you up now. That way, you can pack for me while I make the flight arrangements."

"How far away are you?"

"I should be at your house in the next fifteen minutes."

"I'll call and get the flight times while I'm waiting."

"Thanks, Ma. I'll see you in a few minutes."

The rest of my drive was consumed with thoughts of me and Devon. All of the laughter and tears we've shared over the years. All of the joy and pain. My operation. His coming out *again* party. My move to Atlanta. Most recently, our reunion weekend. Lord, I don't know what I'll do if I ever lose him.

*Honk, honk.* I blew as I pulled in to mama's driveway. She stuck her head out of the door and said, "Be right out." Mama came out in a matter of minutes. We threw her suitcase in my little trunk and sped off.

"How are you holding up, honey?" Mama asked with sorrow-filled eyes.

"I'm doing the best I can. I'm just so worried about Devon. If anything ever happened…"

"Don't even talk like that, Toni. Devon is going to be fine. Now you and I both know that prayer changes things. So we're going to stay prayerful and faith-filled. I don't want to hear you talk like that again."

Clearly I'm not the only one who's on edge. Mama must be going through her own pain. Rarely have I ever heard her speak to me like that. For those reasons I drove the rest of the way in silence.

***

Fortunately for us, we were able to catch the 8:05 flight out of Hartsfield airport. I called Mr. Carlton from the plane to let him know what was going on. He was even more supportive than I thought he would be. He told me to stay as long as needed. He also congratulated me on doing a great job with La Cola. "Toni," he said, "you have shown great leadership ability since you walked through the doors of Carlton International. Don't think our staff are the only ones receiving bonuses. There will be a nice little surprise in your next check. You just go ahead and see about your friend, and don't worry about work. The hard part is over."

"Thanks, Mr. Carlton."

"No, thank you. And, Toni…"

"Yes."

"Mr. Santos told me how you stood up to Bill Blackwell for us. I admire your courage. I'll see you when you get back. Have a safe trip."

"Thank you sir, Good-bye." I hung up the phone. Then I reclined my seat, closed my eyes and tried to pretend this was all a bad dream. Mama must have been sleeping or praying, because she didn't try to talk to me the whole flight. She didn't even ask how my presentation had turned out. Although I'm overjoyed about how smoothly everything ran today, I feel a little funny being happy when Devon is in the hospital possibly fighting for his life. I'm in so much inner turmoil right now, I guess I'll just have to postpone celebrating this milestone until Devon is up and moving around again.

*Lord, I prayed. It's me, Toni, again. I know it seems like I am always asking for a favor, but this one is major. You know I've asked you to spare Devon's life previously during his childhood asthma attack. Here I am again, Lord, humbly asking that you spare his life from this asthma attack. If you would indulge me again I would really appreciate it. Amen.*

***

John picked me and mama up from the airport and greeted both of us with big warm hugs. Then he took us directly to the hospital.

"How was your flight?"

"It was fine," I murmured, turning my head to look out the window.

"Sweetheart, try not to worry too much. I'm sure Devon is going to be fine."

"I know he is, John. I'm just so sad he has to even go through this. Have you heard anything else about his condition?"

"No, nothing. I've tried calling Roger but he's not answering."

"Maybe he's at the hospital. You know it's hard to get a signal inside a hospital."

"That's true."

Mama interrupted, "John, dear, would you mind dropping me off at Devon's mom's house after we leave the hospital. I'm going to stay with her while we're here."

"Sure. No problem."

"Thank you."

From the moment we walked into the hospital my heart started beating fast. My palms began to sweat and my eye started twitching. John took my hand and squeezed it lightly and uttered, "It's going to be okay."

"May I help you?" the receptionist asked.

"Devon Davis's room, please."

"Ma'am, he is on the ninth floor in ICU. Are you his family?"

"Yes, I'm his sister."

"Then you all may go right up. Only family members are allowed in ICU."

"I understand. Where are the elevators?"

"Continue down this corridor and make a right when you get the end. The elevators will be on your left."

"Thank you."

"You're welcome."

"Come on, let's hurry."


I was walking so fast someone could have mistaken me for a speed walker. I didn't know what to expect when I got off the elevator. I never imagined him in ICU. *What on earth could have happened to him?*

"Linda, Toni!" Ms. Davis called out to us as we walked toward her. She ran up and gave both of us bear hugs. "I'm so glad you're here," she said with exasperation. "Devon's room is down the hall. Follow me."

Ms. Davis looked like she'd aged ten years in just a few weeks. When I saw her during reunion weekend she looked fabulous. Today she looks almost homeless. Her salt and pepper hair was bit whiter than I had remembered. Her face looked haggard like she and sleep were strangers. The worry lines in her forehead looked like they were going to make a permanent indentation in her face. I felt sorry for her. Devon is all she had other than mama and me. She has spent her whole life making sure he was okay. Now it seems that his own body has turned against him and is threatening to take away the only man she's ever loved. Her heart has got to be breaking more and more with each passing minute.

"Before we go in, would you share his status with us? We still aren't clear on what happened."

"From what I've been told, Devon was at his house with his friend, Roger. They were horsing around and laughing at something Devon said when he started having an asthma attack. Roger didn't know what was happening so he got scared and called 911. Apparently Devon was trying to point to his inhaler while he was gasping for air. Roger panicked and didn't know what to do, so he picked Devon up and put him in the car to drive him to the hospital.

On the way here someone ran the stop sign and crashed into the car on Devon's side. He lost consciousness. He's in critical condition. The doctors are afraid he might have some internal injuries. They also said that because Devon went so long without air, he may have suffered some brain damage. We won't know anything for sure until he wakes up."

I couldn't believe what I was hearing. I wanted to scream at her to shut up. But nothing was coming out. My knees started to buckle. John caught me.

"Toni, I know this is hard on you. It's extremely hard on me too. But the doctors insist that you remain strong around of Devon. So you are going to have to pull it together before you go in there. They say that sometimes the patients can sense when the people around them are upset, and they get upset too. We can't afford to have anything upset Devon."

"Yes, ma'am. I'm sorry. It's just so hard."

"I know, baby, but we have got to be strong for Devon."

"I'm ready to go in now."

"They are only allowing two people in at a time."

"Toni, why don't you and mom go in. I'll stay out here with Ms. Davis."

"Okay. Come on, Mama," I said, grabbing her hand. Mama looked at me and a faint smile crossed her face. We walked in. Nothing could have prepared me for what I was looking at. Devon's lifeless body lay motionless. Hooked up to a respirator and an IV.

"Excuse me, nurse. What is the IV for?"

"Pavulon."

"What is Pavulon?"

"A muscle relaxer."

"How long are you going to administer that to him?"

"Until he is able to breathe on his on."

I noticed the restraints. "Why do you have restraints on him?"

"Because when patients wake up and realize they have a tube down their throat the first thing they do is try to pull it out. The restraints will prevent him from doing so."

"Do you know anything else about his condition or his injuries?"

"I do know that most of his injuries are from the accident, not the asthma attack."

"Do you all happen to have a copy of the police report?"

"No, I don't think one was filed."

"Not filed! How could that be possible?"

"Please lower your voice, ma'am."

"I'm sorry."

She continued, "My understanding is that the person who brought him in was in such a panic, that he did not wait for the police to arrive. He just left the scene of the accident and brought Devon into the emergency room."

"Do you know who this person is?"

"No, but they may have his name at the front desk."

"Thank you. You've been very helpful."

"You're welcome. I hope your brother gets better,"

The nurse said as she walked out of the door.

"Mama, can you believe Roger didn't get a police report?"

"Who is Roger?"

"He's John's friend. Remember the guy I told you about?"

"The married one?"

"Yep."

"Then that's probably why he didn't get a police report. He wasn't supposed to be with Devon."

"You think so?"

"Honey, I have been on this earth a lot of years, and I know men. Trust me on this one; he was trying to keep his name off of any recorded documents. Didn't you say he was planning to run for office too?"

"Yes. Governor."

"Well there you have it, case in point."

"Poor Ms. D. Mama, what are we going to do?"

"The only thing we can do. Pray and be here for him."

John stuck his head in the room. "Toni, they just announced that visiting hours are over."

"We'll be right out."

"Toni, let's say a quick prayer with Devon."

149

"Would you do it Mama? I think God has had enough of me for one day."

"Take Devon's hand."

I picked up his limp, cold hand.

"Heavenly Father we humbly approach you with bowed heads and heavy hearts. We ask that you watch over this loyal servant. Heal his body and his mind, Lord. Make him well again. We ask these things in Jesus' name. Amen."

"Amen."

# Chapter 16
## Hide and go seek

Drained is a nice way to describe what I felt like by the time I got in bed. After leaving the hospital, John and I dropped Mama off at Ms. Davis's house. We made sure she got settled in before we left. My head ached so bad that it blurred my vision. Any hope I had of being excited about spending my first night at John's house was lost long before I got on the plane. I just needed rest. My purse dangled from my arm as I dragged myself into the house. I'm not sure which was heavier, my legs or my heart. John looked at me with sympathetic eyes as he carried my bags down the hallway.

"Toni, make yourself comfortable. I'll run you a bath."

A nod in John's direction was all I could muster. Judging by the way I looked I guess I needed a bath. From what I could see, my sophisticated up do looked more like a don't. My perfectly applied makeup had turned into war paint. And my power suit was now a suit for the powerless. Let's face it; I looked like hell.

"Here you are, sweetheart; I made you some herbal tea. Is there anything else I can get for you?"

"No. Thank you."

"Whenever you're ready your bath is waiting for you. I turned the jets on to help you relax."

I peeled the clothes from my weary body and cautiously stepped down into the tub. The fragrance of vanilla invaded my nostrils and forced my head back against the bath pillow. The windows to my soul slammed shut and I floated. The water took my body under siege and the power of the jets beat me into submission. I surrendered.

For the first time in days I relaxed. I had a moment of peace. I emerged from the bathroom wearing one of John's robes. To my surprise he'd already turned the bed down and had my white silk nightgown lying across the bed. I smiled at his thoughtfulness, took his robe off and let it gently fall to the floor. Before I was finished dressing, John walked in and saw my partially nude body. I didn't mind. I felt sexy. He walked up behind me and watched me as I let my gown fall effortlessly over my perfectly altered body.

"Am I interrupting?"

"Not at all."

"I came in to see if you needed anything."

"Your timing couldn't be better."

"Why is that?"

"Because what I need is you."

151

John took my face into his hands and let his tongue explore the warmth of my mouth.

My body ached, but this time the aching wasn't in my head. The urge I had was immediate and couldn't be satisfied with Tylenol.

John grabbed me by the hips and lifted me.

I wrapped my legs around his waist giving him the ok to be our compass.

He navigated his way to the bed, holding me like fine china, and slowly lowered me on to it. Then he stood up to unbutton his shirt.

Anticipation got the best of me, so instead I ripped it open and slid my tongue lightly over his erect nipples and down his stomach.

He moaned.

Unbuckling his pants meant that I was one step closer to extinguishing the fire that burned between my legs. So I did it. His pants fell to the floor as I released them. My lips started at the head and expanded as they made the journey down his shaft.

"*Mmmm,*" he groaned, signaling his satisfaction with my technique.

I continued until he couldn't stand it anymore. We switched positions and I rode him like a thoroughbred.

He flipped me over on my stomach without exiting my body. John's thrusting pelvis banged against my behind for twenty minutes before he maneuvered me out of doggie style and onto my back. "Toni, I want to make love to you all night-

Toni, Toni, are you okay in there?" John asked, knocking on the bathroom door. "You've been in there for two hours. Are you all right?"

"Yes, sweetheart, I'm fine. I must have dozed off."

"Are you ready to get out?"

"Yes, I'm coming out right now."

"May I put on one of your robes?"

"Of course."

"I took the liberty of taking one of your night gowns out. It's lying on the bed. I'll leave and give you some privacy. I'm in the den if you need me."

*Damn!* I guess there *is* something to be said for wet dreams. That was by far the best one I ever had.

I finished drying off and dressing and slid into bed. "John," I called out. "Yes?"

"Are you coming to bed?"

"I thought you'd never ask." He smirked. "Let me take a quick shower and I will be right there."

"Don't make me wait too long; I might be asleep when you come out."

John was in and out of the shower in less than five minutes. He slid under the sheets with me, wearing nothing but silk boxers. He looked very sexy but I was

152

still too tired to enjoy it. We cuddled into our spoon position and drifted off to sleep. Finally this terrible day had come to an end.

***

Today is a new day, thank God! I wasn't sure if my emotional well-being could survive anymore yesterdays. Even though a new day offers the opportunity for a fresh start, it didn't change the fact that Devon was still in ICU. My job today is to find out what happened to Roger. We haven't seen or heard from him since he took Devon to the hospital. I'm inclined to believe mama's theory is right. Maybe there is more to this asthma attack story then we think. The moment John comes back from the store, I'm going to ask him about Roger.

I called to check on Mama and Ms. Davis. Mama said Ms. Davis didn't come home last night. Ms. Davis wanted to stay at the hospital just in case Devon woke up. She didn't want him to think he was all alone.

"Toni, did you find out anything else about Roger's whereabouts?"

"Not yet, mama. I was too tired last night to question John about him, but I'm rejuvenated this morning. I plan to launch an all-out investigation. I'm ready to turn this into the adult version of hide and go seek if Roger doesn't show up today."

"Where is John now?"

"He went to the store to get some food for breakfast."

"Are you going to cook breakfast for him?"

"No, Mama, I'm the guest. He's cooking breakfast for me."

"I guess you told me."

"I guess I did." I laughed.

"What time are you coming to pick me up?"

"I'm not sure yet. I'm going to call the hospital as soon as we hang up to find out what time visiting hours start. I'll call you back and let you know what time we're coming."

"Okay, honey, enjoy your breakfast, and I will talk to you in a lil' bit."

"Bye, Mom." *One more call to make.*

"Tallahassee Memorial, how may I direct your call?"

"ICU, please."

"Please hold."

"Thank you."

"ICU may I help you."

"Yes, good morning."

"Good morning."

"My name is Toni Davis. My brother, Devon Davis, is in your unit."

"Yes ma'am."

"I was calling to inquire about the status of his condition?"

"There has been no change, ma'am."

"I'm sorry to hear that. What time are visiting hours?"

"9:00 a.m."

"Do you know what time the doctor will be there?"

"They usually make their rounds pretty early. So my guess would be about 10:00 a.m."

"Do you know if my mom is awake?"

"Yes, I saw her getting coffee a few minutes ago."

"Would it be possible for you to get her to the phone."

"I'll see what I can do. One moment please."

"Thank you."

"Hello?"

"Good morning, Ms. Davis. How are you holding up?"

"I'm hanging in here, sweetheart. How are you?"

"I'm better than I was yesterday, but I'm still worried sick."

"I know what you mean."

"The nurse said there has been no change in Devon's condition."

"That's correct."

"Have you talked to a doctor today?"

"No. They won't be in for a few hours."

"Has Roger called?"

"Not that I know of.

"I hear John pulling up now, so as soon as we finish breakfast we're going to head over there. Do you need anything?"

"Yes, please have you mother bring me a fresh change of clothes and some toiletries. I would also like for you to go into the closet in my bedroom, and on the top shelf there are two blankets. The pink one is Devon's and the purple one is mine. Would you please bring them with you? Those are our special bonding blankets. We use to always use them when we watched girlie movies together. I'm sure having them here when he wakes up will at least bring a smile to his face."

"I'll make sure I get them. See you soon."

"One more thing, Toni."

"Anything you want."

"Please bring me a super stack of pancakes from IHOP. This hospital food is terrible."

"Don't worry we got you covered."

"Thanks, sweetheart. Goodbye."

I hung up the phone with Ms. Davis and opened the door for John. His hands were filled with shopping bags.

"That's a lot of food for breakfast."

"I know. You know the saying, 'Never go grocery shopping while you're hungry.' Well I'm a prime example of why that is. Pancakes, eggs, and sausage has turned into Eskimo pies, steak, charcoal…"

"Charcoal!"

"Yes, I needed the charcoal to grill the steak."

John looked so serious when he said that, that I burst out laughing.

"You poor man. Come here; let mama give you hug." John walked over to me and wrapped his arms around my waist and squeezed me. I looked up and gave him a peck on the lips.

"Ooh, what's that for?"

"Only for being the sweetest man in the whole wide world."

John blushed. "I see somebody is feeling much better today."

"You're right. I'm feeling a bit more optimistic today. And I'm not as fatigued as I was when I got here."

"That's good. For a moment there, I thought there were going to be two of you in ICU."

"Was I in that bad of shape?"

"Yes. You even fell asleep in the tub last night. You were in there for two hours."

"I was."

"You don't remember?"

"No. I remember getting in and laying my head back; that's it."

"You poor thing. I guess you must've been operating on autopilot. Do you remember how things went with your presentation? We never got a chance to talk about it."

"Oh, Yes!" I beamed. "Everything ran like clockwork. My team at Carlton was just phenomenal. Everyone took a personal interest in the success of our presentation. You could just see the pride in their eyes. They worked effectively and efficiently. We had the reps from La Cola eating out of the palms of our hands. Mr. Carlton was so pleased, that he is giving everyone two extra vacations days this year and an extra bonus in their next check."

"That's great news! I'm so proud of you, baby! So does this mean that you are going to use those two vacation days and that bonus check to take me to Africa for our pool tournament rematch?" John asked jokingly.

"Look at you, plotting on a sistah's money already. As a matter of fact, Mr. Collins, I had forgotten about the rematch, but I'm a woman of my word, so I will see what I can do."

"I was just joking."

"No, no Don't try to back pedal your way out of this whooping you have coming to you. Now I'm not promising you it will take place in Africa. But I do promise you a whooping nonetheless."

"Oh, I see you got jokes."

"No, I have skills."

"Okay, we'll see. As soon as Devon is back on his feet, you and I have a date with a pool table, young lady."

"That's a deal. But in the meantime, I need you to make my breakfast."

John looked at me, surprised for a moment, then he headed for the kitchen. "I see the old Toni is back," he mumbled.

"What did you say?"

"I said welcome back."

"Thanks."

\*\*\*

After breakfast John and I headed over to Ms. Davis's house. All morning I had been contemplating how to approach John about the Roger situation. Since they are such good friends, I didn't want to upset or offend John by making any false accusations. I decided to ask questions first and worry about his reaction later. I needed to get to the bottom of this.

"John, have you heard from Roger yet?"

"No," he said, stopping at the light on Monroe Street.

"Did you know that he was with Devon when he had the asthma attack?"

"I remember hearing Ms. Davis saying that."

"Why do you think he left the scene of the accident?"

"Probably because he was scared Devon was going to die and he just wanted to get him to the hospital."

"So you don't think it had anything to do with the fact that he's married?"

"Married. What difference would that make?"

"Well, for starters, why would a married man be hanging out with an openly gay male?"

"True."

"Secondly, if something like that made the news it could hurt his run for governor."

He paused and looked at me. "You have a point. I hadn't given that any thought. I just assumed the brotha was shaken up."

"He *could be* just shaken' up. But why hasn't he been to the hospital?"

"He may have been to the hospital. We aren't sure about that yet."

"Yes, I am."

"How?"

"I spoke to Ms. Davis this morning, and she told me she hadn't seen or heard from him."

"That's interesting."

"My guess is that there is either more to this story than we know, or maybe he is trying to make sure his name does not appear anywhere in connection to Devon."

"You make a convincing argument, but you know Roger is my boy, and I'm sure he has a reasonable explanation for this."

"Then why hasn't he called you?"

"He's probably still shaken up, Toni."

"I guess that's possible. But if he doesn't show up today with some answers, then I just might have to go looking for him."

"What do you mean by that?"

"Just like Roger is your boy, Devon is mine, and I'll be damned if I'm going to let him go through this alone and not find out what's really happening. So all I'm saying is your boy, Roger, better come correct."

"Dang, baby, calm down. I'm sure Roger will turn up with a reasonable explanation. I know for a fact that he really cares about Devon."

"Well he has a funny way of showing it."

"That's not fair, Toni. After all, he did leave the scene of an accident to take Devon to the hospital. Which means that he is going to have to pay for any damage done to his car himself. That's also a criminal offense. If the police find out he left the scene of an accident he could be charged. That, to me, is showing you care about somebody."

"I guess you could look at it that way too."

"One thing is for certain."

"What's that?"

"When Devon wakes up, we'll find out what really went down."

"If he remembers."

"My boy has a memory like an elephant. He'll remember."

# Chapter 17
## It's about time

John and I picked mama up and were on our way to the hospital. When I had a sudden epiphany.

"John, stop! Turn around. I forgot to get the blankets."

John slammed on brakes and the car skidded. He looked at me like I was crazy. "What blankets?"

"The blankets Ms. Davis asked me to get for her and Devon."

"Oh, baby, you scared me half to death!"

"Me too!" Mama added, holding her hand against her chest.

"Sorry about that, y'all. It's just that Ms. Davis asked me to bring them specifically, and I promised her I would.

"Then let's get the blankets," John added, turning the car around.

We drove back to Ms. Davis's house. It was my first time really going inside her new home. Devon told me that ever since he set that trust fund up for her, her taste has improved. I could see that he wasn't lying. The foyer alone is spectacular, with a stunning crystal chandelier hanging from the ceiling and marble floors. A beautiful, jet-black baby grand piano sitting on white carpet serves as your welcome mat to the living room. *I better take my shoes off and leave them at the door.* The last thing I wanted to do is mess up that beautiful carpet.

I continued walking down the hallway and opened the door to the master suite. My mouth dropped open, I couldn't believe the size of it. The east side of the room is a sitting area lined with a comfy, overstuffed couch and a maple wood bookshelf built into the wall. I could see she was a big E. Lynn Harris fan. She had all eight of his novels on the shelf. I'm sure at least a couple of them were gifts from Devon. E. Lynn is his favorite author.

At first I didn't see the closet because I was so overwhelmed by the size of the room. But then I saw a lovely frosted, sliding glass door. When I opened it, my eyes bulged. Ms. Davis had the mother of all closets! Her closet was even bigger than D's; it could be a bedroom all itself. I admired the set up. But I knew I needed to pull myself away. Mama and John were still outside waiting for me in the car. So I retrieved the blankets, made sure the house was locked up, and left.

"Don't forget to go to IHOP," Mama reminded John.

"We have something better than IHOP for Ms. Davis."

Mama leaned forward. "Oh yeah, what's that?"

"A special breakfast prepared for Ms. Davis by that famous Chef Le John Collins," John said in his best French accent.

Mama seized the golden opportunity to mess with John's ego. "Le John Collins, huh? Sorry, never heard of him. He can't be too famous."

John peered through the rearview mirror at Mama. He was checking her expression to see if she was serious.

Mama didn't crack a smile.

"Well, mom I want you to know that I *am* famou;, just ask Toni. Baby, tell your mama I'm famous."

Mama and I made eye contact through the vanity mirror on the passenger side of the car. We burst out laughing. I leaned over and pinched John's cheek. "Yes, you are famous," I said in a baby voice.

John blushed.

Mama put on her sincere face and apologized. "John, I was just kidding. That was very nice of you to prepare breakfast for her."

John grinned. "I'm sure she will appreciate it. After all, there's nothing like good home cookin'."

"Amen to that," I added.


We parked in the visitors lot and made our way across the over pass that lead directly to the hospital. We boarded the elevator and pressed the ninth-floor button. The ride up was solemn. It seems as though we were all saying a little prayer. The doors opened and we stepped off. I lead the way to Devon's room. When we got there, the doctor was examining Devon. I could see Ms. Davis' lips moving, but I couldn't make out what she was saying. I opened the door and stuck my head in.

"Do you mind if I come in?" I asked with pleading eyes.

"Of course not, dear. Please, come in," Ms. Davis replied. "Doctor, you were saying?"

He continued. "As I was saying, Devon's vital signs have improved. He is doing about 50% better than he was yesterday. However, we are not out of the woods yet. I'm ordering a CAT scan to check his brain waves. That will give us an idea 'sof whether or not he suffered any brain damage. However, we won't know anything for sure until Devon wakes up. If he can remember who you are and how he got here, that's a good sign. If he has all of his motor skills, that's a great sign!" the doctor expressed with unbelievable enthusiasm.

"Good morning Doctor I'm Toni, Devon's sister." I extended my hand.

"Good morning," he replied with a firm handshake. We traded smiles.

"What I would like to know is how long will Devon be on the IV?"

"Why do you ask?" he inquired, wearing a puzzled expression on his face.

"Because the nurse told me that a muscle relaxer was being administered to him through the IV."

"That is correct."

I raised my eyebrows and looked at him like *duh!* I continued.

"Then it would seem to me Doctor that, if you take him off of it, maybe he'll wake up and breathe on his own." *I mean, really which one of us is the doctor here? This is not rocket science.*

"Toni, I can understand and appreciate your logic. However, it's a little more complicated than that."

*I detected a bit of sarcasm.* I folded my arms and cross-examined him. "Oh yeah, how so?"

He seemed irritated. "Well, for starters, removing the tube does not mean that he will automatically wake up. Devon's condition is very critical. If we stop administering the muscle relaxer to him and he has another attack the results could be deadly. His esophagus could close up around the tube we have down his throat and cause him to choke to death. So as you can see, it's not that simple."

"I guess not."

"Once his condition stabilizes then we will take him off the IV. I know you are worried about your brother. But trust me, we know what we're doing and we are providing him with the best possible care. Have a good day, ladies," he said and exited the room.

I paced back and forth, declaring, "They better provide him with the best possible care, Ms. Davis. Doc just don't know I have ParksCrump law firm programmed in my cell phone on speed dial. Trust me, Ms. Davis, they don't want that kind of hell!"

"I hear you, Toni. Thanks for having my baby's back."

I put my arm around her and said, "always. You know that goes without saying."

"Did you all remember the food and the blankets? I'm starving."

"Of course we did, I told you, we got you!" She smiled. "John and Mama are outside, let's go and join them," I suggested.

"Hi, Linda, and John." She greeted them with a group hug.

"Hi, Pearl, how are you feeling today?" Mama asked, holding her hand.

"I'm fine, girl. I'm just hungry as heck."

"Then you're in for a special treat."

Her eyes lit up for the first time since we'd been there. "Really? What's that?"

"John, would you like to do the honors?" Mama asked him.

John blushed. "Only if you insist."

"I do," Mama replied.

"Ms. Davis, I took the liberty of cooking breakfast for you this morning."

A shocked look covered her face. Her eyes began to water. "Are you serious? You cooked for me?"

"Yes, ma'am." John beamed with pride.

"I-I don't know what to say," she stuttered.

160

"How about *thank you*," Mama whispered.

"Forgive my rudeness, John. You caught me completely off guard. Thank you. And, please, call me Pearl."

"You're welcome, Pearl." He smiled.

I winked at John and gave him the thumbs-up. *I know he's winning mega cool points with both mama and Pearl. Hell, he's also winning them with me for that matter. Not that he really needs anymore with me, considering he's been nothing but wonderful to me since the day I met him.*

I handed Pearl the food and insisted, "Ms. Davis, you and Mama go to the cafeteria and enjoy your breakfast. John and I will stay up here and sit with Devon."

"Thank you, Toni. I'm going to take you up on that. I could use the break."

Mama wrapped her arm inside Pearl's and nudged her. "Let's go. We have a lot of catching up to do, girlfriend."

"You got that right, sistah!" Pearl laughed.

The two of them headed to the elevator.

John and I took the blankets to Devon's room. "Which one do you think belongs to Devon?" John asked.

Smiling at John, I quipped, "Take a wild guess."

"Don't tell me it's the pink one."

"Okay, then I won't tell you."

"Toni, come on, man. It's not the pink one, is it?" he aske, with a pleading expression. It was as if he wanted Devon to at least be manly in that sense.

"Sorry to disappoint you, honey, but it is the pink one. Pink has been Devon's favorite color since we were kids."

"That's deep!" he said, rubbing his forehead. "Let me ask you something, Toni."

I laid the blanket across Devon. "Go ahead."

"How did you and a gay man become so close?" He looked puzzled.

"Let me ask *you* something. How did *you* and a gay man get so close?" I was referring to his relationship with Roger."

"What are you talking about? I'm not close to any gay men."

"Oh yeah? What about Roger?" I said, folding my arms with a smirk on my face. *Not to mention me.*

"Touché! I forgot about Roger. But I don't see him as gay, though."

"Why not?"

"Because he has a wife and kids."

"He also has a boyfriend. Or did you forget about Devon."

"No, I didn't forget about him. I-I guess I just don't think about it."

"Speaking of Roger, have you heard from him yet?"

"No."

"Would you mind calling him for me? I would really like to talk to him about what happened."

John pulled out his cell phone. "No, I don't mind, I'll call him right now."

The phone rang and rang. When the answering machine picked up. John left Roger a message. "Hey, man, what's up? You've been MIA for over 24 hours. I'm here at the hospital checking on Devon. Yo, man, holla at your boy. Peace."

"Maybe you can catch him at home. Try his home number, John."

"Anything for you, sweetheart," he said as he dialed the number.

"The answering machine picked up again. John left another message. "Hey, you two, it's John. Roger, give me a call when you get this message. I need your help with something. Hit me up on the cell. Peace." He walked over to me and kissed me on the forehead." Are you satisfied now?"

"Yes, thanks."

\*\*\*

John and I sat beside Devon's bed playing Uno for nearly two hours. The nurses came in and out of the room checking Devon's vitals and refilling his IV. I had lots of flowers delivered to brighten up his room. I ordered sunflowers, gladiolas, and roses. I know when Devon wakes up he will appreciate the gesture. Besides, I figured John would enjoy being in a room filled with beautiful flowers  that's is his passion. Mama and Ms. Davis must have had a lot to catch up on; They are still gone. But I don't mind. This is a way for me to spend quality time with my two favorite men.

John's phone rang. "Hello?"

"Hey, man, it's me. Roger."

"Roger, man, it's about time you checked in. Where have you been? Toni and I have been concerned about you."

"Toni? Is she there with you?"

"Yeah, she's right here. She flew in last night."

"Is she asking a lot of questions?"

"What do you think?"

"Look, man, I had to get my head together. This whole thing has freaked me out."

"When are you coming to the hospital?"

"I'm not sure I'm coming."

"What?"

"Look, John, I really need to talk to you. Do you think you can get away from

162

Toni and meet me at Lake Ella?"

"Sure."

"Meet me there in an hour."

"For sure."

*John was starting to use a few too many oneword answers. I knew something was up.* "John, may I speak to Roger?"

"Baby, I'm sorry; he already hung up."

*How convenient.* "Well, what did he say?"

"He didn't say much."

I sensed John's hesitance. He wasn't looking me in the eye. Something was definitely up. "Well how much didn't he say?" I wasn't letting up.

"He said he had some things on his mind."

"When did he say he was coming to see Devon?"

"He didn't say."

"What? What do you mean he didn't say?"

"He didn't say, Toni, Damn!"

"Hold up! Why are you cursing at me?" I demanded as I rose out of my seat.

John looked tense. "Because you're asking me questions I can't answer."

"That's still no reason to curse at me. I don't disrespect you like that, and I would appreciate it if you treated me with the same amount of respect."

"Look, Toni, I'm not trying to disrespect you but I am not trying to stand here and answer fifty questions either."

Now he'd done it! I walked up to his face and stood there looking at him eye-to-eye, nose-to-nose. "John, I'm not about to entertain this bullshit ass conversation. Not while my friend is lying in that bed fighting for his life. Now if you want to tell me what Roger said to you that made you so irritable, then please do. Otherwise, I think you might want to stop before both of us say some things we might regret!"

His eyes darted back and forth while looking at mine. And without another word he grabbed his keys and left.

*Oh no, he didn't just walk out on me like that!* Did you see that? Can somebody tell me what just happened here, because I sure as hell don't know? *Is that the same kind of response I'll get if I tell him about me?*

I sat there staring at the door, wondering what had just happened. One minute we're playing cards the next minute we're having our first official fight. I started massaging Devon's legs. "Well, friend, I guess it's just me and you. Just like old times. Remember when you came to visit me in Paris. We had so much fun. Remember that night we dressed up like working girls and walked the street. We must have gotten hit on twenty times. How about Madame Fifi? Do you remember when she took us to the club to become dancers? How on earth did I let the two of you talk me into that?"

Now I know *you* won't believe this but Ms Toni T. Goodwin has a little bit of a past. Close your mouth; I know you're shocked. But I wasn't always Toni with an I, or a Y. I was once Toni with an E, as in Tone-e. It was all Ms. D's fault. She came out to Paris to visit me for a month during the time I was living as a woman before my operation was complete. That's one of the requirements. The doctors make you live as a woman for a year before you have your full operation. It's kind of like a getting-to-know-your-new-self type of thing. What it boils down to is the opportunity to *try it before you buy it.* Get my drift?

Anyway, D and I became friends with a drag queen named Fifi. She invited us to come down to club Marmalade to see a show. D accepted the invitation for us. That night we both went dressed as women. It just so happened to be the night of the amateur drag queen competition. Of course, D put our names down as contestants. Need I say it? We won! We tied for first place. To this day I still think I was cheated. After all, my breasts were real. D's weren't. From that night on, Fifi constantly harassed us about being performers for the club. We agreed, and that's how I became Tone-e the Teaser, and Devon became Ms. Divine.

I still remember walking on the stage the first night I performed alone. I was shaking like a leaf but when the music started I pulled it together real quick. The smoke-filled room had a little of everybody in it. I could barely see their faces from the stage. They were transvestites, pre-ops, post-ops, bisexuals, homosexuals, transsexual, heterosexual, and gender girls. All of them were there for one reason and that was to enjoy the show. I even saw a few American black men and women in there from time to time. The atmosphere was lively yet very dark. I often saw cross-dressers in there that looked like some of my sixty-year-old professors from college dressed in drag. It's amazing the kind of people you can run into in a club like that.

Devon and I made friends with a gender girl named Kellie. A gender girl is a natural woman. Kellie taught us how to apply our makeup so we wouldn't look overdone. She taught us how to walk in high heels and how to control our gestures so they wouldn't be overexaggerated. That's always a giveaway for T's, also know as transsexuals. T's are known for over-exaggerating their gestures. So D and I have worked very hard to make sure we don't do that. I've perfected it. D only remembers to do it when he's in drag otherwise he is flaming like a burning spear. *Now that was funny!* I wish D would wake up and laugh with me.

"*Oh D,* Please wake up and get out of this bed. I need you Ms. Divine."

# Chapter 18
## The confession

I really hated to treat Toni like that. But I couldn't think of another way to leave the hospital without her getting suspicious. Hopefully I'll be able to make it up to her. Roger sounded so desperate when I spoke to him on the phone; I knew my partner needed me. I'm sure whatever is going on has to do with the reason why Devon is laid up in the hospital.

The clock on my dashboard read 5:02p.m. I made a right off of Tennessee on to Monroe Street. Geez! The traffic on Monroe Street is bumper to bumper. I forgot it was rush hour. I slipped a jazz CD into my changer and calmly waited for the traffic to move.

As I pulled into the parking lot, I spotted Roger sitting on a bench wearing a Seminole baseball cap, some faded blue jeans, and the new Jordans. "Hey, partner, what's up?" I said, giving him some dap. I saw fear in his eyes.

"John, man, I'm going through hell."

"I am not trying to be funny man, but you look like it. When is the last time you had some sleep?"

He shook his head. "I don't know, man."

"Wel,l talk to your brotha. What's up?"

"Where's Toni?"

" At the hospital."

"Does she know you're coming to meet me?"

"N., I had to start a fight with her to get away, so this better be good."

"It's not good, man, but it's worth it. How is Devon?"

"The same. There really hasn't been that much of a change?"

"What did the doctors say?"

"They said he could have suffered some brain damage. But we aren't sure yet. We won't know anything until he wakes up."

Roger put his head in his hands. "*Lord*, he has got to wake up."

I placed my hand on his shoulder. "Man, it's going to work out. Now tell me what's on your mind?"

"Sonya has gotten suspicious."

"About what?"

"She thinks I'm having an affair. She's hired a private investigator to have me followed."

"How do you know?"

"She's constantly calling to check up on me. Last week I had a fraternity function to go to. It was an all male event. By the time I got there one of my frat brothers told me she'd called there three times. She even called some of the other wives to check to see if their husbands mentioned anything about going to a frat function."

"What made her so suspicious?"

"I haven't wanted to make love to her for months. At first she thought I was experiencing a bout with impotence. So she scheduled a doctor's appointment for me and went with me for moral support. The doctor confirmed that there was nothing physically wrong with me. He said the problem was psychological. So she started getting depressed because she thought I wasn't attracted to her anymore. She's still a little self-conscious about her weight ever since she had the baby."

"But she looks good."

"I know. I did my best to convince her that her body didn't have anything to do with my problem. So she tried changing the scenery, and dressing up in kinky lingerie, but I still couldn't get an erection no matter what she did. Then one morning she woke up before me and saw that my dick was hard. So she knew it was still possible. That's when she became suspicious."

"Do you know what the problem is?"

"Yes."

I started to get a little anxious. I checked my watch to see how long I had been gone. "Well, do you care to share that information with me?"

"This isn't easy for me, John."

"I know, man. I guess I'm just a little impatient because I know I'm going to have my own drama to deal with when I get back to the hospital. Continue."

Roger swallowed hard. "John, I think I'm in love with Devon!" he blurted out.

"You're what! *Hell naw, Bruh!* You can't be!" I paced back and forth, shaking my head. "Naw, partner, you just can't be."

"Why not?"

"Because he's a man. You have a beautiful wife and daughter at home and a son in college. Please explain to me how you can be in love with another man!"

"I can't believe you are acting like this John. I thought you understood."

"I do. I understand that you have a problem."

Roger sprang from the bench. "What kind of shit is this, John? Who the hell are you to judge me. You are supposed to be my boy."

"Supposed to be? What do you mean supposed to be? I am your boy! How many men do you know that would still hangout with their boy once they found out he had gay tendencies? Man, how dare you challenge my loyalty!" I was in Roger's face now.

We stood toe-to-toe. "I told you that in confidence!" Spit flew out of his mouth. "Now you're using that to judge me. Fuck you, John! This was a big mistake!" He walked off.

"Roger! Hold up, man. I'm not judging you. I'm just not condoning what you're doing. Look, Roger, we have been friends for 15 years. When you confided in me about the gang rape, I listened and I was there for you.

I know it's not easy for a man to admit that he's been violated. I also understand that being raped by a gang of boys when you're one yourself has got to be devastating. But you've managed to work through your issues with counseling for the most part. And I applaud that. You came to me like a man and told me you like anal sex with men because you feel like it's a way to reclaim your power. Hey," I said, throwing my hands up, "I even went along with you on that. But now you've come to me to tell me that you are about to destroy your family over a piece of ass! I'm sorry, dawg, I can't get with that."

"Man, you misunderstood me. I am not trying to destroy my family. I might not have a choice in the matter. Yes, I do think I'm falling in love with Devon, and if that makes me gay, then I guess I'm gay. However, I have no intention of coming out. I still plan to be Governor of the state of Florida, and there is no way I'm sacrificing my political goals for a love affair. But, like I said, I might not have a choice in the matter."

"Why?"

"Because when I told Devon that I thought Sonya might be having me followed, he did some detective work of his own and found out that my suspicions were correct. She *is* having me followed."

"Do you think she's uncovered your affair with Devon?"

"Not yet. As soon as we found out we cooled off."

"Then how did you end up over to Devon's house the night of the accident?"

"I called Devon and told him I was coming over. I needed to see him. He told me he had other plans, and that I was forcing him to move on with his life. I went over to his house anyway. When I got there I used my key to let myself in and that's when I saw it."

"What did you see?"

"Devon was naked and leaning over the sofa, and Lester was fucking him."

"Who is Lester?"

"Lester McMillan of the Cincinnati Bengals."

I couldn't believe what I was hearing. I just sat there listening to him in disbelief. "Roger, are you shittin' me?"

"Would I lie about something like this?"

*Shit, I wish you were.* "No, I guess not. It's just that I never expected this." *This gay stuff is getting to be a bit much. First Roger, now pro football players. Who's next?*

"Me either."

"So what happened?"

"I went into a rage. They didn't hear me come in so I snuck up behind Lester

167

and hit him over the head with a ten-pound vase. He fell to the floor and I jumped on him and beat him some more. I was totally out of control. Devon tried to stop me, but I pushed him out of the way. Lester did manage to get a few licks in but nowhere near as equal to the beating he took."

"Wow, man! I don't know what to say. Is that how Devon had the asthma attack?"

"Yep. He was so overwhelmed by the fight that he started panicking and gasping for air. I'd never seen an asthma attack before, so I wasn't sure what to do. I called 911 and the operator told me it sounded like he was having an asthma attack. So instead of waiting for an ambulance to arrive, I dragged Lester to his car and left him there unconscious. I put Devon in my car and took off. On the way to the hospital a car ran the red light and crashed into us on the passenger side of the car. Devon was the only one who sustained injuries. He wasn't wearing his seatbelt. I had forgotten to buckle it up. You see, John, this is all my fault."

"That's a hell of an ordeal. I see why you have been laying low."

"Man, I'm so tired I can barely think straight."

"What happened to Lester?"

"That's the scary part. I have no idea."

"What do you mean?"

"After I got Devon to the hospital. I left and went back to his house to deal with Lester but he was long gone. I haven't seen or heard anything about him since."

"What do you think happened to him?"

"I'm hoping that brotha hopped a plane back to Cincinnati and is going to let this one ride."

"And what if he doesn't?"

John looked worried. "Then I'll have to cross that bridge when I get to it. I do know that he has just as much to lose as I do by going public so I don't have to worry about that. But he might try to get me back on the sly. So I've become pretty paranoid."

"Man, this is no way to live."

"Who you telling? I want my life back."

"So do you think you were being followed that night?"

"I was initially, but I went through quite a few twist and turns down some back roads and lost him."

"Are you sure?"

"Relatively sure."

"At least now I know what's up with you. We couldn't figure out why you weren't coming to the hospital or returning our calls."

"What do you think I should do, John?"

"I don't know. What do you want to do?"

"I want to visit Devon in the hospital."

"What's stopping you?"

"I don't want to be followed there. I can't afford to be associated with him. That's why I never filed a police report."

"I have a plan. Check this out: We'll leave here and go up the street to that mom-and-pop gas station. The bathroom is around the back of the building; we'll go in there and switch clothes. Then I'll come out first wearing your clothes and get in your car and drive off. If someone was following you they'll follow me instead. Then you can take my car and go to the hospital to see Devon. If you park in the parking garage, you can walk across the over pass and that will put you directly into the hospital. That way, you can avoid signing in downstairs. Once you get inside, go to the 9th floor. Devon is in ICU."

"Intensive Care? *Man*, I didn't realize it was that serious. Let's get out of here."

"Wait. One more thing."

"What's that?"

"If Toni ask, you haven't seen me."

"I got you covered."

We left the lake and drove down the street to put our plan into motion. We went into the bathroom and exchanged clothes. Before Roger walked out of the door, I gave him a hug. "Good luck, partner. You know I'm still your boy, and I got your back."

"Thanks, man. By the way, what time and where are we going to meet back up?"

"Meet me at my house in an hour. There is no way a private investigator will be able to get past my guard gate. I'll have something for you to eat, and you can take a nap before I go pick up Toni."

"Cool, man. Thanks. I appreciate you looking out."

Roger left the bathroom, got in my car and drove off.

# Chapter 19
## Trick or Treat

After I left John, I turned off of Monroe Street and took a few back roads to Magnolia Street. The hospital was sitting off to my left. I pulled in and followed John's instructions. Our plan was working like a charm. I jumped off the elevator on the 9th floor and found my way to Devon's room virtually unnoticed. *"Thank God! Toni's not in here."* I mumbled under my breath. *"Look at Devon lying in that bed. This is all my fault."*

I walked over to Devon and rubbed his forehead. He didn't move. He looked so peaceful. He almost looked dead.

I took his hand and knelt down beside his bed and spoke to him. "Devon, I'm sorry I haven't been here for you. And I'm sorry for being the one who put you here in the first place. I need you, baby. Please come back to me."

I don't know if I was just caught up in the moment or if it was my imagination but I could swear I saw his foot move.

"Devon? Devon can you hear me? It's me, Roger. Can you hear me?"

He didn't respond. In that moment I heard voices coming down the hallway. I knew it was time to make my exit. I leaned over Devon and kissed him on the forehead. *"I'll be back. Hang in there."* I whispered. *"I love you."*

I knew I had to hurry I could hear footsteps coming closer. I left Devon's room and walked in the direction opposite the voices. I knew I needed to go toward them to get to the elevator, but I couldn't risk running into Toni.

"John? John is that you?" I heard somebody call out to me. I kept walking. I knew it wasn't Toni's voice. It sounded like an older lady. I made a quick right and ran down the stairwell and out of the hospital.

I had to stop running and bend over long enough to catch my breath. *"Whew! That was close."* After I gathered enough air in my lungs to continue walking to the car, I jumped in John's ride and headed for the hills.

*Lord, please let Devon pull through.* Thoughts of Devon kept me preoccupied while I was driving. It took me about eighteen minutes to get to John's house. The guard waved me right in. I pulled into the garage and entered the house through the kitchen.

The aroma of home cooking hit me as soon as I opened the door. "Something smells good in here!" I was licking my lips and rubbing my hands together.

"Man, what took you so long?"

"What do you mean, partner? I am on time with fifty-nine seconds to spare."

"I'm just kidding. So how did it go?"

"It was cool at first. I got inside the hospital and into Devon's room completely unnoticed."

"What did Toni say?"

"Nothing. She wasn't there."

"She wasn't there?"

"Nope."

"That's strange."

"Maybe she went to get something to eat. Anyway, I got a chance to talk to Devon alone. I have to admit, John, the sight of him laying in that bed ain't nothin' nice."

"I feel you, dawg."

"I kept expecting him to crack a joke or say something funny."

"I know. Toni said the same thing."

"What freaked me out was that I could swear I saw his foot move."

"For real?"

"Yeah, but when I tried calling his name again, he didn't respond. Then I heard voices coming down the hallway so I had to get out of there."

"Did anybody see you?"

"Yeah, some lady yelled out 'John, is that you?'"

"Was it Toni?" John said nervously.

"No, it was a older woman's voice."

"Then that had to be either her mother or Pearl, Devon's mother. What did you do?"

"I kept walking, made a quick right, and got the hell out of there!"

"Thank God they didn't get a good look at you. I couldn't imagine having to explain that along with trying to make up for the argument I started earlier."

I walked over and took a lid off of one of the pots on the stove. "So what's in these pots, partner? I'm ready to throw down?"

"Don't you want to shower first?" John wrinkled his nose. "You are a little ripe, playa."

"Oh, so it's like that, huh?"

"I'm afraid so, partner. But listen I took the liberty of washing your clothes for you. I even gave you a pair of briefs from one of my new packs. Everything is laid out for you in the guest room."

I headed for the shower. "Thanks, man. I'll be back in a few."

"Throw my clothes outside the door so I can wash them and put them back on. I don't want Toni getting suspicious about shit."

"I feel you, dawg. Once you get a woman's curiosity up, you can forget it. Just look at me, I'm a living testimony to that." I laughed, but it wasn't funny. It was true.

Steam filled the bathroom in sixty seconds flat. The mirrors fogged up, and my sinuses cleared out. John was right about this shower. I did need it. The hot water awakened something in me. I started to feel alive again for the first time in days. If it wasn't for the burn in the pit of my stomach, I might have stayed in here longer. But no can do. I have got to eat. I dried off as quickly as I could and hurried out to the dining room to eat.

"I thought you might want to relax and watch Sports Center, so I set your food in here."

"Cool, bruh," I said, taking a seat on the couch. "What am I having?"

"Smothered chicken, yellow rice, string beans, and cornbread."

"Damn! You threw down, *Black man!*" I smiled for the first time in days.

"You know I did a little sumthin' sumthin'. Go ahead and dig in. I have to go work on my plan to get out of the doghouse with Toni. I'll be in my office if you need me."

"Thanks man."

I sat on John's leather sofa with my towel wrapped around my waist, eating and chillin'. John put his foot in that food. I knew the brother could cook, but he really showed out on this meal.

Kobe Bryant was on Sports Center conducting a press conference. I couldn't believe that brotha' sat there and admitted to committing adultery. "Naw, Kobe, man, you are going against the code!" I shouted. "What happened to deny, deny, deny?" I yelled at him. As if what he'd done wasn't bad enough, that brotha broke out and started crying! I fell on the floor and rolled around, holding my head. I hate to see another playa fall. We're going to have to burn his card after this one.

I turned the TV off after that. Kobe's situation didn't do nothing but depress me further. He made me think about my own storm. I guess both of us are a little hemmed up. Unlike him, I'm going to deny, deny, deny until I die. This is one secret I'm planning to take to the grave.

*** 

My eyes opened, and John was standing over me, shaking me. "Roger, wake up. Wake up, man. I have to get back to the hospital."

"Huh?"

"Get up, man. You have to get dressed and get out of here. I have to go back to the hospital and make up with Toni."

"Damn, man," I stretched.

"Did you see that shit Kobe got himself into?"

"Yeah. It's pretty jacked up."

I got up and took my plate into the kitchen. "Naw, man, that shit is fucked up! Watching that playa fall like that just drained all of my damn energy. I don't even

172

remember falling asleep."

"I'm sure the 'itis had something to do with that, too."

"You're right about that, playa. That food was off the chain!"

"Thanks, partner. I'm glad you liked it," John said, walking out of the door. He turned and looked at me with a sympathetic expression. "Roger, hang in there."

"I intend to."

"I'll see you later. Lock up when you leave."

"I will... and, John...thanks."

"Don't mention i," he said, closing the door behind him.

# Chapter 20
## Humble pie

Toni was sitting next to Devon's bed reading a book when I walked in. She shifted her eyes from the page, looked up at me then back at her book. I knew that was a silent *dis*.

I tried breaking the ice. "Hi, baby."

Toni lowered her book and looked at me with venom in her eyes. "Hello Jonathan." She returned her book to its original position.

This is going to be tougher than I thought. She called me Jonathan, and that's not even my name. Most men named John have the full name Jonathan, but not me. Mine is Johansen. I guess we never discussed it, so she's just assuming its Jonathan.

I moved in a little closer. "It's Johansen," I corrected.

She raised one eyebrow. "What?"

"My name—- it's Johansen. You called me Jonathan."

"My bad. Johansen," she said with a sistah-girl neck roll.

"Toni, I'm sorry." I knelt beside her.

She wouldn't look at me.

"Look at me baby, I'm on bended knee." I put my finger to her chin and tilted her head back. "I sincerely apologize for disrespecting you. I don't know what came over me." My eyes were begging for her forgiveness. "Please believe what I'm telling you. My intent is never to hurt you. You are my earth; I'm lost without you."

A tear fell from her cheek. "You had me at *I'm sorry*." She leaned in and kissed me. "I don't want to fight anymore, baby." She placed her arms around my neck. Her voice was softer now.

"Me neither." I whispered. Holding the sides of her face. Toni's eyes mimicked what I was feeling, a deep and abiding love.

"I missed you, John."

"I missed you, too, baby."

***

"Cut that Hollywood shit out."

"What did you say John?"

"I said it, tramp." the voice was raspy.

Toni sprang from her chair! "Devon! You're awake!"

"No heifer I'm talking in my sleep! Now get over here and give me some love."

Toni nearly knocked me over trying to get to Devon. She ran over to his bed and hugged him.

"Where is my mama?"

"She's outside with my mama."

"Linda? She came too?"

"Of course she did. You know you're the daughter she never had." Toni teased.

"You got that right, sistah! Well, tell those two old broads to get in here and dote over me. You know how I like attention, and I know this hospital menagerie is *all* about me!"

"Aren't you at least going to say hello to John first?"

"I'm sorry, John. I couldn't see you because somebody is blocking my view and sucking up all of my air. She needs to move so I can get a hug from you. After all, lack of oxygen is what got me here in the first place."

"You don't have to tell me twice," Toni said, moving out of my way.

I walked over and hugged Devon. "Welcome back, Devon. You gave us quite a scare."

"Well, you know how I do it! It's either all-out drama or nothing." He laughed.

Toni rolled her eyes playfully. "Ain't that the truth? This is the biggest drama queen this side of the Mississippi."

"You're just jealous, heifer."

"John, would you please go outside and get our mothers before I have to put sleeping beauty here in a choke hold."

"Watch it, sistah, you don't want none of this!"


I left the room and went outside to get Linda and Pearl. They were nowhere to be found. I figured they must have been in the cafeteria having dinner. I took the elevator down to the lobby only to discover that the cafeteria is on the 2nd floor. Instead of waiting for the elevator to come back, I walked the one flight of stairs up to the 2nd floor. I heard their voices before I entered the dining area.

"Hey, ladies, I have great news."

"Let me guess!" Pearl said with excitement. "Devon's CAT scan came back negative!"

"It's better than that. Devon is awake!"

Pearl jumped out of her chair and screamed at the top of her lungs. Her arms were flying back and forth as she chanted. "Lawd, Jesus, thank you, *Lawd, Jesus, thank you, Lawd Jesus—*"

On the third Lawd Jesus, Linda and I had to usher her out of there.

We managed to calm her down long enough to get her back to Devon's room. When we walked in, she looked at Devon and started the chant again. Only this time she was crying and hugging her baby when she said it.

I put one arm around Toni, the other around Linda, and the three of us joined in with a silent, "Lawd, Jesus, *we* thank you!"

# Chapter 21
## Stranger things have happened

Heavenly Father, I come to you with the joy of thanksgiving in my heart. Once again you have heard my cry and answered the call. Thank you, God, for leaving Devon in our midst. There aren't enough words in the English language to describe how overjoyed I am. So I'm simply going to say thank you, Father. Amen.

*** 

Thank you, *Je-sus!* Whew! I'm about to have a Holy Ghost party up in here, y'all. Devon scared us, didn't he? I know you're just as glad as I am that he woke up. That's one sister-friend I'm not ready to lose. Can I get an Amen to that? Okay, it's time for me to catch you up on what's really been happening.

Yesterday, I was a little confused about what went down between John and I. We go together like peanut butter and jelly. So when the peanut butter part of this duo started acting like a real nut, my radar went off. And you know what that means. It was time to investigate!

I sat down and did a little analysis of the circumstances surrounding our argument. Exhibit A, Roger Calls. Exhibit B, John gives one-word answers. Exhibit C, John hangs up the phone without letting me speak to Roger. Exhibit D, John starts a fight with me for no apparent reason and leaves. Ladies and gentlemen of the jury, I'd say he was guilty of being up to something.

At first I didn't know what to do. Or how I was going to catch him. So I decided to wait until he came to me on his own. But as fate would have it Pearl asked me to go to her car to get her phonebook. On my way back into the building I saw John running across the over pass out to the parking lot. I followed him. When he stopped to catch his breath, I could see that it wasn't John. It was a man wearing John's clothes. I put two and two together and figured out it was Roger. I jumped in Pearl's car and decided to follow him. I called Pearl to let her know that I borrowed her car. Mama got on the phone.

"Toni, what's wrong with John?"

"Why do you ask?"

"Pearl and I just saw him walking down the hall and when I called his name he kept going."

*Bingo. He was cold busted!*

"That's strange, Ma, but who knows? John and I had a fight this morning, so maybe he was in a foul mood. I'll ask him about it when I see him."

"Where are you off to?"

"I have a quick errand to run. I'll be back in a few."

"Drive safely, honey."

"I will, Ma. I'll see you later."

Roger drove directly to John's house. I followed closely behind him. Instead of going in the guard gate I tipped the guard $50 and asked him a few questions.

"Is Mr. Collins home?"

"Yes, ma'am," the gray-haired gentleman replied. "He came home about an hour ago, driving his friends' car. His friend pulled in just before you did, driving his car. Aren't you his lady friend?"

"Yes."

"Well, I'll be happy to let you in."

"No. That's okay. I'm planning a surprise party for him, and I needed to get in to decorate but I can't do it if he's there."

"I understand, ma'am."

"I'll find a way to get him out of the house. Thanks for your help, sir."

"You're welcome, and good luck with the party. I hope he enjoys it."

"Me too. Just remember, it's a surprise, so don't mention it." I waved and drove off.

*** 

On my way back to the hospital I called Sean at home.

"Hello?"

"Hi, Sean, it's me, Toni."

"Toni, how are you? How is Devon?"

"He's still in ICU, but his vital signs have improved. And this morning they removed the tube from down his throat. So things are starting to look better."

"Did you find out what happened?"

"Yeah, he had an asthma attack and on his way to the hospital he had a car accident."

"I'm sorry to hear that. No wonder you were so out of it."

"Sean, I don't mean to change the subject, but I wanted to know how things went in the office on Friday."

"It was business as usual."

" Did you take any messages for me?"

"Only one. It was from a guy named Tommy Jones. He said he'd heard that something happened to Devon and he wanted to see if you knew. I told him you'd already left for Tallahassee."

"Shit!"

"Did I do something wrong, Toni?"

"No, Sean. I just forgot to call him."

178

"You might want to check your voice mail for your other messages."

"I wil,l Sean. Thanks."

"Do you know when you're coming back?"

"Probably the day after Devon wakes up." *Whenever that is.* "I'll keep you post-ed. If we hear anything from Cola, call me."

"You know I will. Take care."

"Bye, Sean."

***

I completely forgot to call Tommy. I wish Sean wouldn't have told him I was here. Now I feel obligated to call and apologize. Hopefully he'll understand.

*Ring, Ring.*

*Good his voice mail picked up.*

"Hello, Tommy, it's Toni. I'm in town. Sorry I didn't call you sooner, but I've been really stressed out over Devon. I'll probably be here until he wakes up. He is still unconscious right now. I guess I'll try you again later. Bye."

That worked out perfectly. Now I can avoid his call until I leave. There is no way for me to entertain the thought of seeing Tommy while I'm staying with John. Hell, I'm under enough stress as it is. I'll be damned if I'm going to let juggling two men add to it. Tommy's not that cute. *But John is.* I smiled.

***

"Just in time," Mama said as I peeked into Devon's room.

"Just in time for what?" I questioned. *Lord, what are they up to?*

"You're just in time to relieve us. We want to go downstairs and have dinner."

"Oh, go ahead. I'll sit here and read my book while I keep Devon company."

"Thanks, Toni, you're such a sweet girl."

"You're welcome, Pearl. By the way, thanks for letting me use your car. Here are your keys and your phonebook."

"Thanks, dear. Where did you park?"

"In the same spot you were in."

"Okay, wel,l we'll be in the cafeteria if you need us."

"Enjoy."

I was sitting down reading my book when John walked in. I had already decided that I wasn't going to make him eat too much humble pie. Yes, I knew he was keeping something from me. But who am I to talk? I have a little mass

179

deception of my own going on. So letting him off the hook right now is the least I could do. Besides, I'll find out what he's up to eventually.

# Chapter 22
## It's good to be home

Mama brought me home from the hospital today. The doctors said that I'm going to make a full recovery. I have to stay off my feet for a while and get plenty of rest. Other than that I am feeling like a new penny. I know how fortunate I am to come through this ordeal with my good health and good sense in tack. So I took a moment to give thanks.

*Hey,* Jesus, it's me, Devon. Now I know it's been a mighty long time since we've talked. And I know I don't keep in touch like I *should.* I have always been bad about keeping in touch. Ask anybody who knows me. Anyway, you know my heart, so hopefully you know I mean well. I just stopped by today, Jesus, to say thank you. Thank you for sparing my life. I know that if you so choose you can pluck a flower like me from this earth at any moment and replant me in your heavenly garden *if I'm lucky.* I know I had a lot of people praying for me and asking you to leave me here. Thanks for making me an answered prayer. Amen.

So like I was saying. I'm out of the hospital, but I 'm not staying at my house. I decided to stay with mama until I'm back on my feet. My house is a two-story, and it would be too difficult for me to get around. Pearl lives in a ranch-style house, so you do the math. Later today we are having a welcome-back cookout for me. Toni and Linda are leaving tomorrow, so everyone decided that we should have a party tonight.

"Devon, telephone!" Pearl yelled from the kitchen.

"Who is it, Mom?"

"Toni."

I picked up the receiver. "I got it Mom."

"Hey, Diva. How are you feeling?"

"Bootylicious," I said, laughing. "*Oops,* no pun intended."

"I guess you're feeling like your old self. I see you still got jokes."

"Yes, Teaser, I 'm feeling good."

"Then what time are we getting this party started?"

" Four o'clock."

"Have your swim suit on because I plan on throwing you in the pool."

"Ya'll ain't ready to see all this here."

"On second thought, you're right. We aren't ready to see all that there. Not in Speedo's anyway." Toni was laughing so I hard I could barely make out what she was saying.

"I see I'm not the only one who's got jokes, heifer."

"Oh, D, you know I'm just kidding. Have you heard from Roger yet?"

"No, not yet?"

"Does he know you're out of the hospital?"

"I have no idea. I haven't seen him since he took me to the hospital. Have you seen him since you've been here?"

Toni hesitated. "Not exactly."

"What is that supposed to mean?" I knew something was up.

"A few days ago, as a matter of fact, it was the same day you woke up. John and I had a fight and he left the hospital."

"Okay, but what does that have to do with Roger?"

"Well, the fight started shortly after Roger called. I'm sure he asked John to meet him some place. Anyway, about an hour later Roger shows up at the hospital wearing John's clothes. He must've gone to see you."

"Hold up, Toni. I remember him being there. I thought I dreamed it. But I remember hearing him saying he was sorry and that he loved me."

"Why is he acting so sneaky, D?"

"I don't know."

"What happened the night of your asthma attack? Do you remember?"

"Yeah, I remember clearly. Girl, check this out! Roger and I decided to lay low because his wife had gotten suspicious and is having him followed."

Toni interrupted, "*What!*"

"Yes, now close your mouth so I can continue with the story."

"Sorry, girl, go ahead."

"Lester called me that night and asked me if he could come over. I told him yes. Then Roger called and said he was coming over and I told him not to. But he came anyway."

"Damn, D, this is better than the soaps."

"Would you stop interrupting me?"

"Look who's talking? You do that to me all the time."

"Sorry, Toni, I don't remember ever doing that," I said with a hit of sarcasm. "Yeah right!"

"Chile, how about Roger let himself in and caught me and Lester fucking!"

"No wonder your ass ended up in the hospital. You probably fainted from getting caught."

"*Okay!*"

"So then what?"

"Roger hit Lester over the head with an imported porcelain vase. Girl, do you know how much I paid for that vase? I'm going to make his ass reimburse me for that—

"Stay focused, D, you're getting off on a tangent. Finish the story."

"I'm just saying, that vase cost me a couple thousand dollars. So anyway, Roger beat Lester down. In all of the excitement I started having an asthma attack. I was trying to point Roger to my inhaler, but he panicked and called 911, not realizing what I was trying to tell him. Eventually I passed out, so I'm not sure of the details after that."

"That's some story, D."

"Yeah, it's a booty call gone bad."

"Well now I understand why Roger has been laying low. He's probably the most wanted man in Tallahassee."

"What do you mean, Teaser?"

"His wife is after him; Lester, I'm sure is after him; and the police are probably after him too."

"The police?" Toni was scaring me now.

"Why would the police be after him?"

"The car accident."

"What car accident?"

"That's right you don't know, do you? On the way to the hospital a car ran the red light and hit you and Roger. That's where most of your injuries came from. You were the only one hurt."

*Me in a car accident.* I put my hand up to my forehead. "Oh, Teaser, I think I'm going to faint."

"Quit with all that damn drama. You've had your moment in the spotlight already."

"You sure do know how to rain on a girl's parade."

"Have you heard anything from Lester?"

"That homophobe? Girl, Lester wouldn't be caught dead coming to the hospital to see me. If anything, he sent flowers to my house under an assumed name, like Bugs Bunny." I said shaking my head at how ridiculous he is. "So chances are he won't confront Roger about anything. He has too much at stake."

"D, you just be careful. This has gotten too far out of control, and you almost lost your life because of it. Not to mention you stole my thunder."

"How did I steal your thunder?"

"I got the news about you being in the hospital the day of my presentation. I was wondering why I didn't hear from you the night before. But I see now, you were to busy getting your grove on."

"Girl, I hope I never get that busy again."

"Amen to that."

"So how did it go?"

"We did an excellent job. They loved it."

"Then I guess congratulations are in order."

"We don't have the contract yet, but we're still contenders."

"You'll get it."

"I hope so. Well, Diva, we better get off this phone. You are the guest of honor at a party starting in less than an hour. I'm sure you'll need more time than that to get ready."

"You know me so well, don't you?"

"Better than you think."

"Ciao!"

"Bye."

***

The barbecue went off without a hitch. Toni, Linda, and John arrived first. They brought potato salad, and baked beans with them. Apparently John is a wiz in the kitchen. Pearl hasn't stop raving about the breakfast he made for her yet. He also volunteered to be the grill master for the party. Of course nobody argued with him about that.

A few of Pearl's neighbors came over and brought salads. We had a DJ and a fierce slide competition going on. Unfortunately, I wasn't well enough to get out there and show them how it's done, but Toni was workin' it. Meanwhile, John was workin' the grill.

I rolled up on John holding a plate. "John, those steaks look good."

"Thanks, Devon. Are you ready to try one?"

"You know I am."

"Give me your plate."

John slapped a mouthwatering sirloin on my plate "Here you are, Devon. I hope you enjoy it."

"Thanks, John. I'll let you know if it meets my seal of approval."

I took a seat by the pool and ate like there is no tomorrow. This is the first time I had regular food since I went into the hospital. And John really did a great job cooking. He will be receiving the thumbs up from me.

"Hey, baby, how's the food?" Mama asked.

"Good," I said with my mouth full.

"Didn't I tell you that John could cook? Toni has got herself a real keeper."

"I know that's right."

"Does he know about her situation?"

"No."

"Is she going to tell him?"

"I hope so."

"I would hate to see her lose him. So she should tell him."

"That's the same thing I told her from the beginning."

"She's probably scared."

184

"I'm sure she is. That's not going to be an easy task."

"No, I guess not."

Linda walked over to us.

"What are you two over here whispering about?"

"We're just admiring that handsome son-in-law of yours."

"Isn't he handsome, Pearl? He's a great catch. I hope he does become my son-in-law."

"When do you think Toni is going to tell him?"

"Mama, stop being so nosey."

"Devon, we're all family here. I don't mind Pearl asking."

"But that's not appropriate behavior."

"Devon, please! Your mother and I are girlfriends just like you and Toni. So she can either ask me in front of you or away from you. But trust me, she was going to ask me either way."

They slapped a high-five "You got that right, sistah!" Pearl said.

"To answer your question, Pearl--- I have no idea. I might try to get it out of her on the plane."

"You make sure you let us know when you find out."

"Will do. Speaking of planes, we better start getting ready to go. I need to pack and get a good night's rest; we have an early flight. Do you need us to help you clean up?"

"No. My neighbors will do it. You all have done enough."

"I'm going to go and grab that dancing diva and let her know that you're ready to go, Linda."

"Thanks, Devon."

I rolled over to John. "If you plan to get a dance in with your dancing queen over there, it's now or never. Linda is ready to call it a night."

"Good lookin' out, Devon! Would you ask the DJ to play *Beautiful Eyes*, by Glenn Lewis?"

"Will do."

John walked up to Toni and took her hand. I told the DJ to play the song. The two of them danced, looking into each other's eyes like they were completely captivated. I could see the love in the air. I just hope it survives Toni's secret.

## Chapter 23
## Decisions, Decisions

*Welcome to the Tallahassee airport,* the recorded greeting said.

John took mama and I to the airport and waited with us. He wasn't allowed into the boarding area so we waited in the lobby. Mama sat there doing a crossword puzzle while John and I sat off to the side talking.

"This trip was nothing like the last one, huh?"

"No, John, not by a long shot. The last time I was here I felt like a teenager again. The fun was nonstop. This trip felt like it challenged every emotion in my body."

"I know what you mean. It was pretty stressful. Not to mention we had our first fight."

I looked at him, smiling. "We did, didn't we?"

"Yep. But it wasn't too bad."

"No, it wasn't."

John took my hand. "Toni, I have something to ask you?"

I slid to the edge of my chair. "I'm listening."

"I don't know how to say this." He took a deep breath.

I stroked his face. "Take your time."

"Toni, I know we said we would take our time and see how this long distance dating is going to workout. So far I think it's working."

"I agree."

"I was wondering if you felt comfortable enough with me to take it to the next level?"

My eyes bulged. "The next level," I repeated.

"Yes, I would like for us to become exclusive," he continued. "You're a beautiful person inside and out. I see how deeply you love just by watching you with Devon and your mom. I want to be a part of that deep loving."

I was so nervous that I couldn't feel anything on the left side of my body. "But, John, you could have any woman you want. You're smart, handsome, successful"

He cut me off. "Toni, this is not about me, baby. This is about us. I could sit here and list the same characteristics about you. But why state the obvious. I am a man who knows what he wants. What I want is you. I'm ready to give myself to you and love you the way a good woman needs and deserves to be loved. The questions is: Are you ready to let me?"

"Flight 279, nonstop service to Atlanta, Georgia is now boarding at Gate number 5," the announcer warned.

186

"Baby, that's your flight. I need an answer before you step on that plane."

Paralysis had taken over my whole body. The only things I felt I could move were my eyes. So I blinked them very fast, trying to stop the flow of the impending tears. "John...I don't know what to say..."

Mama interrupted. "Toni, baby, they just called our flight."

I didn't take my eyes off of John. "I heard them, Mama."

"Then you better come on. Can I get you two lovebirds to let each other go long enough for me to give John a hug?" She took my hands and coaxed them away from him. "Thanks for your hospitality, John," Mama said, hugging him. "You take care of yourself, and the next time you're in Atlanta, the party is at my house, and I'm doing all of the cooking."

"That's a deal, Linda."

"Call me Mom."

John smiled. "That's a deal, *Mom*."

"Toni, are you coming?"

"No, you go ahead Mama. I'll meet you on the plane."

"Okay, don't get left."

"I won't, Ma."

"You see, baby, even your mother approves. So what's it going to be?"

"This is the final boarding call for flight 279, nonstop service to Atlanta, Georgia, boarding at Gate number 5," the announcer warned again.

"Toni, I'm waiting."

I shook my head yes.

"Is that a yes to my question or a yes, you know I'm waiting?"

"It's a yes to your question."

John picked me up and spun around with me around. "I'm going to make you the happiest woman in the world, sweetheart. I promise you." He kissed me.

"John, you better put me down so I can catch my plane."

"That's right, baby. You better go. Call me when you get in."

"I will. I promise." I blew him a kiss and ran down the corridor to my boarding gate.

"Ma'am, you just made it." The flight attendant said, locking the hatch behind me.

***

"So, what were you and John talking about?"

"Look who's all up in my business," I said to Mama with a smirk on my face.

Mama pinched me. "Girl, don't get smart with me. If it wasn't for me you wouldn't have any business."

"Oh, is that right?"

"That's exactly right. Who do you think created you?"

"God."

"Okay, Miss Smarty Pants, whose body did you come out of?"

"Yours."

"Then that has earned me the right to be all up in your business. Now stop stalling and tell me what all of that was about."

I turned sideways in my seat so that I could see Mama's face. "Mama, John just asked me to be his girlfriend."

Mama's face lit up. "Toni, baby, that's wonderful! What did you say? You did say yes didn't you?"

"Yes! I said yes! Can you believe it? This is my first official boyfriend since the Robert incident."

Mama shook like she had chills. "Don't remind me of that horrible incident. But since we're on the subject, did you tell him?"

"Tell who what?"

"Tell John about your special situation."

"No."

"*Ton—i.*"

"I know, Ma, I just couldn't bring myself to tell him."

"You do intend to tell him, don't you?"

"Eventually."

"What do you mean, *eventually?* You need to tell him immediately...Have you slept with him?"

"No, Ma."

"Well, that's a blessing."

"Mama, would you stop making such a big deal out of this?"

"It is a big deal, Toni!"

"Ma, lower your voice. People are starting to stare."

She whispered, "It is a big deal, Toni. You don't want the same thing to happen again, do you?"

"Of course not."

"Then you can't handle the situation the same way."

"I don't intend to."

"Then what are you going to do?"

"I don't know yet. This is all happening so fast."

"Honey, John is a good man. Don't ruin him. At least try to tell him before you have sex with him. You owe him that much."

"I know. I'm going to have to do something soon. I know sex is going to come up. He has already hinted at to it."

"What man wouldn't have? You are lucky he's been patient this long."

"I know. I just don't want to lose him. I love him, Ma."

"I'm sure he loves you too. If you're honest with him, maybe his love for you will supercede any feelings he may have about your situation."

"Yeah, maybe."

*** 

I spent the rest of the plane ride in silence. I was engrossed in my own thoughts. I have a decision to make that will impact the rest of my life with the man I love. I don't want to make the decision, but I don't have a choice. I know that Mama and Devon are right about me needing to tell John, but I'm scared. The last time I confided in a man, I landed in the hospital. Lord knows I don't want a repeat performance of that again. But John does deserve to know the truth. We all have to play with the hand we're dealt. I guess it's my fault that I chose to reshuffle my cards.

Then there is the issue of Tommy Jones. I mean, really, what in the hell am I going to do with him. I need to call him up and just tell him it's not going to work out. But I never gave him a chance. He didn't get to come visit or spend any time with me in Tallahassee. I'm sure he won't let me off the hook that easy. Well, maybe I'll get lucky, and he will see that this long distance dating is harder than he thought. God, I can only hope. Decisions, decisions...

## Chapter 24
### Realizing a Dream

*Welcome Back, Toni!* The banner hanging over my office door read. I smiled at my staff's thoughtfulness, and went into my office ready to work. After being gone for nearly a week, I figured I had quite a bit of catching up to do. I went in early in order to insure that I would have a few hours to myself--- uninterrupted. The first thing I did was check my messages. All three of my girls were on there, worried about me. I intended to call them from Tallahassee but I could never seem to get around to it. The fourth message was from Tommy.

*Hello Toni. I got your message. But you didn't leave a number for me to return your call. I hope Devon's okay. Call me when you get a chance. Take care of yourself. Beep.*

That's just what I was afraid of. Tommy doesn't sound anywhere close to being ready to give up on me. I don't know how I'm going to get out of our agreement without hurting his feelings.

The next message was from Mr. Santos.

*Hello, Toni. This is Mr. Santos from La Cola. I'm sorry to hear about your friend. I hope everything works out. Please call me as soon as you're back in the office. It's concerning the ad campaign. We've made a decision. Beep.*

Mr. Santos automatically jumped to the top of my "to do" list. He will be the first phone call I make today, followed by my girls, and then Tommy.

While I was organizing my schedule according to the changes Sean had made in my calendar, my cell phone rang. I looked at the Caller ID to see who could be calling me this early in the morning. It was Devon.

"Hello?"

"Hey, Teaser."

"Hey D. Is something wrong."

"No girl. I just called to make sure you got back safely."

"Thanks. Yes, we had a smooth flight. I'm sorry I forgot to call you. I spoke to John briefly and then I went to bed."

"Speaking of John... Did you tell him?"

"No."

"Have you decided when you're going to?"

"No, but if I tell him, it has to be soon. He asked me to be his girlfriend."

"That's good news, Toni! But what do you mean, *if you tell him?* I thought we agreed you would tell him."

"No, we agreed that I would strongly consider telling him, which I am doing. I'm scared of losing him, D."

"I know you are, but he deserves to know. Just remember that. Now I'm going to climb down off of my soapbox and go back to bed. Have a good day at work."

"Thanks. Oh, D, I got a call from La Cola. They've made a decision. I'm calling them first thing this morning. So keep your fingers crossed."

"I'll cross my legs and eyes, too, if you think it'll help."

"That will work, every little bit helps. Talk to you later."

"Good luck."

*Seven a.m..* I have exactly one hour left before this place livens up. I better get busy.

***

Sean walked in carrying a box of donuts and two bushels of sunflowers.

"What are you doing here already?"

"I came in early to get a jump on my day."

"I was going to surprise you with these sunflowers, but you ruined it."

"What a lovely gesture, Sean. I'm sorry. Can I still have the flowers and a donut, too, if you don't mind?"

"Anything else, boss lady?"

"Yes. Get over here and give me a hug." I walked from around my desk and hugged Sean. "Thank you for taking such good care of me, Sean. I appreciate your thoughtfulness."

"It's all in a days work." He beamed, trying to be modest. "I'll get your coffee started, because we have quite a bit of work to do today, young lady."

"I'm way ahead of you." I walked back to my chair and picked up the phone to call Mr. Santos.

"Thank you for calling the La Cola Company; how may I direct your call?"

"Mr. Santos, please."

"One moment."

Butterflies formed in my stomach as I waited for Mr. Santos to answer the phone.

"Miguel Santos speaking."

"Good morning, Mr. Santos, this is Toni Goodwin."

"Good morning, Toni. How nice to hear your voice. How is your friend?"

"He's much better, thank you for asking."

"I'm assuming that the reason you're calling is because you got my message."

"That's correct."

"Would you be available for a meeting today, Toni? I know it's short notice, but I don't like to drag these things out."

"Sure. I'll make myself available."

"Will eleven o'clock work for you?"

"One o'clock would be better."

"Then one o'clock it is. Do you mind coming here?"

"Not at all." *Especially if you are going to award us the contract.*

"Wonderful. Then I'll see you this afternoon. And, Toni...Welcome back."

"Thank you."

As I hung up the phone it felt like my butterflies had taken flight. I jumped up and ran down to the executive restrooms. I was praying that no one was in there, because what I was about to do should not be witnessed by anyone. My nerves had gotten the best of me. I have a meeting today that could set my career on fire. I can't afford to have diarrhea...not now!

I stayed in the bathroom for twenty minutes. Every time I thought I was ready to leave, my stomach would turn against me and hold me hostage. Finally, after several deep breathing exercises and some meditation, I was able to pull myself together and go back to my office.

I spent the majority of the morning walking the floor. I wanted to interact personally with every staff member and tell each one, individually, how much I appreciated his or her hard work on the La Cola presentation. I also wanted to let them know that there was going to be a meeting today between me and the team from Cola, and that when I come back from there, we will have an answer.

When I returned to my office, I had a message on my desk. Mr. Carlton wanted to see me. I went to his office and knocked on the door.

"Come in, Toni."

"Good morning, Mr. Carlton."

"How are you, Toni?"

"Fine, sir."

"Have a seat."

"Thank you."

"Is everything okay with your friend in Tallahassee?"

"Yes, he is going to make a full recovery. Thank you for asking."

"That's good news."

"It sure is."

"Toni, the reason I wanted to see you is because there has been a lot of talk going on around here about you."

I raised an eyebrow. "Really, what kind of talk?"

"Talk about your work ethic."

I shifted in my chair.

"It has been brought to my attention that you are the best thing that has happened to this company in a long time." Mr. Carlton was beaming with enthusiasm. "While you were away, I took the liberty of talking to many of the employees. I selected them randomly and asked them all about you and how they liked working with you. Each and every one of them gave you nothing but praise. They love your hands-on approach. They all said you don't ask them to do anything you wouldn't do yourself."

I smiled.

"That's exactly the type of person I am and that's the attitude I want representing this company. Toni, in the few months you've been here you have constantly proven to me that we made the right decision by bringing you on board. If you keep this up, there is certainly a promotion in your future."

"Mr. Carlton, I don't know what to say."

"You don't have to say anything. Just keep on doing what you're doing. Let your work continue to be your testimony."

"Yes, sir."

"As promised, Toni, I have a little something for you." He handed me an envelope."

"Thank you Mr. Carlton."

"No, *thank you* for running my company like it was your own." He extended his hand.

I rose from my chair and shook hands with him.

"Mr. Carlton, I have a meeting at La Cola today. I believe they have made a decision."

"You want to know what I believe?"

"Sure."

"I believe that decision was made before they left our offices a week ago."

"I hope you're right."

"I know I'm right. Just call it a businessman's intuition."

I nodded my approval and walked out of the door. Before the elevator arrived, I was trying to peek inside the envelope he'd handed me. I knew it had to be my bonus, but I was dying to know how much it was. My guess is tow-thousand dollars. The elevator doors opened and I darted inside. I ripped my envelope open, and I couldn't believe my eyes. It was a check for ten thousand dollars and a note that read:

*Congratulations on landing the La Cola account.*
*You deserve this and a whole lot more.*
*Jeffery*

Mr. Carlton had given me a ten-thousand dollar bonus. I guess now I will take John wherever he wants to go for our pool rematch.

***

Twelve o'clock came before I knew it. I had to gather my nerves and my confidence together and hit the road. The last thing I wanted to be was late for my meeting. I jumped in my car, popped in my Carl Thomas CD, and got on the 285 expressway. I turned my cell phone off because I didn't want anything disturbing my mental groove. I'd planned on using the ride as therapy. I often do that when I'm in high-pressured situations and need to have my game face on. Once I'm in a zone, I'm unstoppable. I always get what I want. And today, what I want is the La Cola account, complete with the Latin Grammy's contract.

I arrived at my destination in forty-five minutes flat. I checked my makeup in the vanity mirror to ensure that it was perfect. I smiled to make sure no food was in my teeth. Then I popped a mint in my mouth to assure that my breath was fresh. I closed my eyes and became still. Then I said a little prayer and got out of the car.

Once I was inside, a voice inside of me said, *Go ahead and claim what's yours, Toni. You worked hard for this and you deserve it.* "Sho' you right," I said under my breath as I approached the receptionist, a petite, brunette with breast implants.

Her demeanor was welcoming. "May I help you?" she asked.

"Yes. I'm Toni T. Goodwin; I have a one o'clock appointment with Mr. Santos."

"Please have a seat. I will let him know you're here."

"Thank you."

"You're welcome. Would you like something to drink while you're waiting? We have coffee, tea, Cola, and water."

"I'm fine, thanks."

"You're welcome. Mr. Santos will be with you momentarily."

I nodded in agreement and smiled.

As I sat there waiting for Mr. Santos, I noticed the latest edition of Essence on the table next to me. I smirked and picked it up. Jada Pinkett Smith was on the cover. The title was "How I Learned to Trust Women." I immediately thought about John. *How would he ever learn to trust me if I don't tell him the truth soon?* I quickly let that thought fade. I couldn't allow my internal dialogue to start speaking to me before I handled my business. So I put the magazine back down. I picked up a gardening magazine instead. Looking at the beautiful flowers and greenery immediately returned me to my center.

"Toni, sorry to keep you waiting."

Mr. Santos' voice startled me. I jumped.

"I'm sorry I didn't mean to frighten you."

I was embarrassed but I insisted on not showing it. "You didn't scare me; I was so captivated by the beauty in this magazine I didn't see you walk up. You caught me off guard. That's all." I placed the magazine back on the table and stood to

194

shake his hand. "Where is Mrs. Slutsky today? Will she be joining us?"

"Yes, she is already in the conference room. Right this way." he instructed.

As we approached the conference room, I recognized it as being the same conference room we'd met in previously with the monochromatic accountants. When I entered the room, there were at least ten people gathered around the huge conference table. I was surprised at the number of people present, but I maintained my cool. I pride myself on never letting them see me sweat. And this time was no exception.

"Toni, come right in," Bill Blackwell said. "It's good to see you again."

"You too, Bill." I affirmed as I shook his hand.

"Let me introduce you to the others. Of course you know Mrs. Slutsky."

"Yes," I shook her hand, smiling. "It's lovely to see you again."

"Likewise," she replied.

Bill continued introducing me to everyone in the room. I smiled and exchanged pleasantries until the last hand had been shaken.

"Toni, please take a seat."

He continued, "As I told you in our previous conversation, I don't like to beat around the bush. I'm a direct person, and I get straight to the point. Well, quite frankly, we have made a decision. And although the competition was tough—-

" *Oh here it comes the moment of truth,*

"our decision was made very quickly and unanimously."

I sat up straight in my chair looking him eye to eye. I was prepared for whatever he had to say to me. I was solid as a rock. *Bring it on Bill I'm ready for you.*

"Toni, it is with great pride that we award Carlton International The La-Cola Company's advertising campaign for the 2003-2004 fiscal year. You all did a phenomenal job. You blew your competitors away."

Bill was elated. Everyone in the room clapped and gave me a standing ovation as our test spot played in the background. I felt like I was in a movie. And in a way I was. I was in the midst of realizing a dream. This is my one moment in time, my finest hour, and I was speechless.

Not for long though. I had one more order of business to discuss with Bill before I could officially celebrate.

"Bill, on behalf of Carlton International, thank you. We worked really hard to earn your confidence. However, I do need to know if this is strictly for the Essence account or have we received the contract for the Latin Grammy Awards too?" I caught a glimpse of Mr. Santos giving me the thumbs-up. "Give 'em hell," he mouthed to me from the back of the room.

I wanted to smile but I couldn't, not on the outside at least. I had to maintain my cool yet assertive composure.

Glee appeared in Bill's eyes before he spoke. "Toni, you never cease to amaze me. You are a tough lady. Yes, you do have the Latin Grammys, and all of our other campaigns for the next year."

I stood up and extended my hand. "Thank you, Bill. This is the best news I've heard all day." Now I was excited.

"You're welcome. I'm anxious to see what other ideas you all will come up with."

"I promise, you won't be disappointed."

"There is not a doubt in my mind. I have all the faith in the world that our advertising dollars will be well spent this year."

"I appreciate your vote of confidence."

"Toni, I know you want to get back to work and make the announcement, so we won't keep you. We can schedule a meeting for next week to iron out the details and sign the contract."

"Great! I'm anxious to let everyone know that our hard work paid off."

"Mr. Santos will escort you out." Bill extended his hand. "Welcome aboard, Toni."

"Thank you."

I went around the room shaking hands and receiving congratulatory remarks. I was smiling so much that I thought my face might crack.

I finished shaking the last person's hand.

"Toni, if you're ready, I'll escort you to the lobby."

"I'm ready Mr. Santos. Lead the way."

We boarded the elevator and Mr. Santos let his professional demeanor slip yet again. But this time, I didn't mind.

"You go, girl!" he said, giving me a high-five. All I could do was laugh. He turned out to be a pretty cool guy after all. "Toni, I want you to know that Mrs. Slutsky and I have been waiting for this day for 15 years. It's about time minorities broke through the corporate ceiling. I'm so glad you were the one to do it."

I knew he was sincere so I extended my arms and hugged him. We were two totally different people who shared the common bond of fighting to stay alive in the struggle. Today, we'd won.

We reached the lobby and were exchanging our goodbyes when Mrs. Slutsky came running.

"Toni, wait!" she yelled.

When she caught up to us, she was breathing hard and sweating. "I have got to start my diet," she mumbled.

We all laughed.

She grabbed me and embraced me. "Congratulations! We were pulling for you." Her eyes danced with excitement. "If you need anything, please call Miguel or myself. We want to make sure you do well. We have a vested interest in your success."

"Thank you. It's good to know you have my back."

"Oh, believe me, we have it." She let her corporate demeanor go, too. "Now give me five, sister." She put her hand out and I laid one on her. I wanted to do my power-to-the-people fist and say, "*Solid*," but I might have scared her to death. Instead I gave both of them another hug and left.

I hopped into my car, put the top down, and got my jam on. At one point, my excitement over took me, and I pulled over to the side of the road, sprang out of the car, and did the cabbage patch. I got so caught up I broke out with the prep too. I was shakin' a tail feather, y'all. I started to *drop it like it's hot*, but I was already starting to attract attention by the side of the road. So I got back in the car and sang....*Go, Toni, you got the account. Go, Toni, you got the account. Go, Toni.....*

\*\*\*

I arrived back at the office, feeling like I was on top of the world. I knew that Sean and everyone else were waiting with baited breath for me to arrive and deliver the verdict. That's when I decided to have a little fun with them. I knew that they would think we didn't get the account. Then I'd make an announcement and surprise them.

"Here she comes, y'all," I heard Sean say.

I kept walking, not saying a word to anyone. I wouldn't even make eye contact.

Sean walked over to me and put his hand on my shoulder. "Toni, is everything okay?"

I exhaled, and looked at the ground. "Yes, Sean, everything is fine." I walked in my office and closed the door behind me. I was in there rollin'. I knew I needed to put them out of their miseries soon. So I opened all ten bottles of the sparkling cider I'd hid in my office this morning. I started filling glasses.

"All right, listen up everybody I'm only going to say this once." I stood in front of my office, looking stern.

People stopped working and gathered around. "Sean, would you activate the intercom for me?" I walked over to his desk and began my speech.

"First I'd like to say I really appreciate the all-out effort that everyone has put forth. We really did our best. But as you know, sometimes your best is just not good enough."

197

Looks of disappointment wrapped around their faces. But I continued with the bit.

"That's why it saddens me to announce that we did not get the Essence Music Festival contract."

A loud *Awww*...enveloped the room and threatened to steal my thunder. "I know you are disappointed, but don't be, because we got the contract for the entire year!" I was bubbling with excitement. "We're doing all of La Cola's advertising for the next year, including the Latin Grammy Awards!"

My staff started jumping up and down and hugging one another. Some of them even cried. I walked to my office and got the sparkling cider. "This calls for a celebration!" I proclaimed, handing Sean the first glass.

Someone turned on some music and we partied. If someone from of the street had walked in, they might have mistaken our office for a club. We danced, drank cider, and celebrated for a little over an hour. Then I announced that everyone could take the rest of the afternoon off. I knew Mr. Carlton wouldn't mind. It would be hard to get any work done with all the excitement. And they were only leaving an hour early.

I stayed until the last employee left, and then I called my girls to arrange a "ladies night" out *on me*.

# Chapter 25
## Putting 2 & 2 together

I called Ebony first because I knew she would know where to go on a Thursday night. My prediction was wrong. Ebony suggested that we call Michelle because she'd mentioned this new club called "The Underground Connection."

"Hey, Michelle, it's Toni and Ebony."

"What's up, *sistah-girls?*"

"Nothing much. We're calling to ask you about that new club you told Ebony about."

"Which one? The Underground?"

"Yeah."

"From what my guy friend told me, it's supposed to be da bomb! He hasn't been there, but he said his boy recommended it. It's a mixed crowd, but he heard that the men sometimes out number the women."

"Now this I have got to see," Ebony suggested. "Let's do it."

"Okay, Michelle, get your drag together; we're going out tonight!"

"Oh yeah, what's the occasion?"

"We're celebrating me landing the biggest contract of my professional career!"

"You got the Essence contract?" she screamed.

"It's even better than that. We got all of La Cola's advertising contracts for the next year, including the Latin Grammy's!"

"*Guuurl*, get out! Are you serious?"

"Yes, it's incredible, isn't it?"

"*Oh, Toni*, I'm so proud of you. You deserve it. Count me in! What time do I need to be ready?"

"I'll pick you up at 8:30p.m.. We'll meet Ebony and Cynt at nine."

"Have you told Cynt your news yet?"

"No. I'm getting ready to call her right now."

"You go ahead. I'll see you in a few."

"Okay, *gurls*, I'll see you all later."

I hung up the phone and dialed Cynt's number. I got her recorder, so I hung up and called her cell phone. She answered on the third ring.

"Hello?"

"Hey, Cynt, what's up?"

"Nothing much, girl, what's happening?"

"Well, I was calling to see if me and the girls could have the pleasure of your company tonight."

"That depends."

"On what? Do you have another offer on the table?"

"You know me, I like to keep my options open."

"Excuse *me* then! I thought you would want to celebrate with your girls, but since it's like that, I guess we will just have to do it without you."

"Hold up, Toni. You didn't tell me what we were celebrating."

"Only me landing the biggest account of my professional career," I humbly submitted.

"Are you kidding me!"

"Cynt, lower the volume on your cell phone; you're killin' my eardrum. And no, I'm not kidding!"

"My bad, Toni. Of course I'll go out with you to celebrate. That's terrific! I didn't mean to rain on your parade. I have been in a funky mood all day."

"Is everything okay?"

"Gurl, it's the usual. Men," we said in unison.

"You got it."

"Then this celebration is right on time. The club we are going to is supposed to be packed with men. You will have the opportunity to see some new meat."

"Count me in. This will give me an opportunity to celebrate your victory and replenish my stock."

"Good. I'll see you there at nine  It's called The Underground Connection. You can call Ebony for directions."

"Will do. See you at nine."

"Bye, Cynt."

I hung up the phone and started piecing together my gear for the evening. Whenever I'm going out with the girls I have to be tight work. Those three sistahs have some of the baddest bodies in the A-T-L, and mine is just as fine, so the competition is always fierce. Brothas are usually falling all over themselves trying to talk to us. We're usually so caught up in our own thing that we don't give them too much play. But after hearing the way Cynt was sounding I am sure that lioness will be on the prowl tonight. The good news is that I have a boyfriend now, so I am out of the rat race. I'll just sit back and let my girls handle their business tonight.

\*\*\*

The clock on my dashboard read 8:55 p.m. We pulled into the parking lot and got out of the car. Ebony pulled up next to me; Cynt pulled in about thirty seconds later. Ebony jumped out of the car, wearing a brown mini dress from the Tracy Reese collection.

Her hoop earrings danced as she ran over to give Michelle and I a hug. She backed up and looked at me.

"It looks like somebody hasn't missed a day in the gym."

I blushed. "You know mama has got to keep it tight to keep up with you three." I was wearing a white Givenchy cotton and Lycra pants suit. The top had bare shoulders and a rhinestone neck. The pants fit like a glove; the waist was embroidered with a rhinestone-studded belt. I set my outfit off with my newest pair of Bandolino sandals and my diamond-stud earrings. I have to agree with Ebony. This sistah was taking no prisoners. I looked fabulous.

"Meow," Ebony hissed at Cynt as she walked over to us wearing a black strapless catsuit.

"Go to hell, Ebony," Cynt hissed back. "Hey, you two?" She hugged and kissed Michelle and I.

"Are we ready to go turn this mutha out, *ladies?*"

"Lead the way, boss lady," Ebony instructed.

We entered the club with a serious presence. But no one seemed to notice. I leaned over and whispered to Michelle. "Your friend wasn't lying about the number of brothas up in here."

Michelle's eyes bugged. "I see," she said, looking at this brotha from his penis to his face. "*Dayum!* He's fine!"

The four of us stood there taking it all in. Any type of brotha you ever wanted to meet was in the club. From the everyday brotha to *THE SUPER FINE-YOU-CANT'T-TOUCH–THIS-OR–YOUR-ASS-WILL-BE–WHIPPED-LOOKING–FOR-ME-IN-THE-DAYTIME-WITH–A-FLASHLIGHT-I-MIGHT-HAVE-TO-GET-A-RESTRAIN-ING-ORDER-AGAINST-YOU-TO-KEEP-YOU-FROM-STALKING-ME-BECAUSE-MY-DICK-IS-SO-DAMN-GOOD-TYPE-OF-BROTHA!* In a word, we were in *PARADISE.*

It didn't take us long to notice that something wasn't quite right in Paradise. Michelle went over to the bar to get her flirt on. She was showcasing her double-D's and that tiny waist of hers in a tiny fitted shirt that revealed her cleavage. Her navel ring sparkled every time the strobe lights hit it. Her fishtail skit hugged her curves and flared out in just the right spot. But not one brotha seemed to notice. Instead they all seemed more interested in what each other had to say.

"Ladies, why don't we get a table." Cynt suggested.

"That's a good, idea." I acknowledged.

We walked across the stage to the opposite side of the club and occupied a booth about three feet from the stage.

"Is it me or is there something strange about the vibe in here?"

"No, Cynt, it's definitely not you," I assured her.

"I'm getting a weird vibe too."

Michelle chimed in, "I know what you mean. Not one brotha offered to buy me a drink when I went to the bar. They don't usually treat me and the girls like that."

"What kind of club did your friend say this was?"

"He just said a mixed club."

"It looks mixed alright. I think these brothas are mixed up."

"What happened to your gaydar, Ebony, it should be screamin' by now?"

"It's not screamin' yet, but it's definitely on high alert."

"Ladies may I take your order?" the mahogany, shirtless waiter asked.

"You can take mine," Ebony volunteered.

"What would you like?"

"Your six pack to go!" She was referring to his perfectly sculpted stomach.

He blushed. "That's very kind of you, but I'm afraid I'm going to have to decline."

"Suit yourself. But you don't know what you're missing."

"Ebony, quit flirting with the man and order your drink, damn!"

She smiled. "Pierre, I'll have a sex on the beach. Thank you." Then she turned and glared at Cynt.

"And what would you like?" he asked, looking at Cynthia.

"A blow job, please."

"He didn't ask what you wanted to give him, heifer. He asked what you would like," Ebony countered.

"Ladies, it's all good," Pierre offered.

I interjected. "That's right, ladies, it's all good. Just chill."

"What are you having?" he asked me.

"I'll take a Miami Vice, please."

"And for you?"

"Hypnotiq, please."

"Thank you, ladies; I'll be right back with your drinks."

Michelle and I smiled at Pierre until he was out of sight. Then we turned to Cynthia and Ebony to find out what was up with them.

"Ebony, what's with you two?"

"Don't ask me, ask her. She's the one that's been acting like a fucking bitch for the last few weeks."

"Cynt. What's the problem? You *have* been a little edgy."

She sucked her teeth and sat there with her arms folded.

"You might as well tell them," Ebony encouraged her.

"I found out the guy I was dating is gay," she wailed as she began to cry hysterically. Michelle and I just sat there with our mouths open.

"What happened? Ebony, tell us what happened," I insisted.

"A few weeks ago Cynt and I went to Stone Mountain to exercise. While we were walking around the mountain we overheard these two men having a conversation. It sounded almost like a lover's quarrel, so we decided to eavesdrop. They were talking about the party they'd gone to the night before. It turned out that the guy Cynt was dating—"

"Which guy?" I interrupted.

"Jamie."

"Not Jamie!" Michelle said

"Yes, Jamie was one of the men talking, and he was chastising the other guy for allegedly flirting with some dude at the party. *Chile*, it was too gay for me."

"What did Cynt do?"

"She stopped, turned around, and confronted him."

"He damn near peed in his pants. There he was standing there face to face with both of his lovers. Honey, the look on his face was priceless. Cynt and *Tyrone* were both standing with their hands on their hips, waiting for him to say something."

"What did he say?"

"He told Cynt that he was sorry, but he was in a relationship with *Tyrone* and that he was gay."

"What did Cynt do?"

"She went sistah-girl on him and went off! She slapped the shit out of his face! Then his sissy-ass boyfriend tried jumping in it with some windmill fist action, and I punched his punk-ass one time and knocked him out. Girls, it was on at Stone Mountain that Sunday."

We rubbed Cynt's back as she sat there with her head on the table. "We're sorry, girl. No wonder you've been in such a foul mood."

"Tell me about it! I have been catching hell from this heifer ever since we caught his ass cheating."

"Why is she taking it out on you?"

"I don't know. I guess because I was there. But she needs to chill, because Ms. Ebony is not going to take too much more of her shit."

We touched Ebony's hand. "Thanks for being patient with her this long, Ebony. It's got to be hard on her."

"I know it's hard. Remember, I've traveled this road already. That's the only thing that's been keeping me from knocking her ass out," Ebony sounded irritated. "I don't know how much more of her attitude I can take."

"Well, now that Michelle and I know, it probably won't be that bad. She can talk to us about it when she needs to vent."

The waiter came back with our drinks and placed them in front of us. "Pierre, we're here to celebrate, so keep them coming. You can run a tab on my credit card." I handed him my Platinum American Express Card.

"No problem. Enjoy the show, ladies."

I grabbed his arm before he walked away. "What show?"

"*The all-male review.* It's starting in five minutes." He smiled then walked away.

"Then let's get this party started!" Michelle shouted over the sound of the music. "Okay, ladies, raise those glasses in the air. I propose a toast. *To the best weave-wearing, perfect-eyebrow-having, tailored-suit-buying, just-sealed-a-hellu-va deal...advertising Vice-President we know.* Toni, congratulations. You are our shero."

*Clink, Clink, Clink, Clink.* Just when we finished toasting, the MC came on to introduce the entertainment for the evening.

"Good evening, Ladies and Gentlemen. It's my pleasure to welcome you to The Underground Connection. If you haven't connected to someone in the underground, then you might be in the wrong part of town. Now sit back and relax. As our first entertainer, Undercover Brother shows you how to be a good lover."

The MC left the stage. The house lights went out. We put our glasses down in anticipation of what was going to happen next. The soulful sultry beat of Maxwell's *Urban Hang Suite* CD played. We sat there in darkness, grooving to the hypnotic melody of Maxwell's voice "*Gonna take you in the room, suga', lock you up and love for days; we gonna be rockin' baby till the cops come knockin'...*"

"*Oooh,*" Ebony sang. The house lights came up. A nine-inch dick was tappin' her on the shoulder. She maintained her suitor's gaze and rocked back and forth snapping her fingers.

He slid his dick down her cleavage. "*Six on a Thursday night 'n you be jonesin,' baby, for brother to hold you tight and keep on going...*

*She* licked her lips, and kept on grooving.

He slid his hand between her legs. "*Gimme a call, it's cool the M's all open, I'm wider than oceans, I'll be your lotion, If it's all right...* "

*Oooooh,*" she sang again, this time struggling to maintain his gaze. She lost the battle when he buried his head between her thighs.

"*Please you, tease you, eat you, make you feel so good inside, loving you long if that's alriiiight...*

"It's alright baby, it's alright!" Ebony shouted.

"Let's give it up for Undercover Brother." The MC announced. Ebony ran to the stage and gave him a twenty and her phone number. She came back to the table clutching her chest.

"*Whew! That was the best orgasm I ever had in a room full of people.*"

Michelle high-fived her. "Girl, you are off the chain!"

"Girl, what was I supposed to do? Let a nine-inch dick tap on your shoulder and see how well *you* handle it. I just took one for the team, that's all." She laughed. " Thanks for the celebration, Toni, and since this night is your treat, you owe me twenty dollars for the tip I gave the stripper."

"I don't pay for my own orgasms, sweetheart; I'm certainly not going to pay for yours. You tried me then!"

"Hey, you can't blame a girl for trying."

The MC came back to the stage to announce the next entertainer.

We continued to sit and enjoy the show, but we couldn't help noticing all of the entertainers had names that were suspect: Closet Lover, Rump Shaker, Dick Teaser, etc.

"Y'all, there is something definitely not right about this club."

"What's up with those names? And why are so many men watching a male review?"

"I'm feeling you on that, Ebony. There has got to be about a hundred fellas and twenty ladies including the four of us. Ordinarily, I wouldn't complain about the men outnumbering the women, but when I send Monique and Unique out to do a job, and we come back empty-handed, something's up."

"I agree with you, Michelle. Even though I'm officially off the market. I'm still checking out the brothas and none of them are trying to talk to any of the women."

"But they aren't holding hands with each other either."

"Ebony, we need to get to the bottom of this, and since you are the bold one in the group, I vote for you to go find out what's up.

"I second that motion."

"I third it," Cynt added. "The last thing I need is to be sitting my ass up in some black male gay club after what I've been through."

Ebony got up from the table. "I can take a hint. Ya'll don't have to beat a sistah over the head. I'll go to the bar and find out what the deal is."

As she made her way through the crowd, Ebony noticed that not one brother tried making eye contact with her. She continued working her way to the bar, making sure her ass rubbed up against dick after dick as she squeezed through the sea of men. Still nothing, not even a pinch on the booty. *Either I'm losing my touch or these fellas are not here to meet anyone with estrogen.* She mumbled under her breath. A hand reached out and touched her on the elbow. *Finally!* She said as she turned around, smiling.

"Excuse me," a baritone voice said.

"Paul? What are you doing here?" She reached over and hugged him.

"A friend of mine told me about this place. So I came to check it out.   "What are you doing here?"

"I'm here with some of my girls. We came here to celebrate."

"What are you celebrating?"

"My girl, Toni, just landed a really big account at work. Come on over to the table so I can introduce you to my friends."

"Sure. Lead the way."

Ebony worked her way back through the crowd. This time, she was not paying attention to whether or not the men were checking her out. She was just excited about seeing her old college boyfriend and introducing him to her girls. As they approached our table, my eyes locked in on the 6'6" walnut-colored elongated version of Adonis standing before me.

I knew him from somewhere.

Ebony beamed. "Ladies, I'd like to introduce you to my friend, Paul. Paul, this is Michelle, Cynthia, and Toni."

"Hello, ladies. It's a pleasure to meet you."

Michelle shook Paul's hand. "Hello Paul. Trust me, the pleasure is all ours," she said as she slid over next to me, and patting the seat next to her.

"Please, have a seat," she offered.

"Is that okay with you, Ebony?"

"Sure, you're welcome to join us."

"Hi," Cynthia said flatly.

I reached over and extended my hand. "Hello, Paul. I'm Toni."

Paul sat his drink on the table and slipped into the booth next to Michelle.

"So, Toni, I hear a celebration is in order. Congratulations on landing that account.

"Thanks."

I continued looking at Paul. I tried hard not to stare, but he was too familiar to me.

"So, Paul, what are you doing now?"

"College recruiting for our alma mater."

"How do you like it?"

"It's pretty cool. I like it. I get to travel a lot, which is nice. As a matter of fact, I was home last week doing some recruiting for my old high school."

"Speaking of home, you know, Toni is from Tallahassee too."

"Oh yeah?" Paul said, smiling. "What high school did you go to?"

"Leon. And you?"

"Jefferson. Your biggest rival."

"Are you kidding me? You went to Jefferson?"

It was finally starting to click. My eyes widened as I sat there looking like a deer in headlights. I was astonished. I couldn't believe that my first love was sitting across the table from me and he had no idea who I was.

"Yep. I was their star basketball player too."

"Okay, Mr. Big Shot Basketball Player, you don't have to bore the ladies with your childhood nostalgia."

"How did the two of you meet?" Michelle quizzed.

"Paul is my old college sweetheart. We were an item right up until I went on

206

line for Sigma Gamma Delta."

I choked on my drink.

"Are you okay, girl?" Michelle asked.

"Yes, I'm fine. I guess my drink went down the wrong pipe. I'm sorry. Y'all, continue with the story."

"There isn't much more to tell. Ebony basically cut a brotha loose for no reason."

Ebony punched him in the arm playfully. "You know you need to stop that."

"You know it's true, Ebb."

"Anyway, let's change the subject."

Paul was looking as good as ever. " Toni, do you get back to Tallahassee often?"

"I've been twice in the last few months. We recently had our ten- year reunion."

"I'd heard about that. I started to go. I had a few friends that went to Leon that I would like to catch up with."

"You should have gone. I'm sure you would've enjoyed it."

"Next time, I guess."

"I don't mean to interrupt, but they *are* playing my song. Ebony, if you don't mind, I'd like to steal Paul away for a minute," Michelle said.

"No, go right ahead."

"Paul would you be kind enough to escort me to the dance floor?"

"It would be my pleasure."

Michelle and Paul made their way to the dance floor, arm in arm.

"Girls, you do realize who that is, don't you?" Ebony whispered.

"Yeah, that's the one you were telling John about isn't it."

"Exactly."

"You mean the one who was bisexual?" Cynthia added.

"Yep. So that explains this club. These brothas are undercover. That's why they aren't trying to holla at the ladies. They're here to see each other. We're intruding on their turf. That also explains why they're not trying to make eye contact; they don't want to be recognized by any of us."

"I'll be damned! That's just what I needed." Cynthia looked disgusted.

"I could have been home watching *The Best Man* and eating a pint of ice cream instead of sitting through this shit. No offense, Ton,i but I'm just not feeling this. Not tonight. I'm leaving."

"I understand." I leaned over and kissed Cynthia on the cheek. "Thanks for coming."

"Toni, I'll make it up to you this weekend. Maybe the four of us can have a girlfriends day at my house."

"That sounds good."

Cynthia leaned over and kissed Ebony on the cheek too. "Sorry for being such a bitch. You know I love you, gurl."

"That's okay; you can't help it! I'm just kidding. I know you didn't mean it. Get home safe."

Cynthia waved goodbye to us as she left the club.

"Ebony, Paul still hasn't come out of the closet?"

"No."

"Does he at least realize that you are on to him?"

"No. I never said a word."

"How did he explain being in this club tonight?"

"He just said a friend of his told him about it, and he came to check it out."

"What a waste. He is such a good-looking man. Too bad he's not interested in women."

"Girl, who are you telling? I still miss Diamond. "

"Who is Diamond?"

"His dick. That's what he used to call it. And *gurl*, that thang was hard enough to cut glass too. "*Umm, Umm, Umm.*" Ebony shook her head.

" I guess our friend Michelle is going to be so disappointed when we tell her."

"Yeah, I noticed she was getting her flirt on."

"Poor thing has no idea he likes men." We laughed.

Michelle and Paul made their way back to the table. They'd worked up a sweat.

"Chile, why didn't you tell me Paul was a dancing machine."

Ebony rolled her eyes. "Girl, he's alright; he ain't all that!"

"What's up with the hatin', Ebb? You could give a brotha some credit?"

"My bad! Michelle, Paul is a pretty good dancer," Ebony corrected. "How was that?"

"Better, but you could ease up on the sarcasm a little."

"Well, ladies and gentleman, I don't know about y'all, but I'm ready to call it a night." I unzipped my purse and pulled out my car keys.

"Paul, would you be kind enough to tell our waiter to close out our tab. His name is Pierre; he has my credit card."

"No problem. I'll be right back."

Ebony leaned in once Paul was out sight.

"Michelle, I have to say this quickly, so listen up. Paul is gay, so you can stop flirting with him. You are not his type."

"What do you mean he's gay?"

"Remember the guy I was telling John about the night we went to Libations? My college boyfriend."

"Yeah."

"Well, duh? Put two and two together, dingy."

Michelle put her hand over her mouth. "Oh shit! Say it ain't so."

"Sorry, honey, but it's so."

Damn! All that fineness going to waste: Maybe he's changed."

"I doubt it, sistah! Look at the club he's in. All of these brothas have got to be undercover. That's why Monique and Unique weren't getting their usual amount of attention. Think about it."

Michelle looked down at her breast, admiring them. "Now you're making sense."

"Speaking of gay men... Where is Cynthia?"

"You know you are wrong for that."

"I didn't mean it like that. But where is she?"

"She left while you were out on the dance floor shaking your groove thang."

"Does she know about Paul?"

"Yeah. I think that's what put the nail in her coffin."

"The poor thing. I can't imagine what she must be going through."

"I can, and believe me it's not fun."

Paul returned and handed me my credit card. "Thanks, Paul, but where is the bill? I need to sign it."

"No you don't. I took care of it for you. A lady shouldn't have to pay for her own celebration."

"Thanks, Paul. You didn't have to do that."

"I know, but it's the least I could do for my homegirl." He smiled.

*He's still a sweetheart.* I stood up and gave Paul a hug and a peck on the cheek. "That was really sweet of you. I enjoyed meeting you."

"Congratulations again, Toni. Maybe I'll run into you in Tallahassee sometime."

"Maybe."

"Thanks for the dance, Paul." Michelle grabbed him and pressed her breast tightly against his chest.

Ebony stood off to the side shaking her head. "Look at this heifer trying to put her titties on him like that's going to change him," she whispered in my ear.

"Michelle, would you let the man go so he can breathe?"

Michelle blushed with embarrassment. "Sorry, Paul."

"Don't be, I like a nice hug."

"Then come over here and give me some for old time sake. Ebony stood with her arms extended.

Paul scooped her up and spun her around like he used to. "It was great seeing you again, Ebony."

"You, too, Paul. Here is my number; keep in touch."

"I will. Goodnight, ladies."

"Goodnight, Paul."

## Chapter 26
## Lover's paradise
## There are two sides to every story
## (Side one)

Sean walked up and slapped Mike on the back. "What's up with you, man? Your game was a little bit off today."

"Fellas, if y'all had some of what I did last night! Man, none of you would be here right now."

Trent pulled up a seat. "By all means, my brotha, enlighten us."

"You know that girl I have been kicking it with."

"Which one? The Vivica Fox look-alike."

"Naw, the fine ass one with the big titties. Michelle."

"*Right, Right.*"

"She called me over to her house to come kick it with her last night. She said she had something for me.

So you know me; *I'm trying to do the damn thang!* So I went out and bought a little insurance policy. To make sure a brotha was going to get to tap that ass."

"*Represent, black man, represent!*" Trent shouted.

"I bought her two dozen roses, a bottle of wine, a box of chocolates, and a card."

"Damn, all that?" Ilandus said.

"Like I said, it was an insurance policy."

"*Go 'head, playa, go' head!*" Danny added.

"So I threw my gear on, made sure I was lookin' right, and rolled on over to her place. I told her I had a surprise for her. She stayed upstairs while I set it up. So I sprinkled white rose petals everywhere, from the living room up the stairs and all in the bed and shit."

"*Damn, dawg, you doin' it like that?*"

"*Hell yeah!* So she came out the room and saw the roses and started smiling. Man, when she hit that last step and I saw her ass, I almost passed the fuck out! She had on this lavender teddy and some thongs with the high heels. Man, y'all know how a brotha is about those high heels and big titties! Her shit was lookin' right! I was ready to rip her back out!"

"*Yes, suh!*" Trent said, laughing.

"So she kissed me and thanked me for the roses and the card and stuff. Then she said we had to play scrabble. So we sat there and played scrabble by candlelight. And it was cool, but after a while we started cheating. We wanted to get that game over with so we could get to the main event."

"*Right, Right.*"

"So when we finished, she took me upstairs and I lingered a little bit behind her because I had another trick for her."

"That's what I'm talking about! *Represent, playa!*" Stan cheered.

"She turned on a little music and told me to have a seat on the couch in her bedroom. Then she started dancing for a brotha. Man I just started throwing money at her. She asked me if I wanted a lap dance. I said hell yeah and pulled out a fifty. I was putting money in her thong and playing with the pussy. Man, I felt like I was back in Miami at the Rolexx."

"*Whaaaaat!!!!!*" The fellas shouted, laughing.

"I was getting loose up in that thang, boy. So then we were laying on the floor, kissing and shit. So I told her to look up. *Dawg, your boy had the chocolate syrup and the whip cream ready to turn her ass into a sundae.*"

"Handle your business, playa! You were ready to eat the pussy, huh, dawg?"

"You damn right! Man, Danny, I had to show her what time it was. She had this big-ass smile on her face and told me to do what I had to do."

Trent started laughing. " I like this girl; she was down for *whatevah.*"

"*What!* Then she said to me after I finished, 'You're not the only one who can make a sundae.' So she told me to lie down. Man, she put that chocolate and whip cream on me and started licking me and shit. *Boy, boy, boy!* I didn't know what to do! She told me she was an amateur, but that night she was head of the class. She slid my dick in her mouth and domed a brotha' up! I had a toe orgasm like Eddie Murphy in *Boomerang!*"

Trent stood up and looked at Mike with a puzzled expression on his face. "*She did you like that, dawg?*"

"*Just like that!* So then we were all sticky and shit, so we went to take a shower. Man, we had chocolate everywhere: on the carpet, the shower curtain-- just everywhere. While we were in the shower, she tells me she wants to have sex in the shower because she had never done it before. I told her *cool.* She reached over and pulled out a condom from the cabinet and handed it to me. *Man, I had to high-five her!* That sistah was handling her business. So I bent her ass over and gave her a spinal tap like a real playa would. I was straight up tearing that ass up from the back.

So then we finished showering and went in the room. We drunk a little wine and did a little toast. And then you know what time it was. I pulled back the covers; and she saw those rose petals and it was on! Man, that night started at 10:30 p.m. and didn't end until about four in the morning. We went through five condoms! Now *that,* my brothas, was a night to remember."

Trent stood up and gave me some dap. "You represented, black man!"

Stan followed suit. "For real, tho."

Danny patted me on the back. "Yeah, dawg, you handled your business."

Ilandus asked, "How can I be down?"

"Well, now we know why your game was off," Sean added.

"By the way, Sean, she said she and her girls went to that club you said Jamie told you about. She said something wasn't quite right up in there."

"Mike, man, does she have any friends?"

"I'm glad you asked, Trent. I've done all of you a big favor. We are going to have a get together with the six of us and some of her girls before the cool weather kicks in. Sean, I told her you had a girlfriend. So if you want to bring Jamie, so the fellas can finally check her out, it's all good."

"Naw, man, that won't be necessary. We broke up last week."

All of the boys raised their glasses in a toast. "Then welcome back to the game, dawg."

# Chapter 26
## Lover's Paradise
## (Side two)

"Ladies, are y'all ready for this? Come in, sit down, and get ready to take notes."

"Damn, Michelle, what's up? You glowing and shit."

"You'll find out soon enough, Ebony. Now have a seat. As we all know, I had been kickin' it with that new guy, Mike, for a minute. Well, last night I decided to give him some. But I didn't want this to be no ordinary sex thang. I wanted to show him how the big girls do it. So I decided to start my own sexual revolution."

"*Oh shit*, what did you do?" Ebony asked, covering her mouth.

"Okay, Michelle, you're scaring me," Toni added.

"Girl, get to the good part; you have all of our undivided attention. Toni, pass me the chips and a Corona for this one."

"Well, ladies, it went a little something like this: I called him up and told him to come over and hang out with me. He had no idea what I had in store for him. I had my entire house lit only by candlelight. I also had all of my CD players cued to the exact songs I wanted played in each room. I had Glenn Lewis for the living room, Kem's *Kemistry*, for the shower, and Brian McKnight for the bedroom. I had all of my bases covered.

So when he arrived, he called from his cell phone and told me to unlock the door and ordered me to stay in the room until he told me to come out. So I was like, *oh shit*, a brotha with a plan. So you know me, I can go with the flow, so I indulged the brotha. He came in and I stayed in the guest room while he did his thang. About ten minutes later, he knocked on the door to let me know he was ready. I told him to go downstairs and have a seat. I walked over to the door and opened it. To my surprise, this brotha had a trail of rose petals going all the way down my staircase through the foyer and out to the living room where I had the Scrabble game set up. Honey, I thought I was in *Coming to America* and he was King Jofe Joffer!

"*Girl, you need to stop!*" Toni laughed.

"So anyway, I walked down the stairs, and when I got to that bottom step, that brotha's eyes lit up like a fireworks display. He was like 'oh my god, you look so damn good!' I have to admit I was tight work that evening. I had on a new outfit from Victoria's Secret, complete with a matching thong. I had on some stilettos and my weave was hooked! But I have to give the brotha his props too. He was looking rather fly with his fresh haircut and Ralph Lauren outfit. He'd bought me two dozen long stem roses, a bottle of wine, a box of Godiva chocolates, and a really nice card to commemorate the occasion. He had it all nicely set up and

214

waiting for me when I got downstairs."

"I ain't mad at him!" Cynt added. "*Shit*, if he's doing it like that. You should find out if he has a brother or a friend of like mind?"

"I'm with you, Cynt. Girl, find out if he has two. Hook your sistahs up, please!"

"Don't worry, I got you. But let me finish the story. So anyway, we played Scrabble for about an hour. Then we started cheating because we wanted to hurry up and get to act two. So after I won the Scrabble game, I led him upstairs to my bedroom. I noticed he was lingering behind me but I figured he was just admiring the view. So I didn't think anything of it. I went in the room and hit the play button on the CD remote and told the brotha to have a seat on the couch.

I asked him if he had some money, and he pulled out a wad of cash. So I started dancing. I told him my name for the evening was Seduction. And seduce him I did. Mama was working it, ladies. I asked him if he wanted a lap dance and the brotha pulled out a fifty-dollar bill. So I gave him his money's worth. Then I slid on to the floor and grabbed both of my ankles and was spread eagle with my legs up in the air. He looked at me and then looked up at the sky and said 'Thank you God'. He leaned near my pussy and started putting money in my thong. I looked at him and said, 'This is how the thirty and older sistahs do it'. He couldn't help but smile. We started kissing, and all of a sudden he stopped and looked up, so I was lying there wondering what he was looking at. He nodded his head for me to look up too. Y'all, let me just say there is nothing like a man with a plan. That brotha had snuck in the chocolate and whip cream on me. I was so damn proud of him. I said, 'You go, boy! I'll be your sundae'".

Ebony jumped up and high-fived me. "*He better work it!*" she shouted.

"And work it he did. At first, I told him maybe we should get on the bed, because I didn't want him to mess up my Berber carpet with the chocolate. But then he assured me not one drop would leave my body and if it did he would pay to have my carpet cleaned. I couldn't pass up a deal like that, so I told him, 'handle your business, black man!'"

"And did he?"

"Toni, that brotha licked his plate clean! Not one drop left my body for any place other than his mouth."

"Well hot damn, you know I like a man who keeps his word!"

"Me too. However, y'all, I have to admit that I got a little caught up after that. I told him he wasn't the only one who could make a sundae. I got the chocolate and whip cream, and I sprayed it on him. Chile, let's just say I am still getting chocolate out of my hair and off of the carpet. I made somewhat of a mess, and all we could do was laugh and go take a shower, because we were so sticky."

"Okay, Michell. I'm going to need you to tighten up on your sundae making skills," Ebony insisted.

"For real. My sistah, you can't be embarrassing us like that."

"I'm working on it, Cynt. But may I finish my story please?"

"Keep going, girl."

"As I was saying, we got into the shower and while we were in there, I told him I always wanted to do it in the shower but never had because I always forget the condoms. He asked me, 'so what's up with tonight?' I told him, I'm one step ahead of you, brotha! I reached over and pulled a condom out of the bathroom drawer. He was so impressed, the brotha high-fived me and said, 'handle your business, sistah!'

So I assumed the position, and we got to work. After the shower was over, we went back to my room and had a little toast to new beginnings. Then he pulled back the covers to reveal the rose petals, and it was on. We were rockin' until about 3:30 this morning. We fell asleep in each other's arms and stayed there all night long. This morning when we woke up there was a rainbow of condoms in the trash: red, yellow, blue, green, and orange. Ladies, it was all good!"

"I'll, drink to that!"

"Hell, Ebony, you'll drink to anything."

"Girl, you showed out!"

"It sounds like y'all had a lot of fun. I think I'm going to have to take a page out of your book the next time me and John hook up."

"You mean you're finally going to give that man some?"

"Don't act so shocked, Cynt. I've been seriously thinking about it."

"It's about time you let somebody come in and sweep out those cobwebs."

"Dang, what's this, gang-up-on-Toni-night?"

I put my arm around Toni. "No it's not. We just think its time for you to stop acting like a born again virgin and get your freak on like the rest of us. Speaking of which: Cynt and Ebony, remember when you two asked me if he had any brothers or friends."

"Yep, what you got for us?"

"Calm down, Ebony. Mike and I are going to host a post Labor Day jam. We're only inviting his boys and my girls."

"Well, do I still get to come even though I have a man?"

"Of course you do. You can even bring him if you want to. He mentioned that one of his friends has a girlfriend that he may want to bring."

"Thanks for the hook up, girl. I know I'm ready to meet some new men."

"Me too. Some new *straight* men that is."

"Don't worry, Cynt. They are all straight. I already asked that question."

"Good lookin' out."

"You know I got you."

"So when is the party?"

"It's the last weekend in the month, so that gives you two weeks to tighten up."

"Girl, speak for yourself. I have been sticking with my Shemar workout program. Everything on me is tight."

"Well on that note, I guess we can get our spades game started. Toni, deal the cards."

# Chapter 27
## Lover's Quarrel

I know by now you're starting to wonder what's up with me. I hope you're paying attention because I'm only going to tell this story once. My name is Sean, and I am a closet homosexual. There. I said it. Are you happy now?

I guess I can't just leave you hanging like that without at least giving you a little bit of my history. As you already know, I come from a hard working family. My father has about as much testosterone as any man can get, so if he ever found out about my lifestyle it would kill him. That's why I've been hiding it from my parents my entire life.

I've known I was gay since I was old enough to know the difference between boys and girls. I knew I was a boy and that I was supposed to be attracted to girls, but I wasn't. Boys turned me on. I often caught myself peaking at them in the locker room when they weren't looking. Whenever one of my teammates patted me on the butt to say *good job*, I found myself liking it a little too much. I even fantasized about them as I masturbated. Now don't get me wrong. I like women, but I am just not sexually attracted to them.

Growing up, I tried forcing myself into the stereotypical macho role that was expected of me. I dated women and talked shit about them like most men do. And from the outside I looked the part. On the inside I was dying. I felt my soul slowly melting away like candle wax as I continued to suppress my desires. I was getting burned out.

My father signed me up every year for optimist football, basketball and baseball. He taught me how to play golf when I was eleven years old. By the time, I was six-teen years old, I excelled in every sport I played. That was my way of dealing with my repressed sexuality. I became an overachiever in both athletics and academics. In some ways, it backfired on me because I received more attention than I wanted, especially from girls.

My senior year in high school, I was captain of the basketball team. I led us to the national title. I was voted best all-around and most likely to succeed by my senior class. I maintained a four-year relationship with a lovely young woman named Tasha. I even had sex with her. She was my first. We broke up when I went to Morehouse and she went to Harvard. I was so relieved.

One of the reasons I chose Morehouse, aside from it being a phenomenal, historically black college, was because it was all male. I don't mean that in a sexual kind of way. I mean that in a I-could-finally-feel-comfortable-in-my-own-skin kind of way. I figured by going to school with all men I wouldn't have as much pressure on me to date someone from campus.

Everybody's girlfriend went to a different school. So nobody would really know

218

if I was dating someone or not.

I did date while I was in school, though. I dated Leslie. He was attending Georgia Tech at the time. I generally like men with unisex names. That way, I can talk about them to my boys and they always think it's a woman. Especially Mike. He's been my roommate and my boy for so long, and he has absolutely no idea that I'm gay. I started to tell him one time. But I lost my nerve when I heard him say that he hates faggots. Even though I knew he was just blowing off steam because a guy had just tried him. I knew I couldn't take the chance of losing him as my best friend. So whenever Mike or any of the fellas pressure me about meeting my lady, I either say we just had a fight or I get my good friend Jackie to hook me up with a friend of hers for the evening. So far I've been successful. However, I'm always nervous that one day my luck might change.

It almost happened a few weeks ago. My partner Jamie and I went to Stone Mountain to walk and talk. It's a pretty popular spot in Atlanta to go and exercise or just hang out. We like going there because it's easy to go unnoticed. Most people are so busy doing their own thing, nobody is paying attention to us. Besides, gay men in Atlanta are like black women wearing weave. You see it so much that it becomes the norm.

Well on that particular day, Jamie and I were having a fight. We got into it about him accusing me of flirting with this guy at a party we'd gone to the night before. I was trying to explain to him that the guy came on to me. The ladies walking in front of us stopped and turned around and confronted Jamie. Apparently, Jamie had been leading a bisexual life style without my knowledge.

So there he was face to face with two of his lovers. He did admit to the lady that he is gay, and she slapped him so hard we all started fighting. The one thing my father forgot to teach me was how to fight. So I can't really say I was holding my own. I'm fairly manly in every other aspect of my life except fighting. Fortunately no one has ever tried me. Needless to say, after all of that drama, Jamie and I broke up. The irony of the situation is that Jamie was accusing me of being deceptive when he was deceiving both of us. So now I'm just laying low.

I guess it is all working out for the best because about a week ago, I was hanging with the fellas and Mike told us he is having a party. He had invited a group of young ladies to come over. He told me I could bring Jamie, and just like always, we'd just broken up. So I managed to dodge that bullet again. My plan is to go to the party and socialize with the women like I'm a straight man. If they offer me their numbers, I'll take them but I won't call them.

I mingle really well in mixed company, so no one will suspect anything. From the outside looking in I appear to be a charming, well-dressed ladies man. *Um,* if only they knew. I sincerely hope Mike doesn't try to hook me up because if he does, that's where I will have a problem. Even though he means well, if Mike sets me up with someone, he will constantly call me to check our progress. If I tell him she's not my type then he'll interrogate me as to why she's not my type. Then he'll eventually give up and set me up with someone new and start the process all over again. I know there will be more guys than girls at this party, so I'm going to arrive late and hope by the time I get there that everybody has already paired off. I'll be home free and able to enjoy myself.

## Chapter 28
### It's party time

I ran up to Devon and grabbed him the moment I laid eyes on him. He was kind of hard to miss, wearing a wide-brimmed pink hat. "D, you look great!" I yelled, squeezing him tightly.

"Thanks, girl. I see you still have good taste. But do you think I'm overdoing it with this hat?"

"I know you didn't just ask me that, Diva."

"Yes, I did, so answer me."

I shifted my weight to my left leg and placed my hands on my hips. "Yes, you are overdoing it."

"Good, that's what I was hoping you'd say." He pinched my cheek, smiling. "That means I still got it."

I extended my arms to D again. "Oh, D, you are so crazy. Give me another hug. I'm so glad you're back to normal. You gave us quite a scare."

"Chile, I scared everybody including myself. Do you know how many people would be put out of work if I decided to leave this earth? Honey, I got flowers from my dry cleaners, my tailor, my hairdresser, my cleaning service, the *entire* mall, my travel agent, the limo service, and the country club-- just to name a few. Girl, those people thought they were all going to lose their best costumer. Every card read '*get well soon and receive 50% off!*'" D laughed.

"I know you're lying now."

"Would I lie about a thing like that?"

I folded my arms and looked Devon in the eyes. "Yes."

"Okay I would, but not this time," he said, laughing. I even brought one of the cards with me so you could see it."

"Then you can show me when we get home. Right now we need to get all of your luggage in the car and try to beat this rush hour traffic."

We placed three of D's bags in the trunk. He had to put the fourth one in the front seat with him.

"How long are you planning to stay?"

"A week at the most."

"Then don't you think four bags is a *little* excessive?"

"Girl, look who you're talking to. I don't believe you tried me like that."

"You're right; forget I asked."

"*Oh, honey,* will you look at the traffic! I didn't know traffic in the ATL was this bad?"

"It's terrible. I was hoping we wouldn't get caught in it, but your plane delay threw us off schedule."

"Did you have something planned for us?"

"No, not tonight. I figured we would do our ritual. I already have our ice cream and movie waiting for us. We need to catch up."

"You're right about that. I need to hear all about you landing that La Cola account."

"And I need to hear about you and Roger."

"Oh, before I forget to tell you. Tomorrow we're going to a post Labor Day pool party, so I hope you brought something cute to wear."

"Everything I buy is cute, Ms. Thang."

"My bad! Well do you have something appropriate for a pool party?"

"Actually I did bring a cute little something with me that should be perfect for the party. But I would like to go to the mall to buy some new sunglasses."

I got off the highway in Buckhead. I figured it made more sense to go to the mall now and get it out of the way, rather than sit in rush hour traffic for an hour.

"D, since we're near Lenox Mall, let's just go now and get it out of the way. That way, we can kill two birds with one stone. You can get your sunglasses, and we won't have any traffic to deal with when we leave."

"Sounds good to me. Is this a popular mall? Will there be a lot of brothas there?"

"More than likely. It's a pretty hot spot."

"Ooh, chile, lead me to the mens."

"Okay, D, behave yourself and quit clapping."

"Why? I came here to have a good time, and behaving myself is not on the agenda!"

I just sat there shaking my head. " D, what am I going to do with you?"

"Walk faster so I don't miss anything. Come on Ms. Thang, *hustle.*"

D and I walked every square inch of the mall. I think D spent more time looking at men than looking at glasses. The funny thing is the men were looking at him too. Now, granted, Devon is over six feet tall with perfect skin. Every woman I know wishes she had his eyelashes and cheekbones. He is quite simply a good-looking man. So even if he wasn't as flamboyant as he is, he would still turn a lot of heads. However, today I think he's getting so much attention because of that hat. I tried to convince him to leave it in the car, but he wasn't having it. One lady walked up to him and asked him where he got it and how much he paid for it. A group of sissies walked up to him and started giving him major props. They even invited him to hang out with them while he was in town.

They promised him free drinks all night long if he decided to go to the club with them. D was loving every bit of the attention he was getting. The whole time we were in the mall, he kept flashing that killer smile. Person after person stopped to talk to him. Our one-hour trip to the mall turned into three hours and four telephone numbers. By the time we left there, my dogs were beyond barking. They were howling, and D still didn't have any sunglasses.

*** 

"Home at last!" I shouted as I turned the lock on my front door.

"Oh, quit overreacting, heifer! We weren't in the mall that long."

"Is that so? Then how do you explain the three runs I have racing down my pantyhose. Not to mention my feet. These things are so swollen they look like Flintstone feet. I think you've ruined my pedicure."

"Girl, soak those things in the foot fixer while we watch the movie and they'll be as good as new."

I shook my keys at D. "They'd better be or else."

"Or else what?"

"I haven't thought of that part yet, but there will be hell to pay, trust me."

"Yeah, yeah, yeah, look here, Wilma, are you going to show me around Bedrock, or do I have to give myself a tour of your new pad."

"It's not new anymore, I've been here for ten months now."

"Well it's new to me. I haven't been here at all."

"Give me two of your bags, and I will show you to your room and give you the grand tour all at once."

I took D room by room throughout my four-bedroom house. I showed her my den first. It's my favorite room in the house. I have everything I need right at my fingertips, from my 52" projection TV and entertainment center to my fireplace and mini refrigerator.

"Girl, I love this room. It has such warm undertones."

"Thanks. It's my favorite place to be."

"I can see why, but you know you're wrong for the refrigerator."

"Girl, that's the best thing I could have done. The kitchen is up the stairs and on the other side of the house. When I'm down here chillin' and need something to drink or snack on, I can just walk over there and get it rather than climb a flight of stairs and walk another thirty feet to the kitchen."

"It still seems lazy to me but I guess you have a point."

"Call it what you want; I call it convenience. Come on, let me finish showing you the rest of the house."

I took D back upstairs to the main floor and across the hallway to the kitchen.

"Toni, I love this kitchen! Check you out with the stainless steel accents! Oh and look at this island. I always wanted a kitchen with an island."

223

"You have the money and the space; install one."

"I never thought about it like that, but you're right; I can have one installed. I'm going to have to put that on my things to do list when I get back home."

"Come on let me show you my office and the workout room."

I have a passion for cherry wood furniture. My home office is almost an exact replica of my office at work. I have a picture-perfect cherry wood desk, with a high-back Italian leather chair, just like the one I ordered for my office at work. The difference is the fountain and the music. My fountain at home is more of a waterfall that stands about five feet tall and is built into the wall. The music in my home office is strictly Jazz. At work I rarely have time for music, and when I do listen to the radio it's usually R&B. I listen mostly for the commercials so I can hear what kind of ads are out there.

"I like what you're doing with the gym. Having the TV mounted to the wall is perfect for using the treadmill or riding the bike. But what's up with the punching bag? Don't tell me you're thinking of becoming a man again?"

"Very funny, D. No, I'm not thinking of becoming a man again. I read recently that a lot of celebrities are using boxing as a way to stay in shape. I just thought I'd give it a try."

D clutched his heart. "*Whew*, you had me worried for a minute."

"Are you ready to go upstairs to the bed rooms, drama queen?"

"Lead the way."

I took D to the guest room, so we could put his stuff down.

"This is your room, D. Please make yourself comfortable."

"Did you decorate this room in pink just for me?"

"Who else?"

"That's so cute! Thanks, Toni."

"You're welcome. Come on, let me show you how real queens sleep."

I opened the wooden double doors to reveal my master suite. The paint on my bedroom walls is a creamy café au lait. The warm neutral color is just right for all four seasons. My huge sleigh bed is nestled comfortably on the right side of the room. It's positioned perfectly for admiring my lake front view. Situated in the opposite corner of the room is my pride and joy-- the custom-made bookshelf, aligned with my favorite books.

"Now this is a cozy little nest you have here, Ms. Goodwin. Too bad you aren't sharing it with a man on a regular basis."

"Don't speak too soon."

"*Gurl*, don't tease me like that. What are you planning?"

"Nothing yet, but I have been seriously thinking about giving John some."

"It's about time! Did you tell him your secret?"

"No."

"But you will, before you have sex with him, won't you?"

I walked away from D and plopped down on the bed. "D, we've been through this before. I'm not sure when or if I'm going to tell John. You need to get off of my back about it."

"I'm not trying to sound like a nag. But if you lie to a man about your sexuality, then you're challenging his. The results of your actions could prove fatal. Do you want that?"

"Of course not, D. However, I don't want to lose the man who could possibly be the love of my life, either. Everything has gone so smoothly between John and I, and I don't want to risk ruining it by telling him."

"Maybe you won't. John is a sensible man. He may be cool with it. Then again maybe he won't. But you will never know until you tell him. You've got to tell him Toni."

"No, I don't! What he doesn't know can't hurt him."

"Are you sure about that?"

"What's that supposed to mean?"

"Suppose you and John get married without you telling him. What happens when John tells you he wants children?"

"I'll tell him I'm barren, I can't reproduce."

"Assuming he buys that. How are you going to explain the fact that you don't even have a period?"

"I'll tell him I had my plumbing removed a few years ago."

"Do you really expect him to believe that?"

"Sure, why wouldn't he?"

"Give me a break. Would you believe it?"

"If the woman hasn't given me a reason to think otherwise, sure I'd believe it."

"Okay, I see you have this all figure out. So I'll just leave it alone."

"Good. Can we at least go and enjoy our movie ritual?"

"Of course we can. But tell me something, Toni. Have you asked John how he became such good friends with a gay man?"

"Yes. What's your point?"

"What did John say?"

"He never really answered the question. Why? What are you getting at?"

"My point is that if you find out why John is so accepting of Roger, you may be able to determine how accepting he would be of you if he knew the truth. Just something for you to think about."

"You make a good point. Maybe I'll try asking him again."

"Good. Now we can go exhale."

"I'll race you to the den."

"Honey, you're talking about running down two flights of stairs. I concede defeat. You win."

"Oh, D, don't be such a wimp."

"Sticks and stones honey. Sticks and stones."

\*\*\*

"D, I'm leaving without you!" I shouted from the bottom of the stairs. We were running about thirty minutes late for the party. Michelle had just called me for the third time.

"Girl, what is taking you so long?"

"I'm waiting on D to get his drag together."

"Girl, tell him it's not that serious and come on."

"Honey, you don't know him like I do. It is that serious."

"How much longer do you think he's going to take? We're ready to get the spades tournament started."

"Wait for us. We're going to leave right now."

"Okay, tell D we can't wait to meet him."

"Did you tell Mike that D was coming and that he's gay?"

"Yeah. He said as long as D doesn't hit on any of his boys everything will be cool."

"I'll make sure I tell D to behave."

"Good. Now hurry up and get here."

"Alright, I'll see you in a few."

I hung up the phone and grabbed my keys and beach bag off of the counter.

"D, this is your last boarding call. The Toni T. Goodwin train is pulling out of the station."

D appeared at the top of the stairs with his hands on his hips. "Heifer, what is your problem? How am I supposed to get myself together if you are constantly screaming my name?"

"Look, Diva, you better come on before I leave you."

"Chile, what is your rush?"

"Michelle has called me three times, they are waiting on us."

"Good, then I can make a hell of an entrance."

"Keep it on the low. D, all of the men at the party are heterosexuals. Please don't flirt with any of them."

"Don't worry, I'll control myself. I'm not trying to cause any problems."

"Good. Let's ride."

We got to Mike's house in twenty minutes flat. The moment we pulled into the driveway, the door swung open, and Ebony ran up to the car. Before I had the

226

opportunity to introduce them, Ebony leaned into the car and screamed, "Devon, I have been dying to meet you!"

D looked her up and down. Then flashed those killer dimples and said; "Let me guess-- you must be Ebony?"

"In the flesh. Now get out of that car and give me a hug."

Devon hopped out of the car and scooped Ebony up into his arms.

"Um, you're a good hugger. I like that."

"I'm good at a few other things, but we won't get into that," Devon joked.

"D, you promised," I said, pinching him.

Ebony hit me on the arm. "Oh, Toni, let the man have his fun."

Michelle stuck her head out of the door. "Are y'all going to just stand out here talking or come inside so we can get this party started?"

"Say no more; we're coming."

We walked over to Michelle, and I gave the introductions.

"Michelle, this is my favorite person in the whole wide world. This is Devon."

Michelle extended her hand.

"Girl, are you kidding me? Toni talks about the three of you so much, we're practically family. Give me a hug."

"I'm so glad you said that. I'm a hugger too. But I didn't want to intrude on your space. You know some people are funny about that."

"Well, honey, I'm not one of those people."

"It's good to finally meet you, Devon. Come on in. We were just getting ready to start a spades tournament."

"Michelle, why don't you introduce us to everyone first," I suggested. "I like knowing the names of the people I'm going to beat up on before I play them."

A handsome brotha started walking my way. "That sounds like a challenge to me, fellas. You must be Toni."

As he extended his hand, I noticed the Ralph Lauren watch. Bingo! "Yes, I am, and you must be Mike." I smiled as I shook his hand. Then I turned to introduce Devon. "Mike, this is my friend, Devon."

D gave Mike a very firm handshake. I could tell he was trying his best to be masculine. I smirked as I watched the exchange.

"Good to meet you, Devon."

"Likewise."

"Okay fellas, listen up. Now that all of my girls and our friend Devon are here, I'm going to go around and introduce everyone."

"Hold up Michelle, we are still short one person. I'm waiting on my roomie to get here."

"So should we wait for him or can I continue?"

"I guess you can go ahead; he'll just have to introduce himself when he gets here."

"Trent, Ilandus, Stan, and Danny. This is Toni, Ebony, Cynthia and our boy, Devon."

Everyone shook hands or hugged. Cynthia eased over to D. "My, you're even better looking than Toni described. I'm Cynthia."

"I knew who you were without introduction. Toni described you perfectly."

"I hope that's a compliment."

"It is. You are a lovely woman."

"Thank you." Cynthia blushed. "How long do we get to keep you in Atlanta?"

"I'm considering staying for a week."

"That's great! Me and the girls have been waiting far too long to meet you. We were hoping we'd all get a chance to go out. From what Toni says, you are the life of the party."

"I can see that Ms. Toni has been telling all of my business." Devon smiled.

"Only the good stuff," Cynthia whispered.

"If you are finish flirting with Devon, we need to go take these boys out on the card table."

"Are you coming, Devon?"

"No, you girls go ahead. I'm going to get me a drink and chill."

"If you need anything, just holler, D."

"I will."

Michelle and I teamed up against Mike and Trent. Ebony and Cynthia played against Stan and Danny. Ilandus sat there and watched us talk shit.

"Michelle, I hope you're ready to put it on them. We need to whoop these fellas."

"I got your back, sistah. It looks like a Boston to me."

"Trent, these ladies are talking much trash. I think we're going to have to school them."

"*For sho!* Deal the cards, partner."

Mike dealt the cards and they beat us the first hand. But once we got warmed up we beat them mercilessly. Ilandus couldn't bear to watch his boys get spanked, so he went into the den to watch TV with Devon.

"Who's winning?" Devon asked.

"The ladies are. I couldn't bear to watch the slaughter."

"That's my Toni. She's a pretty mean card shark."

"I heard *that*. Is she your lady?"

"No, just my best friend."

"That's a fine best friend you got there. Are you sure you're not tapping that...?"

"Definitely not. We grew up together."

"Cool. That means I can holla at her."

"Hey, man, we're all adults here. Handle your business."

"I will. Thanks, Devon. Ilandus got up and went back into the living room. "Are you ladies finish beating up on my boys?"

"*Awww, man,* how are you going to play us? Trent, you see how Ilandus has turned on us."

Trent's brown eyes peeked over the top of his beer bottle. "I'm checking him out."

Mike shook his head. "And I thought we were boys."

"We are boys. I'm not turning on you, dawg. I'm just stating the obvious."

"It looks more to me like you're trying to impress the ladies."

Michelle and I looked at each other and smiled.

Ilandus continued. "What's with the playa hatin', fellas? It's all good."

Mike picked up Michelle's hand. "I know it is. My lady is sitting right here at the table with me."

"Look, man, if you want to play, you can take my spot. I need another beer anyway." Trent got up to leave the table. "I'll be back for a rematch, ladies. Don't think you are going to get away with that injustice?" He smiled revealing the braces on his bottom teeth.

"You know where to find us when you're ready," Michelle said.

"*Oh,* so it's like that?"

"Just like that!" I assured him.

"Then it's on. I hope you ladies don't have any other plans for today, because we're going to have to spank that ass!"

"Don't mess around and get spanked," I flirted.

Michelle looked at me and winked. She knew I was flirting. I knew it too but I couldn't help myself. It's a female thang. I'm sure he's not taking me seriously.

"Michelle, it's looks to me like Trent is writing a check he might not be able to cash."

"I'm feeling you on that, my sistah."

We looked at each other and shouted, "Girl power!" and gave each other a high-ten. "It's awfully quiet on that other table. Cynthia and Ebony, I hope y'all are representing."

"Trust me, we're holding it down," Ebony said.

"Yeah, we should be wrapping this up in less than five minutes," Cynthia added, laughing.

"Dang, Stan and Danny, are y'all going to let them handle you like shorties?"

"Unfortunately, Mike, man, we may not have a choice."

\*\*\*

229

After Michelle and I beat up on Ilandus and Mike, I took a break to check on Devon and to get something to drink.

"Are you enjoying yourself, D?"

"More than you know."

"What do you mean by that?"

He leaned toward me and whispered, "I met somebody."

"What do you mean you met somebody? I told you all of the men here are straight."

D raised one eyebrow and looked at me. "Are you sure about that?"

"Yeah. That's what Michelle told me. Besides, I've met all of them, and my gay-dar has not gone off at all."

"You haven't met the guy I'm talking about. He came in while you were playing cards."

"Where is he now?"

"In the bathroom. He'll be back in a minute. Wait here with me so you can meet him."

"What makes you think he's gay? Did he try to hit on you?" I whispered.

"No, I don't think he's open about it, but I feel it in my soul. I just know he's family."

"If you say so." I shrugged.

"*Shhh*, here he comes now."

As I lifted my head and focused my eyes on the image before me, time came to a crashing halt. I couldn't believe it!

"Toni! What are you doing here?" I looked at him, speechless.

Devon looked confused. "You two know each other?"

"We more than know each other; Toni's my boss."

Devon looked at me with a look that said, *say something.* So I did. "Hey, Sean."

"I didn't know you knew Mike," he said.

"I don't. I'm a friend of Michelle's."

"Oh, I get it. These are your girlfriends who you're always talking about."

"So, is this the Devon that was in the hospital not too long ago?"

"Yes."

"Wow! It's a small world."

"Yeah, *too small.*"

Sean put his arm around me. "Devon, you gave this lady quite a scare. She fainted when she heard something happened to you."

"*Really!* Toni, you didn't tell me that."

"I guess I forgot." I tried snapping myself out of the trancelike state I was in. I knew I had to get out of there. "Well, I was on my way to get something to drink; can I get either of you something."

"No, I'm cool. Thanks," Sean said as he took a seat.

Devon bent down and picked up his glass. "I'm still nursing this glass of wine so I'm okay."

"Alright, well, I'll call you when the food is ready."

"Thanks, Toni," Sean said. He was completely clueless about what was going on.

I tried to hide my surprise but I know he had to see the look on my face. Fortunately for me, he's probably thinking it's because we ended up at the same party. And not because Devon told me he thinks he is family. I'm straight trippin'. Never in a million years did I think I was going to run into Sean at this party, much less have Devon uncover his sexuality. *Damn!* Why does it always have to be the cute ones? What in the hell am I talking about? I'm one of the cute ones too. *Okay, Toni, you really need to get it together.* I have to pull Michelle aside and ask her about Sean.

I continued on my way to the kitchen to get something to drink and bumped into Michelle in the doorway. I grabbed her by the hand and said, "Gurl, I need to talk to you!"

"*Oooh, this sounds juicy!*"

"Where can we talk in private?"

"Let's go outside by the pool."

I followed Michelle out to the patio. "Okay, girl, tell me what's up? No, let me guess: It's Trent, you like him, don't you?"

"*Girl, please!* No, it's not about me."

"Then tell me, the suspense is killing me. I know what it is. It's about Cynthia flirting with Devon. What's with her and gay men lately?"

I grabbed Michelle shoulders and shook her. "Will you be quiet and just listen for a minute?"

"I'm sorry, Toni. I was getting caught up. What is it?"

"What do you know about Mike's friend, Sean?"

"All I know is that they were roommates in college and that they're best friends. Why?"

"Did Mike ever say anything to you about Sean being gay?"

"No!"

"*Hmmm,* then he probably doesn't know."

"Know *what?* Toni, what is this all about?"

I turned around to face Michelle. "You have to promise me you won't say anything."

"Okay I promise. Cross my heart and hope to die, stick a needle in my eye and all that good stuff. Is that good enough for you?"

"That will do. Let's walk to the other side of the pool; I don't want anyone to overhear us. Sean is my executive assistant."

"What's so secretive about that?"

"Nothing. Devon and Sean met while we were playing cards. When I went over to check on Devon, he told me he met someone he thought was gay."

Michelle covered her mouth and her eyes widen. "*Oooooh*, are you saying that Mike's best friend is *gay?*" she whispered.

"I don't know. But Devon is rarely wrong."

"He works for you, doesn't he."

"Yeah."

"Well, did you ever think he was gay?"

"Not really. I just thought he was one of those men who are a little bit in touch with their feminine side. You know how some men get when they work around women too long. But I never thought he was gay."

Michelle started walking towards the house. "Damn! When Mike finds out, he's going to have a fit."

I jumped in front of her. "And just how do you suppose Mike is going to find out?" I inquired with my arms folded across my chest.

Michelle regained her composure. "I meant *if* Mike finds out."

"Michelle, remember, you promised me."

"I know. I'm not going to say anything. Besides, I don't want to bear the burden of possibly breaking up a great friendship."

"Remember, nothing is confirmed. Devon is just assuming this based on his instincts."

"Well, you did say he is hardly ever wrong."

"That's the truth. His gaydar is usually on point. It's going to be really interesting to see how this unfolds. I know I'll be paying close attention to Sean from now on." Raindrops started falling while we were talking. " Girl, we better get inside before it really comes down. I can't afford to get my hair messed up. I just paid Luxurious Locks seventy-five dollars for this do."

"I'm feelin' you on that."

Michelle and I grabbed each other and ran toward the house arm in arm. Mike met us at the door with a towel. "Toni, were you and Michelle out there trying to get your signals right for the next round of spades?"

I put my hand up to my chest and dropped my mouth open like I was appalled. "*Why, Mike,* are you accusing us of cheating?" I said, using my best southern bell accent.

He laughed. "Not exactly. I'm accusing you of conspiring to cheat."

"For your information, we don't have to conspire against such amateur card players like you and your cohorts. We could beat all six of you with our eyes closed."

"You talk a lot of noise for a corporate executive."

"What does that have to do with anything?"

"I don't mean that in a bad way. I'm just saying, executive women are usually a little uptight. But I can honestly say all of you ladies are pretty cool people."

"Thank you-- I think."

"By the way, Sean told me you're his boss."

"Yes, I am. We had no idea we were going to the same function this weekend."

"It's a small world, huh?"

"You got that right."

Mike turned to Michelle. "Baby, you know Sean was the one who told me about that wack-ass club I referred you to the other night."

Michelle gave me a questioning look. "Oh really?" she said. "Then I'm going to have to get on him about that."

"Don't bother. I already got on him for making me look bad. He said his friend Jamie referred him to the place. He hasn't been there before."

"In that case, I guess we can let him slide. Baby, Toni and I are going to go to the bathroom to dry off and freshen up. We will be right back."

"Go ahead. When you come out the food will be ready."

Michelle and I hurried to the bathroom. "*Gurl*, did you hear what he just said?"

"Yes, loud and clear," I said, pacing back and forth.

"So you know what that means, don't you?"

We looked at each other and screamed, "Cynthia!" Then we ran out of the bathroom.

"Michelle, we have got to find her and Ebony before they cause a scene."

"Let's check in the den to see if they're in there."

When we walked to the den, Devon, Stan, and Ilandus were sitting in there eating.

I slid over to Devon. "Where is Sean?" I whispered.

"I think he went outside with Cynthia. Why?"

"I don't have time to explain it right now, but come with us."

We looked in the backyard near the pool but nobody was out there. And it was still drizzling. "Let's check the porch," I suggested.

"Good idea," Michelle said.

"Will one of you please tell me what's going on?"

"Not now D! I said through clenched teeth, trying not to raise my voice. "I'll tell you later."

We walked back through the house trying not to draw attention to ourselves. We got to the front door and eased outside. I spotted Cynthia, Ebony and Sean standing next to Cynthia's car. "They're over there. I pointed. We rushed over to where they were standing.

"Lower your voice; Toni's coming." I heard Sean demand as we approached them.

"I'm not lowering anything," I heard Ebony say.

"She is my boss, dammit!" Sean said through clenched teeth.

The three of us walked up to the three of them. "What's up, guys?" I said, trying to break the ice. The tension was so thick you could feel it.

Sean tried to be cool. "Nothing much, Toni. We were just getting acquainted."

"In the rain?" I asked.

"We were already out here when the rain started."

"Well is everything alright? Ebony, you look a little upset."

"I am. This is the—"

Cynthia cut her off. "This is *not* the kind of weather for a pool party. Ebony is just upset because she couldn't get in the pool and show off her new bathing suit." Cynthia nudged her. "Right, Ebony?"

Ebony continued to stare at Sean. "Yeah, whatever you say."

Sean gave Cynt an appreciative look.

"Look, people, I don't know about y'all, but I'm not trying to ruin my silk outfit standing out here in the rain. I have a plate of ribs calling my name, so I'll see y'all inside."

"I'm going inside with you, Devon," Ebony said as she brushed past Sean.

"Toni, are you coming?"

"In a minute, D. I need to speak to Cynthia alone for a second. Sean and Michelle, do you mind giving us some privacy?"

"Not at all," Sean said with a nervous look in his eyes.

Michelle wrapped her arm inside Sean's. "Come on, Sean, let's go get something to eat before Mike thinks nobody likes his cooking."

"He is a little sensitive about his cooking, isn't he?" Sean joked.

The two of them left arm in arm. Cynt and I stayed outside.

"Let's get out of this rain and sit in your car," I suggested. Cynt hit the remote on her key chain to unlock the doors. We climbed inside.

"So what do you want to talk to me about?" she asked, looking remarkably calm.

"Sean."

"What about him?"

"Is he the one you saw at Stone Mountain with Jamie? Is he Jamie's gay lover?"

"Maybe you should ask him that."

"C'mon, Cynt, you're my girl, just tell me."

"I *am* your girl, Toni. But you are his boss. I'm not sure it's my place to be discussing him with you."

234

"Okay, then tell me why was Ebony so upset?"

"Maybe you should ask her that."

I reached for the handle and opened the door. "Okay, I will."

Cynthia grabbed my arm and yelled, "Wait! Close the door, Toni. I'll tell you what's happening. But you have to promise me this will not affect Sean professionally."

"It won't. I promise."

She lowered her eyes. "The answer is yes."

"Yes what?"

"Yes, Sean is the one that was with Jamie."

"I knew it!"

"How did you know it?"

"Michelle and I just put two and two together. That's why we came running out here we wanted to keep you from making a scene in front of the rest of the fellas."

"Why did you think I was going to make a scene? You know that's not my style."

"True. But you were so upset about what happened, we just figured when you saw Sean you might go off."

"Sean didn't do anything to me Toni, Jamie did. He was being cheated on just like I was. My beef is not with him. It's with Jamie."

I relaxed my posture in the seat. "Well, that's a relief."

"Don't feel too relieved."

"What do you mean by that?"

"Ebony is the one you should be concerned about."

"Why Ebony?"

"She is the one who was fighting with Sean on the Mountain that day. She's still mad. That's why she was so upset. Sean begged her not to say anything to you. He doesn't want you to know he's gay."

"That's understandable."

"He said nobody knows. Not even Mike. So do me a favor, Toni, act like you still don't know."

"I will, but what are we going to do about Ebony?"

"I'll pull her to the side and talk to her. Maybe once I tell her that I've moved on she will too.

After all, Sean does seem like a really nice guy."

"He is."

"Not to change the subject, but have you had anything to eat yet?"

"No."

"Me either and I'm starving, so can we just forget about this whole thing and enjoy the rest of the party?"

"Absolutely. Let's go."

Cynthia and I got out of the car and went back into the house. We piled our plates high and ate every ounce of food on them. The fellas just looked at us in amazement.

"Who would have guessed those lovely little bodies could hold that much food." Danny remarked.

Cynthia and I smiled and kept on eating.

Devon and Sean spent quite a bit of time playing checkers. I heard Devon telling Sean to crown him during one of their games and I giggled to myself. Ebony and Trent disappeared to a quiet area of the house to try to get to know each other better. Ilandus, and Stan were engulfed in a heated battle over some video game. Michelle and Mike were curled up on the couch watching it all unfold.

At 10:30p.m. we called it a night. Everyone said there good-byes, and Devon and I got in the car and drove home.

**A Few Months Later**

# Chapter 29
## Seasons Greetings

Before I knew it the Holidays were here. I'd been extremely busy at work, preparing ad campaigns for all of our upcoming events. My staff and I worked long, hard hours. My relationship with Sean grew even stronger. I never mentioned to him what I had found out that night at the party. Nor did I change my attitude towards him. As far as I'm concerned, he is still in the closet. Initially when we first got back to work, he was acting a little strange. You know the way that you do when you think somebody knows your business. But I quickly realized why he was behaving so strangely and did not react to his distant behavior. You see, I know what it feels like to be in his shoes. That's why I'm so glad I finally freed myself and traded in my 'Gators for Stilettos. Maybe one day Sean will trust all of us enough to reveal his true self. In the meantime, his secret is safe with me.

Michelle and Mike are an official couple now. The girls and I agreed that he is a pretty cool brotha, and he is always down for whatever, which never hurts. Ebony and Trent hooked up and are currently kicking, it but there hasn't been any commitment made yet. They're still weighing their options. They're what single people classify as dating. Which basically means that they are seeing each other and other people too. The rift between Ebony and Sean was mended about a month later at a party hosted by Cynthia. During that evening, over a game of Clue, they apologized to one another and became friends. Cynthia is still searching for a rich *straight* man although she does call Stan on occasion to come over and hit it. They're what we call friends with privileges. Ilandus was crushed when I told him I was already involved in a serious relationship, but he rebounded pretty well. He showed up at Stan's Halloween party with a sexy-looking cat woman. Danny is still single and searching. *Hmmmm*, maybe he and Cynthia should hook up.

Devon and Sean did exchange numbers but nothing ever came of it. D said Sean never admitted he was gay. He thinks Sean was too afraid I would find out the truth about him if he became friendly with D, so they had one phone conversation and that was it. Devon is still seeing Roger and whomever else he chooses too. Roger's wife finally called off her private investigator once Roger started spending more time at home with her and the baby. Lester was last seen running fifty-five yards for a touchdown.

I wrote Tommy a letter and told him it just wasn't going to workout between us. I haven't heard from him since. John and I are just as in love as ever. For Thanksgiving he invited me, mama, Devon, and his mom over and prepared a gourmet meal for us.

*"Honey, that John can cook!* You've got yourself a good man there, Toni," Ms. Davis said, wiping her mouth.

"Yeah, he sure would make a fine son-in law," Mama added, acting like she just happened to let that comment slip. I gave her the evil eye. "Alright, Mama!" I warned her.

John put his arm around me and kissed me on the forehead. "Sweetheart, let them have their fun. I don't mind."

Devon didn't have much to say because he and I were still fighting about me not telling John. So he mostly stayed in the background making faces and mouthing obscenities at me like, *"Tell him, bitch."* A few times I laughed out loud at him, and everyone looked at me like I was crazy. I had to dismiss their concerns by telling them that I was just thinking about something Ebony said. Each time that happened, D would slide out of the room giggling.

All in all Thanksgiving was good. For Christmas, everybody is coming over to my house. I even invited Mr. Carlton and his family. I really want Mama and John to meet him. He and Sean are the only two people I invited from work. I told Sean to feel free to bring his parents with him. I never got a chance to thank his father personally for the cleaning referral. So I figured I could do that by having them over for Christmas dinner. Which is only a week away. I enlisted Ebony's help this afternoon to go grocery shopping and to help me find nice little trinkets to give to all of my guest. She's pretty good with that sort of thing.

For Christmas, I'm planning to take John to Hawaii. Thanks to Mr. Carlton's generosity with my bonus and vacation time, we're going to have a funky good time.

***

*Buzz.*

"Yes, Sean?"

"Ebony is here."

"Tell her I'll be right out."

"Will do."

"Toni said she will be right out. You may have a seat if you'd like."

"That's okay. I'm sure as soon as I sit down and get comfortable, I'll have to get back up. So what's new with you? Are you ready for the holidays?"

"No, I still have a ton of Christmas shopping to do."

"I hear you. I'm hoping to finish mine while we're out today."

"Is that where you two are headed?"

"Sort of. We're supposed to be going shopping for Toni's Christmas party. But I figured I can kill two birds with one stone and get some of my own shopping done

239

while we're out."

"That makes sense to me."

"Hey, girl, sorry to keep you waiting." I walked over and gave Ebony a kiss on the cheek.

"No biggie. Sean and I were out here chatting away."

"Are you ready to go?"

"As ready as I'll ever be to go shopping in 30 degree weather."

"Have a cup of hot chocolate for me ladies." Sean waved.

"Don't worry; I got you." Ebony winked at him.

"I'll see you on Monday, Sean. Have a good weekend."

When we got outside the Hawk was kicking.

"Girl, hurry up and open this door and turn the heater on high."

"I'm moving as fast as I can. Nobody told you to wear a leather mini in this cold weather."

"Excuse me, but I'm still fashionable when it's cold."

"You can be fashionable and covered too."

"Touché, Miss Thang." Ebony laughed. "So where are we going first?"

"The nearest drive-thru. I need some coffee to warm me up."

"Make that two cups."

* * *

We began our shopping trip at the fabric store. I wanted to buy some material to make two matching tablecloths for my Christmas dinner party. Ms. Davis told me that if I Fed-ex the material to her, she will make them for me and bring them with her on Wednesday. I'm so excited about having this party. It's the first party I've thrown this year. Mama is really excited too. We're going shopping tomorrow for her gift to John.

"*Ooh,* Toni, pull in there," Ebony said, pointing.

She was so excited that I wasn't quite sure where she was pointing. "Where Ebony?"

"Over there."

"You mean *Ross?*"

"Yeah."

"For what?"

"I haven't gotten Trent or Cynthia's present yet, and you know they sell famous name brands for less."

"Oh, you are wrong for that!" I said, laughing as I pulled into a parking space.

"No, I'm not. I haven't forgotten how evil that heifer was treating me a few months ago. And Trent *still* hasn't made a commitment. So the way I see it, the two of them are going to get name brand stuff at affordable prices. It's a win/win situation."

"Whatever you say, sistah girl. Just be quick about it. I want to get to the mall before it gets too crowded."

Ebony spent about forty-five minutes shopping for their gifts. I have to admit, she bought some pretty cute stuff for under two hundred dollars. She bought Cynthia a lovely red *DKNY* zip-up jogging suit, with a matching sports bra. For Trent she bought a man's valet set and matching luggage.

"Ebony, I have to admit you did get some nice gifts for less. But what made you buy Trent luggage?"

"Chile, if that Negro doesn't make a commitment soon, I'm going to kick his black ass to the curb. So I figured the luggage would be cute for me to pack his *shit* in when I tell him to get to *steppin'*," she said stomping her feet.

I hollered. "Girl, you are too stupid."

She laughed. "*Scandalous* is more like it. *Girl*, I can't have that Negro sitting up here wearing out my pussy and not making a commitment."

"How long are you giving him?"

"Until the end of January."

"That's a decent amount of time."

"I think so. I like him a lot and we spend quite a bit of time together. I think it's a natural progression. I'm not asking him to marry me. Just to be in a monogamous relationship with me. *Hell,* I even let him leave some clothes and a toothbrush at my house, and you know how funny I am about that kind of stuff!"

"Yes, I do."

"So what do you think? Am I asking too much?"

"Not from where I sit. I think you're entitled to at least that much. Have you two discussed it?"

"A little bit. He seems open to it, but he still hasn't made a move."

"Maybe he's just scared or waiting for the right time. He may even do it during Christmas or New Years."

"God, I hope so."

"Gee, Ebony, I've never seen you like this over a man. It's kind of cute."

"That's because I've never felt like this about any of those trifling-ass negroes I've been out with."

"I know what you mean. John has my nose wide open, too, and I like it. Being in love is so refreshing. It's like the feeling you get on the first day of spring. When the flowers are blooming, the birds are chirping, and the warm sun hits your cool skin." I put the car in park and gave myself a hug with my eyes closed. There's nothing like it." "Amen to that! Now let's end this conversation and get in this mall and shop 'til we drop."

"I only have one thing to say to that."

"What's that?"

I snatched my American Express Card out of my purse and yelled, "Charge!"

# Chapter 30
## A new beginning

My Christmas party was lots of fun. Unfortunately, Sean's parents couldn't make it; they had a prior commitment. Everyone who attended got along well. We played charades, Uno, *and* spades of course. In the midst of our caroling someone suggested karaoke so we did that too. Everyone laughed and sang and had a good time. I'm not sure whose gift I loved the most. As far as I'm concerned, Mr. Carlton and John are tied for first place in the gift-giving department. Mr. Carlton announced to everyone how pleased he was with the way I was handling my responsibilities at Carlton. "Therefore," he said, "on top of the generous bonus I gave her for landing the La Cola account, I'm giving Toni three weeks vacation with pay, starting today!" He caught me totally off guard. I was elated. I knew I had a week of vacation time coming, so for John's present, I booked us a trip to Hawaii for New Year's. John was speechless when I handed him the gift-wrapped envelope. He opened it up and saw two first class tickets to Honolulu.

"When do we leave?" He asked with excitement.

"Sunday!"

"How long are we going to be there?"

"Five days."

"That's perfect."

Everyone stood around watching our exchange. I'm sure they were thinking the same thing I was. *What's with all the questions?*

"Perfect for what?" I asked John, puzzled.

"You'll understand when you open your gift." John handed me a substantially large box.

"What's this?"

"You have to open it to find out."

"Well, it's not a ring, judging from the size of it. Unless he bought you the rock of Gibraltar," Devon blurted out.

"Ms. Davis, would you *please* get your son before I have to hurt him in front of God and all of these witnesses?" Everyone laughed. I ripped the paper off of the box like little kids do on Christmas morning. Only to realize it had a lift up top. I was a little embarrassed but I didn't care. I love gifts and I was anxious to see what was inside of that box.

"Toni, maybe you should read the card first," John suggested.

I opened the card and noticed John's handwriting. It read:

*You are cordially invited by Mr. John Collins to:*
*Where: Nairobi, Kenya*
*When: Saturday January 3, 2004 at sunset*
*What: Billiards rematch!*

I dropped the card and started shaking. I didn't know whether to laugh or cry, so I did a little bit of both. I jumped up and hugged John as tightly as I could.

"I got you, didn't I?" he whispered in my ear as he gripped me tightly around my waist.

"You sure did."

"Would someone please fill us in on what's going on? Toni, you didn't show us what the box has in it."

I released the grip I had on John and wiped my eyes. "I'm sorry, Mama. I didn't finish opening it, did I? Everyone, please forgive us. We don't mean to be rude. It's just that John caught me by surprise," I said. I pulled mosquito netting, a backpack, sunglasses, a safari hat, and passports out of the box.

"What's all of that for?" Trent asked.

"John is taking me to Africa!" I screamed.

All of the ladies in the room screamed with me, including Devon. Mr. Carlton walked over to John, shook his hand, and patted him on the back. "Now that's the way you're supposed to treat a woman. Sean, I hope you and all these other young fellas are paying attention."

Sean smiled politely, but he looked uncomfortable. I caught Trent and Ilandus glaring at John. Stan got up and went to the bathroom. It was obvious that John's romantic gesture made them all feel a little uneasy.

"So, Toni, what did the card say?

"Here, you can read it. I'm sure John won't mind."

Cynthia picked up the card and read it. "He invited you to a Billiards rematch?" she said with a frown on her face.

"Oh, I get it," Devon said, smiling.

"Well clue me in because I don't."

"Clue all of us in." the other ladies said in unison.

"I'm sure Toni told y'all that when she and John met, he took us out on his yacht and beat her in a game of pool. *Chile*, he beat her like she stole something!" Devon said, laughing.

I glared at him. "Shut up, D, and just tell the story."

"Sorry, Teaser. Anyway, they made a bet before the game that the person who won could call a rematch at anytime and anywhere at the expense of the loser. Toni told him she wanted a rematch in Africa at his expense.

I'm sure you can figure the rest of it out."

"Oh, sweetheart, that is so romantic. He gave you your wish even though you lost," Mama said, hugging me. Then she went over and hugged John.

"You take such good care of my baby. Thank you, John, for being a part of our family."

John hugged Mama back and said, " No, I should be thanking you for creating such a beautiful person."

Devon couldn't stand it. He nearly gagged on all of the pleasantries. Ebony went and grabbed Trent and told him he should be taking notes. Mike and Michelle were happily trying on the gifts they gave one another. Danny came over and congratulated the two of us on our major vacations and said he was going to have to call it a night. Shortly after he left, everyone else did too. Mama, Devon, and Ms. Davis retired to the den to watch *The Preacher's Wife,* and John and I cuddled quietly in front of the fireplace and watched the lights on the Christmas tree blink.

*** 

Hawaii was wonderful. It's funny how you don't realize how much you need a vacation until you go on one. John and I spent most of our time lounging around. We went on sightseeing tours during the day and enjoyed romantic dinners at night. We did a little bit of island hopping while we were there too. We spent two days on the island of Maui.

Then we flew back to the main island just in time for the New Year's Eve celebration. The celebration was spectacular. We watched them roast a pig, and then the belly dancers came up to our table and pulled John on stage. I nearly spilled my drink laughing at John trying to do the hula. It's a good thing I videotaped it, otherwise I wouldn't have any blackmail material for when he acts up. We spent the entire evening eating, drinking, and laughing. I have to give it to them, the Hawaiian people really know how to have a good time.

The next day we didn't get out of bed until 1:00p.m. We were still a little hung over from the night before. We slept through breakfast and damn near missed lunch. We had appointments to go snorkeling at 3:00p.m; and since it was our last day on the Island, I didn't want us to spend it sleeping. I woke John up and told him we needed to get dressed and have a snack before snorkeling.

He rolled out of bed looking whipped. "Oh, somebody is looking a hot mess." I said.

He didn't say anything; he just stumbled into the hot shower I had waiting on him. I ordered room service while he was in the bathroom. Thirty minutes later John emerged from the bathroom looking like new money. He was freshly shaven and smelling good. I couldn't resist running into his arms and kissing him all over his face. He spun me around and said, "Now that's a good morning."

We finished eating our snack and made our way down to the beach just in time for our snorkeling lesson.

"John, I'm a little nervous about this snorkeling lesson."

"Just follow my lead. I'm an old pro."

"Whatever you say, Jacques Cousteau," I mumbled.

"May I have your attention, please?" the instructor announced. "My name is La'wai. I am going to teach you the proper way to snorkel. Please pay close attention so that you won't get hurt. Do I have anyone here who knows how to snorkel already?"

John raised his hand.

"The gentleman in the back." He pointed to John. "What's your name, sir?"

"John. John Collins," John said, sticking his chest out.

I rolled my eyes. I knew John was getting ready to embarrass himself. He told me the only time he'd been snorkeling was in his mama's tub when he was a little boy. Now he's trying to act like Aquaman in front of all of these people.

"John, would you mind coming up to the front. I would like for you to help me demonstrate the proper technique."

John looked at me, and his Kool-Aid smile faded. "Uh-oh," he said as he made his way to the front of the group.

I laughed. "Go ahead, baby, show us how it's done," I taunted him.

"Everyone, give John a hand for being kind enough to volunteer to help me out," La'wai insisted. "The first thing we need to do is to make sure we have all of the right equipment. Everyone, please check your bags to make sure you have goggles, flippers, an air hose, and alcohol pads."

La'wai went on to teach John snorkeling. He had John put on all of the equipment including the flippers. Then he had him walk out into the water, by the stingray farm, and hold his hand underwater with squid in it. Before John could get his hand under the water good, a stingray swam between his legs. John damn near jumped out of his shorts. We all laughed, and I took plenty of pictures for the scrapbook.

"That's okay, John try, again!" La'wai shouted.

John composed himself and did it again this time two stingrays came swimming towards him. The larger one sucked the food out of John's hand and swam away. The group cheered. La'wai started them chanting, "Go John, you can do it, go, John, you can do it." Before I could stop the group participation, John was in the water doing the running man. Can you say *embarrassing?* John was so caught up that he almost got stung when he stepped on the tail of one of the stingrays. Fortunately he didn't. We spent that afternoon snorkeling with the stingrays and jet skiing. We had a ball.

The next morning we got up, packed our bags, and headed to the airport. We were on our way to Africa!

***

Before we went to Hawaii we'd altered our reservations and changed our plane tickets. We re-booked them from Atlanta to Hawaii, from Hawaii to Nairobi, and from Nairobi back to Atlanta.

While we were in the airport, we shipped all of the souvenirs and extra clothes we bought back to Atlanta. We called Mama and asked her to pick up the boxes from the airport.

The flight to Nairobi took eighteen hours. We slept most of the way. The first day we got there we were so jet lagged we stayed in our suite the whole day. On day two we did some sightseeing and shopping. I bought a lot of African art and some material for Devon's mom. I tried on a gorgeous dress made out of burlap. It was hand painted with different African designs. Underneath the shell of the dress was a silk slip to keep the burlap from touching your skin. I looked beautiful in the dress. John told me to get it but I felt it was too expensive. They wanted five hundred dollars for it. So I left it right there. I figured before we leave I'd go back and barter with them for it. We shopped some more and then returned to our hotel room to shower and get ready for dinner.

While John was in the shower there was a knock at our door.

"Who is it?"

"I have a package for a Ms. Toni T. Goodwin," a man's voice said. I stared at the locked door, wondering who would be sending me a package. Then I cautiously opened the door. "Yes, may I help you?" I said, sounding skeptical.

"Are you Toni Goodwin?"

"Yes, I am, but I didn't order anything."

"This package is for you ma'am." The charcoal-colored gentleman handed me a package wrapped in tissue paper and tied with a beautiful bow.

"Do you know who this is from?" I asked him, still admiring the wrapping.

"No, ma'am but there is a card attached." He tipped his hat and attempted to walk away.

"Just a moment!" I insisted. "Let me get you a tip."

He smiled and said, "The tip has already been taken care of. Enjoy your stay."

"Thank you," I said and closed the door.

I laid the package on the bed and opened the card. It read; *Be dressed and ready to go in twenty minutes.* There was no signature attached to it. It was type written. I figured it had to be John, but typing is not his style. Besides, when would he have had the time to do it?

The suspense was killing me. I pulled the beautiful mud cloth bow off of the package and on the bed lay the burlap dress. You would think by now I would be used to John and his surprises. But honestly, I pray I never get used to it. I picked the dress up and held it up to me in the mirror. It was absolutely beautiful. John walked out of the bathroom door and saw me admiring myself in the mirror.

"Thank you, John!" I shouted as I leaped into his arms.

"I knew you really wanted it. You're welcome. Now get dressed; we're leaving in twenty minutes." John patted me on the behind as I hurried to the bathroom to take a shower.

When I emerged from the bathroom looking like a million bucks. John was nowhere to be found. He left a note lying on the bed. *Meet me downstairs* was all it read. Then there was a knock at the door.

"Who is it?"

"Ms. Goodwin, we're waiting for you."

*Who is this 'we'?* I said to myself. I opened the door and two beautiful ladies, clad in African attire, stood at my door. A trail of rose petals lay behind them. I was straight up trippin'. "Who are you?" I asked, bewildered.

"We are your escorts. Please come with us and don't ask any more questions." I raised a single eyebrow and gave that sistah a look like, *don't try any sudden moves. I will beat your ass.* Then I smiled politely and followed her instructions. I walked down the hallway lined with rose petals to the elevator. The doors opened and there were more rose petals. When we got to the bottom floor there was red carpet that ran from the elevator to the outside. The escorts stepped out ahead of me and started dropping rose petals on the carpet before me. *Hot damn!* I thought. *Michelle thought she was Coming to America. I'm living it! Mike don't have shit on John!* The other guests in the hotel stopped what they were doing and just stared at me with sheer amazement. I couldn't believe it either. As we approached the sliding glass doors, a white Rolls Royce pulled up with a man inside. The bellman opened the door. John leaned his head out of the car and said, "Don't just stand there, get in. We have reservations for 7:30PM." He reached his hand out towards me. I took his hand and the bellman helped me into the car.

"Carry on, driver," John instructed.

"What about the escorts? Aren't they coming?"

John laughed. "Oh, I see you've gotten spoiled already."

"What do you expect? You can't get a girl used to being treated like a queen and then take her escorts away from her." I leaned over and kissed John, and we both laugh. Then I looked at him and said, "Have I told you how amazing I think you are?"

"No, not lately."

"Well, then I'm telling you now.   John Maurice Collins, I think you're amazing and I love you!"

Now it was John's turn to be speechless. He was shocked by my declaration of love for him. It was the first time I'd said it out loud. I shocked myself.

"I love you, too, sweetheart," he said as he kissed me passionately.

"Un-Um," the driver cleared his throat. "Sorry to interrupt you, sir, but we have arrived at our destination."

"Thank you."

The driver got out of the car and opened the door. He escorted me out of the car and then waited for John to exit. John whispered something in his ear as he placed a considerable tip in his hand.

"What are you up to?" I quizzed him.

"Didn't the escorts instruct you not to ask anymore questions," John said sarcastically.

"No, you didn't try me like that, Mr. Collins."

"Yes, I did. Now *shhh* and come on."

We entered a beautiful tent. I could see that this restaurant was a popular tourist attraction. We were the only American black folks in there. As we maneuvered to our seat, several of the ladies in the restaurant complimented me on my dress. I overheard one lady whisper to her husband, "That's the dress that I wanted."

"Well, if you had eight-hundred dollars you could have bought it," he said. I smiled and kept walking. John had really hooked a sistah up.

Our table was a nice little secluded booth in a more private part of the restaurant. The staff waited on us hand and foot. I didn't eat much because I was so filled with excitement that I didn't have much of an appetite.

"Are you okay, sweetheart?" John asked.

"I'm perfect."

"You didn't eat too much. Do you like the food?"

"I love it. I'm not very hungry due to all of the excitement."

"Are you ready to go?"

"Whenever you are."

John snapped his fingers and my escorts appeared. I'm sure my smile lit up the entire restaurant. My girls started dropping the rose petals as I began to walk. Everyone stopped eating and watched. I overheard the same white lady asking her husband, "Can I at least have some goddamn rose petals!" Then she hit him with her purse. John leaned over and whispered to the man, "Sorry, playa!" Then we left the restaurant.

An hour later we arrived in what looked like the middle of nowhere. The driver helped me out of the car once again. John whispered in his ear and then the driver left. By then I had gotten the hang of, it but I couldn't resist asking the question.

249

"John, where are we and why did you let the driver leave us out here all by ourselves?"

John clapped his hands like he was auditioning the clapper, and tiki torches lit up all around us. In the middle of the torches stood a mahogany pool table. It was beautiful!

"Dessert, madam?" John asked.

"Oh, you are *too* much! How are you doing all of this?"

"Ancient Chinese secret," John claimed.

"Well, you can tell me. The Chinese won't know. We're in Africa," I pleaded.

John laughed. "Look, are we going to have this rematch or not?"

"You want to play pool in these clothes?"

"Why not?"

I wrapped my arms around his waist and pressed my breasts against his back so he could feel how much my nipples had swollen. Then I lowered my voice and said, seductively in his ear, "For one thing, you look so cute in your black Armani tuxedo that I might lose my focus and not play well..." I let my hands fall and brush up against his dick "...or fair for that matter."

"Oh, ho, I see you got game, huh?" John said with a crooked grin on his face.

"Naw, baby, I got skills."

"Then, rack 'em."

"If you insist."

I racked the balls on the table and handed John a pool stick. "Winners go first," I insisted. While John lined up his shot, I took one of the chocolate covered strawberries off of the platter, leaned my head back, and sucked it off the stem. John missed his shot.

"My turn!" I yelled.

"Oh, I see how you are." John laughed. "Two can play at that game."

While I lined up my shot, John took a strawberry and tilted his head back and licked it until all of the chocolate was gone. He had my juices flowing, but I played it cool and made my shot. On my next shot, he took his jacket and tie off and performed a mini striptease for me. I made my shot again; this time, two of my balls went into the hole. I lined up to take my next shot. John popped open the buttons on his shirt and started massaging his chest with oil. I don't know where the oil came from. I barely made that shot, but again I knocked two balls in the corner pocket. John got desperate. As I went to make my next shot, he came up behind me and pressed his rock hard dick against my ass. I scratched and lost my turn. Then I missed the next shot too.

It was John's turn. He approached the table, smiling, not knowing that I had a trick in store for him. I positioned my body directly in front of the pocket he was aiming for and spread my legs. Thank God John missed that shot!

"That's not fair...you're not wearing any underwear," he protested.

"All is fair in love and war, darling. And this is a little bit of both."

"So it's like that right there, huh? You're just going to spread your legs in front of a brotha, with no panties on and make him miss his shot."

"John, baby, don't take it personal. This is just business." I winked at him as I made my next shot.

"I only have one more to go before the eight ball. Whatcha got for me?"

John looked at me seriously for a minute. "Boy, you got a brotha's back against the wall now." he said, pacing back and forth. "I hate to have to do this to you, Toni, but I'm going to have to put God on you."

"God?"

"Yep, I'm just going to say a little prayer."

I laughed and took my shot. I made it! "And for my finale, Mr. Collins, since you have been such a great sport, I'm going to introduce you to the Toni T. Goodwin split with the eight ball in the side pocket."

"What on earth is that?"

"Watch and learn, grasshopper," I slipped my dress off and climbed on to the table, wearing only my stilettos. I did a diagonal split across the table. John's mouth dropped open. I took the pool cue in my right hand, placed my left hand on the table in front of me, and lined my fingers up in a V. I whispered the shot.

"The eight ball in the corner pocket."

John stood motionless. As I made the shot, I lifted my body just enough so that the stick didn't rub me raw. John nearly passed out when it went into the corner pocket. He looked up to the sky and said, "Thank you, Jesus!"

"Now you can have dessert," I boasted.

John brought the bowl of strawberries over to me. "These are nice, but that's not the kind of dessert I'm talking about. Come to Mama..." I pulled him on top of me, and we made love on top of a pool table under the stars in Africa. It doesn't get much better than that. At least that's what I thought.

\*\*\*

The next morning, John and I were up bright and early. We had to make it to the airstrip by 5:00a.m. We took a flight over to Camp Wakosua. John had us scheduled to go on Safari at 7:00a.m. We arrived on time and boarded a single-engine plane for the camp. As soon as we landed, the tour guide met us and gave us the microwave version of safety while on safari. Then he told us to get inside of the jeeps.

Four groups of tourists piled into the jeeps, and we headed for the bush. It was an exciting adventure. We saw lions, giraffes, and elephants. John and I took lots of pictures. We laughed when we saw two deer humping. "I guess they're getting it on in the bush too," I whispered in John's ear.

We arrived back at the camps and headed straight for our tent. We were both exhausted. John and I decided not to go to dinner that night with the rest of the group. We opted to stay in our tent and eat the snacks we'd brought with us. We were too tired to go anywhere, and we had to be up at five again the next day.

Morning came before we knew it. John and I woke up and showered together. I heard the servant telling the people in the tent next to us to grab their breakfast before the baboons take it. I looked outside and some of our fruit was already missing.

"Mr. Collins, we're leaving in five minutes," the driver shouted.

"Okay, we're coming now." John yelled back. Toni, grab your backpack and let's go."

"Where are we off to this morning?"

"The sky."

"The sky?"

"Yes. Now *shhh.*"

"Oh, here we go with the *shhh* again. Why do you keep *shhsing* me?"

John grabbed me by the shoulders and kissed me. Then the jeep stopped.

"We're here," the driver announced.

John let go of me and I couldn't believe my eyes. In front of me was a large hot air balloon.

"Is that for us?"

"It sure is" He smiled.

I hopped out of the jeep, grabbed his hand, and ran over to the hot air balloon.

"Are you ready to fly ma'am?" the guide asked.

"I'm already flying, sir," I said as I looked into John's eyes.

"Sir, we should get going while the wind is on our side."

"By all means." John said, breaking our starry-eyed gaze. He and the guide helped me into the basket.

The guide explained safety tips to us and told us that the landing would be somewhat brutal. Then he fired up the engine and we took off.

"Oh, John, look at the antelope running beneath us."

"I see them. Do you see the hippos?"

"This is so beautiful. I feel like you have shown me the world!"

"I will if you just say yes."

I turned my head to the right and John was no longer towering over me. He was down on one knee with the rock of Gibraltar in his hand.

"Toni. T. Goodwin, will you marry me?"

Tears streamed down my face as I stood there, speechless. It was the same feeling I had in the airport when he showed up with that beautiful rainbow of flowers. I knew he really meant he would give me the world.

"Well, Miss. We're waiting?" the guide said.

John and I laughed. "Yes, baby, we're waiting."

I shook my head yes. "Yes, John, I'll marry you!"

I bent down to kiss him and the basket swung. "Whoa!" the three of us screamed.

"Sir, I think you better stand up and let her kiss you."

I agreed. "That's a good idea."

John stood up and we kissed as we sailed through the sky. During the final fifteen minutes of our balloon ride we watched the animals run wild. We saw a heard of buffalo migrating. We saw elephants grazing and zebras running. Our landing was as brutal as the guide had promised. We hit the ground hard. Then we had to roll out of the basket.

"Thanks, it was beautiful," I said to the guide.

"You're welcome, and congratulations."

"Thanks," John and I both said.

Our driver was awaiting our return. We hopped in the jeep.

"So how was it?" he asked.

"Beautiful! Look what I got." I bragged as I stuck my left hand out.

"Now, that's a rock!" the driver shouted. "Are you ready for breakfast?" he asked.

"We already had a little something before we came."

"*Shhh*," John said.

This time, I just shut up and went along with the program. Ten minutes later, we arrived at our destination. We were in the remote part of nowhere and there stood a lovely table filled with china and crystal. Complete with a butler wearing white gloves. He walked up to me and stuck his arm out.

"May I escort you to your table, madam?"

Without saying a word, I nodded. I wrapped my arm inside of his and followed his lead. John walked behind us. Once we were seated, he returned with menu cards that had our names on them. They read:

*Toni and John's Champagne Brunch*
*A toast to a new beginning*
*January 4, 2004*
*Nairobi, Kenya*

The waiter returned with a bottle of Dom Perignon. He poured John and I a glass.

John took my right hand. "I'd like to propose a toast." I lifted my glass. "To a new beginning."

"To a new beginning!"

**THE END.**

For Now...

The Sequel,

**True Intentions,**

Coming Soon...

# Special Thanks

Book Layout and Back Cover Design:
Green Creative
greencreativefirm@yahoo.com

Cover Art and Design: Mario Cadenas
Mariocadenas725@yahoo.com

Website Designer:
Clark Solomon
celgin2002@hotmail.com

Author Photo:
B & B Photography & Video
Moses Bell
(954) 321-6767

Publicist:
Annette Breedlove
786-303-3031
sistahnet@juno.com

Author Biography:
Treva J. Marshall and Larcenia Dixon

Media Kit:
TJM Communications, Inc.:
Treva J. Marshall
1025 Greenwood Blvd.
Suite 300
Lake Mary, Fl 32746
(407) 708-1823
www.tjmcommunication.com
treva@tjmcommunications.com

Legal Representation:
ParksCrump
Attorneys At Law
240 N. Magnolia Drive
Tallahassee, Florida 32301
(850) 222-3333
www.ParksCrump.com

# About The Author

Literary newcomer, Hallema discovered her writing talent as a senior in high school in her hometown of Miami, Florida. Her undergraduate education prepared her for a career in law, as she holds dual Bachelor of Science degrees in criminology and political science from Florida State University. Upon graduating from FSU, she was awarded a full scholarship to Stetson University College of Law, where she attended and later decided to focus on nurturing her writer's voice.

Hallema returned to her roots in Miami and became a local favorite as a spoken word artist in South Florida by reciting her original and dramatic poetry. Building on her growing celebrity, she founded *Just Us Girls,* a book club for inner-city teenage girls. Community service has been a guiding principle throughout her life. As a member of the Dade County Alumnae Chapter of Delta Sigma Theta Sorority, Inc, The Universal Truth Center, and The Black Alumni Association of Florida State University, she actively participates in projects that benefit the community.

Professionally, Hallema has enjoyed an impressive career as a marketing consultant for two Fortune 10 companies. However, her burning desire to be a published author could not be extinguished. In July 2003, she resigned her position as a financial consultant to devote herself totally to her craft. She completed Mass Deception on August 15, 2003. Hallema believes that writing is her true purpose in life. She credits her strong faith in God, her partners in prayer, and a supportive network of family and friends for giving her the strength to step out on faith and realize her dream.

A prolific storyteller, Hallema takes her audiences through an in-depth look at her characters, their inner selves and their life issues. Her first project highlights her ability to entertain, inform, and even surprise her readers. Hallema has built an impressive resume of education, career, and social endeavors, but it is her arrival on the literary scene which evinces her ultimate gift and purpose.